TOGETHER FOREVER

CLARK SELBY

Library of Congress Control Number: 2025913768

ISBN
979-8-89641-085-0 (Paperback)
979-8-89641-086-7 (eBook)
979-8-89641-084-3 (Hardcover)

1

The year was 1951 and it was a hot September morning, with the golden Kansas sun shining brightly. Chance Clark approached the large red brick school with considerable apprehension. He was beginning the ninth grade in a new school in a new town; he couldn't help but wonder what lay ahead.

Chance was a tall boy at fourteen, six-foot-one, with lightbrown wavy hair, green eyes, and a freckled face. He was just an average small town American boy, without any outstanding features, except he was slightly taller than most other boys his age.

Chance was born in the middle of the Great Depression to parents, who were farmers trying to scratch out a living on a rented east Oklahoma farm. Before Chance was two, his father had to give up the farm and find a job in town so his family could keep eating.

His father was a hard worker and Chance knew his father could do more work then any two men. His father never went back to the farm after he found work in the natural gas business. His dad's work had brought them to this new town only a month before school started. Chance had not met anyone in Webster before the opening day of school and he was looking forward to talking with someone his own age.

As Chance passed through the gate of a high fence surrounding the school grounds, he began picking up his pace, caught in the stream of students hurrying to begin a new school year. Once inside, Chance was on an entrance landing with a wide stairway up, flanked on each side with narrower stairways going down. Up the wide stairway he went, and when he reached the top of the stairs, he went into the school office where a few days earlier he and his mother came to enroll him.

The school office was a mad house; students were wall-to- wall and Chance barely had been able to squeeze through the door. He had to pick up his class schedule and he thought with the crush of people, he would be lucky to have it by lunchtime. The office staff was working at a dizzying pace, giving out class schedules and directions to homerooms. In no time at all, he was at the counter and was surprised that before he could open his mouth, the young woman behind the counter said, "Chance Clark, isn't it?

"Yes," Chance answered as he quickly realized this was the same young woman who helped him enroll. She searched through the ninth-grade boys schedules, found his, and as she handed him the schedule, she said, "Chance, you are in homeroom 214, Miss Fowler, go up the stairs to my left and then to the end of the hall."

Chance walked through the door of classroom 214 to yet another surprise. Miss Fowler was the youngest teacher he ever saw. She was slightly overweight for her five-foot-five height, with long blonde hair, blue eyes hidden behind dark-framed glasses, and a peaches and cream complexion. Chance thought she looked sexy. Just what sexy looked like, Chance wasn't really sure, but whatever it was, he knew Miss Fowler looked it.Miss Fowler said, "You must be Chance Clark because the rest of my class is here and at their desks."

"Yes ma'am."

"Well, Chance, I saved you a desk right in front by me," and she pointed to the desk right in front of her desk. "That way, I can keep a close eye on you." Chance quickly went to his desk and sat down. He thought to himself that he could keep a pretty close eye on her as well, and he would.

The rest of the day passed quickly. Chance was in his last classof the day, Algebra, room 112, with Mr. French. Mr. French wasbalding, in his late fifties, and Chance took a quick liking to him.Mr. French had a seating assignment chart on the door so as eachstudent came into the room; they would know exactly wherethey were to sit. Chance found his name on the chart and wentto his desk. He sat down and watched the rest of the kids findtheir names and desk assignments. Chance was pleased with theway things were going. The teachers and the kids were open and friendly, unlike some of the other schools he had attended.

Chance watched as the last student came in the door. She had been talking with Mr. French in the hallway and her desk was directly across the aisle from him. He watched her move to her desk and sit down. She wore a skirt in the latest nineteen- fifty fashion, just above the ankles, and a white peasant blouse. All during class Chance wondered what her name was. Chance kept glancing over at her. He couldn't understand why he was attracted to this tall, skinny girl.

When class was over, the tall girl was quickly out the door, met by two other girls, and then lost in the crowd of students leaving after the end of the first day of the new school year. Chance waited until the other students left and then he stopped to look at the seating chart. He found his name on the chart again and then looked at the name across from his. Chance read, "Ann Harris." So that's what the skinny girl's name is.

He liked it and said her name softly out loud to himself, "Ann Harris."

Mr. French said, "Did you say something to me young man?"

"Oh! No, sir, uh, good night"

Chance headed for the job he got the first week he came to town. He was going to work for a local grocery chain store as a stock boy and sacker. He wanted to start to work when he first moved to town, but had to settle for beginning after school started since other employees were leaving to go to college at that time. The walk to the grocery store was only about six blocks, so Chance arrived very early. He was not supposed to be at work until 5 p.m.and school let out at 3:15. Chance went directly to the office to see the store manager,

Mr. Bruce. Mr. Bruce was one of the company's brightest, sharpest, young managers. He was only twenty-seven years old and had come up the ladder of success rather quickly. During his climb, he held every job at the store: sack boy, stock boy, cashier, check-stand manager, produce manager, meat cutter, meat market manager, and now, one of the youngest managers in the Super-Duper store's organization. He was certainly destined for bigger and better things in the future. When Chance opened the office door, Mr. Bruce looked up from reading a paper from the stack f reports piled on his desk "Hello, Chance, you're a little early for work, aren't you?"

"Yes, sir, I am, but I thought I would come in a little early to give myself time to find out what I am supposed to do about time sheets, learn where the aprons are kept, and what my duties are before actually starting work." Chance had worked in a grocery store in the last town he lived in, so he knew something about working in supermarkets.

"That's very thoughtful of you Chance and shows real initiative. That's the kind of get-up-and-go that makes us at Super-Duper, the kind of chain store that's going to grow. You're going to do all right here."

Mr. Bruce got up from his desk and put on his store jacket, he told Chance, "We'll go downstairs to the stock room and I'll show you around."

They headed down a back stairway to the stockroom, with its stacks and stacks of brown cardboard boxes. The boxes were in neat rows, and everything in the area was as clean and orderly as the front of the store.

"Chance, I believe the stockroom should look as good as the front of our store. If we don't stay in the habit of keeping our stockroom perfect, the rest of the store will suffer. If you can't keep up the place where you live and work, you can't develop the habits needed to make our store perfect. That's the only way I will have it."

Just then, a heavy-set young man came through the back door. He was almost as tall as Chance but must have outweighed him by thirty pounds. He had piercing blue eyes and short, curly brown hair. He spoke softly. "Good afternoon, Mr. Bruce."

"Hi, Don. I want you to meet the newest member of our Super-Duper team, Chance Clark."

"Chance, this is Don Smith."

"Hi, Chance," Don answered, extending his hand to him.

Chance took his hand and shook it. Don had a firm grip, unlike some of the other kids he met. Shaking hands with some of them was like shaking hands with a cold, dead fish.

"Hello, Don."

"Chance, Don works in our meat market in the evenings"

Mr. Bruce explained. "Say, you two should be in about the same grade. Aren't you in the ninth grade, Don?"

"Yes, I am, just started my first day today at South Webster Junior High."

Chance said, "That's funny, so did I."

"Well, since you two have so much in common, I'm going to let Don show you about signing in and getting you a stock apron, and Don, have Mary Ann make up a nametag for Chance. Chance, I'll be back in about twenty minutes to get you started on restocking shelves."

Mr. Bruce went back up to his office.

Don spoke first, "So, you started at South Webster today. I don't think you are in any of my classes, are you?"

"No, Don, I don't think I am. Whose homeroom are you in?"

"Miss Robinson's you know, she teaches Government, its room 213. Whose homeroom are you in?"

"Miss Fowler's just next door in 214."

"Say, Chance, you wouldn't want to trade homerooms would you, that Kay Fowler is super-sexy. Speaking of super, we better get you signed in here at Super-Duper and get your stuff before Mr. Bruce comes back and blows his stack."

They had just managed to pick up his apron, have Mary Ann make up his nametag and get back to the stock room as Mr. Bruce was coming down the stairs.

"Thanks, Don, for showing Chance around. I had to get that order in to our warehouse before four thirty this afternoon so our stock can be delivered tomorrow."

As Don turned to go into the meat market, he said, "Chance, I'll look for you at school tomorrow."

Mr. Bruce began explaining, "Chance, I want you to start in aisle one and check every item to see that the shelves are full. You know, you can't do business with empty shelves. If we don't have the merchandise in our stock room to fill the shelves, I want you to do two things. First, stack the cans or boxes to the front of the shelves so they look full, and then, make a note of the items we don't have and leave it on my desk."

Chance walked to the front of the store in aisle one and began to list the items missing from the shelves. Chance began bringing the items on his list from the stock room and filling the shelves. He had been able to locate most of the items and as he marked the price on each can, he began to think about his day. A new school, a new town, a new job and a new friend he liked the idea of doing new things, going to new places and meeting new people.

Time was passing fast--September, October, and now it was the middle of November. Chance was going into the gym after lunch. This week had flown by it was already Friday. Every week, South Webster Junior High had a Friday lunch time dance in the gym.As Chance walked by a group of girls, he was surprised as Betty Smith called to him. Chance stopped as she came up to him. Betty Smith was a nut but also a very lovely girl and Chance couldn't imagine what she wanted to talk to him about.

Betty said in her sweetest little-girl voice, "Chance, who do you like?"

"What do you mean, who do I like?"

"Oh, you know what I mean, a girl friend."

Chance saw Ann Harris sitting with the group of girls Betty had just come from.

"Who are you asking for, you?"

"No! You know I'm going steady with Jack Rodgers. I'm asking for Ann Harris."

Chance thought about the skinny girl who a strong wind would blow away and then he heard himself answering something he couldn't believe he was saying.

"You tell her I like her. Ann Harris." Betty left so quickly Chance became self-conscious standing there, so he walked over and sat down on a bleacher. Chance turned and watched Betty talking with Ann Harris. Betty almost picked Ann up from her seat and brought her over to where Chance had sat down.

Ann was shy, but she suddenly gathered all her courage to speak. "Chance, Betty told me you liked me."

Chance's experience with girls; just talking with girls, was absolutely non-existent. He wanted to, but couldn't bring himself to do it. For some reason though, Ann's courage gave him courage.

"Yes, Ann. I do like you."

Ann sat down next to him. Chance wondered what to say or do next. Just then Betty walked off with a laugh, leaving the two of them sitting by themselves. Chance's mind raced, what can I say to this girl and what can I do?

Suddenly he blurted out, "Ann would you like to dance?"

Yes, Chance, I would."

Uh, Ann, the truth is, I don't know how to dance."

Ann smiled. "Come on, I'll show you. It's easy."

Chance got up slowly from the bleacher and reached for Ann's hand. When their hands touched, it was like completing an electrical circuit. Power flowed from one to the other. For the first time Chance really looked at Ann, looked beyond seeing a skinny girl of fourteen. She was tall, at least five-foot-seven, she had big blue eyes, and her hair was light brown with a small white streak of hair in the center of her forehead. She was pretty, really pretty. He later found out Ann didn't bleach her hair to keep up with current fashion. Ann's white streak was natural; she didn't have any pigment in that part of her scalp. Chance loved it.

Ann put her arm around Chance's neck and told him to move with the music. She was showing him how to move his feet, just as the bell rang.

"Ann, can I see you after last hour? Maybe I can walk you home."

Ann smiled, "OK Chance, after class you can walk me home."

The rest of the afternoon took forever to be over. Finally it was time for the last hour class. Ann was already at her desk when Chance came in. She smiled up at him as he sat down at his desk. Chance stared at her all through class. He watched her every movement. He could have given a report, on the number of times her heart beat. She was even prettier then he thought earlier.

When class was over, Ann turned to Chance. "Are you going to walk me home? I have to pick up some things from my locker before we go."

Ann got up and Chance followed behind her like a little puppy. She put her books in her locker and picked up her gym clothes. "Chance, are you going to take your books home over the weekend?"

"No, I'll put them in my locker downstairs on the way out."

Ann went down the hall and down the steps, with Chance right behind her, as they were about to pass the last row of lockers.

Ann said, "Chance, I thought you were leaving your books in your locker."

Chance stopped, turned around and went back to his locker.

"Sure I am, but since I started following you, I can't even find my locker."

Ann laughed. "Don't blame me if you are lost!" "I always knew where my locker was before. It must be your fault I've lost it." Ann laughed again. "Are you going to walk me home or are you going to spend the rest of the day looking for your locker?"

Quickly, Chance put his books in his locker. He thought she has a good sense of humor to go with her good looks.

Out the school building they went, down the steps, through the gate and as they started walking west Chance realized he didn't know where Ann lived just as they passed the end of the school yard's fence.

Chance asked, "Where do you live?"

"Right here."

There were two lovely old homes next door to the school and Ann lived in the one on the corner.

Chance commented, "That was a pretty long trip, don't you think? We sure had a long time to talk."

Ann began laughing again. "Come in and have a coke or something."

"Are you sure it is OK with your folks?"

"Sure, I have girls here after school almost every night. My mom is working, it's all right."

"Maybe you hadn't noticed, but I'm not a girl."

"That's what I like about you."

Ann unlocked the door and motioned for him to come in. Chance followed her into the house. It was a beautiful old house with large windows, high ceilings, and lovely old woodwork. The kind of a house

Chance had never lived in. Ann's house was well furnished and perfectly decorated. Ann went into the kitchen and soon came back with two glasses of ice and cokes.

She said, "Why don't we sit here on the couch."

She handed him his coke.

Chance took his coke and sat down next to her. She even smelled good. She was unlike anyone he had ever been around.

"You know Ann I have to go to work at five what time is it?" Ann glanced at the clock. "Only five minutes to four. Where do you work?"

"I work at the Super-Duper store over on Fifth Street."

"Well, that's not far from here. How long does it take you to get there?"

"Only about ten minutes, if I walk fast. Ann, could you teach me some more about dancing?"

"Sure. Let me put on some music and I can start your dance lesson right now."

Ann got up and went over to a big, blonde-wood console record player. She turned on the machine, raised the arm on the record player and lifted the records that were already on the player she pushed the reject button, and watched as a record fell onto the turntable.

"Come on, Chance."

Chance got to his feet, held out his hand for hers, and when her hand touched his, he felt that strange power again. Ann was very patient with him, showing him over and over each step, how to turn, when to pause. Time passed quickly. Chance was beginning to show some improvement before he stepped lightly on her foot.

"Sorry."

Chance was very embarrassed.

"It's all right, Chance. Maybe you need a few more lessons."

"Are you sure you're all right?" "Sure, I'm tough."

"You don't look too tough to me."

Then he said, "Ann, could you go to the movies on Saturday with me?"

"I don't know, Chance. Why don't we try to go next Saturday? I will have to ask my mom and I'm not sure I could talk her into it by tomorrow."

"OK, Ann, I'll hold my breath until you let me know."

"You might get pretty red in the face by then."

"Bye, Ann, I'll see you on Monday."

Chance was out the door and on his way to work because he only had ten minutes to get there. He was going to have to walk very fast because he couldn't let Mr. Bruce down.

The weekend passed at a snail's pace for Chance, even though he worked ten hours on Saturday. On Sunday, he went with his folks to visit his aunt and uncle on their western Kansas farm. He always enjoyed going to his aunts, but this time all he could do was think about Ann, wondering what she was doing.

Monday dragged by until it was finally time for last hour. Chance hurried to get to Mr. French's room, but as he walked through the door, he saw Ann's empty desk. He sat down and waited, but class started and Ann still didn't come. After school, Chance found himself walking slowly toward Ann's house. He wondered if he should stop and see about her. God, how he wanted to, he summoned up every ounce of courage he could, walked to her door, and rang the bell. What if her mother came to the door, what was he going to say?

The door opened slowly. Ann was wearing a blue bathrobe and blue pajamas. She was as pale as a sheet of white paper and her blue eyes expressed surprise at seeing him there.

"Hello, Chance."

"Hi, Ann, are you all right? I missed seeing you at school so I thought I would stop and see about you."

"I'm OK, Chance. I will be back in school tomorrow. Do you want to come in?"

"Are you sure it's all right. You don't have anything catching, do you?"

"Hardly."

Chance went into the living room with Ann and sat down on the couch beside her. "Are you sure you feel well enough for me to be here?"

"Sure I do, I have been in bed with a migraine headache all day, but I feel better now."

Chance looked tenderly at Ann, wondering what he could say.

Then he told her, "I hope you'll be back in school tomorrow."

Ann smiled, "Chance, it is really all right; I will be OK tomorrow and be back in school."

Chance felt he should not stay too long, so he got up to go.

"Ann, I think I'd better get to work. I'll see you tomorrow." Ann reached up and took his hand.

"Chance thanks for coming to see me and my mom said I could go to the movies with you on Saturday."

The next day, time went by a little faster then on Monday. As Chance came into Mr. French's class, he saw Ann sitting at her desk. Chance felt relieved that she was there. It was funny how much better the day got, just because he could see her.

After class, Chance asked, "Can I walk you home?"

"Sure, let's go, but are you sure you can make it that far?" Chance laughed. I'll do my best. If I can't, you can carry me." "Sorry, I don't carry big boys."

For the rest of the week Chance walked Ann home and stayed to learn more about dancing. On Friday he met her for lunch and went with her to the school gym to dance. They looked very good together. Chance was tall enough to complement Ann's height and she was just right for him. They caused several people to stare because, together, they took on a completely different look. They appeared to get better looking when they were together.

Saturday night, Chance came by at seven. He rang the bell and Ann opened the door. She looked like a dream. She was wearing a one-piece orange playsuit. Her hair was combed to the side, with her white streak covering a large portion of her hair.

"Good evening, Chance."

"Hi, Ann, you look great"

"A little better then I looked Monday afternoon, I hope."

The movie was a nondescript Western. At least, the good guy won the girl in the end and didn't go off in the sunset with his horse. The hero even kissed the girl. Movies were getting better then ever!

"Do you want to stop and get a coke?"

"Chance, are you sure you can afford it? I don't want you to spend all your money on me."

"I'm a working guy, remember? Besides, I just got paid today." They stopped at the Cash Drug Store and found a booth in the back.

"Ann, would you like to have something besides a coke?"

"You know what I'd really like to have?" "No."

"A banana split. They make great ones here and I didn't have dinner."

The waitress came just then and Chance ordered two banana splits. Chance reached across the table and took Ann's hand. Every time they touched, Chance could feel this power flowing between them. When the banana splits arrived, they ate them hungrily and when they finished, Chance went to the counter to pay for them. The waitress said to Chance, "Did you see the man who was sitting at the counter? Well, he paid for your banana splits."

Chance exclaimed, "You're kidding, who was he?"

"I don't know, maybe he was just a guy who wants you to go through life wondering who paid for your banana splits."

"Thank you, ma'am!"

Chance and Ann were shocked, and what the waitress said would turn out to be true. For the rest of their lives, they would always wonder who paid for their banana splits.

Ann and Chance walked toward her house. As they came to a small park on the way,

Chance asked, "Do you want to sit down for awhile or are you too cold?"

"No, I could sit down for a few minutes, if you sit close and keep me warm."

As they sat down, Chance looked at Ann and said, "You know what?"

"No what?"

"You've got blue eyes!"

Ann laughed, "You are a nut you know it?"

"Well, it's true. You do have blue eyes, but I guess we'd better go because I can hear your teeth chattering. You must be freezing."

They walked on to Ann's house. When they reached her front porch, Chance took her hands in his. "God, your hands are cold."

"You know, cold hands, warm heart."

"Ann, can you go to the movies next Saturday?"

"I don't think so. Next week is Thanksgiving and I am going with my folks to Missouri."

"I had forgotten about Thanksgiving."

"I could go the next Saturday after that."

"Ann, that's great!"

He looked into her eyes. "You really do have blue eyes."

Then he leaned down and kissed her tenderly. She kissed back and then he kissed her harder. She moved back.

"Goodnight, Chance. I had a good time, thanks. And thanks for the kiss."Ann took out her key and opened the door. Chance waited until she went inside and turned on the lights. He walked away on cloud nine. He had really kissed her and she kissed him back. He knew right then she was his one and only love.

2

Thanksgiving week was a busy week for Chance at the Super Duper store. He had to go in early every night so he didn't get to see Ann after school at all that week. Chance thought life was tough not seeing and talking to her every day.

Ann left with her folks on Wednesday afternoon to spend Thanksgiving with her grandmother in Missouri. When Chance, finished work Wednesday night, his folks picked him up and they drove to Oklahoma to be with his grandmother for Thanksgiving. Chance loved to be with his grandmother. She was his biggest booster. In her eyes, Chance could do no wrong. Everyone needed someone like her; someone who's every action emits love. She was constantly building up his ego and making a fuss over him.

It was almost two o'clock in the morning before they got to his grandmother's house. Chance woke up as they turned onto her street. He could see she had the porch light on for them. As his dad stopped the car in front of the house and turned off the engine, the front door opened, as if some magic link was connected between the car's ignition and his grandmother's front door. Chance could see his grandmother coming through the door in her nightgown and robe and she smiled as she saw Chance running up to her. She held out her arms for him and as Chance kissed and hugged her, he almost picked her up off her feet. He had forgotten how muchtaller and stronger he had become than she was.

His grandmother insisted on fixing sandwiches, coffee, and cake. She knew they must be starving after their trip, and she knew Chance would not have eaten since lunch. She didn't think about his mother fixing him food and bringing it with her for him to eat in the car. Regardless of how sleepy they might be, they ate the food she prepared. Food always tasted better when you have loved ones to share it with, even if you weren't hungry. It was three-thirty before Chance went to bed and his folks and grandmother were still talking ninety to nothing. The sound of their voices was like a sleeping pill to Chance he was soon fast asleep.

Thanksgiving morning started with a bang. Chance sat straight up in bed for he heard a tremendous noise. Chance ran toward the source of the noise, the kitchen. His grandmother was standing on the top step of a kitchen stool, looking down at assorted pots and pans on the floor. Chance laughed when he saw the source of his alarm clock.

He asked, "Are you going to cook in those or just throw them around?"

His grandmother began laughing. "I just can't make up my mind yet, which do you think I should do?"

"I guess it won't make much difference with all of the food mom brought, but if you are going to throw them, at least wrap them up so they don't make so much noise. Some people are trying to sleep around here!"

Just then, his dad came into the kitchen. "What are you two doing out here? It sounds like you are tearing the house down."

Chance grinned, "Grandma is trying to decide if she should cook in these pots or just throw them around."

"With two of you together, I should have know you were just clowning around."

His Dad was yawning as he left the room to go and to get dressed.

"Are you going to help me clean up this mess or just stand there?"

Chance began picking up the pots and pans for his grandmother. She took a small roaster from him and placed a ham in it. Chance watched as his grandmother began pouring a sauce over the ham.

"Chance, do you think this ham will be big enough?"

"Sure, you already have a turkey in the oven and mom brought a piece of roast beef that looks like it's half a cow."

His grandmother said. "I just want to be sure we have enough."

"Grandmother, I have a girlfriend."

"That's really great Chance. What's her name? Does she go to school with you and is she nice?"

"Her name is Ann Harris and she is in my Algebra class."

"What do your folks think of her?"

"They haven't met her yet."

"Chance, you didn't tell me if she was nice."

"Grandma, she's wonderful. She's really pretty and she makes me feel wonderful when I am with her. Grandma, I love her and I'm going to marry her."

"What do your folks think about that?"

"I haven't told them yet. I haven't even told Ann yet."

Their conversation ended as Chance's folks came into the kitchen and Chance left to get dressed. The rest of the day went as Chance remembered all of their family get-togethers did,

plenty of food, lots of laughs, the ritual card games, and joshing his grandma about politics and his grandfather. His grandmother was a staunch Democrat who never forgave herself for voting for Herbert Hoover. Why she ever did that she would never know, except the Democrat running against him was a Catholic and she was a Southern Baptist.

Chance's uncles-in-law loved to tease his grandmother and get her started on the Republicans. She could always fairly well lay-them-out, Chance thought. She could take care of both the Republicans and his uncles. Chance was as proud of her as she was of him.

Chance always had a fun time with his mother's sisters and their husbands. One of Chance's, uncles-in-law, Roy Roberts, was a born clown, he had a quick wit and kept everyone laughing during family get-togethers.

One thing his Uncle Roy taught Chance when he was a little boy that always brought a smile to Chance's face was his uncle's little poem.

The poem was in answer to a question his Uncle Roy would ask. "Why is a fire truck painted red?" No one ever knew, but Roy's poem explained it perfectly.

Why are fire trucks painted red?
Because one and one is two.
Two and two are four.
Three fours make twelve.
Twelve inches makes a ruler.
Queen Elizabeth was a ruler.
Queen Elizabeth was a ship.
Ships sail the sea.
Fish swim in the sea.
Fish have fins.
The Fins fought the Russians.
The Russians are called Red.
Therefore, fire trucks are painted red
Because they are always rushing!

Chance learned this poem when he was about six years old and would always remember it and his Uncle Roy, regardless if now days some fire trucks were painted other colors. Obviously, those fire departments just didn't know why their fire trucks should be painted red!

Monday, Chance was looking forward to seeing Ann. Hurry up day, he thought. He wanted to see her and wanted to know how her trip had been. Also, he hadn't seen her since he admitted out loud to himself and his grandmother that he loved her. The day didn't go as quickly as Chance would have liked, but it was finally last hour. Chance walked as fast as he could through the halls without knocking people over. He went through the door with great expectations. His heart sank, as he thought, what if she wasn't there? But there, sitting at her desk, was Ann. Thank God! Nothing happened to her on her trip. She was watching for Chance and when she saw him, her eyes brightened and a big smile came to her face. Chance casually said, "Hi Ann."

He couldn't let her know how much seeing her meant to him. What if she didn't care that much about him?

"Hi Chance."

She reached out her hand to touch him as he sat down and said.

"I missed you. Did you have a nice Thanksgiving?"

"Great! We went to my grandmother's in Oklahoma. Ann, can I see you after school?"

"Sure."

Ann began to say something, but stopped when Mr. French started class.

After school, Ann and Chance went straight to her house. As soon as they were inside, Chance took Ann's hands, looked into her eyes and began kissing her. They sat down on the couch, still embracing and kissing. Finally, Ann had to get a breath.

"Chance, do you want a coke?"

He let her question fade away without answering.

"Ann, you don't know how much I missed you. Please don't go away and leave me again."

"Chance, I have to go with my folks on their trips to Missouri. I like to see my grandmother."

Chance thought about his own grandmother.

"All right, Ann, I understand, but I can't get by without seeing you every day."

Ann put her arms back around him and began kissing him again. They spent the rest of the afternoon locked in each other's arms, with their lips glued together. Chance realized it was getting late and that he had to go to work.

"Ann, if you do have to make these trips with your folks, I hope you will be as miserable as I am."

"Dearest Chance, I was, I was miserable without you. Did you know Friday is my birthday and my folks are taking me out to dinner? Could you come with us?"

"I'm supposed to work Friday night, but I will see if I can get off. Have you asked your folks if it's all right if I come?"

"My dad asked me what I wanted for my fifteenth birthday and I told him I wanted to invite you to my dinner party."

"What did he say?"

"Do you mean, eventually?"

She laughed and said, "What else could he say, but yes. After all, I'm his only daughter. I want my folks to know you."

"I'll come I'll get off somehow,"

Chance told her. "I wouldn't miss your birthday, but I'd better get to work right now or Mr. Bruce will let me off work permanently." With that, Chance was quickly out the door and moving at his top walking pace so he would be at work on time. He couldn't afford to be late and lose his job, not with what he had on his mind. When Chance got home after work, he asked his mother to take him uptown to help him find a birthday present for a girl. Chance's mother was surprised, as Chance had never said anything to her about having a girl. She knew he went to the movies with this girl, but she had no idea how he felt about Ann.

His Mother asked, "Chance is this someone you work with at the store?"

"No, mom, I met her at school."

"What's her name?"

Chance always knew his grandmother could be trusted with anything he told her; this reinforced his trust in her. She hadn't said a word to his mother about Ann.

"Mom, her name is Ann Harris. She invited me to her birthday party Friday."

"Is it a large party?"

"No, she asked me to go to a dinner party with her folks. I just have to get her a present."

"She must like you a lot to have you go with her on a family birthday party."

Chance admitted, "I hope she does, because I like her a lot."

His mother dutifully drove him to a large drug store, the only place open that late at night. They went inside and began looking for a present. What could he get her? Whatever it was, it had to be special for it was going to be the first present he had ever given her. Finally, he found what every girl in the romantic movies always had, something they would touch and then get a dreamy, faraway look in their eyes, a musical powder box. This one was rose colored, with an eighteenth-century dancing couple on the lid and it played the *Blue Danube Waltz*.

Friday night came and Chance searched through his clothes closet, trying to find something to wear. He didn't own a suit. His mother had been trying for months to get him to go to town with her and buy himself a new suit. He wished now he had listened to his mother. She had been telling him for months that when he was little, she could always take him to town and keep him in clothes. Now, he was either working or in school. Chance finally found a pair of slacks and a sweater that matched and he put them on.

Chance rang Ann's doorbell and Ann answered it immediately.

"Come in Chance, I want you to meet my folks."

As he came in the door, Chance handed her the musical powder box his mother had gift-wrapped for him.

"Happy birthday Ann!"

He winked at her as he said it.

"Mom, dad, this is Chance Clark. Chance, this is my mother and father, Julie and Jack Harris."

Chance could sense they were not exactly happy to see the boy their daughter insisted on taking with her for her birthday dinner party, but they were pleasant and friendly in their greetings. Chance thought they probably would just like to see him disappear, forever! The dinner party was nice. Ann's father was in a congenial mood and Chance had already heard from Ann that his bark was worse then his bite. All through dinner, her father was either teasing Ann or her mother.

As the waitress brought her birthday cake, her father said. "Ann, how dare you?" Ann was shocked by the tone of her father's voice.

"What did I do?"

"I'll tell you what you did. You keep getting older, that's what!"

He started laughing. "If you're getting older, what do you think that's making your mother and me?"

"Daddy, you'll scare Chance to death. He doesn't know your sense of humor."

The waitress set Ann's cake on the table and her father began singing Happy Birthday to her so, Chance and Ann's mother joined in. The candlelight revealed the sparkle in Ann's eyes. How Chance could have ever thought of Ann as a tall, skinny girl a few months ago was beyond him now. He could see she was a lovely young woman.

Mr. Harris started the engine of their new Caddy, backed out of the parking space, and headed the big blue car back to town. It had started snowing. This was going to be an unusually cold hard winter if it was snowing in early December in Kansas.

Her father said, "Chance, I think I better drive you home after Ann opens her birthday presents. This snow looks like it could get rough after while."

The snow was beginning to cover everything. The flakes got bigger and bigger and as Mr. Harris pulled the car into their drive, the cars light shining on the new fallen snow gave the Harris's house the appearance of a Christmas card Chance once saw. It was such a beautiful sight that none of them wanted to get out of the car and destroy the looks of such a perfect picture. Mrs. Harris moved closer to her husband and Ann had been sitting almost on Chance's lap since he got in the car. Chance felt rather embarrassed when he gotten in the car after closing Mrs. Harris's door and Ann's door since Ann moved across the huge back seat of the Caddy right next to him. Chance thought he wouldn't have the nerve to do something like that in front of his parents.

Mr. Harris finally broke the magic spell by asking Ann.

"Say, do you want to open your birthday presents tonight, or maybe we could wait a little longer and you could have them for Christmas?"

With that, Ann was across the seat, out of the car and halfway across the front porch before anyone else could move.

Ann yelled back at them, "Come on, nobody's going to cheat me out of my birthday presents."

As they started getting out of the car, Ann called to them.

"Would you hurry up? I'm freezing out here!"

Her dad got to the door, unlocked it and turned on the light. He picked up her birthday packages and handed them to her. Ann sat down in the middle of the floor with her packages around her.

She opened Chance's package first and when the paper was torn away, revealing the music box, she exclaimed.

"Chance, it's just want I always wanted. Thank you."

With that, Ann jumped up from the floor and came over to thecouch where Chance was sitting. As she did, she wound the musical powder box and it began to play the familiar tune, The Blue Danube Waltz. She kissed him, and then, just as quickly as she came over to the couch, she was back at the packages, tearing away at the next one. It was a beautiful long, camel-colored coat with a hood.

Her mother told her, "Now, maybe you'll quit freezing all the time."

Ann had the coat on in a flash and sat back down on the floor to begin opening another box Chance thought looked like more clothes. When the tissue paper was pulled back, Ann's face got bright red, for staring back at her were several pairs of white panties and bras.

Upon seeing Ann's red face, her mother told her.

"Don't worry, Ann, I'm sure Chance has seen girls underwear before. Besides, you've outgrown all of your bras."

Ann pleaded, "Mother!"

She laid the package aside and immediately began opening the last of her birthday presents. It was a small rectangular box with a large green bow. Ann opened it with care, and then shouted.

"Daddy, it's beautiful! Look, Chance!"

Ann was holding a very expensive yellow-gold watch and in the center of the watch box was a large sapphire mounted in a yellow-gold ring.

"Now, dear, you can't tell me when you're late, you didn't know what time it was and the sapphire matches your eyes."

Ann put her arms around her parents and gave each of them a kiss. She put on her new watch and sapphire ring and began turning around in circles, laughing. She was the happiest she had ever been in her life, she told her father.

"I'm going with you to take Chance home."

Chance almost forgotten how late it was and that tomorrow was another workday Saturday for him. Ann and her father started out the door. Chance thanked her mother for letting him share the family birthday party. Out in the snow again, Ann got into the front seat between her father and Chance. As Chance sat next to her, he could feel the warmth of her body through her new coat. Maybe her mother was right, maybe her new coat would keep her from freezing to death.

After Ann's birthday, it was only a few days until the Christmas school vacation was to begin. Ann was busy helping her dad at the store since Christmas is the busiest time of the year for jewelry stores. Ann told Chance that fifty percent of the year's business was done in the jewelry store between Thanksgiving and Christmas.

Chance and Ann didn't see each other during the Christmas vacation. Ann went with her folks to Missouri to be with her grandmother as soon as their jewelry store closed on Christmas Eve. Chance went to Oklahoma with his parents the same night to be with Chance's grandmother and his mother's sisters and their families.

At the end of the first day of school after Christmas vacation, Chance met Ann after their last class and they went to her house. As soon as they left the school grounds, they started holding hands and when they got into Ann's house, they began kissing. Both realized how much they had missed seeing each other.

Ann told Chance, "I have something for you. It's your Christmas present."

Ann gave him a small oblong package, wrapped in shiny gold paper with a big red ribbon.

Chance felt like a jerk, he had not bought anything for Ann and he promised himself that would never happen again in his lifetime. He said to Ann, "I'm sorry I didn't get anything for you."

Ann smiled and said, "It's OK. You already gave me a birthday present and my birthday is so close to Christmas, it was a birthday-Christmas present combined. Besides, I wanted to give you a present to remind you of me."

Chance opened the box and found a beautiful ID bracelet inside. On the top of the bracelet was engraved "Chance" and when he turned it over "Annie" was engraved on the back.

Chance never had any kind of jewelry before, other then a ring when he was a baby. His bracelet looked just like one he had seen Alan

Ladd wear in several movies. Chance knew he would love it forever. He thanked Ann for his beautiful present and gave her a big hug and kiss.

He told her, "I love it. Now I'll always have a part of you with me. I feel really feel bad about not getting you anything for Christmas."

Ann replied, "You gave me everything when I saw the look on your face when you opened my present."

Chance could only hold her and give her another kiss and whisper, "Thank you, Annie!"

3

The school year was passing rapidly. Ann and Chance spent every afternoon after school at Ann's house. They went to the movies every Saturday night and they were together all day on Sundays. They started going to church together to give them an excuse to be together every Sunday morning. No one in Webster could criticize a teen-aged couple attending church every Sunday. Chance had been waiting for Valentine's Day to ask Ann a special question. They had been going out only with each other, but he had never asked her to go steady. He had been waiting for this day, since he thought Valentine's Day symbolized the very essence of romance and love. Chance bought the biggest heart- shaped box of candy he could find. It was a beautiful red satin box with a doll on the top. He asked his mother to bring Ann's Valentine present to him after school, because it was too big to get into his locker. Chance told Ann he had to go to a meeting after school and would meet her at her house afterwards. Ann told him she could wait for him in the hall until his meeting was over and this caused Chance to do some pretty fast talking to change her mind. He finally insisted it would be better if he came over to her house after school because he didn't want her waiting around the boy's dressing room where the meeting would was being held. He was certain she thought that was strange, because she always waited for him there when he played basketball. Reluctantly Ann agreed, but Chance knew she would forgive him for lying to her since he only wanted to surprise her.

When Mr. French's class was over Chance almost ran out of the classroom. He didn't want to talk to Ann again. He wasn't good at lying to her he knew Ann could look at his face and read his thoughts. Chance's mother was waiting for him on the street away from Ann's house. He thanked her for bringing Ann's Valentine. By the time he arrived at Ann's front door, his heart was pounding with excitement. He wondered how he could get the box in the house without Ann seeing it. He decided to lay it down by the door before he rang the bell. Chance hoped she wasn't watching for him at the window as she normally did on weekends when he was coming over. He rang the doorbell and when she didn't answer it, he rang it again. What if she wasn't here? What if she waited for him at school after all? Then he heard her coming through the house. Ann opened the door as she was straightening her clothes. "Sorry, Chance, I was in the bathroom. I didn't think your meeting would be over this soon."

"It's all right, Ann." Chance said as he came in the house, leaving her Valentine leaning against the house next to the front door.

"Do you have a coke? I need something to drink."

As Ann left the living room to get a coke, Chance opened the front door and set the Valentine on the couch. Just as Chance closed the door. Ann ran back into the room almost bumping into Chance who had started into the kitchen.

"Chance, I thought you left. I heard the door close." "No, we just didn't get it closed when I came in."

Ann took his hand and led him into the kitchen.

"Here, right here, you sit down while I finish fixing the cokes. I want to be able to keep an eye on you. You've been acting funny all day."

"Annie, I wanted to ask you something." Chance said with his heart in his throat.

"All right." Ann said as she finished putting ice in their cokes.

"You have my undivided attention."

Chance said as he reached for her hand, "Let's go into the living room.

"OK, but you are really acting funny."

Chance replied, "Who's acting? I am funny."

Chance took Ann's hand and led her into the living room. As they entered the room, Ann's eyes went straight to the huge heart-shaped box.

"My god! Do you think that's a big enough box of candy? Chance, it must be ten pounds!"

Chance said as he turned her toward him and begins kissing her.

"Not nearly as big as the love in my heart for you Annie, I wanted to ask you to go steady."

"Yes, Chance, but I already thought we were, at least I felt like we were."

"I know, Ann, but I thought we should put it in words."

Chance began kissing her again and he touched her breast.

Immediately, he pulled his hand back and said, "I'm sorry, Ann."

"Don't be sorry," she said, taking his hand and putting it back on her right breast.

"I love you, Chance."

"I think we better have those cokes and maybe if you have an extra piece of candy around you could spare, we could have that, too. If we keep this up, I don't think I could stop. Besides, I have to go to work after awhile and I don't want to be wearing wet clothes. Being with you like this is giving me that problem.

"You're right. I'm not too sure if we kept this up, I would want you to stop."

With that remark Ann pulled away from Chance and went back into the kitchen to bring back the forgotten cokes.

"You know what, Ann?"

"No."

"You really do have blue eyes!"

"You nut! I love you."

Chance grabbed Ann and kissed her again, spilling their cokes all over them and the carpet.

Chance laughed and said, "Well, I guess that's one way of cooling us down. I've heard of throwing cold water on dogs, but cokes on people?"

They laughed and began picking up the ice and putting it back in their glasses. Ann got a wet cloth and wiped up the carpet.

As she was putting the finishing touches on the clean-up job. Ann said to Chance, "I guess you will be wearing wet clothes to work anyway, not only wet, but sticky."

"You think they weren't sticky before? You should be ashamed of yourself causing me to have wet pants."

Ann replied, "Mine aren't too dry, so you'd better get out of here and get to work or you're going to be late.

As Chance went out the door, he turned and shouted. "Annie, I love you! And, you really do have blue eyes." "Goodbye, you nut! I love you, too!"

The following Friday, an article on the front page of the school newspaper announced the hottest pair of new steadies in school was Chance Clark and Ann Harris. On the very next page of the newspaper, you could read that the editor-in-chief of the school paper was Ann Harris. That week Ann even covered the news story on the front page.

The rest of the school year flew by. Chance and Ann were always together. He started going to her house before school to walk her to school. They had lunch together every day and they left school together every afternoon. Since it was against school policy to hold hands or show any kind of affection on school property, they waited until they passed through the school yard gate before holding hands. He called her every night when he was working. Sometimes, Chance thought maybe he was not quite as good as an employee for the Super-Duper stores as he might have been since he spent most of his time thinking about Ann. She had become the most important thing in life for him.

However, even with this handicap, Chance was still one of Mr. Bruce's best employees. He apparently had acquired his father's work habits. He could do as much work as any two other employees in the store and still have time to think about Ann.

The school year was drawing to a close and the big ninth grade prom was getting very close. Ann was very excited about the prom. She wanted her mother to help her find the "perfect" dress.This was going to be her first prom, and she wanted everything to be just right. Ann's mother worked every day running a small fountain service in a large department store and she also managed an apartment building owned by a church. She was a very busy woman, but she promised Ann she would take next Thursday afternoon off, two weeks before the prom, and help Ann find her "perfect" prom dress. Ann continued to worry she would not be able to find a dress like the one she had pictured in her mind. She wanted Chance to be proud of how she looked and more importantly, she wanted Chance to think she was the best-looking girl at the prom.

Finally Thursday arrived and Ann told Chance she was meeting her mother right after school to go shopping. Chance acted very upset with Ann because he didn't want to give up his time with her. He couldn't understand how going shopping could be more important than being with him. He became very quiet.

Ann said, "Are you going to pout the rest of the day?"

She had never seen this side of Chance before and said, "You're acting like a baby who can't have his own way."

Chance couldn't make her understand being with her was the most important thing in life to him and every minute away from her was like a year.

When the school day was over, Chance rushed out of Algebra class before Ann even had a chance to pick up her books. She couldn't believe how Chance was acting. How could Chance treat her like this, when all she was doing was trying to find a prom dress that would make him proud of her? By the time Ann got home to meet her mother, she was in tears.

"Mother, how can Chance act like this?"

Mrs. Harris didn't know what Ann was talking about and couldn't understand why Ann was crying.

"Ann, what in the world are you crying about? What has Chance done?

"Mom, Chance is mad at me because I'm going shopping with you. How can he act like that?" She didn't give her mother a chance to answer. "I just wanted to find a dress to make Chance proud of being with me."

Mrs. Harris said, "Ann, don't try to understand boys or men.

They can find any little thing to get mad about if they don't get their own way all the time. One thing I can tell you is he will get over it and everything will be all right."

With that, Ann cried even louder and then stopped.

"Mom, let's go!"

They got into the Harris's car and started to town. Mrs. Harris guided the blue Caddy down Main Street and headed to the King Dress Shoppe, one of Webster's best clothing stores. By the time they parked the car, Ann's tears were gone and she almost managed a half-smile at the thought of at last finding her "perfect" prom dress.

As Mrs. Harris and Ann entered the store, they were greeted warmly by Mrs. King. Last summer, Ann worked for Mrs. King, helping to take care of her mother just before she passed away. Mrs. King was about sixty years old and had been a very attractive woman in her youth and still managed to look very good.

Mrs. King hugged Ann and said, "Ann, it's so good to see you. You have grown into such a beautiful young woman since I saw you last summer. I want you to know how much I appreciated your help looking after my mother. She thought you were such a dear. How can I help you, or are you looking for something for your mother?"

Mrs. Harris said, "Heavens no, we are looking for Ann's first prom dress. She thinks she knows just what she wants and it would save us all a lot of time if you have it."

Mrs. Harris and Mrs. King both laughed. Ann was not so sure what her mother said was all that funny.

Mrs. King took Ann's arm, "Come on, love, let's see if we can find a dress as lovely as you."

They headed to the back of the shop where Mrs. King kept her party and prom dresses. Ann's eyes opened wide when she began to push one after another of the dresses across the clothes rack. She found dresses in mint greens, blues, pink, pale yellows. Then she saw it: her "perfect" prom dress, just as she had pictured it in her mind. It was as white as snow. The dress had a cape made of lace that would cover her shoulders and fastened around her neck. She quickly took the dress to the dressing room to try it on.

When she came out of the dressing room wearing the white prom dress, Mrs. King said, "Honey, you look just like an angel. I can't believe how grown up you are."

Mrs. Harris agreed Ann looked like a full-grown woman in the dress and the white color of the dress just set off the white streak in her hair.

Mrs. King told Ann, "Honey, that dress is you!"

Ann couldn't believe she found the dress she had seen in her mind. Now, would her mother agree to buy it for her?

"Mom, it's just what I want it's my "perfect" dress."

Mrs. Harris couldn't believe the forty-dollar price tag either. Mrs. King said she would give them an employee discount since Ann worked for her last summer.

Mrs. King said, "Ann, you've got to have that dress."

Mrs. King told them she would let them have the dress for thirty-two dollars.

Mrs. Harris hesitated for a moment and then agreed. "OK, after all, it's her first prom."

After Mrs. Harris paid for the dress and it was placed carefully in a box, they left the store and Ann told her mother she would need new shoes to go with the dress and a strapless bra so she would be able to take the cape off. Her mother agreed and off they went in search of the rest of Ann's prom ensemble. By the time they found Ann's shoes and a strapless bra, it was time to pick up her dad from his jewelry store.

Jack Harris was a master jeweler and watchmaker. He was a remarkable man. When he was nine years old, his older sister's boyfriend came to call, and Jack was showing off by swinging from a tree limb, he fell to the ground breaking his leg. Since they lived in rural Nebraska, it took his parents sometime to get him to a doctor and by the time he got treatment, gangrene set in, causing him to lose part of his leg.

The problem got worse and before he recovered, he lost his leg up to his hip. It took Jack over a year of being in and out of hospitals before he completely recovered. From that time on, Jack Harris used crutches to get around. He was the most active handicapped person you would ever know. He fished he hunted, loved to drive and could walk a two-legged person into the ground. He loved life and loved people and he certainly loved his daughter. Ann got her sense of humor and quick wit from her dad.

The Harris's decided to make a night of it and go out to eat since they were already in the car and Mrs. Harris had not started dinner. By the time they returned home from dinner, it was almost nine o'clock. As their car pulled into the drive, the lights reflected on someone waiting on their front steps. It was Chance.

Mr. and Mrs. Harris went into the house, leaving Ann alone with Chance. Chance blurted out, "Annie, I am sorry for acting like such a jerk."

Ann reached out for him and they literally fell into each other's arms.

Chance just kept saying over and over, "Annie, I'm sorry."

Finally, Ann said, "It's OK, you're here with me now."

Chance told Ann, "I can't believe I was so mean to you just because you wanted to buy a dress for the prom. I didn't even ask did you get your dress."

Ann replied, "Yes! I found my "perfect" prom dress."

Chance said, "I've got to get home, my folks will be worried about me since I haven't been home since this morning."

They kissed and Chance headed home. Ann went into the house to show her dad her dress.

Mr. Harris could hardly believe it was Ann--his little girl--in that dress! She looked wonderful. She was beautiful!

Mr. Harris said, "You will always be my girl."

"I know, daddy."

Prom night finally arrived and Chance's dad drove him to Ann's house to pick her up. Since she lived next door to the school, they would just walk to the prom. He told his dad he would walk home after the prom. Chance was wearing a new suit his mother helped him pick out at Penney's. It was dark blue and with a white shirt and new red tie, he looked like he was ready for the prom. His grandmother sent money to help him buy a suit for the prom because she thought it was important for him to look good for his first prom. He was ready for the prom all right, but he was not ready for how Ann would look.

Chance rang the doorbell and Mrs. Harris promptly answered it. She told Chance Ann was almost ready. When Ann came into the room, Chance was shocked by this vision of loveliness. Ann was absolutely beautiful in her white dress, cape. She had found her "perfect dress," all right, perfect for her. Her hair was pulled to the side, with the white streak the smallest he had ever seen it. She had it fastened on the side with a gold clip. Ann was stunning!

Mrs. Harris wanted to take pictures of them before they left for the prom. Chance had forgotten until then about the corsage he had for Ann. He offered the small white box to Ann and her mother helped her pin it on her dress. Ann gave Chance a white carnation for his lapel. He had never, ever, had anyone give him a flower before and he was touched. Ann insisted on pinning the carnation on Chance's jacket. As she worked to get it just "right," Chance let out a little scream and jumped back, making Ann think she had stuck him. Then he laughed and Ann cried out he had better stand still or she really would stick him.

Mrs. Harris began trying to take their picture, but with the way she was moving the camera around Chance thought if she was going to get a picture this had better be a movie camera. A week later when the pictures were developed, he found he was right. All of the pictures of them together were blurred. The only picture that turned out good was the one he took for Mrs. Harris of Ann by herself.

Ann and Chance left the house filled with excitement. They were looking forward to the prom and since it was their first one, neither knew what to expect. By the time they arrived, the music was going full blast and most of their friends were already there. Don and his girlfriend, Sue, had saved them a place at their table. Sue went to the other junior high in town and Chance and Ann had gone to the show with them a couple of times, so they already knew her. Sue was a strange, kind of "stuck-up" rich kid from the other side of town and Chance couldn't figure out why she was going with Don. Chance guessed it was their business and not his. The junior high gym was decorated to look like a nightclub from a movie set. Around the dance floor were small tables that seated either four or six people. Chance thought the decorating committee had done a pretty good job converting the junior high gym to a New York nightclub considering how far away Webster was from New York City.

Chance and Ann headed for the dance floor and began dancing every dance together. They were having a good time, although they could have had just as good of a time by themselves.

Don and Sue began fighting, as always. Sue wanted to dance and Don wanted to talk to his football buddies. Sue finally called her daddy to come and get her and she went home. After that, things got a lot happier at their table. Don began smiling, making jokes, and having a great time.

In the middle of the prom, the committee planned a floorshow. Chance almost for got Miss Fowler roped him into being a part of it. If Miss Fowler had not been such a nice teacher, young and good looking, Chance probably would have found some way to say no, but she was all of these things. So Chance said yes. He was to be a dance student that kept stepping on his dance teacher's feet. For the kind of dancer Chance was, acting this part was not very hard for him. He was to act the skit with Betty Lovelace. Chance could never get over her name and he wondered how someone ever got a last name like Lovelace. Betty was only about five-foot- one and since Chance had grown another inch since school started, his six- foot-two really towered over her.

The skit was going great. Chance thought the kids were laughing at every line and Betty was so cute and bubbly it was easy for him to play his part, right up to his next-to-last line! He looked at Betty and couldn't remember his line. Betty could see the panic in Chance's eyes and she just made up something up to say and Chance responded. Betty saved the skit and him. No one ever knew he had forgotten the line except Betty, Miss Fowler, and, of course, Ann, who helped him practice his lines. Chance was so happy to get back to the safety of his table and into Ann's arms; he vowed never to do that again.

The rest of the prom went by quickly and it was soon time for the next-to-the-last dance of the evening. This was a special dance, a balloon dance, where balloons were tied to each of the boy's legs and tied to the girl's legs. The winner was the couple who didn't get their balloons popped or the ones who had the most balloons left at the end of the dance. The object was to try to break everyone else's balloons without having your balloons broken. Chance and Ann were doing pretty well. Several people tried to break their balloons, but they had managed to avoid them. Suddenly, Don and several of his football buddies decided to make sure Chance and Ann were the winners. They just made a circle around them and began breaking anyone else's balloons that came close to Chance and Ann. Before long, Chance and Ann were declared the big winners and received their big prize, two Milky Way candy bars.

Just after Chance and Ann got their prizes. The last dance of the evening was announced, than they heard a loud clap of thunder. It shook the whole gym. The rain began pouring down as if someone pulled the plug on a giant bathtub. Don said he would take Chance and Ann home in his car and left to bring it as close to the door as possible. When Chance and Ann got to the door, they were met with mass confusion. Everyone that had a car was trying to get as close to the door as possible, along with all the parents who had come to pick up their kids. Finally, Chance spotted Don's black two-door ' Chevy and they made a dash for it. Once inside the car, Ann announced they had all been invited to a party over at Sylvia Smith's house. Chance didn't really know Sylvia except she acted like she knew a lot of things the rest of them didn't know. Although Chance was sure Sylvia was really younger then he was, she talked and acted like she had been around.

When they arrived at Sylvia's house on "A" Street it was an old, very large, house with a huge circular front porch. Sylvia greeted them as they rushed through the rain and onto the porch. Several of their friends were already there, and Sylvia had all kinds of snack foods, small sandwiches, and drinks. Chance and Ann were not used to seeing beer and liquor bottles sitting out for everyone. Chance and Ann took sandwiches and stuck to drinking cokes. Don and some of his buddies started making screwdrivers, with vodka and orange juice. Chance asked Sylvia about her mother and found she and her boyfriend had gone to Wichita for the weekend, so they had the house to themselves.

Chance and Ann began to dance and since it was a pretty small area of the dining room Sylvia was using for dancing it was more like just standing still, holding each other and listening to the music.

Although the lights were turned down very low, Chance recognized several couples who were sitting in the corners of the rooms, kissing and pawing each other. The rain continued to come down outside and at times, the rain was so loud they couldn't even hear the music. After they had been at Sylvia's house for about an hour-and-a-half, Chance realized it was almost one-thirty in the morning and he had to be at work at seven. Chance found Don wrapped in Sylvia's arms on her bed and both were startled when Chance came into the room.

Chance said, "Hey, Don, I've got to get Ann home and we both have to be at work at seven in the morning."

Don and Sylvia both sat up and began straightening their clothes. Chance quickly left the room and Don was right behind him. Don said something about it being a good thing Chance coming in because things were getting out of control. Sylvia soon came out of the bedroom and her clothes were not exactly straightened, but her prom gown's skirt was not twisted around her as it had been. She thanked Chance and Ann for coming over and they thanked her for a great time. Sylvia grabbed Don and kissed him as he was trying to go out the door.

It had stopped raining as quickly as it had started. Don put the old Chevy in gear and off they went to Ann's house. Chance walked her to the door, they kissed and Chance hurried back to Don's car. As Don drove Chance into the alleyway behind his house, Chance was surprised to see his folks' '47 Plymouth was not in its usual parking place. Chance hurried into the house and up the stairs to his bedroom.

His mother called out to him, "Chance, is that you? Your father has been looking all over town for you. He went to the school to pick you and Ann up when it started raining. He is so worried something happened to you. He's been to Ann's house and her folks didn't know where you two were either. Are you OK?"

"Mom, I'm all right.

We just went over a friend's house after the prom." "Well, you'd better get into bed before your dad comes in. I hear him pulling into the driveway now."

Chance's mother didn't have to tell him twice, he was instantly in bed. When his dad came up the stairs, all he heard was his mother saying.

"It's all right, Chance's home and in bed."

Chance thought to himself, thanks mom you've saved me again.

The next day when Chance got a lunch break, he called Ann to make sure she was not in trouble with her folks for being out so late. Chance was worried about what Ann's folks thought when his dad stopped by their house looking for him and finding that the Harris's didn't know where Chance and Ann were either. Ann said her folks were not happy with her for not telling them they were going to someone else's house for a party after the prom. Ann told them she didn't know they would be going there, since they had been invited at the end of the prom. It appeared both Chance and Ann's parents were not too pleased with them, but they were happy they were all right.

Ann told Chance, "I think it's best for you not to come over tonight after work and we let our parents cool down. Chance quickly agreed with Ann's wisdom. Chance and Ann's parents were all shocked when the couple stayed home on Saturday night and nothing else was ever said about prom night by either set of parents.

On Sunday morning, Chance stopped for Ann to go to church, as they had been doing every Sunday for sometime. Ann was happy to get out of the house and Chance was thrilled to see Ann. They held hands all the way to the Methodist Church. The sermon must have been designed especially for them. It was titled "Honor Your Father and Mother." Chance and Ann looked at the church bulletin, then looked at each other, and almost died on the spot. They knew they had not quite lived up to that commandment a few nights ago. After church, they walked slowly back to Ann's house and before they got there, they decided perhaps each of them should spend the rest of the day with their parents, as a little more penance. Chance kissed Ann goodbye and headed home. Both sets of parents were pleased to have them home for Sunday dinner, but surprised! By now, their parents thought of Chance and Ann as a set, something like salt and pepper. You didn't have one without the other.

The school year was winding down. They had a big awards assembly and both Chance and Ann received several honors. Both were honor roll students, both worked on the school newspaper and they had been captains of their homeroom sports teams. Chance's homeroom boy's team won the school championships for softball, volleyball, and basketball. Ann's homeroom girl's team won the school championship for softball and basketball. Ann was honored for her outstanding citizenship and Chance for being a student athlete and for his music. Together they had become the darlings of the faculty and of a lot of the students. It just couldn't get much better for either of them. Most importantly, they had each other.

One of the last things Chance had to do in his Social Studies class was to write a self-evaluation for Miss Robinson's class. Social Studies, was one of Chance's favorite classes, but he certainly did not like doing this assignment. Chance wrote he had a very bad temper and had been known to take his temper out on objects, sometimes destroying them with his bare hands.

The next day, Miss Robinson asked Chance to come back to her room after school, because she wanted to talk with him. Chance liked and respected Miss Robinson a lot. She had devoted her life to teaching and traveling. She had never been married and often talked about people she had met in her travels, some of who were very famous. Chance told Ann he was asked to meet with Miss Robinson after school and as soon as he could, he would come over to her house.

Chance would never forget the meeting with Miss Robinson, although it took him several years to completely conform to her teaching.

Miss Robinson began her conversation. "Chance, I read over your self-evaluation very carefully. What do you want to do in your life?"

Chance said, "Well, I want to be a Supreme Court Justice, so I want to study law."

"Chance, you wrote you have a bad, sometimes mean temper. Is that right?"

Chance replied, "Yes I do, that's true, just like I said on my paper.

With that Miss Robinson said, "Chance, I like you a lot and I'm going to give you some advice. You know, I wouldn't give a nickel for a person that didn't have a temper, but Chance, I wouldn't give a penny for someone that couldn't control it. You think about what I just told you. I think you can be anything you want to be, but you've got to learn to control your temper."

Chance thought about what Miss Robinson just told him and he said, "Thank you for taking the time to talk with me and I will certainly think about what you said."

Miss Robinson told Chance, "I hope you will and good luck in life, Chance.

She then closed her books and walked out of her classroom.

Chance hurried over to Ann's as fast as he could.

When Ann opened the door, she said, "Chance, what did, Miss Robinson want with you anyway? Are you in trouble?"

"No, I'm not in trouble; she just wanted to give me some advice about my temper."

"What did she say Chance?"

"Oh, just something about her not giving a nickel for someone that didn't have a temper, but that she wouldn't give a penny for someone who couldn't control it. That's all."

Ann looked at Chance and said, "That's a funny kind of thing to say to someone, isn't it?"

"I guess so." But Chance understood a lot more of what Miss Robinson said to him then he acknowledged to Ann.

The last day of school came too soon for Chance. There were parties in every classroom that day. When he went to Miss Fowler's home room for the last time, he was surprised when she told him. "Chance, I had you sit up here by my desk to be able to keep an eye on you, but you never gave me one minute's worth of trouble." With that she laughed and said she had enjoyed her first year as a teacher and she was going back to Ohio next year to teach. As Chance was leaving her room, she reached up and gave him a hug. She said, "I hope you and Ann continue to be sweethearts through high school. You are both special people."

For a moment Chance couldn't say anything, but he finally got out, "Thank you and good luck, Miss Fowler." After the end of Mr. French's class, Ann and Chance started out the door together when Mr. French stopped them.

He said, "I understand you two met in my class and you are two of my top students. I hope you stay together when you get to high school next year."

Ann replied, "Thanks, Mr. French, I really enjoyed your class this year and I think I got a bonus by meeting Chance."

Mr. French smiled and winked at Ann, then said to them both, "Good luck and good-bye."

Chance and Ann walked out of Mr. French's class room and out of South Webster Junior High School for the last time, but they didn't hold hands until they cleared the front gate. They both hoped their next school year would be as great as this one had been for them.

4

As school vacation went by day by day, Chance and Ann spent every minute together except when Chance was working or they were sleeping. They ate almost every meal together, they took walks together, they danced, they went shopping and they went to the movies three or four times a week. No one ever saw one of them without the other. They loved being together. Sometimes they talked non-stop; other times, they just sat without saying a word--just looking and touching each other.

July came and Ann was going to Rockaway Beach, Missouri with her friend Betty Shaw with Betty's parents. Ann had been going with Betty and her folks for two weeks every summer for the past four or five years. However, that was before she met Chance. Betty's folks owned a big printing company in town and were friends with Ann's parents.

Ann always had a great time on these trips. Betty's folks let them do everything. They went horseback riding, rented paddleboats, looked through the local shops and checked out all the boys on the beach. Ann's favorite pastime was hanging around the stable talking with the boys who took care of the horses and going horseback riding. There was one boy she liked very much--a blond, muscular cowboy called Robbie. Robbie was probably about seventeen or eighteen years old and Ann made a mistake by telling Chance about "this nice boy" who always got their horses and rode withthem every day. Although she told Chance about Robbie months ago, Chance remembered her talking about him. Ann sensed then just hearing her speak of Robbie made Chance jealous.

Now Chance brought it up again. "I guess when you go to Rockaway Beach; you'll be going horseback riding with Robbie." Ann tried to pass the remark off by saying, "He's probably not even there any more."

But Chance wouldn't let her off that easily. "Ann you remember you are going "steady" with me and leave the cowboy to his horses." Ann resented this remark and retorted, "You better do the remembering, and watch out for all the girls here in Webster. Don't let Don lead you astray while I'm gone."

With that, Chance grabbed Ann and began kissing her, saying between kisses, "Don't worry about me. You are the only girl for me. Now and forever."

Then Chance said he had to go home so he could get up and go to work by seven in the morning. He kissed Ann very hard and finally said, "Ann, I hope you have a lousy time on your trip and you're as miserable as I'm going to be without you."

With that, he left her standing on her front porch.

As Chance walked down the steps, he called out to Ann, "Please come back to me. Stay safe and as sweet as you are. I love you."

Chance was so insecure when it came to Ann. He knew he loved her and that she was the most important thing in the world to him and he just couldn't believe Ann could feel the same way about him. She was just too perfect and he was just too ordinary.

The next two weeks were even more miserable for Chance than he thought possible. He marked off the days on the calendar each morning as soon as he got out of bed. He kept thinking about Ann at Rockaway Beach having a wonderful time, riding horses and Robbie flirting with her. He couldn't stop picturing Ann kissing Robbie and letting "that cowboy" put his hands all over her. No matter how hard he tried to get this picture out of his mind. The picture just became more "graphic." He was going nuts with jealousy without having any reason to be jealous.

On Thursday he got a postcard from Annie, saying she was having an awful time without him. That made Chance, feel a lot better.

Ann also said she had been right; Robbie wasn't working at the stable anymore. One of the other stable hands remembered Betty and Ann and how Robbie always took care of them. He told them Robbie was in the Army in Korea. Just what Chance needed to hear; now Robbie was probably going to be some kind of war hero, like Audie Murphy!

One thing about Chance's imagination; when it went to work, it really came up with great images. Now he could see Robbie coming back to Rockaway Beach wearing his uniform with all kinds of metals and telling Ann, "I just had to get back to see you while you were here."

What a jerk Chance could be and how could he have been so mean to the girl he loved by telling her to have a miserable time on her vacation, now Chance felt really bad.

From Thursday on, Chance got a card from Ann every day and he kept marking off the days on his calendar until Ann was coming home. On Friday night, Chance finally agreed to go with Don to get a hamburger and catch a movie. When they got to the movie Chance was so tried he went to sleep and slept through the whole picture. He hadn't been sleeping very much since Ann had been gone and his body just had to get some sleep.

Chance thought, just one more day Ann would be gone--one more lousy day! He only had to make it through Saturday then Ann would be coming home on Sunday. He would be waiting at her house for her, no matter what time she got there. He had to see her; he just couldn't make it without her. She had to be with him every day!

Saturday was very busy at the store and Chance was so busy he almost didn't have time to think about Ann. Finally, it was time for him to go home. He left the store and walked home as quickly as he could. When Chance turned the corner and saw his house, he couldn't believe what he saw, there was Ann running down the sidewalk to meet him. In a flash, Chance was there to meet her.

Ann jumped into his arms, wrapping her legs around him and saying over and over, "Chance, I love you and missed you."

When Chance caught his breath, he said to Ann, "How did you get here? You were not supposed to come home until tomorrow.

"Well, it has been raining in Rockaway Beach for the past three days and the Shaw's said they were tired of seeing Betty and me moping around the cabin, so they said, "Let's go home.""

It seems Betty also had a new boyfriend and she wanted to get home to see him.

Ann said the Shaw's told both of them, "From now on, when we go on vacation we are leaving you girls at home. Rockaway Beach just can't compete with your new boyfriends!"

Chance had been so tired when he left work, but now all of that tiredness was gone. Chance and Ann stayed together on Chance's front porch, holding each other until it was almost midnight.

Chance's mother finally came out on the porch and said,

"Chance, you better get Ann home, it's getting awfully late."

Chance walked Ann home and as he was leaving her, he said, "Ann, you don't know how much I love you and need to be with you every day."

Ann simply replied, "I know how much I missed you and how much I love you."

Ann's folks thought Ann wasn't coming home until late Sunday night, so they had planned to visit some friends in western Kansas the next day and would be gone all day.

Ann told Chance, "Come over as early as you can and we will have the house all to ourselves all day."

Chance was back at Ann's house by ten the next morning. He saw the Harris's blue Caddy was already gone. Chance rang the doorbell and then rang it again. The second time he heard Ann coming to the door and when she opened the door, she was still in her pajamas. She stood back from the door so no one could see her and let him in.

Chance leaned down and kissed her, "Good morning, darling."

Ann said, "Chance, I've got to brush my teeth."

She turned to go into the bathroom.

Chance sat down in the living room and began looking at the movie magazines Ann bought while she was gone. Ann came back into the living room dressed in white shorts and a white blouse.

She said, "Now, Chance, what were you saying about "good morning,'" and she leaned over and began kissing him.

They continued kissing and holding each other for a long time until Ann suddenly said, "We better stop and have something to eat."

Ann headed to the kitchen with Chance right behind her, pulling on her waist, and saying, "What, you'd rather eat then kissing me?"

Ann said, "Of course not."

But she continued into the kitchen.

As Ann began looking for something to fix, she opened a can of pork and beans. She put them in a small pan and placed them on the stove. Chance thought to himself he had never eaten warmed up pork and beans before his mother just opened the can and they ate them cold. Then Ann opened a package of wieners and put them in water and placed the pan on the stove.

Then she got cokes and ice out of the fridge and opened a bag of chips.

As Chance sat at the kitchen table watching Ann work fixing their lunch, he thought, why can't this be our house and she could make my lunch every day?

Ann put plates, silverware, and paper napkins on the table, along with the cokes and potato chips. When the wieners were hot, she warmed up the hot dog buns and added them and the warmed pork and beans to the table. Ann sat out catsup and mustard and asked Chance if he wanted an onion.

Chance answered, "Only if you are eating them."

Ann laughed, "I can't eat a hot dog without onion." Ann chopped up half an onion and sat down with Chance to eat their lunch.

This was the first time they had ever eaten a meal at home by themselves. Chance thought how wonderful it would be if just the two of them had every meal together. They finished their lunch and Ann began cleaning off the table.

Chance moved his chair away from the table to get up and help, when she walked by his chair. He pulled her down on his lap and said, "Thanks, Annie, you're a great cook!"

She smiled at him and Chance let her get up and he began helping her clean up the kitchen. Chance washed the dishes and Ann dried them and put them away in the cabinets.

After they got everything cleaned up, they went back into the living room where they immediately started kissing and holding each other again. Ann stopped and said she had to go to the bathroom.

When Ann returned she said, "Let's go into my bedroom. I have something for you from Rockaway Beach."

They went into Ann's bedroom. She had not had time to make her bed and she still had clothes from her trip lying around the room. She made an effort to push her dirty clothes into a corner and began to straighten her bed.

Ann took a package out of her suitcase and handed it to Chance. Chance quickly opened it and found a yellow terrycloth pullover shirt. Ann insisted he put it on, so he unfastened his jeans, pulled his shirt tail out, unbuttoned his shirt, and took it off. Then Chance put on his new shirt. Ann watched all of this very carefully. The shirt fit fine. Ann was concerned it might have been too small. Chance refastened his jeans and belt and was looking for a mirror to see how he looked in his new shirt. He liked the way it looked and it fit fine.

Ann had another surprise. She had bought herself a shirt that matched his. Chance told Ann she had to put it on so they could see how they looked together. Ann took her shirt out of the suitcase and went back into the bathroom to change. When she came back into her bedroom, Ann was wearing her matching yellow terry cloth shirt.

Chance smiled and said, "We look like we're twins, well at least a set!"

Later that summer, Ann and Chance walked to a small park near a railroad track a few blocks from Ann's house. Chance told Ann they had to get married and he took a small knife out of his pocket. He told Ann they would get married like the Indians did in a movie they recently saw called Broken Arrow with Jeff Chandler, Debra Paget, and Jimmy Stewart. In the movie, Debra and Jimmy were married by an Indian Holy Man. Chance took the knife, ran it across the middle finger of his left hand until it began bleeding.

Then he started to cut Ann's finger the same way the Holy Man cut Debra Paget's, but he couldn't do it. He couldn't bring himself to hurt Ann, so Ann took the knife from Chance and ran it across the middle finger on her left hand until it, too, was bleeding. Chance put his finger over Ann's and said, "Our blood is now mixed together. We have become one, and from this day forward, we will always be one. After their private ceremony, they knew they were married, even if no one else did. They knew they were to be together forever.

Summer was slipping by fast and before long it was time to start back to school. This would be Chance and Ann's first year at Webster High School and they would no longer be the big shots at school, only lowly sophomores. In addition, they would be mixing in the students from North Webster Junior High. Chance wondered how things would go if all the students from North Webster were as dingy as Don's girlfriend, Sue. Surely, he thought, they were not all like Sue.

Don came by Chance's house every morning and picked him up. Then they stopped by Ann's house for her, then to Sue's house for her and then on to school. They followed the same routine every morning. At lunchtime, they all met at Don's car and drove out on West Fourth Street to the Golden Drumstick for lunch.

Each day the four of them would put in their lunch orders for the next day so Mrs. Golden could have their lunch on their table when they came through the door. Mrs. Golden and her husband ran the cafe by themselves, she waited on tables and he did the cooking. Taking their orders was not really too hard, since they all had burger baskets and cokes, except Don always had an extra hamburger. Some days they got a surprise in their burger baskets because Mr. Golden would put in a piece of fried chicken for each of them. Chance thought the Golden's were a very nice couple. Chance guessed they were, in their sixty's and they had never had any children, so they kind of fell for Chance and Ann.

After school Chance and Ann walked to Ann's house when Don went to football practice. Usually they would stop at the Rainbow. Bread Bakery and buy a loaf of un-sliced bread, right off the cooling rack. Then they would hurry to Ann's house and consume the loaf of warm bread in about ten minutes. Nothing could have tasted as good as the fresh, hot bread and butter. It was wonderful! Chance would then rush off to work and Ann would straighten up the house before her mother came home. Ann would help her mother fix dinner and then go with her to pick up her dad from his jewelry store.

Chance would stop by his house after work for dinner with his folks and then go to Ann's until bedtime. His folks kept asking if he was just going to move in with Ann because he was never at home. They kept up this routine for the first nine weeks of school and then Chance and Ann got their first report cards from Webster High. They were both shocked! Ann's grades were OK, with A's and B's, but Chance had a D in Geometry and a C in Bookkeeping. The only classes in which he was doing OK were English and Speech. Chance thought it was something special to getting an "A" in Speech. Because, he always just made up his speeches on the way to the front of the classroom when it was his turn to give one! Chance didn't like his Geometry teacher, she was a very old lady and Chance just couldn't understand anything she was trying to teach. However, the real truth was Chance could only think about Ann and wanting to be with her. He just didn't care about school anymore. In fact, he didn't care about anything, except Ann. Chance and Ann were together every minute of every day. They didn't want to do anything else or be with anyone else.

At work Chance got the news his boss, Mr. Bruce, had just been promoted to become the regional supervisor of ten Super Duper stores. Chance always knew Mr. Bruce was going to be a big wheel in this up-and-coming grocery chain. Chance didn't think he was going to be as pleased with his new store manager who he hadn't even met yet.

The new manager was coming from one of the Wichita stores and where he had been an assistant manager. His name was Charlie McCoy and he would be in Webster next week to start his new job.

Chance and Ann tried to get involved in school activities. They went to the high school football games and they tried other high school activities, but the truth was they only cared about being with each other. Chance's sixteenth birthday was in September and his dad took him to get his driver's license. Since his folks had only one car, Chance didn't have a chance to drive often. Chance and Ann didn't even care they didn't have a car they just walked everywhere, because that way they could be together longer. In early December Ann's 16th birthday came and soon after that, Chance and Ann decided they were going to quit high school and get married. They tried to decide how to get their folks to agree to give them permission to get married and after several days they came up with a plan.

They decided to talk to Chance's mother first and get her to help them with Ann's folks and Chance's dad. Chance and his mother had always had a very close and special relationship, so Chance thought she would be easiest of their parents to convince.

Chance knew his mother went to the movie by herself that Sunday night, so they walked uptown and found her car. No one in Webster ever locked their car, so they got in her car and waited for Chance's mother. Finally, Mrs. Clark came to get into her car. She was surprised to find Chance and Ann waiting there for her.

Chance said, "Mom, Ann and I have a problem."

Mrs. Clark asked what kind of a problem and Chance blurted out, "Ann and I have to get married."

Mrs. Clark struggled to regain her composure and asked, "Ann, are you going to have a baby?"

Ann replied, "No, Chance and I just can't wait three more years to get married!"

Mrs. Clark asked if they talked to Ann's mother about getting married and Ann said, "No, Chance felt you could help us by talking with my folks better then we could."

With that, Ann began to cry.

Mrs. Clark soothed Ann and said, "Don't cry. Everything will be all right. I will talk with your mother if you're sure that what you two want to do."

Chance asked, "Mom, when can you talk to Mrs. Harris?"

His mother said she would do it right away.

Ann said to Mrs. Clark, "I think it will be better if you talk with her by yourself. I don't think my folks will understand me wanting to quit school to get married."

Chance told Ann, "My mom can help us. We just have to get married now. I love you and need you. I just want to be with you and I don't care about anything else."

Chance's mother promised to go to Ann's house and talk with Mrs. Harris right away and she said to Chance, "You better let me talk to your dad. He's not going to be happy about you quitting school."

Chance and Ann got out of the car and started walking in the direction of Ann's house. Mrs. Clark backed the car out of the parking space and drove around the block on the way to Ann's house. Chance thought to himself they had asked a lot of his mother to talk with Ann's folks, but it was done now and there was nothing they could do to stop her. She would be at Ann's house before they could get there.

By the time Chance and Ann reached Ann's house and came up on the porch, they could see Chance's mother through the window, sitting on the couch and talking with Ann's mother.

When they came into the house, Ann's mother turned to Ann.

"Why didn't you tell me about this?"

Ann said, "I didn't know how."

Chance realized Ann's father was not at home. Mr. Harris had gone back to the store to finish a repair job on a piece of jewelry he had promised a customer for tomorrow. Chance thought that was probably good because it gave the two mothers a chance to talk. The evening ended with Chance's mother telling Mrs. Harris she would meet her in the morning and they would decide what Chance and Ann would have to do to get married.

Chance found out later their folks were concerned if they didn't help them get married, Chance and Ann might run away. Chance hugged Ann and kissed her goodnight. He promised her everything would be OK and he would see her in the morning. As Chance and his mother were driving home, his mother asked, "Chance, are you sure this is what you want to do?"

Chance responded quickly, "Mom, I love Ann and I just want to be with her. We just have to be together. We've just got to get married."

His mother replied, "All right Chance, I'll help you all I can."

The next morning Chance's dad had gone to work early and left home by the time Chance got up. His mother was preparing to go over to Ann's house and meet with her mother.

Mrs. Clark told Chance, "I talked with your father last night and I can tell you he was very upset about you quitting school. The only good thing he said was at least Ann was a nice person and he thought her parents must be good people. Chance, you and Ann might as well go on to school today, and I will talk to Mrs. Harris to decide what to do next."

Chance blurted out, "Mom, we can't do that, we just can't."

Mrs. Clark told him, "Chance, you can do this for me after what you asked me to do for you."

Reluctantly Chance said OK, about that time he heard Don's car, so he went out the door and got in the car just like he had been doing all of the school year. Chance didn't say a word to Don and Don didn't speak either. They drove the few blocks over to Ann's house in complete silence, both acting like they were lost in their own problems.

Ann came out the door as Don's car pulled into the drive. Chance got out of the car and Ann kissed him and said, "Good morning." After she was in the car, she said, "You two are sure in a good mood," neither of them replied.

Chance wondered how Ann could be putting on such a front, as though nothing was wrong. He would find out in life it was Ann who had the strength, not him.

Finally Don told Ann he broke up with Sue the night before because she told him she had their lives planned. She told him they would finish high school, get married, and move to Kansas City. Don would become a store manager for one of the Super Duper stores and they would have three children, two boys and a girl.

Don told Ann, "I don't know what I want to do next week, much less have someone plan out my life for me."

He said after Sue told him her plans, he told her they were finished; he took her home and left her crying in the driveway.

Ann said, "Don, girls like to make plans for their lives and I guess sometimes they make mistakes telling what their plans are."

Don replied, "She sure made a mistake trying to tell me what I was going to do with my life!"

They arrived at school and Don found a parking place. The three of them walked up the steps and into the building just as the first bell was ringing, each left for their first-hour class.

The morning dragged by, but it finally ended. Don, Chance, and Ann drove to the Golden Drumstick for lunch. Each was very quiet, lost in their own thoughts. If the morning was slow, the afternoon was a hundred times slower and Chance thought this school day would never end.

After school, Chance met Ann at the front door of the school and they walked down the steps together, not paying any attention to any of the other students around them When they reached the bottom of the steps, they saw Chance's folks' '47 blue Plymouth parked at the curb. Both Mrs. Clark and Mrs. Harris were waiting for them in the car. Chance opened the door and Mrs. Harris got out letting Chance and Ann into the back seat of the two door car. After the car pulled away from the curb, Mrs. Clark told Chance and Ann they got all of the information they needed to get married. Chance's mother said, "You will have to have blood tests and get a marriage license. Then you will have to wait three days after applying for the license before you can get married."

She continued, "We made an appointment for you to get your blood tests in the morning. Then we can go to the county courthouse and you can apply for your marriage license."

The next morning Mrs. Clark drove Chance over to Ann's house to pick up Ann and her mother to take Chance and Ann for their blood tests.

When they arrived at the lab scheduled to do their blood test, the lab tech told them, "I'm going to take the bridegroom first. I've had so many of them pass out when they see me stick a needle into their little bride's arm."

With that, he put a small rubber tubing around Chance's left arm and stuck him with a needle. Chance didn't feel too good and couldn't believe they were going to fill up that whole big tube with his blood, but somehow he managed not to faint. When the lab tech finished with Chance, he turned to Ann and repeated the procedure. Ann hardly even made a face, except to smile at Chance.

Next, they went to the courthouse to apply for their marriage license. The clerk had them fill out the forms and after she looked them over, she told them they would have to have one of their parents sign for each of them, since they were not eighteen years old.

Chance's mother signed for him and Ann's mom signed for her. Then the clerk said she would have to have a judge sign the form giving Chance permission to get married at sixteen years old.

Chance asked if the judge had to sign for Ann too, but the clerk said as long as a girl had permission from her parents, she could get married at fourteen and didn't need a judge's approval. The clerk told them they didn't need to worry, since Chance's mother had signed the consent form, the judge would sign it too.

In a few minutes the clerk came back with the judge's signature and told them they just needed the blood test results and to wait for the three-day waiting period before picking up the license to get married.

Chance and Ann then tried to meet with the minister of the Methodist Church they had been attending every Sunday, but found he was out of town and wouldn't be back until Sunday morning. After their three-day waiting period, the first day they could be married would be the following Monday, so they decided to contact Chance's parents' minister at the First Baptist church. After several tries, Chance got the minister on the telephone and the minister told Chance he could marry them early next Monday morning at the parsonage.

On Thursday afternoon they dropped off the results from their blood tests at the courthouse and the same clerk who helped them with their marriage license application gave them their license.

She told them, "I sure hope this works out OK for you two young kids. Good luck!"

The only thing left to do was to ask Don and Ann's friend, Betty Shaw, to stand up with them. Both agreed.

5

The Sunday before the wedding, Chance went to Ann's house so they could go to church together. When he arrived, Mrs. Harris answered the door and Chance asked if Ann was ready to go. Mrs. Harris told him he better go and see Ann in her bedroom.

Chance knocked softly on Ann's bedroom door and he heard her say, "Come in." Chance opened the door and went into Ann's bedroom, closing the door behind him. Ann was in bed and looking as pale as a bright white sheet.

Chance asked, "What's the matter?"

Ann cried, "I've got one of my migraine headaches."

Chance went over to her bed and sat down, taking her hand in his and asked, "Do you think you will be OK tomorrow? We are getting married in the morning. We've got to get married. I don't care about anything else, but you."

"Chance, are you sure that's what you want?"

"Now you are beginning to sound like my mother. That's the same thing she asked me. Ann, what else do I have to say to you? I love you, I want you and I need you."

With that, Ann rose up and kissed him.

She said, "My dad asked my mother to take me to buy awedding dress yesterday and look what else he brought to us last night from his store."

Ann took a small blue cloth-covered box from under her pillow in it was a Keepsake diamond engagement ring and a diamond wedding band. Encircling them was a man's gold wedding band. Chance couldn't believe what Mr. Harris did for them.

"Ann, that's wonderful, I can't believe he would do that for us."

"My daddy told me getting married at sixteen was not exactly what he had planned for me, but if you were what I wanted it would have to be all right with him."

"Ann, I am so happy your dad is acting this way. I was really afraid he might want to shoot me."

"Darling, my daddy wouldn't do that, he likes you and besides, he wouldn't do it to me, he knows I love you."

Chance stayed with Ann for about two more hours, but couldn't stand seeing her in so much pain. Ann told him, "When I'm like this, I would really rather be by myself."

Chance spent the rest of the day with his folks. His dad was having a hard time with Chance getting married in the morning. Chance's dad just couldn't bring himself to talk about it. He was never one for doing a lot of talking, but today he would hardly say a word.

After supper, Don came over to spend the night with Chance so they could get up and get to Ann's house early the next morning. Chance and Ann were to be at Reverend Thomas's house at nine the next morning for the wedding service.

Don said, "I've been working all day and haven't had anything to eat."

Chance said, "Ok I'll go with you and have a coke while you have something to eat."

By the time they started back to Chance's house, it was snowing very hard; huge snowflakes were coming down. Chance thought what, if we can't get to the minister's house tomorrow? Kansas, weather could be so unpredictable. As Don turned the corner on "B" Street to go north on Poplar, the little black Chevy's rear end began sliding and before Don could react, the car slid into and up over a high curb.

The car became high centered on the curb and it would not move, the rear tires would spin but they were not touching the ground. Chance and Don climbed out of the car and both realized the temperature had dropped below freezing and they were suddenly very cold.

Chance said, "We've got to get this car off the curb. It's getting late and we might be here all night."

Then Chance remembered something he saw his dad do once. He asked Don if he had a jack in the car and Don said he did. Don began digging around in the car's trunk, looking for the jack in the dark the snow was getting deeper by the minute. Finally Don found the jack and the jack handle.

Chance got under the car and located the rear axle of the car. He placed the jack under the right side of the axle and began raising the right side of the car. Chance told Don to get in the car, start up the motor and put the car in gear. Don agreed to do it, but said the rear wheels aren't touching the ground.

Chance told him, "When I yell at you, let out the clutch and give the car as much gas as you can."

Don started the car and put it in low gear. Chance yelled at him to let the clutch out and give it the gas. Don began slowly letting out on the clutch and giving the old '35 Chevy the gas.

Chance put his right shoulder against the right side of the car and pushed with all his strength. Suddenly the jack fell over and the tires hit the ground, the little Chevy jumped off the curb. Don almost couldn't get the car stopped. It slid around sideways in the snow.

The car was now stopped and facing back toward the curb Chance had just pushed it off of. In the car's headlights Chance could see the jack and jack handle in the snow, so he picked them up and threw them into the trunk.

Chance got into the car and said to Don, "Let's try to get home safely. Please take it easy, will you?"

Don slowly started the car moving again and took great care driving to Chance's house. They made it safely there and when they went inside the house.

Chance's dad said, "I was getting worried about you two in all this snow. Are you OK?"

Chance replied, "Yeah, we're OK. It just took a little longer than normal to get home."

The next morning, Chance was up early and dressed in the blue suit he bought for the ninth-grade prom. He woke Don and he was soon dressed and ready to go. When they went outside, they found the snow had stopped sometime during the night and Chance's dad had all of the snow cleaned off Don's car.

On the way to pick up Ann, Don told Chance, "Listen, I better not ever hear about you mistreating Ann. She's special. If I do, I'll come over and kick your rear end until you're not able to sit down! Do you understand me?"

Chance understood Don had real feelings about Ann, but he just answered, "You don't have to worry about that, I would never hurt Ann."

They arrived at Ann's house and both of them went to the door to get her. Ann was wearing a new cream-colored dress that was very beautiful, but made her look older then her years.

Chance asked if she was "OK" and she assured him she was. Ann told them Betty was driving her own car to the minister's house and would meet them there.

When they arrived at the minister's house, Betty was sitting in her car waiting for them. They got out of the cars and walked up the sidewalk that someone had shoveled. They climbed the stairs to the front porch, Chance rang the bell, and the door was quickly answered. Reverend Thomas introduced himself and each of them did the same. Then Reverend Thomas asked them to come into a small parlor just off of the entrance hallway. He asked them for their marriage license and Don gave it to him.

In the same tone of voice in which he had been talking to them, Reverend Thomas began the wedding ceremony. Chance did not even realize the wedding ceremony had begun until Reverend Thomas asked him. "Chance, do you take Ann to be your lawfully wedded wife. To honor and love, to have and to hold from this day forward, in sickness and health, for richer or poorer, and forsaking all others and keeping yourself only unto her until death do you part, and then pledging yourself to her even in death?"

Chance answered, "I will."

Then Reverend Thomas said to Ann. "Ann, do you take Chance for your lawfully wedded husband. To honor and obey, to have and to hold from this day forward, in sickness and health, for richer or poorer, forsaking all others and keeping yourself only unto him, until death do you part, and then pledging yourself to him even in death?"

Ann answered, "I will."

Reverend Thomas continued, "Inasmuch as you both have pledged your troth to each other and by the power of God and under the laws of the State of Kansas, I pronounce from this day forward, you are husband and wife. Chance, you may kiss your bride."

Chance began kissing Ann just as the grandfather clock in the hallway began striking. One, two, three, four ... nine times it struck, just like it had been prearranged to do so for a movie.

Chance thought now, the whole world knows Ann and I are one.

Don kissed Ann and Chance kissed Betty. Reverend and Mrs. Thomas congratulated them and Don gave Reverend Thomas an envelope Chance had given him earlier with twenty dollar for his services.

So Chance and Ann were married on a cold and snowy day on December 22, 1952, in the central Kansas town of Webster and their life together had begun.

After they left the parsonage, Chance, Ann, and Don got back into Don's car and Betty told them she would meet them at Ann's house. When they arrived, their mothers were waiting for them. Although it was only about 9:30 in the morning, their mothers had a wedding cake, ice cream and punch waiting for them. The mothers gave Chance and Ann big hugs and kisses and congratulated them.

Chance and Ann cut their wedding cake and each began to relax a little bit. Their smiles began to grow. For the first time in a long time they were both really happy. They had gotten what they wanted more then anything else in the "world"--each other. They were married. They belonged to each other.

After the cake and ice cream, Betty gave them a wedding present. It was a beautiful set of matching yellow towels and wash cloths. Then Betty had to leave to help her folks with a large printing order that had to be delivered before Christmas. As Betty gave Chance a kiss on the cheek, she told him, "You better take good care of my best friend."

Betty turned to Ann and held her in her arms for a long time and said, "This changes a lot of things in our lives, and I guess from now on, you have a husband that who will comes first over your friends."

For the first time, Ann thought I have a husband!

Ann replied to Betty, "We will always be friends."

Betty said, "Sure we will," and she left.

Then Don said, "Well, Chance, I have to go to work. Since you aren't going to be working for a few days, somebody has to keep the old Super Duper store running."

Don shook hands with Chance and said, "You be sure you remember what I told you this morning."

Chance grinned and said, "You know I'll always take care of Ann. Besides, I wouldn't want you kicking my rear end."

They both laughed.

Don gave Ann another hug and said, "Well, I guess the best man is entitled to one more kiss."

He gave Ann a big kiss directly on the mouth.

Chance said, "I'm not sure you worked that hard being best man to deserve that much of a kiss."

Again, they both laughed the way close friends will do, even when a joke is not that funny.

After Don left, Mrs. Harris said, "Let's go to the store and see your daddy and let him know everything went all right with the wedding."

Chance, Ann and their mothers drove downtown to the Harris's jewelry store.

When they arrived at the store, Mr. Harris was busy with a customer. He saw them come in and could see the pleased looks on Chance and Ann's faces, so he knew everything was OK. Mr. Harris finished making the sale and as soon as the customer left the store, he announced.

"It's almost lunch time and since I just completed a sale for almost a thousand dollars, I think I can spring for lunch for the wedding party."

Mr. Harris led them to a small cafe a few doors from his jewelry store. Many of the tables and booths were already filled with the lunch crowd. Several people were clerks from nearby stores and most of the people spoke to Mr. Harris as the wedding party made their way to a table. Mr. Harris acted like he was happy for Ann. When the waitress came over and handed them all menus.

Mr. Harris said, "What do you think of my brand new sonin-law?"

The waitress said, "I didn't know your daughter got married." Mr. Harris replied, "Well, she just got married this morning!" Hearing that, the waitress said, "Congratulations you two!" Chance and Ann answered in unison, "Thanks," and they smiled at each other with smiles that could only come from two people who were very happy.

After lunch Mr. Harris asked Chance and Ann what they planned to do that afternoon.

They thought for a few minutes and Chance said, "I don't know, but we will find something to do."

Mr. Harris went back to the store and Chance, Ann and their mothers drove back to the Harris's house.

Mrs. Clark said she needed to go home so she would be there when Chance's dad got home from the plant. She wanted to tell him the wedding went all right. Mrs. Harris put a large piece of wedding cake on a plate for Chance's father. Then Mrs. Harris went to the kitchen to wash the dishes from the morning's wedding reception.

Chance and Ann went into Ann's bedroom. After Chance closed the door, he took out the little blue box from his coat pocket containing the rings Mr. Harris gave to Ann for them. Taking Ann's left hand in his, he placed the engagement ring on her ring finger then he took the wedding band placed it on her finger and said, "Ann, with this ring I thee wed, and I promise to love you forever." Ann took his ring from the ring box and placing it on his ring finger of his left hand and said to him, "Chance, with this ring, I thee wed, and I promise you, I will love you forever."

Ann asked Chance, "Why didn't you tell the minister we had wedding rings?"

"I guess he thought we were too poor and didn't have rings, so he didn't ask. I was so worried I couldn't say all the words that went with exchanging the rings, I didn't say anything."

"But, Chance, you just said most of them."

"This is different; this is just the two of us. I can do a lot of things when there is just the two of us that I couldn't do with other people around."

Chance said, "Let's do something to celebrate our wedding let's go to the show."

"OK, Chance, if that's what you want to do, but I want to change clothes and take off my high heels shoes."

Chance sat down on Ann's bed and watched as Ann took off her shoes, then her nylon stockings. She unbuttoned her wedding dress and let it fall to the floor. She wore a beautiful cream-colored lace slip that matched her dress. Chance got up from the bed and put his arms around her and told her how much he loved her, and kissed her harder then he had ever kissed her before. She took off her slip, Chance sat back down on the bed. Ann was standing before him wearing just a bra and panties, like she had been undressing in front of Chance all her life.

As she put on a blue robe and heading for the bathroom, she told Chance, "Find me something to wear."

Chance opened her closet door and began going through the clothes hanging neatly on hangers. He found a light blue wool skirt and a white sweater and laid them on the bed. He always liked her to wear white since it brought out the white streak in her hair. However, the blue skirt was not nearly as blue as Ann's eyes. Chance thought she had the most beautiful blue eyes he had ever seen. They sparkled like diamonds in the sunlight or maybe it was just a touch of devilment. Whatever made them sparkle, Chance loved it. Ann came back into the room and said, "You didn't get me any get shoes to go with this outfit. I need a pair of flat blue shoes that are in the closet."

Chance found the shoes.

Ann asked, "Chance, are you going to wear your suit?"

"I guess I will, since I don't have anything else here to wear."

When Ann finished dressing, they told Mrs. Harris they were going to the movies. Mrs. Harris told Ann that her dad made arrangements to go out to dinner that night and then to play cards with friends, so they could have the house to themselves for almost the whole night.

Hand in hand Chance and Ann walked to the State Theater. Chance bought two tickets for seventy cents. They got cokes, popcorn and, of course, the Black Crows Ann liked. She always had to have candy to go with her popcorn, either Milk Duds or Black Crows. They didn't really see any of the double feature they only saw each other. In fact, neither of them even knew what was playing at the movie.

By the time they left the theater it was dark outside. They walked back to Ann's house just as they had so many times before. Ann found the key in her purse and unlocked the front door. She turned on the lights in the living room and asked Chance if he wanted something to eat. They decided to raid the icebox. They found cold chicken Ann's mother left for them with baked beans and potato salad. They filled their plates and ate their wedding dinner. They toasted each other with cokes. After they finished eating, they worked together, putting the leftovers into the fridge and piling the dirty dishes in the sink. Then they went to Ann's bedroom and began undressing for bed.

Chance took off his shoes and socks, then his suit pants, tie and shirt. Ann was watching him and when he got down to his cotton briefs, he suddenly felt funny undressing in front of Ann. He thought to himself, I don't know why I feel like this, after all, she is my wife and we will see each other naked for the rest of our lives, so he took off his under shorts and got into Ann's bed.

In the meantime, Ann had already taken off her skirt and sweater. She took a long white nightgown out of her dresser drawer. She took off her bra and laid it on the dresser. Chance thought she was so beautiful! Ann pulled her gown over her head and down over her panties.

When she got into bed, she told Chance, "I love you and I'm so happy we will be sleeping together forever."

Chance held out his arms and pulled her over to him. "I love you, Mrs. Clark." That was the first time Ann had heard herself called Mrs. Clark and she liked it. It had been a long day, filled with much happiness, but sometimes the body just has to have rest. Their bodies had all they could take for one day and Chance and Ann soon fell asleep in each other's arms.

6

The next morning Chance woke up to find it was after nine. He was so used to getting up at 6:30 every morning he couldn't believe he was just waking up. And for just a moment, he couldn't believe his eyes to see Ann sleeping on his right arm. Chance had dreamed of this so many times in the last few months, waking up in the morning with Ann in his bed, but this was real. He tried to lie very still, so he wouldn't wake her. He watched her softly breathing and thought, my God, she's so beautiful. I don't know how or why she would fall in love with me. He just knew, somehow she had and he felt so lucky.

As he continued watching Ann sleep, he realized his right arm was hurting, in fact, he couldn't feel anything at all in his arm. He tried to move it out from under Ann and when he did, she woke up.

Ann opened her eyes and looked up at Chance and said, "Good morning, husband. I love you."

All Chance could do was jump out of bed and begin rubbing his arm.

Ann said, "My God, what's wrong?"

Chance said, with a little pain in his voice, "My arms asleep. I guess you have been laying on it all night and cut off the blood circulation."

While Chance spoke, he kept moving his arm around and it began to feel better. Once Ann knew Chance's arm was OK, she put on her robe and went to the bathroom and Chance soon discovered what Ann had been telling him was true--it was really cold in her bedroom.

He quickly put on his shorts and socks. He pulled on his white shirt, buttoned it up, and was just pulling up his suit pants when Ann came back into the bedroom.

Chance said, "I guess we need to go over to my folks' house so I can get something else to wear besides my suit."

"Well, if you really think you need something else to wear besides your suit! But I do think you looked pretty good in it!"

Ann put on some jeans and a sweater and they went into the kitchen for breakfast. They had juice and toast and set out for Chance's house. When they arrived, Chance opened the door and yelled, "Hey, anybody home?"

Chance's dad answered, "Yeah, we're here, come on in." Chance and Ann went into the house. It was the first time Chance had seen his father since he got married. Chance's dad was not much of a talker and almost never shown much affection toward Chance, but Chance always knew his dad loved him.

Mr. Clark said to Ann, "Come here and let me give my new daughter a hug."

Ann walked over to Chance's dad and Chance was surprised when his dad put his arms around Ann and gave her a big hug. Mr. Clark said, "Ann, welcome to the family."

Again Chance was surprised, but he was very pleased with what his father said and was very happy with his father.

His dad said to Chance, "Congratulations, son, I think you've got a good girl here."

Chance couldn't respond because this wasn't anything at all like his dad. He never talked like this. Chance decided his mother must have done a lot of talking to his father. Just then, Mrs. Clark came into the room. Chance and Ann sat down on the couch and Chance said, "I thought I'd better come and get some clothes to wear, something besides my suit. Also, Ann and I wanted to tell you something."

Chance's mother said, "What do you two want to tell us?"

"We wanted to thank you for helping us get married. We couldn't wait three more years to get married. We just wanted you to know that mom. I'm going to my room and change clothes. Do you want to come with me, Ann?"

Ann got up and followed him upstairs to his bedroom. Chance took a pair of jeans out of his closet and selected a shirt to wear with them. He hung up his suit and put on the jeans and shirt. The two of them went downstairs holding hands.

Chance's mother said, "I'm fixing some lunch. Why don't you eat with us?"

Chance said, "It sounds like a good idea to me."

Ann said, "I'll help your mom fix lunch if you want to talk with your dad.

Ann went into the kitchen with Chance's mom and Chance went into the living room where his dad was working on a small tabletop radio.

"Whose radio is that, dad? I don't think I ever saw it before."

"It belongs to one of the men I work with at the plant."Chance sat down by his dad as his dad continued removing the tubes from the radio and inspecting each one very carefully. Finally his dad found one that was very dark in color around the base of the clear tube.

His dad said, "I think this must be the bad tube. Let's take this tube down to the Super Duper store where you work. Don't they have one of those self-checking tube testers in the front of the store?

"Yes, they do, and if they have a replacement tube, I can get an employee discount on it for you."

"Chance, we better check with the women to see if we have time to go to the store and check-out this tube before they have lunch ready."

Chance stuck his head in the kitchen and asked, "Mom, do dad and I have time to go check this radio tube before lunch is ready?"

"If you hurry, you do."

Chance and his dad drove to the Super Duper store and went to the tube-testing machine in the front of the store next to the check stands. Mr. Clark put the tube in the tester and sure enough, the tube was bad. Chance asked one of the checkers to unlock the cabinet door in the bottom of the tube-tester to see if they had a replacement tube. The checker soon found the right tube and rang up the tube on the cash register. After taking off Chance's employee discount, they owed a dollar and eighty-five cents for the tube. Chance's dad gave him five dollars to pay for it and told Chance to keep the change.

They hurried home and Mr. Clark slipped the radio tube back into its socket. He plugged the radio into the electrical socket and it came to life. Chance's dad began tuning in a station just as Ann and Chance's mother came to announce lunch was ready as a familiar song started playing on the radio.

It was Nat King Cole and he began singing, "They tried to tell us we're too young, too young to really be in love."

Chance said, "That's Ann's and my song."

His dad answered, "I'm sure it is they must have had you two in mind when they wrote it."

After lunch Chance and Ann walked up town. Chance wanted to go to the First National Bank to take his money out of his savings account. When they got to the bank, Chance gave the teller his passbook and said he wanted to close his account. The teller took his passbook and paid him the full balance in his account, thirty-seven dollars and fifty cents. This, plus the change his dad let him keep from buying the radio tube, was the amount Chance and Ann had to start their married life. No, that wasn't right; Chance found he had another two dollars in his billfold and Ann had almost six dollars, so together they had a grand total of forty-eight dollars and sixty-five cents.

They had no place to live, although they knew they could stay with either of their parents, but that's not what they wanted. They hadn't gotten married to live with their parents. Chance did have a part-time job, but he couldn't make enough money working parttime to support them. They didn't have a high school education and they were only sixteen years old. It was probably a good thing they didn't know the odds against them in life or they might have given up right then. The odds of making their marriage last must have been millions and millions to one.

They stayed at Ann's house again that night and promised to stay with Chance's folks the next night, the night before Christmas. They also promised to go with Chance's folks on Christmas Day to Oklahoma to introduce Ann to Chance's Grandma Cooper. Chance wanted his grandmother to meet Ann, since she was the first person he ever told about his love for Ann and that he intended to marry her. At the time, he said it; he didn't know how soon it would come true.

Chance and Ann were again fast asleep after their day of planning the next few days of their life. They didn't know how tired they were and how much of a strain these last few weeks had been on them, but they felt safe and loved when they were in bed with each other.

The next day they stayed busy all day long moving Chance's clothes over to Ann's house. They decided they would have more privacy staying in Ann's room then they would have in Chance's old room. They also packed clothes for their trip to Oklahoma. Chance found it was a lot harder for Ann to decide on the clothes she would take and she needed so much more "stuff" then he did. He had one pair of shoes, so they matched or didn't match whatever he was going to wear. He enjoyed every minute of watching Ann taking clothes out of her closet and matching up each piece, then finding shoes, underwear, stockings, and God only knew what else she had to have for each outfit.

Chance thought to himself, we're only going for two or three days and Ann was taking more outfits to wear on this trip then he had in his whole wardrobe. Still, he enjoyed every minute just watching her every movement.

After awhile, Ann said, "You're sure a lot of help."

Chance thought a moment and said, "I don't know anything I can do to help you. Besides, you look like you're doing "OK" to me and you look great doing it. Of course, no matter what you have on or don't have on, you'd look good to me."

"Well, you're prejudiced because you love me, but I want to look special for your grandmother."

"You are special and my grandmother will love you because I do."

Ann finally selected the outfits to take with her and then she said, "What do you think I should wear through?"

"Wear where?"

"You know, wear through."

"You sure talk funny. I never heard about wearing through.

Why don't you just wear jeans?"

Ann didn't like Chance's remark about her talking funny and she certainly wasn't wearing jeans on this trip. She told him, "I said you weren't any help and now you'remaking fun of how I talk!"

Chance just learned his first lesson about married life, sometimes it is best to keep your mouth shut. After thinking for a minute, perhaps he should try to change the subject.

So he asked Ann, "What are you wearing to go to dinner with your folks tonight?"

Ann could see right through his scheme of trying to change the subject, but decided it was not worth pursuing the subject any longer. She went back to her closet and took out a box that contained a new outfit. Ann said her folks had given this outfit to her for Christmas. Her mom had taken Ann to pick it out for herself, but with all that had happened she almost forgot she had it. She quickly slipped out of her jeans and sweater and put on a copper-colored skirt with small black velvet dots and a black wool high-necked sweater. In her new outfit Chance thought Ann looked like a model he had seen in a magazine.

After dinner, Ann's folks gave them their Christmas presents. Chance was shocked to find they had given him as many presents as they gave Ann. The one he liked the most was a ruby ring in a gold setting that matched a ruby ring Ann had. Somehow Ann found a way to buy him a corduroy "three quarter" length coat and he loved it. It was just perfect along with a white silk scarf Ann's folks had given him.

When Ann's folks dropped them off at Chance's house, his parents were already in bed. His mother yelled to them they had better get to bed since they were leaving early in the morning. Ann was really tired and she sat down on the floor, put her head down on an end table, and closed her eyes. She was sitting right in front of the Christmas tree. Chance took his camera and snapped her picture. Later, after he had the film developed, he would carry that picture in his billfold and often remark he had a picture of "the best Christmas present I ever got, my Annie!"

The next day was Christmas and true to Chance's mother's words morning came early at four am, his dad called, "Get up; we've got to get going." Sleepily, Chance and Ann dressed and made their way to the car. They almost forgot to take their suitcase to the car. After all of the work Ann had gone through picking out her wardrobe and packing it, she would not be happy getting to Oklahoma without it.

When they arrived at Grandma Cooper's house, Chance and Ann had been awake for only a few minutes. They slept almost all of the way from Webster to Miami.

Chance's dad kidded them, "Hey, you two are you going to sleep the whole Christmas Day away?"

As soon as the car stopped, Chance was out of the car dragging Ann along with him. By the time they got to the front door, Ann was shaking from going from a warm car into the December cold. Chance tried the door and it was unlocked. So Chance and Ann went inside the house. Chance heard his grandmother working in the kitchen and he called out for her.

She answered, "Is that you, Chance?"

"It's me, and I've brought Ann to meet you."

Grandma Cooper came out of the kitchen, reached for Chance, and said "Merry Christmas."

Then she spotted Ann.

"Grandma, this is my wife Ann."

His grandma replied, "I know, your mother told me on the phone Monday."

She spoke to Ann for the first time, "How do you do, Ann?"

Taking Ann's hand, she said, "Let me look at you."

Ann was embarrassed she thought Chance's grandmother must be inspecting her like Chance just bought a new horse or something. But then, Chance's grandmother said, "You're right, Chance, Ann is a beautiful girl. No wonder you fell in love with her. Did you tell Ann you told me you were going to marry her right after you first started going with her?"

"No, and you're not supposed to tell everything you know about me either."

By this time, Chance's folks arrived in the house and Grandma Cooper turned to greet them and wish them Merry Christmas. Soon, all of Chance's aunts, uncles, and cousins would be there and Chance didn't think he had prepared Ann for what she would be in for. Chance's mother had one older brother and four younger sisters.

Chance's grandmother had not had an easy life. When her youngest daughter, Mary, was eight weeks old, his grandfather went to town from their farm, left his team of horses and wagon, and never came home. No one in his family or his children ever saw him again. Chance's grandmother soon lost their farm to bank foreclosure and she picked up her six children and moved to Miami. There she found a job working in a dry cleaning shop. She raised the six children by herself except for what her children could do to help themselves.

Chance's mother took on many of her mother's duties, looking after her four younger sisters. Chance's Uncle Charlie took any kind of work he could get to help feed them. He was thirteen when his dad left and he would never forgive him. Chance's grandmother would never say anything bad about his grandfather and Chance always thought she would have taken him back into her life until the day she died.

Chance was right, he had not prepared Ann for the teasing Chance and she got from his uncles-in-law. They loved to give him a bad time anyway and Ann was such a nice person she was the perfect person to pick on. Somehow she survived all of their kidding, although a few times she sensed Chance was about to blow up and tell them to just shut up.

However, they must have sensed this because the uncles switched over to giving Grandma Cooper trouble. She knew how to handle them from long experience and would tell them, "Just shut up about Donald!"

That was Chance's grandfather's name. When that happened, her daughters would put a stop to the teasing by jumping all over their husbands. To an outsider, it may have looked like these people were mad at each other, but the truth was they were about as close as any family could ever get.

When Christmas Day finally came to an end and all of the relatives left, Chance's grandmother gave Chance and Ann her bedroom and his folks took the spare bedroom. His grandma would sleep on the couch.

Ann told her, "You don't have to give us your bed; we can sleep on the floor."

"No, you're sleeping in my bed," and with that, Grandma Cooper took her nightgown and robe and left Chance and Ann in her bedroom.

Over the next few days, they made the rounds getting acquainted with Chance's aunts, uncles, and cousins. Ann was a big hit with all of Chance's relatives. When they got ready to go back to Webster, Chance's grandmother took Ann aside and told her, "Ann, you are a very nice girl and you've got a very good person in Chance. Take good care of him and he will always be there for you."

7

The day after they returned to Webster, Chance went to talk to Mr. Charlie McCoy his new boss at the Super Duper store. Chance was asked to wait outside Mr. McCoy's office for a few minutes and Chance could hear Mr. McCoy bawling out one of the checkers. Chance didn't know what the fellow had done, but he really felt sorry him since Mr. McCoy was really laying him out. The conference ended and Mr. McCoy asked Chance to come in.

Chance said, "Mr. McCoy, I have been off work for a few days, because I was getting married. I wanted to know if I could start working full-time."

Before beginning speaking Mr. McCoy sat back in his chair and looked at Chance across his desk. "Chance, I'm aware you were off, because you were getting married. Frankly Chance, I don't approve of someone sixteen years old getting married and as far as working here full-time without completing your high school education, it's not in the cards. Also, I'm not sure I want someone like you working here even on a part-time basis. This town is not very big and already people have begun talking about you getting this nice girl in trouble and marrying her."

Chance couldn't believe what he was hearing.

He said, "Mr. McCoy, are you saying my work is not satisfactory?"

"No, your work is fine; it's just your kind of boy that's not satisfactory to me. You know, I've got three girls and I'm going to teach them about boys like you."

Chance didn't know what to say. He couldn't believe what he just heard. Chance had been counting on getting on full-time at the store. He thought about his relationship with Mr. Bruce, his former boss and he had thought maybe in eight or ten years of working hard, he could become a store manager.

Chance decided the only thing he could say was, "Thank you for your time Mr. McCoy."

Chance got up to leave and Mr. McCoy told him, "I guess you can keep your part-time job until you can find something else."

Chance said, "Thank you, sir."

How was he going to tell Ann about this conversation? After he left the store walking through the parking lot, Mr. Bruce drove into the lot and parked.

Mr. Bruce called out, "Hey Chance, I heard you got married."

"Yes, I did."

Chance went over to Mr. Bruce's car and asked if he could talk with him.

"Sure Chance, but get in, it's too cold to talk out here."

Chance told Mr. Bruce about the meeting he just had with Mr. McCoy. After listening carefully, Mr. Bruce told Chance, "I'm sorry, but he is the store manager and I can't interfere with personnel matters. The best I can do for you Chance is to give you an excellent written recommendation."

Chance was disappointed, but he understood what Mr. Bruce told him. Chance thanked him and began walking back to Ann's house. When Chance got there, he saw Ann watching out the window for him. She opened the door and could read the look on Chance's face before he said a word.

"What's the matter?"

Chance told her about his two conversations. When he finished, she said, "Well, you'll just get a job somewhere else and Super Duper will be the ones missing out."

Chance felt better and told Ann, "As soon as the new year comes, I'll go to the Kansas Employment Agency and see if they can help me find a full-time job." "You'll find something, don't worry." On New Year's Eve Chance and Ann had promised to go with Ann's parents to Kansas City to see two of her aunts and uncles. As soon as the jewelry store closed for the New Year's weekend, Ann's parents planned to leave.

Wednesday evening, Chance loaded the suitcases into the trunk of the big blue Caddy. Mrs. Harris stopped at a service station to fill the car with fuel before they got to the jewelry store. Everything was ready when it was time for the store to close so they could get on the road. Finally it was eight o'clock and a few minutes after that, the last customer left the store shortly after that, Mr. Harris came out to the car and got into the driver's seat.

He put his crutches down next to the car door, loosened his tie, and said, "Let's go!"

Mrs. Harris brought along some bologna sandwiches and pieces of longhorn cheese, which Mr. Harris insisted calling "bull dog cheese."

It seems when one of Ann's cousins was little, he used to say, "Mommy, I want some bull dog cheese."

Everyone in the family thought it was funny, so they continued to call it that.

After having their sandwiches, Mr. Harris began to sing, "Yonder comes a man with a pack on his back, honey, yonder comes a man with a pack on his back, babe." Mrs. Harris, then Ann, and finally Chance joined in the singing. Chance was finding out what a great guy Jack Harris was to be with. They continued singing until no one could think of another song to sing.

Chance didn't know how fast his father-in-law was driving and at time Kansas didn't have any speed limits on the highways, except for something called "reasonable and proper." Chance had never made the trip from Webster to Kansas City before, but he heard it was about a four-hour trip; they made it in just a little less than three hours.

They went directly to Mrs. Harris's brother's house. Although it was almost midnight, all the family was still up waiting for the Harris's to see the new son-in-law and their cousin's new husband. Mrs. Harris introduced her brother and his family. There was Frank Kennedy, his wife Betsy, their two sons, Tom and Chuck, and their youngest child, a daughter, Lori. It turned out Tom was a year older then Ann, and Chuck was a year younger. Lori was only six years old. Chance took an immediate liking to Ann's uncle and aunt.

The family was just getting ready to watch a movie on KCMO-TV. This was the first time Chance had ever seen television. Betsy made a big dishpan full of popcorn and she and Lori brought cold cokes and dishes for the popcorn to everyone. Chance fit right in with this family--popcorn, cokes, and a John Wayne movie. You couldn't get any better then that. By the time the movie was over, Lori was sleeping on the floor. Her dad picked her up and carried her to their bedroom. The boys were sleeping on the floor in the living room, because the Harris's were taking their beds. Ann and Chance got Lori's bedroom.

The next morning they went one block from the Kennedy's and Mrs. Harris introduced Chance to her eldest sister and her husband. Mrs. Harris's sister was about fifteen years older then Ann's mom and her husband must have been twenty years older. When Chance met Ann's aunt and uncle-in-law, Elizabeth and Robert Keane, he thought they must be as old as his Grandma Cooper. He found they were very "gentle" people and loving toward each other. Chance approved of Ann's relatives at once; they were just common nice folks without any airs. They made you feel welcome in their home.

The Keane's had a son and daughter and both of them had children older then Ann. The Keane's children lived in the Kansas City area, but Chance and Ann would not meet them on this trip, as they were busy with their own families.

While Mrs. Keane fixed breakfast for all of them, Mr. Keane and Ann's dad sat in the front room talking about their fishing and hunting trips together. Chance sat listening to their stories and Mr. Keane turned to Chance and said, "Your daddy-in-law is the best hunter and fisherman I ever saw. He can catch a fish out of a pothole in the road after a rainstorm and can shoot the eyes out of a hummingbird a hundred yards away."

Chance tried to imagine someone even trying to see a hummingbird from a hundred yards away, much less trying to shoot out its eye. The image quickly dissolved from Chance's mind when Ann came into the front room and announced, "Aunt Elizabeth's says breakfast is ready."

The men got up and headed for breakfast.

Chance learned a lot about his new daddy-in-law in the last two days and he liked what he learned. He wondered why he had been so afraid of him when he first met Ann.

The following Monday after New Year's, Chance was one of the first customers of 1953 at Webster's Kansas Employment Services. He had to get a full-time job to support Ann and himself. The clerk was very kind, but not very hopeful.

She kept asking, "Chance, are you sure you're not going to go back to school?"

Chance kept telling her, "No, I got married just before Christmas and I need a full- time job."

The clerk finally told him if he wasn't going back to school, they would need to give him some aptitude tests. She set up a time for him to take the tests that afternoon. Chance came back to take the tests and when he had finished. The clerk told him, "You're a very bright young man; it's too bad you don't have a high school diploma. It would sure be easier to find you a job"

The clerk told Chance his test results actually showed he could do well in almost any type of job, but would be best working in an office. She said his test scores showed he had not done very well in the mechanical section so she didn't think they would look for a job for him working with tools.

She told him not to expect them to find something right away. "I have your telephone number at your mother-in-law's house. If I find something for you, I'll call you."

Early the next morning, the clerk from the Kansas Employment Services called and said she thought she might have a job if Chance was interested. Chance told her he needed a job, any kind of job, and the clerk told him to come to her office. Chance walked there as fast as he could. When he arrived, he had to wait for his counselor, since she was working with someone else. After a few minutes, she finished and asked Chance to come and sit down by her desk.

The clerk he had been working with gave him a small, postcard-size card that had the name of a company and the person he was to see about the job. The clerk told him, "This is a job with an office supply company. When I saw it, I thought it might be a good starting place for you."

Chance took the card and began walking south on Main Street. The store was about ten blocks from the Employment Services office. When Chance reached the store, he went in and asked for Mr. Jack Robinson.

Mr. Robinson was in the storage room in the back of the store, but he soon came out and took the card the Employment Services clerk had given Chance. Mr. Robinson was friendly, but very business-like in his interview. Chance thought Mr. Robinson was almost as nervous as he was. The job was "delivery boy" of office supplies for Robinson's Printing and Stationery. The starting pay was thirty-two dollars and fifty cents a week, and Chance would be delivering supplies on a strange-looking bicycle. The bicycle had a huge basket in the front of it for packages and a very small front wheel. Mr. Robinson said, "If you want the job, it's yours."

Chance only asked, "When can I start?"

"You can start right now if you want to," Mr. Robinson replied. Chance wanted to and soon loading packages in the basket of this strange-looking bicycle. He had a job! Not much of a job, but he had a job. Chance began checking where most of the packages would be delivered. He discovered most of them went to the three largest buildings in town, the Main Street Building, the Dillon Building, and the First National Bank building. Chance decided he would start with the offices in the Main Street Building since it was on the same side of Main Street as Robinson's Printing and Stationery store.

Chance rode the bicycle to the Main Street Building and picked out the packages for the offices there. After he had delivered all the packages, he returned to the bike, rode it up to the Dillon building, repeated the same process as he had before and finally made the deliveries to the First National Bank building. When he returned to the store, he turned in the delivery receipts to the accounting department as Mr. Robinson had told him to do.

Mr. Robinson asked, "Chance, are you back from those deliveries already?"

"Yes, sir."

"We're not used to having our delivery boy back this quickly, Chance. The last one would have made it back to the store just in time to go home."

"Maybe I was just lucky everyone was in their office when I made their deliveries."

"I doubt that was the reason, I have to think it was the fact you worked at getting the job done."

Chance finished his first day on the job at Robinson's after meeting a couple of the young men who worked in the store. One was Bill Walters, who was the inventory control clerk and worked as an "inside store salesman." The other young man, Jack Stein, was in charge of shipping and checking in of the inventory when it arrived at the store.

Chance hurried home to Ann to tell her he got a job and already started working. Ann was pleased Chance was successful in landing a job so soon. She had been with her mother and had hit upon her own success. She had found them an apartment, if Chance thought it was OK. After dinner Ann's mother drove them to look at the apartment at the corner of "B" and Monroe Streets on the West Side of town. Ann had the key the landlady let her have so she could show the apartment to Chance.

As you entered the apartment, there was an iron bedstead just to the right of the door. The room was big enough to have a couple of small chairs with an end table between them with a small lamp on it. The room also had a small chest with three drawers and a small closet. The cutest thing in the apartment was a booth in the little kitchen. Chance thought the booth looked like one from some cafe he had once been in. The floors were all covered with linoleum, but the worst thing was they would have to share a bath with people in two other apartments, not only did they have to share the bath, they had to walk upstairs to the second floor to get to the bathroom. The other two apartments that shared the bath were upstairs. The rent on the apartment was seven dollars a week, including utilities.

Chance and Ann decided they had better take the apartment. At least it was some place to start and it would be their first home. The next day when Chance went to work, Ann rented the apartment. Ann's folks gave them a silverware set made by William Rogers. The pattern was "First Love" the set of silverware was probably worth more then everything else in the whole apartment. Chance's folks bought them a set of pots and pans and a set of white dishes with a dark green ring around each piece. Between Ann and Chance's mothers, they found the newlyweds towels, blankets, sheets, pillows, and pillowcases. Not much of their things were new, but they would certainly be OK for Chance and Ann to set up housekeeping. By nightfall, the newlyweds moved into their first home. Ann cleaned and scrubbed everything in the apartment before unpacking or putting one thing in place. Chance carried Ann across the threshold to make this, their first home, official.

On Friday, Ann met Chance for lunch at the Cash Drug Store, two doors south of Robinson's Printing and Stationery store. Chance was pleased to see her. They sat at the counter and ordered toasted tuna salad sandwiches and cokes. Chance was surprised to see Ann was very dressed up just to meet him for lunch.

"I've got something to tell you, I got a job working across the street at Rainer's Department Store."

"You didn't tell me you were going to get a job."

"I just decided to try to get one this morning. I went into Rainer's and talked to the manager, a man by the name of David Dallas and he gave me a job as a sales clerk in the baby department. Chance, they're paying me thirty-seven dollars and fifty cents a week, plus a commission of one percent of my sales every month!"

"I can't believe it, it's wonderful. You know, you're making five dollars more a week then I am."

"No, I didn't even think about it."

"When do you start working?"

"I start next Monday."

The course of true love doesn't always run smooth and it was even true in the first year of marriage for Chance and Ann. If you had a machine to test the strength of their love for each other, using a scale of one to ten, theirs would have been a twenty. This must mean the first year of married life is very hard.

It was filled with highs and lows. Sometimes they had differences of opinion about everything. They had verbal fights about little things, dumb things meaning nothing to either of them. Generally, they couldn't even remember what they were fighting about, but making up was easy, because they loved each other so much.

In February, they were in the local Sears store with Ann's mother, just looking around and they found a lovely blondewood combination radio and record player. After talking with the sales clerk, he told them they could buy it for a twenty-dollar down payment with payments of seven dollars a month. Chance and Ann decided to buy it.

The clerk took them to the credit department and turned them over to a clerk there. After filling out the form needed to acquire credit for their purchase, Chance gave it to the clerk in the credit department. She said Mrs. Clark would also have to sign the credit application. After Ann signed it, the clerk told them she then needed to have the credit manager approve the application.

A few minutes later, the credit manager came out and asked them to come into his office. He was very nice and pleasant to them, but said he was sorry he couldn't approve their application because of their age. He said under Kansas Law, no one under the age of could enter into any type of legal contract. He did suggest they could get one of their parents to co-sign with them. Chance said he didn't really want to do, but told the credit manager they would think about it. As they got up to leave, the credit manager said, "Why don't I keep this application for a few days and you can think about it?"

Chance thanked him and they left his office. By this time, Ann's mother came to the credit office and was waiting for them by the counter. She asked if they had gotten everything taken care of and Ann told her, "No, they couldn't approve the credit application because we're not old enough to sign contracts in Kansas without a co-signer."

Ann's mother said, "If that's all it takes, I'll sign the papers for you," and she told the credit manager who had followed them out of the office, she would sign for them. She did, and their application was approved. Chance and Ann just had their first experience of buying something on the installment payment plan.

Mrs. Harris gave Ann the twenty dollars for the down payment, and Chance and Ann loaded the combination radiorecord player in the trunk of Mrs. Harris's Cadillac. They now had their first piece of furniture and their first debt.

Late in March, Chance received a refund check from the IRS in the amount of eighty-five dollars and fifty-two cents for the income tax withheld from his paychecks from the Super Duper store in 1952. Chance thought they might be able to find a car and use the tax refund for a down payment. After looking around, they found a 1941 Olds coupe for three hundred ninety- five dollars at the Davis Motor Company. The sales manager told them they would need a twenty-percent down payment, plus the three-percent sales tax, or a total of ninety dollars and eighty-five cents. The payments each month would be thirty-two dollars and seventy-six cents. Chance and Ann agreed to buy the car and again filled out a credit application. Chance knew they would want a co-signer and he had already talked to his mother about signing for them and she had agreed to co-sign for them.

However this time they had a surprise, because GMAC approved the credit application. When they asked the general manager about the age problem, he told them GMAC said since they were married, they didn't need a co-signer. Under Kansas Law, they were now considered adults and could sign legal contracts.

Now they had a twelve-year-old car, an apartment of their own with a shared upstairs bath, a radio-record player; dishes and other household goods and both had jobs. Most importantly, they had each other. What else could they need or ever want?

Ann had a problem at work with an older lady named Marie who would come over and take over Ann's customers to get the commission on the sale. Marie worked on commission and if she wasn't busy with a customer of her own or if Ann's customer was buying several items, Marie just took over. One day during lunch hour, Chance and Ann were meeting for lunch at the Cash Drug Store as they did almost every day. When Ann came in, Chance was seated at one of the small round tables with wire chairs which nearly ever drug store fountains used in those days and by looking at Ann he could tell something was wrong.

Ann sat down and said, "I can't believe Marie! I had a customer who was buying a complete layette for a new baby and Marie came over and took her away from me. Chance that was my sale and it amounted to over a hundred dollars. I just can't believe that woman. I've talked with the other clerks about it and she's done it to every one of them."

This made Chance mad.

He asked Ann, "Did you complain to David Dallas about Marie?"

Ann replied, "No, the other clerks told me one of them said something about it to Dave and he just said Marie was his top sales clerk. Besides, she only does it when David is not around- -she's slick."

After awhile, Chance and Ann came up with a plan that might work. Ann would just have to be ready the next time Marie tried to pull her little stunt. Ann didn't have long to wait.

The next day, a lady came into the store and Ann asked if she could help her. The lady was about forty years old and told Ann she didn't know what she needed, but that she was having a baby. Ann asked her if this was her first and the lady told her no, she had a son going to the University of Kansas.

As Ann began helping this mother-to-be select all the items she would need for the baby, Marie came up and said, "Ann, don't forget a supply of receiving blankets."

Than Marie tried to take over Ann's customer as she had done several times before.

Ann said to Marie, "Excuse me Marie, but I believe I was doing a good job of helping this lady."

Turning to her customer, Ann asked, "Would you prefer to have Marie help you or do you think I am doing OK?"

The customer said to Ann, "Well, frankly, I was very happy with your advice and help. If it's all right with you, Miss, I would prefer if you continued helping me."

Ann promptly replied, "It's a pleasure helping you."

David Dallas overhead the whole conversation between Ann, Marie and the customer, he walked up to the three of them and asked, "Marie, if you're not busy right now, could you help me in the storeroom?"

Marie meekly replied, "No, David, I'm not busy right now."

Marie and David went into the back storage room that was the last time Marie ever tried to take one of Ann's customers.

At lunch that day, Ann told Chance what happened.

She said, "Oh Chance, I was so nervous and upset I didn't think I was going to be able to do it."

"I'm proud of you for sticking up for yourself."

He gave her a big kiss right in the drug store. People all stared and one of his co-workers gave a little wolf whistle.

In early May, Mr. Robinson asked Chance to sit down he wanted to talk to him.

Mr. Robinson said, "Chance, I have been very pleased with your work. This company has been around for a lot of years and you are the best delivery boy we've ever had."

"Thank you, Mr. Robinson. I have been doing my best."

Mr. Robinson continued, "Bill is leaving us. He's going into the Army for the next three years and I want to promote you to his job.

I want you to know I'm bypassing some of our employees who have been here longer, but to tell you the truth, I think you can do a better job. Also, Chance, there is a ten dollar a week increase in your salary, starting next week."

Chance was thrilled to hear the news, a promotion and an increase in pay. He had almost caught up with Ann. Well, he had passed her in weekly salary, but with her commissions every month, he thought she would still be a little bit ahead of him.

"I want to thank you very much and I'll do a good job for you. I won't let you down."

"I know you won't. If I thought you would you wouldn't be getting the job."

Chance was the last delivery boy Robinson's Printing and Stationery ever had that made deliveries on the old bicycle. After Chance, they couldn't get anyone to take the job using the old bicycle. The company had to let delivery people drive their own cars and pay them for using their cars. The old bike was put in one of the storage rooms permanently.

Over the Memorial Day weekend, Chance's folks went to see his grandmother in Oklahoma and Ann's folks went to her grandmother's in Missouri. Chance and Ann both had to work on Saturday morning and sometimes, Ann had to work all day on Saturday. This Saturday, however, she only had to work until noon. In the afternoon they decided to drive about eighty miles to Kanopolis Lake and stay overnight in their car. After paying rent, the car payment, and other costs, they had only about ten dollars between them. They filled the Olds with gas and drove to the lake. They brought along enough food and drinks to stay Saturday night and Sunday.

They arrived at Kanopolis Lake and drove past "The Dam Sandwich Place" a little combination grocery store and café at the entrance gate of Kanopolis State Park. Chance always thought this was a strange name for the place, but he liked it, it was different. They drove around the beach and picnic area and found a spot overlooking the lake. It wasn't too far from the public toilets and they could park the car right beside one of the concrete picnic tables. They unloaded the ice chest from the car, which they filled with cokes, sandwich meats, candy bars, and potato chips. They arranged the picnic table just right (and Chance learned no matter what else might happen Ann had to have "everything in its place"). Ann was neat, clean, and organized--three things Chance loved about her. After getting their campsite in order, they took a walk on the beach. The weather was beautiful and warm for this time of year, even for Kansas. As they strolled by the beach hand in hand, they thought how lucky they were and how much they were in love with each other. Sometimes they could be with each other for hours at a time and never say a word to one another. Then there were the times they talked non-stop. This was one of the quiet times.

They were too busy just being with each other, no words were needed. Few people were lucky enough to have that kind of love.

Chance and Ann returned to their campsite, fixed their sandwiches and enjoyed being outdoors. Later, a full moon came up over the dam, as if it were part of a movie set. Chance thought sometimes it was really funny how things in his life happened which seemed more like a movie then real life and this was one of the times.

As Chance and Ann had been enjoying watching the moon rise over the dam, they began enjoying each other. They had spread an old quilt on the ground and put a blanket over it. Sitting on their "ground bed," watching the moon come up, Chance began kissing Ann's hands, traveled up her arms to her neck, and then began kissing her neck and nibbling on her ears. She was not too fond of that, so Chance stopped. God, how he loved her. He needed her and she needed him. As the moon continued to rise above the dam, they made love by moonlight and then fell asleep in each other's arms.

The next morning they were up with the sun. They had moved inside the car during the night to sleep as the temperature dropped and Ann got cold. They made breakfast out of cokes, candy bars and cheese. Then they thought they would load the car and drive around to other area of the lake and just go exploring. They passed "The Dam Sandwich Place" as they drove out of the State Park and headed south on a dirt road away from Kanopolis Lake.

Traveling from Webster to Kanopolis Lake took some doing, as several of the roads were not paved. To get from Webster, you left town traveling north on Plum Street and after you traveled about forty miles north, you came to Highway U.S. 56 and turned left. You only stayed on this highway for about five miles and then you took off across a maze of dirt roads until you finally reached Kanopolis Lake.

Chance had the car traveling about fifty miles an hour when the road curved to the right. He slowed the car to make the curve and safely made the turn. After making the turn, he pressed the gas pedal to the floor to return to his previous speed. The '41 Olds engine responded, and then, bang, a loud noise came from the engine and it suddenly stopped.

Chance tried to restart the engine as he guided the car toward an opening into a field. He managed to coast the car inside the opening into the field before the car came to a halt. Chance tried again to restart the engine--nothing. The starter would not even turn over the engine. They got out of the car to look under the hood to see if they could see anything wrong. Chance raised the hood on the car and on his side of the engine, he couldn't see anything wrong.

Ann said, "Chance, look over here. There's oil coming out of the side of the engine." Chance looked and there was a hole in the side of the engine block. The engine had thrown a rod through the right side of the engine block.

Chance told Ann, "We had better start walking. It's almost eighty miles home and both of our folks are out of town for the weekend."

They locked up the car and started walking down the dirt country road south. Chance wore jeans and a light-colored nylon shirt, one of the first no-iron shirts ever made and sold in America. Ann was dressed in jeans and a white blouse. Hand in hand, they started walking home. Neither of them had any idea whether they could actually walk that far, but they didn't seem to have too many choices. There was no public transportation available. Since they got married, they had so little in common with their former school classmates they didn't have much to do with them. Chance and Ann had perhaps four dollars between them left after filling their car with gas the previous day.

After they walked about two miles, a local farmer came by in a pick-up truck and stopped. He asked if they would like a ride. When they said, they sure would, the farmer asked, "Was that your car parked in the field a couple of miles back?"

Chance replied, "Yes sir, we threw a rod through the engine block."

The farmer asked, "Where do you kids live?"

Ann told him, "We live in Webster."

The farmer asked, "You going to walk all the way home?"

Chance smiled and said, "Well, we're going to try."

The farmer took them as far as Highway 56, but he was going to turn west on the highway to Little River to meet a friend for lunch, so he let them out of the truck. As he was pulling away, he shouted "Good luck, hope you get home OK."

They shouted back, "Thank you, thanks for the ride."

Chance and Ann crossed the highway and began walking east to the town of McPherson and toward their turn-off to Webster. They had only walked a little ways on the shoulder of the highway when a car stopped beside them. The man in the car asked if they needed a ride and they said they could sure use one. They got in the car and the man told them he was a preacher from eastern Kansas. He had been a guest minister in a church in Little River, just west of there. He said he was a friend of the regular minister who was sick, so he was there to help out his friend. Chance told the minister they really appreciated the ride, but would get out in only a few miles since they needed to be on the road going south to Webster. Chance and Ann thanked the minister again for the ride as he dropped them off at the intersection of U.S. 56 and Plum Street.

Chance and Ann started walking again. Several cars passed traveling south, but they didn't stop and Chance and Ann did not try to hitch a ride. After walking for about an hour, they stopped and sat down on a small bridge that crossed a ditch beside the road.

They rested a few minutes until Chance told Ann, "We were making pretty good time until we had to walk. It was sure nice of those men to give us rides."

"Well, you could find one more to take us the last forty miles."

"Sure, no problem, but in the meantime, how about start walking?"

Chance got up and Ann followed. They walked only about five more minutes when a couple in a new Ford convertible with the top down stopped and asked if they could use a ride.

Chance said, "We would sure appreciate one. Our car broke down up by Kanopolis Lake and we are trying to get home to Webster."

The woman opened the door and said, "Get in, we just got this new car yesterday and we're just driving around."

Ann got in the back seat and Chance followed. The fellow driving the car said they lived in Salina and he worked for a grain company there. The sun and wind from riding in the back of the convertible was really taking its toll on Chance. It seemed like his nylon shirt acted like a magnifying glass on his skin. By the time they arrived in Webster, you could see his chest was already turning as red as an overripe tomato. The couple in the convertible took them almost to their apartment.

Chance asked if he could give them some money for gas, but the woman said; "Don't be silly, we were just riding around anyway."

"Ann and I sure appreciate your bringing us to Webster. I don't think we could have walked all the way here." As they were getting out of the car, the young man told Ann, "I think you better get some medicine for your husband's sunburn."

"I'll take care of him as soon as we get home."

Chance and Ann thanked the couple again and started walking the last few blocks home. Before they could get home, someone called out, "Ann. Ann Harris."

Ann turned to see who was yelling at her. It was one of Ann's friends from grade school, who moved to California with her parents sometime ago. Chance had never met Edith before, but Ann had spoken of her to him. They were soon all introduced. Edith said she heard Ann had gotten married and she had a surprise for Ann. Edith was married a month ago in California and her new husband was in the car.

Edith introduced them to her new husband Willie Davis. Chance could see he was a lot older then Edith and themselves. He looked like a tough guy who didn't always win all the fights he was in, but didn't know enough to quit fighting. Chance could see he was not someone who fit in very well with Ann and him. Willie told them he was an auto mechanic and he and Edith decided to get away from his friends in California and start a different kind of life then they had in LA. Chance thought maybe Willie was not such a bad guy after all.

Ann invited them over to their apartment. On the way, Chance told Willie what had happened to their car.

Willie said, "Do you want to go get it? I can pull your car back Webster with this old Studebaker."

Willie kept insisting. So Chance said, "OK, but it's getting pretty late tonight. What if we drove up tomorrow? Ann and I are pretty tired."

Ann chimed in, "And I have to get something on Chance's sunburn."

They decided to go up the next day to bring the car back to Webster. Early the next morning, Willie and Edith came to the apartment and the four of them started back in Willie's Studebaker to get the Clark's car.

Willie had a chain he attached to the front bumper of the Olds. Chance and Ann got into their car and Willie and Edith got back in the Studebaker to begin the trip back to Webster. Willie told Chance he would have to do the braking for both of the cars otherwise Chance's car would run into the back of Willie's car. Willie told him to do everything he could to keep the chain tight between the cars at all times.

As they started Chance found it was a pretty hard task to keep the chain tight. When the chain got slack and then tightened up, it jerked both of the cars badly. Chance began to get better at keeping the chain tight, but Ann was not happy. She kept thinking Willie was going to pull them right into something or that Chance would run into the back of Willie's car. She could have been right either way, but somehow they made it back to Webster OK. They put the car in the yard where they normally parking it.

Chance told Willie he really appreciated him helping them to get their car home. Willie said if they wanted him to he could get another engine from a salvage yard and put it in their car for them.

The next day was a workday, but Chance's sunburn was so bad he couldn't go to work. Ann went a little store across from their apartment to use the pay phone and called a doctor to come and see Chance. The doctor stopped at the house after his office hours and gave Chance medicine for his sunburn. He said Chance needed to stay in bed for a couple of days and stay out of the sun for awhile. After calling the doctor, Ann went onto work and worried about Chance all day. She got home before the doctor arrived and found Chance was still in awful pain. He had been taking aspirins all day and putting cold towels on his chest and back.

Two days later, Ann was having one of her migraine headaches. It was so bad she could hardly get out of bed to go upstairs to go to the bathroom. So they were both too sick to go to work. Chance's mother came over mid-morning to see how Chance's sunburn was and found them both sick in bed.

She said, "I don't know about you two!"

9

Chance and Willie couldn't find a car at any of the auto salvage yards around Webster that had an engine to fit into the old Oldsmobile. They finally found a '38 Olds on one of the used car lots and Willie said he could make the engine work in the '41 Olds, so Chance bought the car for $120. It took Willie and Chance two weeks to pull the motor out of the '38 Olds and get it into the '41 Olds and they had to work every night until nearly midnight and two weekends to do it. Chance told Willie he could sell the '38 Olds to a salvage yard and whatever he got for it would be his for helping change out the engines.

Willie decided the old car had a couple of tires in better shape then two on his Studebaker, so he changed those over and sold the '38 Olds to a salvage yard for forty dollars.

Chance and Ann had transportation again and the '41 Olds with the '38 engine lasted through the summer before the transmission went out. This time, they parked the car they didn't have enough money to fix it. They were back walking again. Months went by and they learned to get by without a car. It was not easy and they missed having a car, but they were young and they could get by, they had each other.

Their first wedding anniversary was coming up soon and by that time they had settled into a pattern of living, working, and hoping things would get better. They moved out of their first apartment on "B" Street to one on East 8th Street. It was not much larger then their first one, but it was in a better part of town and they only had to share a bath with two single women. They also didn't have to walk upstairs to go to the bathroom. However, they did have to walk farther to work.

On their anniversary, Chance and Ann were invited to a Christmas party in the evening for all of Rainer's employees. At the end of the party, David Dallas, who said he hoped they both had a "wonderful Christmas", gave Ann a red envelope. Chance and Ann hurried out to Chance's folk's car which they borrowed for the evening and Ann opened her envelope. She began counting and it had four twenty dollar bills in it! They were thrilled. They drove the car back to Chance's folks and his dad drove them to their apartment. Chance's parents were very happy about Ann getting eighty dollars from the store for a Christmas present.

The holidays were soon over. Chance and Ann enjoyed a great time and they did have one big laugh. Chance got a Christmas bonus, but when he opened his envelope, he found ten dollars, a little different then Ann's Christmas bonus. Still, in 1953, ten extra dollars was ten dollars and Chance appreciated it Chance and Ann paid off the debt on their radio-phonograph and their '41 Oldsmobile, and the radio still worked great. They were out of debt! Chance made arrangements to sell the old car to an auto salvage yard for twenty-five dollars and they came and towed it away. Soon after that, Ann's folks said they wanted to help them get a car.

Jack Harris found a nice little two-door blue 1951 six cylinder Ford for them and he wrote out a check for the down payment of two hundred dollar. The Ford was a lot different for Chance and Ann then their Oldsmobile. They had to get insurance for their new car and after going to several companies, Chance finally found a small insurance agency who said they would send in an application for an insurance policy called an "assigned risk" policy. Chance found out this meant insurance companies in Kansas had to take a certain number of "high risk" drivers, such as he was considered because of his age. It was almost like the drawing of a raffle ticket, except if the insurance company got one of the tickets, they felt they lost.

In the middle of February 1954, Chance received a telephone call at work at Robinson's. He was surprised to hear David Dallas's voice, who said, "Chance, this is David over at Rainer's. Ann just passed out and I think you had better come over."

"I'm on the way."

Chance told Mr. Robinson about the call and left the store.

He ran across the street to Rainer's. When he arrived at the store. He could see several people gathered around Ann, she was still was lying on the floor. As Chance got closer, he could hear Ann saying, "I'm OK. I want to get up."

David said, "Ann, just stay there for a few minutes until Chance gets here."

"You didn't call him, did you?

Before David could answer, Chance told her, "I'm already here."

Chance pushed between two of Ann's co-workers and took her hand in his.

He said, "Ann, are you OK?"

"I'm OK. I just want to get up."

Chance helped her to her feet.

David said, "I think you'd better take Ann home and let her lie down. Ann can sit in my office while you get your car."

When Chance got back with the car, Ann looked much better then she did when he left. She began to get back her normal color.

David said to Chance, "I think she will be OK now, but maybe you had better have a doctor look her over. After we told her we raised her feet over her head and her skirt fell back showing her undies, she started getting some color in her cheeks."

David laughed, but you could see he was concerned about Ann.

Chance helped Ann to the car and started driving home.

"Chance, I was so embarrassed. I was just standing at the morning staff meeting and the next thing I knew, David was asking if I was OK and I was laying on the floor."

"Don't worry the important thing is you are all right."

"My head is hurting and I feel so weak. I guess I hit my head on the floor when I fainted."

Chance asked Ann if she wanted him to take her directly home or to the doctor. She said she just wanted to go home.

Then Ann told Chance, "I had gone into the bathroom at the store before the meeting because I felt kind of sick, and threw up."

"I think you better go to the doctor's office now."

Ann agreed, but said, "OK, but I don't think he's at the office this early; he's probably still making rounds at the hospital."

As usual, Ann was right. The doctor wasn't in his office yet, so Chance made an appointment for her late the next afternoon.

The next morning Ann felt a little better, but she still didn't feel well. Again, she threw up before leaving for work, but she found eating a few soda crackers made her feel a little better. Ann left work to go to the doctor that afternoon and since the doctor's office was only two blocks from the store, she walked.

Chance's mother made arrangements to pick up Chance and Ann from work that afternoon she had bought tickets for them to see the Harlem Globetrotters that evening. She picked up Chance from work and he told her Ann had gone to the doctor, so they drove the two blocks to the Main Street building. As Chance started getting out of the car, Ann came out of the building. Chance opened the car door and got out so Ann could slide into the front seat next to his mother.

Chance asked, "Are you OK? What did the doctor say?"

"Tonight I feel OK the doctor told me I was going to have a baby!"

Chance was stunned, he was truly surprised. Ann began to cry and Chance's mother didn't say anything.

Chance turned to Ann and told her, "It's OK. We'll be OK."

Chance's mother said, "It will be fine Ann, you'll see."

Chance was holding Ann in his arms and he began to softly crying with Ann. He didn't know how he felt about having a baby. He wasn't sure if he was happy about it or not, at this moment all he knew for sure was he was scared.

Mrs. Clark asked Ann if she still wanted to go to see the Globetrotters or if she would rather go home.

Ann quit crying and said, "Mom, let's go ahead to the game.

Chance loves basketball and he has been looking forward to seeing the Globetrotters."

Chance immediately said, "Ann, are you sure you are up to going?"

"Of course I am, I'm not sick, I'm just having a baby."

They went to the game and although they each enjoyed seeing the antics of the Globetrotters, each was lost in their thoughts about having a baby. Mrs. Clark was thinking about becoming a grandmother, before she was forty years old. Ann was not sure how she should feel knowing that a little tiny human being was growing inside her body. Chance tried to think about what this would mean to him--being a father--and how it would change his and Ann's relationship. Finally the game came to an end. The Globetrotters beat the Washington Generals, which Chance felt must happen every night.

Four weeks later, Ann woke Chance up about 1:30 in the morning and said she was having a lot of pain. Chance dressed and took Ann directly to Mercy Hospital in her Robe and nightgown. At the hospital, they took Ann into an examination room and called her doctor. Chance was left waiting outside the examining room.

It seemed like only five minutes later Dr. Jones arrived. He spoke to Chance and went directly in to see Ann.

Dr. Jones proceeded to examine Ann and she was softly moaning in pain as he pushed softly on her abdomen. When he was finished, he checked for signs of bleeding. He ordered a shot for her pain and said he was going to admit her into the hospital for observation.

Dr. Jones told Ann, "Don't worry; we will get rid of the pain for you. I don't think you are going to lose your baby, but I don't want to take any chances."

The nurses told Ann they would get her a room and let her get some rest, and the doctor told Ann, "I'll see you in the morning. Right now, I better tell Chance what's going on."

As Dr. Jones came out of the examining room, Chance was standing right next to the door. Dr. Jones said he was sure Ann and the baby would be OK, but he was admitting her to the hospital overnight so they could keep an eye on her. Chance thanked the doctor and thanked

God with another prayer. That's all Chance had been doing since Ann woke him up, praying she and the baby would be all right.

The nurses came out of the examining room with Ann on a cart, taking her up to her room on the fourth floor. They told Chance he should go home and get some rest, but he wasn't leaving Ann.

When they got Ann to her room, they started an IV in her arm to make certain she didn't lose too much fluid. They already gave her a shot for pain and then they gave her something to help her sleep. Chance thought she looked like a little, pale doll lying in all the white of the hospital bed. Chance thought how different she looked in their bedroom. There, she was a desirable woman here she looked like a little girl, sick and lost.

Chance sat down next to her and took her hand in his.

He said, "The doctor said you and the baby will be all right." "He told me."

"I love you and nothing is going to happen to you."

Ann smiled at him and said, "I know you do. You had better go home and get to bed. I'm sorry I had to get you out of bed."

"You just quit hurting. I'm staying right here."

The sleeping pill took over and Ann was soon fast asleep. Chance continued to hold her hand and watch over her as he done so many times in the past few months.

About four o'clock, a nurse came in to take Ann's vital signs and asked Chance if she could get anything for him. Chance asked if she had something to drink and she told him to come with her. Ann was back asleep already. Chance followed the nurse to a small room behind the nurses' station. The nurse was fixing some chicken soup and asked if Chance would like some. He said he would and quickly drank down the hot liquid. It felt good in his throat and he began to feel better himself. The nurse asked when Ann's problem started and Chance said she began hurting around midnight. Chance thought the nurse was very kind and she told him Dr. Jones was a very good doctor and she was sure Ann would be OK.

Chance went back into Ann's room and sat back down in his chair.

Ann said, "Where have you been? I woke up and you weren't here. I thought you had gone home."

"I was just getting something to drink from the nurse," but before Chance finished speaking, Ann was back asleep and Chance soon fell asleep in his chair.

The next thing Chance knew, Dr. Jones and two nurses opened the door to Ann's room and came in.

Dr. Jones said to Ann, "You look a lot better this morning than when I saw you earlier this morning."

Dr. Jones asked Chance if he would leave the room since he wanted to check Ann over. After the doctor checked Ann, he said, "Ann, I'm going to let you go home this afternoon. We want to do some tests on you while you're in the hospital."

Dr. Jones left the room and told Chance he could take Ann home later in the day after some tests. The doctor also said he wanted Ann to come to see him at his office next week.

Chance went into Ann's room and told her he had to go to work and he would call her boss and tell him Ann was in the hospital.

Chance said he would also call their folks to let them know she was in the hospital. As he was leaving, Ann asked him to bring her some clothes to wear home when he came back to get her. Chance kissed her good-bye and left the hospital.

About two-thirty that afternoon, Ann called Chance from the hospital and told him her mother would bring her home from the hospital and stay with her until Chance got home from work. When five o'clock arrived, Chance was the first one out the door and was home in record time. Ann's folks' car was still parked in front of the apartment. Chance found Ann sitting on the couch, talking with her mother. She had her make-up on and her hair fixed. She looked like herself now and not like the pitiful little girl he left in the hospital that morning. In fact, she looked radiant- a word he had heard many times describing pregnant women. It fit Ann to a "T."

Chance asked her how she was feeling as he leaned down to kiss her hello. Ann said she was feeling OK. She said she took the tests the doctor ordered for her, but would not know the results until she went to the doctor next week. Just about that time, Chance's parents arrived with dinner Chance's mother fixed for them.

Ann's mom said she had to leave to pick up Ann's dad and get something for them to eat. Chance followed her out to her car and said, "Thanks, mom, for picking up Ann and looking after her while I was at work."

Mrs. Harris told Chance, "It's OK. I'm just glad she is OK now."

The following week when Ann went to see Dr. Jones, he told her that her test results all appeared to be normal, but he wanted to see her every other week so he could keep a close watch on her progress. He also suggested she should stay off her feet as much as possible. Ann asked about working and when Dr. Jones learned she was standing most of the day while working in the store, he suggested she quit.

When Ann told Chance about the conversation with the doctor, he said, "You need to give your two weeks' notice right away, we can't take any chances with you or the baby."

So the next day, Ann gave her notice at Rainer's, saying she was quitting because the doctor told her she could not spend so much time standing. The next two weeks went by without any problems. Chance and Ann had a serious discussion about how they could make it without her pay check. Ann suggested maybe they should move in with her folks until the baby was born, and Chance thought this would be the right thing to do, so they decided to move in with Ann's folks.

Ann's "parents" thought it was a good idea, too, so Ann gave notice to their landlady they were moving.

After they had been living with Ann's folks for a few weeks, Chance got very sick. He thought he had strep throat, which he had problems with all his life. He was running a high fever and the glands in his throat began swelling. Dr. Jones came to the house to see him and announced Chance had the mumps! The doctor was very relieved to find Ann had the mumps when she was a little girl. He didn't think her baby was in any danger of getting them.

However, Dr. Jones warned Chance he had to stay in bed and take care of himself because someone with the mumps at seventeen could have real problems. The doctor was right; the mumps did go down on Chance, causing permanent damage to him.

10

Chance joined the National Guard the previous February and was scheduled to go to summer camp during the first part of August. Chance didn't think this should be any problem since their baby was not due until early September. Monday evening was the normal weekly drill night for Chance's unit and they spent the entire evening getting their equipment ready to load for their annual summer camp. The unit was scheduled to leave early on Saturday morning.

Early Friday morning, the day before Chance was scheduled to leave for summer camp, Ann told Chance, "I think the baby is coming. I need to get to the hospital."

Chance woke Ann's mother, she quickly dressed and took them to the hospital. By the time Ann got checked into Mercy Hospital, her contractions were getting closer together. The only thing Chance knew was his Annie was hurting and that's all that mattered to him.

The nurses took Ann to a labor room to prep her. Ann's contractions continued in regular intervals. Finally a nurse told Chance and Ann's mother they could come into the labor room with her. Chance was so scared for Ann, he was sure his being in the labor room with her could not possibly be helping her, but he put on a brave front for her.

She was lying on a small bed, dressed in a hospital gown. Every time a contraction began, she started moaning and each contraction was hurting worse then the one before. It was nearly more then Chance could stand, but he continued holding her hand, telling her he loved her and everything would be OK.

The nurse kept coming into the room and checking on Ann's progress every few minutes. Chance didn't know what the nurse was checking, but he did know she kept telling Ann, "You're doing fine, honey. Your baby is going to be here real soon."

In the meantime, Ann was hurting worse and worse and Chance was getting more and more scared for her. He didn't understand why they couldn't give Ann something to ease her pain. Ann's mother kept telling her, just hang in there it will be over in just a little while.

The nurse finally came in and told Ann, "It's time to go get your baby now, honey," and she told Chance and Mrs. Harris to go to the waiting room and as soon as the baby arrived, the doctor would come and talk with them. When they got to the waiting room, Chance's mom was waiting for them. Ann's dad called her to let her know what was going on, so she came right to the hospital. Chance couldn't say anything he was too busy saying prayers for Ann. He kept saying to himself, please, God, let Ann be OK. Let our baby be OK, and Father, don't let Ann ever have to go through this again.

About thirty minutes later, Dr. Jones came into the waiting room and told Chance, "Ann's OK, and you have a boy!"

Chance asked when he could see Ann, and the doctor told him, "The nurse will be out to get you in a few minutes and take you to Ann."

Chance kept saying, "Thanks God. Thank you for keeping Annie safe."

It was over their baby was born on August 6, 1954, at seven- fourteen in the morning. He weighed in at five pounds, six ounces and was born a month early.

When Chance finally got to see Ann he was close to tears, but he held them back. Ann asked Chance if he had seen their baby yet and Chance told her no. The nurse came to check Ann's vital signs, Ann was doing fine. The nurse told Chance his son would soon be taken to the nursery and Chance could ask the nurses working there to bring his baby to the window so he could see him.

Chance held Ann in his arms and told her he was sorry she had to go through all of the pain and how much he loved her.

Ann just said, "It's OK."

Chance and Ann decided to name their son Chase Clark. Chance went to the office to give them the name of their new baby for his birth certificate. Ann told Chance to be sure to spell his name right.

Chance was scheduled to leave for National Guard camp the next morning at six o'clock and he would be gone for two weeks. On his first day of him being a father, Chance had to get everything ready to leave Ann and the baby the next morning.

When Chance arrived at the hospital that evening, the nurse told him, "I'm sorry, but you can't go in to see your wife right now. The baby is with her."

A few minutes later, the nurse went into the room to take the baby back to the nursery. Instead, she came out of Ann's room and told Chance to come in. Ann told the nurse Chance would be leaving in the morning for two weeks for summer camp with the National Guards, so the nurse let them have the baby in the room with them for a few minutes. Ann gave Chase to Chance. Chance took him into his arms for the very first time and straight into his heart. He couldn't believe how tiny their baby was.

Ann and Chance counted each of his little fingers and toes. He was perfect and he had Ann's patch of white skin in the same spot of his forehead. Too soon, the nurse came back and told Chance she had to take the baby back to the nursery. Chance kissed his son on the forehead and handed him to the nurse, "Good-bye, Chase, I'll see you soon."

Chance stayed with Ann until visiting hours were over and then a little past. She was certainly doing better now then she was this morning. This would the first night they would be apart since they were married. Two weeks apart was going to be an eternity for both of them. They kissed over and over. Ann kept telling Chance to be careful and Chance kept telling her to take care of herself and Chase. Finally he could stay no longer and with one more kiss, he was gone.

The next two weeks would prove to be the hardest two weeks of Chance's young life. He thought he was miserable when Ann went to

Rockaway Beach. Those two weeks would prove to be a walk in the park compared to these two weeks!

Ann was concerned about Chance leaving for Guard camp. She knew he was worried about going to camp before Chase was born now she thought he would be worrying even more about them and about finishing his recruit training. She felt sorry for him, but didn't know anything she could do to help him. The doctor came in to see her about seven o'clock and she kept thinking, I wonder where Chance is. Did he get to the armory on time? Is he OK? Is he thinking about Chase and me?

The doctor checked her over, looked over her charts, and asked how she was feeling. Ann told him she was feeling fine, not like she was feeling yesterday at this time. Dr. Jones told her she did just fine and he understood how much it hurts to have a baby. Ann couldn't help but think, sure, he knows. He's a man. He doesn't have any idea of the pain I suffered to have my baby. Ann was a kind person though, so she let his remark pass about knowing about the pain of having a baby.

"How's my baby doing?"

"I have my associate, who is the expert on babies, looking after your son. Do you remember Dr. Shaver? I introduced you to him in my office last month."

Ann said she remembered him and Dr. Jones said, "Dr. Shaver will be in to see you in a few minutes. He's checking your baby over now. You should be ready to go home tomorrow afternoon. I'll see you in the morning."

This gave Ann something else to worry about besides Chance. She thought, is my baby all right? What does Dr. Jones know he didn't tell me? Before Ann could get herself too upset, Dr. Shaver came into her room.

Dr. Shaver was of the same mold as Dr. Jones. He was soft- spoken and very professional.

He said to Ann, "Hi, I'm Dr. Shaver, Dr. Jones associate and I'm looking after your baby for you."

Dr. Shaver didn't get another word out before Ann asked, "Is my baby OK?"

"Well, Ann, as far as I can tell everything is perfect, but he has lost weight from his birth weight."

"What does that mean, doctor?"

"We're not sure it means anything. Sometimes, premature babies lose weight after they are born."

"Do you think he will be all right?"

"Ann let's give him a couple of days and see how he's doing. I know Dr. Jones told you could go home tomorrow afternoon, but I'm afraid we will have to keep your baby a little longer."

"How much longer?"

"Let's talk about in a couple of days."

He turned to Ann as he was leaving her room and said, "Ann, don't worry. Everything is all right with your son right now. I'm sure he will start gaining weight in the next couple of days."

Telling Ann not to worry was like telling a naked man in a tropical rainstorm, "Don't get wet!"

Ann would worry. She was a new mother and mothers worry about their children. Ann would worry about her baby for the rest of her life. He was a part of her, he grew inside her body and she suffered the pain to bring him into this world. She felt she earned the right to worry and she would.

Dr. Shaver had a nurse bring Chase to his mother to try to relieve some of her concerns. The nurse asked if Ann wanted to give him his bottle. Ann certainly did, she was going to help him gain back the weight he lost. Holding Chase did make Ann feel much better. She fed him his bottle as though she had been taking care of babies all of her life.

Ann and Chance's parents came to the hospital during each visiting period allowed by the hospital. During these visits, Ann would go with them to look at her baby through the big picture window of the nursery. They tried to decide who Chase looked like and decided he looked like himself.

Ann's Sunday started just as Saturday had, with Dr. Jones coming into her room and checking her over.

He told her, "I can tell you now, Ann, when you were sick earlier this year and in the hospital, I didn't think you would be able to carry your baby. We were afraid you would lose him. You did a good job of taking care of yourself. I'm going to dismiss you later this afternoon. Dr. Shaver and I agree we need to watch your baby for a couple more days."

Soon after the doctor left, the nurse brought Chase to Ann so she could feed him. When the nurse left to do her other duties, Ann had Chase all to herself and she looked him over from top to bottom. He looked fine to her, except he looked very long and very thin.

Later that afternoon, Ann's folks came to take her home from the hospital. Ann and her folks went to look at Chase once more before they left the hospital. Ann felt she almost couldn't leave without him. It just wasn't fair, she brought him with her when she came to the hospital, and she should be able to take him with her when she left.

Mr. Harris said, "You really did well, Ann. He's a goodlooking boy. I'm taking you to get a steak, you need some protein." They drove to the Blue Grill Cafe on south Main Street. Her dad ordered the biggest T-bone steak they had for his girl. Ann ate every bit of the steak, even chewing the meat away from the bone. She thought she had never tasted anything as good as that steak.

Besides Chance's army work, he still had plenty of time to worry about Ann and Chase. He didn't know Ann had been released from the hospital, or that Chase had been kept there until he gained back his birth weight. Chance didn't know any of this until Wednesday evening, when a clerk from battery headquarters came to the barracks and bawled, "Mail Call."

Chance was thrilled to get a letter that soon. He opened the letter from Ann and it contained a picture of Chase taken only a few minutes after he was born. The picture was black and white and very grainy. Chance thought his baby's face looked as if it were made of leather. He was sure Chase hadn't looked like this the few minutes he held him on Friday night. Chance was concerned, but became much more concerned after he read Ann's letter and found she was home and doing fine, but the doctors kept Chase in the hospital to be sure he was OK and to gain some weight.

Ann went to the hospital every time she could get in during visiting hours. Since she was no longer a patient in the hospital, she could only see Chase through the plate glass window, like any other visitor. On Tuesday morning, Dr. Shaver met Ann at the hospital and said she could take Chase home.

Ann's mother drove them both home. That evening, Chance's parents and Ann's folks just stood by Chase's basket and watched his every breath. Ann got Chase's bottle and had to wake him up to eat. He would take a little of his formula and then quit sucking and go back to sleep. Ann kept putting the bottle's nipple back and forth in Chase's mouth to keep him eating. Ann held him against her shoulder and gently patted him on the back to get him to burp. When he had accomplished that, Ann put him in his basket and spent the rest of the night sitting on a kitchen chair, watching him sleep.

The next morning Ann was so tired all she wanted to do was sleep and now Chase was awake and wanting to eat.

Mrs. Harris told Ann, "You can't just sit by that baby's basket every night, young lady. You have to get some rest yourself."

"I know, mom, but I was afraid I wouldn't hear him if he woke up."

Ann's mother assured her she would.

Since Ann had Chase she was using all of the items that a few months ago she had been selling in the baby department. She quickly learned Chase loved his bath; he liked the water from the very first time she gave him a bath. Even though Ann was only seventeen years old, from the very beginning she was the kind of mother every baby born into this world should have. She was loving and caring and very protective about looking after him. No one is perfect, but she would be as close as any mother would ever Ann was worrying about Chance. She couldn't be at Camp. Carson to look after him, she could only pray for him and take care of his baby boy. She missed him and wanted him to come home.

It was Friday before Chance got Ann's letter with the news she had Chase home with her. Chance read this and shouted out loud, "Thanks God."

Everyone in the barracks looked at him, but no one said a word. He had two good bits of news that day -- he finished his basic training and Chase was OK and home with Ann. Now he just had to make it through the weekend and be in the field all of next week before he could go home.

Chance got a weekend pass and went into town he started walking down one of Colorado Springs main streets leading to Manitou Springs. He bought a box of Karmel Corn and a coke and thought about Ann and their stops at the Karmel Corn shop next to the Fox Theater in Webster. It was funny how everything he did or thought about reminded him of Ann. How he missed her and how he wanted to be home with her! He knew he could make it through another eight days before he saw her, but he felt bad he didn't have enough money to telephone her. He didn't want to call collect; Ann's folks had done enough for them already without him running up their telephone bill.

Before Chance got to Manitou Springs, he came to a small city park and decided to go in. He sat down on a bench, took out Ann's letter and read it again. He closely looked at Chase's picture again. Ann had written on the picture, "Hi, Daddy." When Chance first looked at the picture, the only thing he had noticed was that Chase's face looked like it was made of leather. Chance knew he didn't look like that when he held him a week ago, but he was concerned.

As Chance studied the picture again, he saw Chase's two bright little eyes staring back at him. Chance thought soon this little guy was going to be calling him daddy and looking for Chance to take care of him. Now, not only did Chance have the responsibility of taking care of Annie and himself, he also had to take care of Chase. For the first time, Chance realized the enormity of the task ahead of him. Chance realized having babies was a part of life. He was determined to be a good father and whatever it took, he and Ann would handle it together.

Ann was keeping busy with the more practical side of parenting. She was trying to keep up with bathing, feeding, changing diapers, and making formula for a week-old baby. In addition, Chase seemed to have his internal clock hooked up backwards. He wanted to be up all night and sleep all day. Ann had her hands full.

The rest of the weekend Chance spent the same as he had Friday night. Trips by bus into Colorado Springs, walking around the city, and sitting in the little park, thinking and worrying about Ann. It was amazing to Chance how one person in the world could mean so much to someone that every moment they weren't sleeping, they were thinking about that other person. He couldn't help himself. Ann was the only thing Chance was interested in, just Ann!

Ann's weekend continued to be busy, but she still had time to think about her love out in Colorado. She missed Chance and she wanted him to come home. Her mother bought Chase a new outfit on Saturday and Chance's folks came over every day and brought Chase more clothes or rattlers or stuffed toys. Ann finally told them Chase was not going to be able to wear all of his newborn baby clothes before he outgrew them. She asked them to wait awhile because he would need bigger clothes very soon.

Chance's convoy rolled into Webster just before 9:30 pm on Saturday two weeks after they left Webster. By the time the vehicles were stored, it was almost 10:30 pm. Chance telephoned Ann's folks, told them he was in Webster and asked if they could come pick him up from the armory. In about ten minutes, which seemed to Chance like ten hours, he saw Ann's folks' car turn the corner headed for the armory. When the car stopped, Ann jumped out of the right-front passenger's seat and right into Chance's arms.

Ann held him and said, "Thank God you're home and you're all right. Don't ever leave me for this long again."

Chance could hardly talk, he could only whisper, "Annie, I love you. You sure look different then when I left you in the hospital. You look beautiful."

"Chance, come see who's in the car looking for his daddy."

As they got into the car, Ann's mother handed Chase to Chance and he pulled back the baby's blanket. Chance thought how beautiful his baby was and his skin certainly didn't look like it was made of leather, as he thought it did in the picture Ann sent him. Chance couldn't speak, he could only smile and try to hold back his tears. He was so happy to be home with his Annie and their baby.

Chance offered a prayer to God in his mind, "Thank you, Father, for bringing me safely home to my loved ones. In my Savior Jesus' name, I pray, Amen. Thank you God."

11

Going back to work at Robinson's the following Monday seemed awfully dull after what Chance did for the past two weeks. He had a new baby he completed his recruit training in the National Guard and survived his first summer camp. The store was very busy and he had a lot of inventorying to get caught up with since many of their stock items were very low. By lunch time Chance was back in the real world of Robinson's Printing and Stationery and by the end of the day, Chance wasn't sure the last couple of weeks really happened.

When Chance got home for supper, Ann's dad said to him, "I've got an idea on how you can get a better job with some benefits."

"What's your idea?"

"You'll have to listen for a few minutes, because it's going to take a little while to explain it to you."

"Go ahead."

Ann and Mrs. Harris were also very interested in what Mr. Harris was going to say, but Chase was more interested in the bottle Ann was feeding him.

Mr. Harris started, "First, I want you to start working with me in the evenings learning how to fix clocks. You can earn some extra money working on the clocks since I don't have time to fix them, also I can get you clocks from four or five other jewelry stores in town to work on. Let's face it; watchmakers make a lot more money fixing watches then working on clocks."

"That sounds great and Ann and I can sure use the extra money." "That's just the start of my plan."

Ann asked, "Dad, what do you mean the start of your plan?" "Just give me time and I'll tell you. A friend of mine is a combination watchmaker and carpenter. He can't decide which one he wants to be. His name is Don Pigeon and he repairs the parking meters for Webster. Don is a civilian employee of the police department, but every winter he quits his job and goes to Florida for the winter and works as a carpenter. Don comes back in the spring and the city gives him back his job, because they can't find anyone else who knows enough about clocks to work on their parking meters."

"Do you think I could learn enough in the next three or four months that I could qualify for the job? One of the things my tests indicated when I took them at the Kansas Employment Services was mechanical work was the least of my abilities."

Mr. Harris answered, "No, you won't be ready this winter, but come next year, you will be and I can teach you to fix clocks better then anyone else in this town, including Don Pigeon. The benefits of working for the city are really good, insurance, uniforms, and they give Don a jeep to drive to do his job and he can drive it back and forth to work and they have a great retirement plan!"

Chance didn't think about what a retirement plan could mean to him at this stage of his life, but the rest of it sounded really good to him. Mr. Harris had laid out a plan to help Chance and Ann get a better life. One thing Chance learned quickly about Mr. Harris, when he set out to do something, he did it. Chance also found out where Ann had gotten her "actions speak louder then words" persona -- from her dad, Jack Harris.

The next night after supper, Mr. Harris looked over the newspaper for a few minutes and said to Chance, "Let's go to work I've got six clocks waiting for you to repair."

Chance, who always had been a worker, replied, "OK, dad, let's go."

That was the first time Chance ever called Ann's father "Dad." He decided he liked it and Mr. Harris acted pleased Chance started calling him "Dad."

Night after night, they worked at the jewelry store repairing clocks. Chance's skills at clock making were coming along faster than even Mr. Harris had expected. After several months, Chance started coming directly from Robinson's to work on the clocks. Mr. Harris was able to get Chance clocks to repair from all of the larger jewelry stores in town. As Mr. Harris said, watchmakers didn't want to spend their time working on clocks when they could make twice the money working on watches.

Chance and Ann's love continued to grow. They made love almost every night. Chance told her, "This makes my day complete and makes me feel we are truly one. When we make love, I feel our souls are joined."

Chase was growing very fast and was a happy, healthy baby. Chance and Ann delighted in dressing him up and taking pictures of him. He was a great plaything for them. The three of them actually grew up together.

One day in the summer of 1955, Chance was working on an electric clock that looked like a black cat and when it ran the tail and eyes moved back and forth. Chance cleaned the clock, lubricated it, plugged it into the electrical outlet and it began to run. The next day Chance noticed the clock was losing time. Chance really liked working on electric clocks, since they either worked or they didn't. He never had one that lost time before and said to Mr. Harris, "Dad, I need some help."

"What's the matter?"

Chance explained the problem. Mr. Harris started looking over the cat clock. He checked Chance's work and suggested maybe Chance should try cleaning the clock again and relubricating it.

Chance did everything again and plugged it back into the electrical outlet. The next day, the cat clock was slow again. Mr. Harris decided he would take a hand at fixing the cat clock. He worked on the clock for about an hour, then he plugged it in and again the next day it lost time.

The following day the customer who owned the cat clock came into the jewelry store and Mr. Harris told him they were having problems repairing it. The customer replied it was funny since as long as he lived in California the clock worked fine. Mr. Harris asked the customer if he could keep the clock another week and the customer agreed since it wouldn't run right after moving to Kansas.

Suddenly, Mr. Harris realized what the problem was. In those days, the electricity in the United States was not standardized. Several areas in the United States, including parts of California, had 110 volt, 50 cycle instead of 110 volt 60 cycle as Kansas did. Mr. Harris removed the motor, checked it and sure enough, it was a 50-cycle motor. He replaced it with a 60-cycle motor.

When Chance arrived at the jewelry shop later that day, Mr. Harris smiled at him when he came into the store.

He said, "Well, I figured out what was wrong with your cat clock."

"What did I miss?"

Mr. Harris related his conversation with the customer, about moving from California, and explained to Chance some of the areas of the United States had not standardized on 110 volt, 60 cycle electric, although all of the power companies were required to do so before 1960. Chance couldn't believe how hard they had worked on that darn cat clock and the problem turned out to be something so strange.

It was soon time for Chance to go to summer camp with the National Guard again. His second camp would be much different from the previous year. Even the name of their camp had changed to Fort Carson. Chance had been promoted to corporal and Ann was coming on the bus on Friday to spend the weekend with him. Ann's folks were going to look after Chase for the weekend. It would be the first time Ann would be away from Chase overnight since the doctors let him come home from the hospital and she was worried her folks would have a problem if he got sick. Ann was an expert about worrying about everything.

When Ann arrived Friday night, Chance was waiting at the bus station in Colorado Springs. They went to a small hotel near the center of downtown Colorado Springs. Chance had never stayed in a hotel before. When Ann traveled with her folks they stayed in auto tourist courts, but like Chance she had never stayed in a hotel. They went into the hotel and Chance told the clerk behind the desk they would like a room for two nights. The desk clerk told Chance he would have to sign the guest register, and Chance signed, "Mr. and Mrs. Chance Clark, Webster, Kansas."

The desk clerk asked, "Are you two married?"

Ann replied, "We certainly are."

As she showed the desk clerk her wedding rings.

Chance piped up, "Yeah, you can see my ring, too."

The clerk said, "OK, but you both look awfully young."

He gave them a key to room 28. It was on the second floor and had its own bath.

Chance unlocked the door of room 28 it was a very large room with little furniture. It had a double bed, a table with a lamp and one chair. The room had a very high ceiling, with a single bulb hanging from it. The room had hardwood floors and there was a braided rug on each side of the bed. Ann looked into the bathroom. It had an old-fashioned stool, a wash basin and a huge bathtub.

Ann said, "That tub looks great after that bus trip."

She was soon stripping away her clothes to get into the tub.

As Ann soaked in the tub, with the hot water steaming into the room, Chance took off his clothes and joined her in the tub.

Chance smiled and said to Ann, "You don't know how much I love you or how pleased I am that you are here with me."

"Sure, I do!"

"God, what a difference a year makes in how I feel. I was feeling so bad this time last year I was so lonely without you."

The next morning they took a city bus up to Cheyenne Mountain to go to the zoo. After about an hour-and-a-half of walking and climbing, they found they actually climbed almost to the top of the mountain and were inside Seven Falls. They mingled with a group of tourists and followed them down the stairway to a little snack shop and souvenir shop. Chance and Ann calmly sat down on a couple of counter stools and had cokes.

They decided they better get out of Seven Falls as soon as possible since they had come in over the mountain and hadn't paid the entrance fee. They both heaved a sigh of relief as they left the entrance area of Seven Falls. They really weren't trying to get into the park without paying they had just been climbing the mountain and ended up inside the park.

Chance took Ann to his little park and showed her where he spent his free time last year. It was wonderful having Annie to share things with she was the only one in the world who understood him. She knew everything about him and he knew everything about her. The rest of the weekend was spent making love, eating and walking the streets of Colorado Springs and Manitou Springs. It was hard for Chance to put Ann on the bus to go back home, but she needed to get home to her other baby.

After Chance returned home from his second National Guard summer camp, time seemed to fly by. Labor Day came and went and summer was over.

One Friday morning in early October, one of his associates, Vern Miller, who worked at Robinson's, told Chance to be sure to look in the evening newspaper, because he thought Chance would find something very interesting in it. Vern Miller had worked at Robinson's for about seven years. He was in charge of inventory control and incoming orders. Chance knew Vern had been a captain in World War II and graduated from the University of Kansas. He didn't know much more than that, but Chance liked Vern. He was a smart, hard worker and always looked out for Chance.

Chance kept asking Vern what he was going to find in the newspaper that would be so interesting, but Vern wouldn't tell him. Finally about four o'clock, Vern told Chance he was leaving Robinson's and going to work for someone who had real money. No matter how hard Chance pushed Vern, he wouldn't tell him where he was going to work.

Chance hurried home and found the Webster News still on the walk in front of the house. Chance opened the paper and found looking back at him on the front page was a picture of his friend, Vern Miller. The article in the newspaper under Vern's picture said Vern had been appointed as the City of Webster's first purchasing agent. The story told all about Vern and his family, his war record, and his education. Vern would be working for the city manager and the article went on to say

Vern was to start his new job in a week. Vern was right Chance was very interested in the news and the city certainly had lots of money to spend.

Chance ran into the house and yelled to Ann, "Ann, come here and look at this newspaper article."

"Hi to you, too!"

"Sorry, but look at this story about Vern Miller."

"Who?"

"You know, Vern Miller from Robinson's."

Ann read the story and said, "Well that's nice for him, but why are you so excited about it?

"Well, maybe I will get his job at Robinson's and an increase in pay.

"Well, that would be good news!"

The following day, after the Saturday morning staff meeting. Jack Robinson asked Chance to come into his office. Chance thought Mr. Robinson is going to give me Vern's old job. Chance was wrong. Instead, Mr. Robinson told Chance he had decided to give Vern's old job to another of the young men, over whom Chance had been promoted over earlier. Chance was very disappointed. Mr. Robinson told Chance he deserved the promotion, but the company felt since the other young man had been with the company five years longer and he deserved the promotion at this time.

Mr. Robinson continued, 'Besides we would have to train two people at the same time if we moved you up and moved someone else into your job."

Mr. Robinson could see Chance was really disappointed and he closed their conversation by telling Chance he was giving him a five dollar a week increase in salary, not exactly what Chance had been looking for. Ann was as disappointed in the news as Chance.

Chance continued to work almost every night on the clocks at the jewelry store. One of the other watchmakers for whom, Chance repaired clocks, Gordon Smith, was a man who had been an apprentice watchmaker under Mr. Harris. He was a nice guy and Chance liked him a lot. He gave Chance a lot of clocks to repair and that made him even nicer.

Gordon was a World War II navy veteran and told Chance the most incredible story Chance had ever heard. Gordon's ship was sunk somewhere in the Pacific during the war and Gordon was injured. Gordon told him he had on his life vest and was floating in the ocean without anyone else near him, when he saw the dorsal fin of a shark heading toward him.

Gordon said, "I passed out from losing blood from my wounds and shock, and the next thing I knew when I regained consciousness I was being pushed through the water by a dolphin."

Gordon said he had two or three dolphins around him and they kept pushing him until they pushed him up on a beach on some island in the Pacific. Several days later he was found by a navy rescue team and flown to a hospital. Gordon never knew how far the dolphins pushed him or what island he was found on. He only knew it was a long time between the time his ship went down and the time he was pushed up on the beach. Gordon was one of the few survivors from his sunken ship several of Gordon's shipmates were eaten by sharks while waiting to be rescued.

Chance didn't know if all of the details of Gordon's rescue were true, but he had read stories about sailors being helped by dolphins and Chance had seen the scars on Gordon's body, arms and legs. Chance also knew Gordon spent over two years in hospitals and rehabilitation before working as an apprentice with Mr. Harris under some special GI training bill. Chance felt the story must be true, because Gordon was a straight shooter.

Gordon was very big in the Masonic lodge and although Chance didn't know much about Masons, he thought it must be a good organization since Gordon was always talking about some project or another they were doing.

Two or three weeks past since Vern Miller went to work as Webster's purchasing agent. One day Vern came in the back door of Robinson's just as Chance was leaving for lunch.

Chance told Vern, "Listen, if you ever hear Don Pigeon, the guy who works on the parking meters for the police department quits, let me know. I want that job."

Then Chance related to Vern the story his father-in-law told him about Don quitting his job with the city every winter to go to Florida and when he came back in the spring, the city would rehire him.Vern assured Chance if he heard anything like that, he would let him know. Thanksgiving came and went, then Ann's birthday. Time kept passing by, but Chance heard nothing about Don Pigeon quitting his job. On a Wednesday in the second week of December, just before noon Vern Miller came into the back of Robinson's store and said to Chance, "I need to talk to you."

"Sure, Vern, what's up?"

"The police chief just left the city manger's office a few minutes ago and was he hot!"

Vern said he was talking to the manager when the chief came in and told the city manager, "That damn parking meter maintenance man quit again this morning."

The chief told them, "That's the last time that son of a bitch does this to me. He's done it for the last five years and by God, I'm going to find somebody to take his place."

Vern said, "I think you should go see the chief as soon as you can and get in your application."

Chance thanked Vern and said he would stop by the police department right after lunch. Chance's lunch hour was from 12:30 to 1:30, so he ran home to tell Ann the news. She couldn't believe that what her dad said more than a year ago had come true, at least the part about Don Pigeon quitting his job. Chance almost ran back to the police department so he would be there by one o'clock. Chance was guessing the chief would be back from lunch a little after one. Chance was wrong; the chief was working in his office and would see Chance right away.

Chance introduced himself to the chief. It was the first time Chance had met the chief of police.

The chief introduced himself to Chance and told him his name was "Karl Spruce, you know, like the tree. What can I do for you and please sit down."

Chance told the chief he understood the man who repaired the parking meters was quitting and he would like the job.

"My God man, he just quit two hours ago. How did you know that?"

"Well, I don't know if my source would want me to identify him, so let's just say I understand the meter man is quitting."

"You mean you're not going to tell me who told you this?

"I would prefer not to, sir."

The chief liked the fact somebody could keep his mouth shut. Then he said, "You look awfully young, how old are you?"

"Nineteen."

"What makes you think you're qualified to do this job?"

Chance told him he had been studying clock making under his father-in-law, Jack Harris.

"I know your father-in-law. He's only got one leg and walks with crutches. He's a good man and an excellent watchmaker. He's done some work for me."

"Yes sir, that's him."

The chief asked Chance if he had any other references and Chance said, "Well, I currently work at Robinson's Printing and Stationery store, I used to work with Vern Miller, the city's purchasing agent."

The chief now knew how Chance found out so quick about the meter man quitting.

Chance continued saying he also did clock work for Gordon Smith and the chief could check with him about his work. Chance didn't know it, but the chief and Gordon were lodge brothers in the Masons.

The chief told Chance, "I tell you what I'll do. You come back to see me on Friday at this same time, and after I talk with your references, I'll let you know."

It took a long time for one o'clock Friday to come, but as Chance discovered, appointment times and future dates eventually arrive.

Chief Spruce told Chance, "Come in to my office. I checked on your references and the only thing I know is you must really have something on everybody you gave me for references, because I never got such glowing reports on anyone in my life. Even your father-in-law spoke highly of you. That's going some, when a guy's father-in-law says something nice about him, you must be OK. The job is yours. When can you start?"

"Thank you sir, I need to give Robinson's two weeks' notice because they have been very good to me.

"You need to be at work with us by December 24th."

Chance told the chief that didn't give him quite two weeks for his notice, but he would be at work on December 24th, he would work it out.

The chief was thrilled to get Chance for the job, because it meant the end of a guy who kept quitting on him every year and the chief thought Chance could do the job with his background in clock repair.

Chief Spruce said to Chance, "You didn't ask what this job pays, but it starts at two hundred fifty-six dollars a month, plus all of our other benefits."

"What time do I come to work?"

"Seven in the morning and I'm sorry to tell you this, but your first day will be Don Pigeon's last day, so I hope you have a chance to learn a little something from him."

On December 24, 1955, Chance arrived just before seven o'clock to meet Don Pigeon and work with him checking meters.

Don introduced himself to Chance and said, "If I had known you wanted this job, I would have quit a long time ago."

Chance didn't think Don meant what he said at all, because Chance felt Don had every intention of coming back next spring and getting his job back, just as he had been doing for the past five years. Don and Chance got into the police department's 1947 jeep station wagon and began checking for broken or jammed parking meters on the main business streets of Webster. Chance found there were a little over nine hundred meters in operation on the streets of Webster. By nine o'clock they finished driving by and checking each meter. Before they returned to the police station, Don repaired or cleared jams on about fifteen meters as Chance watched.

When they returned to the police station, Don took Chance up to the room he used as his parking meter repair shop. The shop was up a very steep flight of stairs that was almost two full stories high. Don unlocked the shop door and led Chance inside. Don reached up and pulled a string attached to one single one hundred, watt light bulb hanging from the ceiling. Chance was shocked to see his new workshop. The workbench was an old library table. The legs of the table were sitting on wooden blocks, so the top of the table would be high enough to be used as a workbench. All of the walls were painted dark green. Parking meter mechanisms were sitting on the floor, boxes of parts were everywhere. Chance had seen junkyards cleaner and better organized than this shop. This wasn't a shop, it was a black hole.

Don said to Chance, "Well, you picked a good time to start this job. We will be finished working here by noon and then you don't have to be back until Tuesday. It's the same deal next week for New Year's. Let's go over to the kitchen and have a cup of coffee."

They walked down the hallway only a few feet from the shop and entered a door on the left of the hall, leading to the jail kitchen. The only person in the kitchen at the time was a trustee named Harold Hess.

Don told Chance, Harold's in the jail all the time. "He lives here; he does a lot of the cooking and fixes everything in the place." "What does he do to get put in jail?"

"Nothing much, he just drinks to get back in jail."

Chance didn't drink coffee, so Don had a cup by himself and then Don and Chance returned to the meter shop.

Don said, "Let me go over a few things with you. In this drawer, I keep the extra keys to the meters."

As Don opened the only drawer in the library desk, he showed Chance the little boxes with different key combinations in them.

Next, Don took out a key ring from his pocket and gave it to Chance. He began telling Chance what each of the keys were for, keys for the meters, the shop door and the jeep. After he finished showing Chance, the keys and explaining what they were for, Don announced: "Well, kid, it's all yours. I'm going home."

With that, Don got up from the old wooden chair he was using for a workbench chair and left.

Chance tried to decide what he should next. It was only a little after 11 and he had been told he should work until noon. Chance thought, maybe I can try to move some of this stuff around so I can at least walk through the shop. Chance began moving parking meter mechanisms around, trying to put them in some kind of order. He put the one-hour meters in one pile, the two-hour meters in another and then he found some that were twelve-minute meters. He had at least moved the meters around so he could now almost, but not quite, get to the other end of the shop. Chance thought what a mess!

Chance checked his watch and it was nearly ten minutes after twelve. As he started down the stairway and headed home, he thought, well, this parking meter business can't be all bad! I've worked five hours and get two-and-a-half days off. Mr. Harris's plan worked just as he laid it out to Chance and Ann in the kitchen almost eighteen months ago. Chance had a much better job, with benefits and the chance to make a much better life for Ann, Chase and himself.

Just as Chance reached home and was going inside, a police squad car stopped in front of his house. The police officer stepped out of the car and asked, "Are you Chance Clark?"

"Yes, sir. What can I do for you?"

The officer answered, "I've got a delivery for you."

He brought Chance a ham and a bushel basket full of apples, oranges and all kinds of nuts.

The officer told Chance, "Merry Christmas from your friends at the police department."

Chance said, "Thank you and Merry Christmas."

Chance, Ann and Chase would have themselves a very merry Christmas.

12

Webster had a very bad snowstorm on January 2, 1956, and Chance had a hard time checking the parking meters the next day. It was hard to drive, and it was almost impossible to see through the plastic domes of the parking meters to tell if they were OK or broken. In addition, the snowplows had plowed the snow up against the meter posts and when Chance found a problem meter, he had to climb over the snow piles. Chance began to understand why the man who had the job before him always quit and went to Florida for the winter.

Chance continued making his rounds, checking and repairing the meters. He found a broken meter directly in front of Robinson's Printing & Stationery store, his old employer. Chance got out of the jeep and began climbing over the snow bank. Just as he got to the top of the snow bank, it gave way, and Chance went tumbling down, ending up almost inside Robinson's front door. Mr. Robinson and several of his former co-workers saw him fall. Mr. Robinson opened the door to see if Chance was all right. Chance's only injury was to his pride and it didn't help much when Mr. Robinson asked if Chance didn't think it would be safer for him to come back to work at Robinson's.

"It certainly looks like it would be today."

"Anytime you want to come back, I have a job for you."

"Thanks. I'll remember that, but you better get back inside the store before you freeze."

Shivering, Mr. Robinson said, "I think you're right, Chance. I'll see you later."

Mr. Robinson went back inside the store.

Chance opened the meter and found it had a coin jam. He quickly cleared the jam and got back inside his jeep. Chance felt good Mr. Robinson cared enough about him to come out of the store to be sure he was all right. It was also very nice of him to tell Chance he could always come back to work at Robinson's if he needed a job.

Over the next few weeks, Chance found he was having a lot of problems repairing the meters. He was not having any problems with the timers in the meters, but he was having lots of problems with the coin-handling portion of the meters. Chance decided his father-in-law might be able to help him with this problem. Chance talked with his father-in-law and Mr. Harris agreed to try to help. They decided to work the following Sunday in Chance's shop at the police department.

On Sunday, Chance and Mr. Harris drove to the police station before nine in the morning. Mr. Harris parked his car in Chance's parking space for his city jeep. They left Chance's jeep at home since only police department personnel could ride in the vehicle. Chance hadn't thought about how difficult climbing the steep stairs to his workshop would be for his father-in-law.

Chance said, "Dad, I forgot about how hard it is for me to climb these stairs, maybe we better forget working in my shop. I can get some meter mechanisms to take home."

"I think I can make these stairs all right," and with that, he put both of his crutches in his left hand and with his right hand on the hand rail, he began climbing the stairs, one at a time.

Chance was concerned Mr. Harris might lose his balance and fall backwards down the steep stairs, so he got behind his fatherin-law to be ready in case he fell. As usual, however, Mr. Harris was able to do whatever someone with two good legs could do. He went up the stairs almost as quick as Chance could.

When they got the top of the stairs, Chance unlocked the door of his shop and turned on the light. Mr. Harris was appalled to see Chance's shop.

He said, "My god, son, is this what you are supposed to be working in as a shop? This place is a disgrace. You don't even have any lights in here. I don't know how you can work in such a place. Trying to work on clocks with no more light then you have you'll be blind in a year."

"Dad, I'm going to talk with the chief to see if I can get some money to fix it up, but right now I don't feel like I'm doing a good enough job with the problems I'm having trying to fix the meters. I haven't said anything to Ann, but I'm worried I might lose my job before I have time to figure out how to get the coinhandling part of the meters to work. If I said anything like this to Ann, well you know your daughter, she is the champion worrier."

Mr. Harris chuckled and replied, "Ann's always been a worrier. She has always been able to find things to worry about and now that she's a mother, she probably worse then ever."

"You've got that right, dad. I thought she was bad before, but now that we have Chase she can find even more things to worry about."

Their conversation ended as Mr. Harris said to Chance, "I wouldn't worry about losing your job. You'll figure out how to get these things fixed. Besides Chance, people like you and they're going to do whatever it takes to help you."

Then Mr. Harris began to examine one of the meter mechanisms Chance had been trying to fix for the last week. When pennies were put into the meter, the first two pennies would each register twelve minutes of time on the meter just like they were supposed to. Then on the next pennies the mechanism would either give no time or only six or seven minutes. Mr. Harris studied the mechanism very carefully and then asked Chance if there was some way to make adjustments on the meter.

Chance explained Don Pigeon told him to adjust the meter you moved a part called a winding ring, either forward or backward from the winding pawl, a part located in the coincarrier assembly.

To make the adjustment there were two flat nuts, one on each side of the winding ring that would allow the winding ring and wheel to be closer or farther away from the winding pawl.

Chance showed Mr. Harris how this was supposed to work. By using a special adjustment wrench, Chance moved the winding ring and wheel closer to the winding pawl. When Chance put a penny in the mechanism, it gave thirty-six minutes for the penny instead of registering twelve minutes.

Mr. Harris laughed and said, "The public will like it, but the city fathers might be a little upset if the meters gave three times the amount of time for every penny."

Mr. Harris took the adjustment wrench from Chance and began moving the winding ring back and forth by using the two adjustment nuts. Then he would insert pennies and test the mechanism. Try as he might, no matter where he set the adjustment nuts, the pennies would not give the right amount of time for each of the ten pennies. Finally, Mr. Harris said, "Chance, I think we better set this meter aside and work on something I can help you with. Working on watches I find sometimes you have to just go away and come back later. Then you see something you had been missing."

Chance agreed and they began cleaning, oiling and repairing timers Chance found in the shop that Don Pigeon had taken off meter mechanisms. Don replaced the timers with different ones, but never bothered to fix the old ones. As the day wore on, Chance and Mr. Harris cleaned and repaired all of the timers and had them working perfectly. Chance knew there wasn't a watch or a clock in the world his father-in-law couldn't fix. Chance wasn't so sure anybody could fix the coin-handling mechanisms though. Chance felt he needed help from someone who really knew about the meters.

Mr. Harris asked Chance how he and Ann were doing and Chance replied, "We're doing great! We love each other more every day."

Mr. Harris smiled at Chance and said, "That's great. I'm really glad for both of you. When mom and I first got married, I almost lost her the first week we were married."

"What happened?"

"I'll tell you, but don't ever say anything about this to her because she still gets mad at me every time she thinks about it."

Chance thought to himself he could hardly believe his ears that Mrs. Harris would get made at dad, because she worshipped the ground her husband walked on.

"When mom and I first got married we lived in Missouri and I had a bunch of coon dogs. One night after we had been married less than a week, I was dreaming my dogs were jumping up on me as I was bringing them their food. Well, in my dream, one of them started licking me in the face, so I took my arm and belted him one. The problem was I belted your mother-in-law instead of the dog in my dream and she was fast asleep and I knocked her out of bed and onto the floor."

Chance pictured in his mind how startled Mrs. Harris must have been, sleeping soundly and suddenly being hit and knocked out of bed onto the floor.

Mr. Harris said, "For God's sake and mine don't ever tell her I told you this, because she gets mad at me every time she thinks about it."

Chance laughed and told Mr. Harris, "Your secret is safe with me."

Chance wondered if Ann knew this story. She was the only one Chance would ask or tell; they didn't have any secrets between them.

By five o' clock that afternoon, Mr. Harris and Chance had repaired, cleaned and lubricated all of the broken clocks Don Pigeon never fixed.

Mr. Harris told Chance, "I'm sorry I couldn't be more help on the coin mechanisms Chance. You'll figure it out; just give yourself a little more time. After all, you've only been working on the meters for a little over a month."

"Thanks dad, for your help and the encouragement."

Chance and Mr. Harris had developed a strong bond between them. They both loved Ann and learned they liked each other as friends. In fact, Chance felt closer to Jack Harris then he did to his own father.

The next day, Chance went into Chief Spruce's office after he finished making his morning inspection rounds of the meters. Chance asked if it was possible to do some work to fix up the parking meter repair shop.

The chief told him, "I'll have our trustee Harold Hess, come up to see you. You tell him what you want and he will make it for you."

"What I really need are some lights in the shop, before I go blind."

"That's not a problem. I'll have Dave Wilson put some lights up for you. You've met Dave, he's the man who takes care of the traffic signals for the city and he is a master electrician." Chance thought to himself, since this is going so well I better ask for everything I need.

Chance said, "Chief, do you know if the company who make the meters has some type of school where I can learn more about the meters then on my half-day working with Don Pigeon? Fixing the clocks is no problem, but I'm really struggling with the coin- handling mechanisms in the meters."

"In the first place Chance, I want you to know how happy I am that I finally have somebody looking after our meters who cares enough to not only want to fix up that hellhole of a shop, but wants to learn more about the meters so you can do a better job. I like that Chance and I'll contact the meter company to see what they can do to get you some training."

"Chief I really appreciate what you said and I appreciate you fixing up the shop. I hope I can get some training on the meters because that would really help me. Thanks again for your help."

Chance went upstairs to his shop and less then thirty minutes later, Harold Hess came into the shop. Harold told Chance the chief told him to "Build you whatever you want."

"I want to have cabinets built along this wall, with drawers and a couple of doors to store meter mechanisms. Also, cabinets along this back wall with doors for more storage of meter mechanisms. I almost forgot I need two knee spaces under the work bench so I can sit down at the bench and work on the meters."

"OK, I know what you want. I'll put together a bill of materials for the things I need to build your cabinets. What kind of covering do you want on the top of the workbench?

Chance thought for a minute and replied, "Yellow linoleum. That's what I have on my watch bench at my father-in-law's jewelry store. It's easy on the eyes."

Almost as soon as Harold Hess left the shop, Dave Wilson came in.

Dave said, "The chief says you need some lights in here before you go blind. I can't see why you should be having any problems you've got a 100-watt light bulb hanging in the middle of the room. You can probably see the light if you lit a match and searched for it."

Dave pulled out his tape measure and took some measurements of the shop. He told Chance, "I'll get you fixed up. It looks like you need some electrical outlets too. Don't worry I'll take care of you."

A few days later, Dave came into the shop with his helper and before the end of the day Chance had lights and power outlets.

What a difference lights made in Chance's shop. Now he could see just how bad his shop really looked. He couldn't wait for his workbenches to be finished. He went downstairs to where Harold had been working on the benches. Chance looked around and asked if anybody had seen Harold. He found out Harold had been released from jail this afternoon, so work on his benches came to a standstill.

Chance went into the chief's office and asked the chief if he knew Harold had been released from jail.

The chief replied, "Yes I know it, but he will probably be back in jail by tonight or no later then tomorrow."

Sure enough, before ten o'clock that evening one of the beat patrol officers arrested Harold for being drunk on a public street and put him back in jail. Chance saw Harold the next morning as he was coming back from police court. By noon, Harold was back in his trustee police coveralls working on Chance's benches.

In less then two weeks from the time Chance asked the chief about fixing up his shop, Harold was ready to install the work benches in his shop.

Harold said, "I think we should paint the walls before we put in the work benches. What color do you want?

"White."

When Chance came into the police station from making his inspection rounds of the meters a few days later, Harold and several other men from the jail were carrying his benches up the stairs. The walls had been painted a few days before and were dry. Harold was directing them just like a foreman running a construction project.

After lunch, the workbenches were installed and as Chance was looking over the finished work Harold had done, two men came into the shop with two new secretarial chairs, with yellow leather-like material on the seats and backs. One of the trustees who Chance didn't know said, "The chief told us to bring up these new chairs for you. He said he thought you needed these to go with your new shop."

Chance couldn't believe how much the chief had done to help him. Now, the shop looked like a decent place to work in. Later that day, the chief came into the shop and asked Chance, "What do you think?"

"I think it's unbelievable how much better this place looks in three weeks. Thanks again, chief."

After seeing the quality of the work Harold Hess did building his cabinets, Chance couldn't understand how someone with that much talent could waste away his life drinking and ending up in jail. Chance thought to himself what a waste!

The following week, one of the beat patrol officers stopped by Chance's jeep as he was working on a meter on South Main Street. The officer told Chance, "The chief called me on the radio and asked me to tell you to come to his office as soon as possible."

Chance finished repairing the meter and drove directly to the police station. He parked his jeep and went into the chief's office. When he arrived in office, the chief was talking to someone Chance didn't know, but the chief saw him and told Chance to come on in.

The chief said to Chance, "This is Elliot Mc Mann. He is a service engineer for Superior, the people who make our parking meters. He's here at my request to teach you about repairing the meters."

Chance extended his hand to Elliot Mc Mann and Elliot shook Chance's hand, as Chance was telling him he was Chance Clark.

Elliot was an Irishman, born and raised in Chicago. Chance would learn later he could have added another word to his description, a "wild" Irishman from Chicago.

Elliot told Chance, "If you're ready, let's get started."

Chance assured Elliot he was ready to learn as much about the meters as he could. Chance led Elliot up the stairs to his "new" meter shop. On the way up, Elliot told him he had been calling on Webster for about three years and knew Don Pigeon. Chance unlocked the door to the shop and flipped on the light switch as he walked inside the shop.

Elliot was right behind him and when Elliot saw Chance's new shop he gave a wolf whistle, "Wow! This place doesn't look like it did the last time I was here."

Elliot said, "You know I travel six states for Superior and I can tell you, you have the best looking shop of any of the cities I call on. I can't believe the change you made in the looks of your shop. You've gone from one of the worst shops in six states to the best one."

Chance was pleased someone recognized the work that had been done to improve things and now, maybe Elliot could help him do a better job fixing the meters. Elliot began going over exactly what each part in the meter was, what it did and how it related to the other parts of the meter. By lunchtime Chance had a much better understanding of how each part in the meter worked with the next part.

Elliot said, "It's lunch time. Let's go to lunch."

Chance answered, "I really can't go today my wife is expecting me home for lunch. If you're going to be here tomorrow, I'll make arrangements to go with you."

They agreed to meet back at Chance's shop at one-thirty. Chance was so excited about having Elliot to teach him about the meters, he wanted to get home and share the news with Annie. Ann was almost as happy as Chance that someone was here to help him learn more about the meters. No matter how hard Chance tried to hide his concerns about not being able to do the job as well as he wanted, Ann could tell he was worried. She always could see right through him.

Before one-thirty, Chance was back in his shop. When Elliot came back from lunch, he said, "Let's go over everything we talked about this morning."

Elliot asked Chance to go through each part of the meter and tell him the name of the part, what it did and how it related to the other parts. Elliot was impressed, because Chance went through the meter parts and their functions as though he had been doing it for years. Elliot was definitely impressed!

Next, Elliot said, "Let spend some time trouble-shooting some of the mechanisms you have in the shop that need to be repaired." Chance pulled out the mechanism he had tried to get working and couldn't, the same one Jack Harris tried to adjust and couldn't. Chance explained to Elliot, "I've tried to get this mechanism adjusted to keep it from skipping on pennies, but it either gives no time or it give too much time on some pennies."

Elliot took the mechanism from Chance and carefully examined it to be sure Chance had put it together correctly. Elliot began putting coins into the meter and it worked just as Chance told him. Elliot turned the mechanism upside down, resting it on the work bench and began moving the two adjustment nuts, moving the winding ring and wheel closer to the winding pawl.

Elliot set the mechanism back up and began feeding pennies in it. After several more adjustments and almost an hour of time, Elliot set the mechanism down and said, "Well, it beats the hell out of me why I can't adjust this mech to work right."

Chance suddenly remembered during his four hours of working with Don Pigeon, Don showed him how to fix meters if he was having this kind of problem. Chance asked Elliot to hand the mechanism back to him because he just remembered something Don Pigeon had shown him. Elliot handed the mechanism to Chance and Chance began putting in pennies. The first three worked perfectly, but when the fourth penny was put into the meter, it skipped, giving no time. Chance picked up a large screwdriver and placing the end of the screwdriver behind the stainless steel winding ring, just behind the fourth tooth of the ring, he began prying on the ring. When Chance put down the screwdriver, Elliot jumped out of his chair and began yelling like a mad man. Chance could only sit there and wonder what was wrong with this guy.

Elliot regained his composure and said Don Pigeon's is a stupid son of a bitch!" Chance didn't say anything because he didn't understand why Elliot was so upset. Elliot kept raving about Don. "I knew the guy was lazy, but I didn't know he was just plain dumb!"

Finally Chance said, "I don't understand."

Elliot became calmer and explained to Chance what happens when you pried or bent the winding ring the way Don told him to. Elliot showed him by picking up one of the clocks that was not installed in a mechanism. He mounted the winding ring and wheel assembly on it as it would be when it was installed in the mechanism. Elliot explained by prying on the winding ring, you were bending the shaft on the main wheel of the timer. After this happened and a timer was cleaned, oiled and put back in the mechanism. The bent shaft would never be back in exactly the same position as it had been, so you could never adjust the meter to work right on the coins.

To prove his point, Elliot had Chance disassemble the mechanism and remove the timer. Chance took the timer completely apart and installed a new main wheel assembly. Then he reinstalled the timer in the mechanism and put the rest of the mechanism together. Chance began coin checking the meter. He moved the winding ring forward to put it closer to the winding pawl and the coins worked perfectly, all ten pennies.

Elliot told Chance, "Don Pigeon must have really screwed up a lot of meters, bending the shaft on the clock's main wheel assembly."

Elliot then asked, "How many new main wheel assemblies do Chance opened the parts drawer of main wheel assemblies and he had about twenty.

Elliot said, "I'll need to go through your parts inventory and write up an order for you." The next day Elliot prepared an order. One clock main wheel assembly was ten dollars and eighty - five cents. When Elliot finished writing up the parts order to get Chance's inventory up to what Elliot felt it should be the order was almost eight thousand dollars.

Elliot and Chance went to the chief's office to get approval for the parts order. When Elliot gave a copy of the order to the chief, Chief Spruce said, "Wow, this order is for more money then we spent all last year for parts."

Nevertheless, the chief approved the order.

Elliot asked Chance if it would be all right if he talked to the chief by himself. Chance excused himself and went upstairs to his shop. After Chance left the office, Elliot told Chief Spruce Chance was the quickest learner on the parking meter mechanisms he had ever seen in his ten years as a service engineer for Superior. Then Elliot told the chief about Don Pigeon screwing up thousands of dollars worth of parts by bending the main wheel assembly shaft of the timers. The chief's reaction was almost as bad as Elliot's was when he saw Chance prying on the winding ring.

The chief said, "I knew he wasn't doing a good job for us, he never took that much interest and he had no pride in his job. I think we have a good kid working for us now."

Elliot agreed and told the chief, "In a year, I think this kid will be one of the best parking meter servicemen in the country."

Elliot came back to the workshop and spent a few more hours talking with Chance. Chance asked about Elliot's job with Superior. Elliot said, "He traveled Kansas, Missouri, Nebraska,

Iowa, South Dakota, and Illinois for the company, teaching city servicemen to repair meters and making new parking meter installations. Chance thought it sounded like something he would like to do someday.

Elliot told Chance he was a marine in World War II and when he came home after the war, he got a job working for Superior's Maintenance Company in Chicago, fixing meters on the street of Chicago. After two years, he got a job as a company service engineer. Elliot told him Superior had seven service engineers covering the USA. Chance also found Elliot was married and had a daughter two months older than Chase.

A few weeks later, Chance met the Superior Parking Meter Distributor for the states of Kansas and Missouri, Karl W. Jones. Mr. Jones arrived in town on a Wednesday evening and checked in at the Hilton hotel. The next morning, Mr. Jones drove his new Cadillac to the police station to meet Chance.

Chance was already working in his shop when Mr. Jones arrived. Mr. Jones went in to see the police chief first, to see if anything was going on about expanding the parking meter system. The previous year the city fathers discussed a plan to add between eight hundred and a thousand new metered parking spaces to Webster's parking meter system.

The chief told Mr. Jones, "Karl, you must be able to smell an order all the way in Kansas City."

Karl laughed and said, "I sure try to."

Chief Spruce said, "We will be adding several hundred meters to our installation in the next two or three months."

"I understand you have a new serviceman."

"Come on Karl and I'll introduce him to you."

Chief Spruce and Mr. Jones opened the door to Chance's shop and walked in. Chief Spruce said, "Chance, I want to introduce you to Karl Jones. Karl is our Superior Parking Meter Distributor."

Chance said, "How do you do Mr. Jones?"

"Please call me Karl and I'm doing fine."

Mr. Jones looked around Chance's new shop and said to Chief Spruce, "Boy, this shop sure looks different than when I was here last fall."

The chief swelled with pride and replied, "Well, we have a real serviceman now for our meters and we couldn't expect him to keep working on an old library table on wooden blocks could we?"

Mr. Jones said, "This is the best-looking shop in my territory. Chance, you must really be proud to have a place like this to work in."

"Yes sir, I sure am and thanks to Chief Spruce he got it fixed up for me."

Chief Spruce told Mr. Jones, "I've got to go to a meeting with the city manager, so I'll let you visit with Chance and I'll see you later Karl."

Chance guessed Mr. Jones was about sixty years old, with pure white hair and very thin on the top of his head. He was about five - foot-nine inches tall, with a ruddy round face and he was kind of heavy set, not fat, just well filled out. Chance liked Mr. Jones right off. Mr. Jones told Chance he lived in Kansas City, Missouri, and traveled Missouri and Kansas selling Superior Parking Meters. He had been the Superior Distributor since 1945. As Chance and Mr. Jones continued talking, Chance learned Mr. Jones was a lawyer and had practiced law for twenty- five years in Kansas City before becoming a Superior Distributor.

Chance asked how he went from practicing law to selling parking meters and Mr. Jones said at first, he represented Superior as an attorney, helping them win orders in three cities, including Kansas City. The vice president of sales for Superior than asked if he would like to become the distributor for them. Superior told Karl he could make a lot more money as a distributor than he earned from them as their attorney. Mr. Jones told them he would try it for six months to see how he liked it. Mr. Jones told Chance when he started as a distributor, he practice law three days a week and worked selling parking meters two days a week and when he first started he didn't even have a car. He traveled by train or bus to make his sales calls.

By the end of the day, Chance knew a lot about Karl W. Jones. He knew he was married him and his wife never had any children - although with a twinkle in his eye, he told Chance he and his wife were still trying."

Chance also found out Mr. Jones graduated from the University Of Kansas School Of Law. Mr. Jones had been in school with Buddy Rodgers, who was married to Mary Pickford. Chance didn't know much about Buddy Rogers or Mary Pickford except he knew she had been a star in silent movies. The more Chance found out about Mr. Jones the more he liked and respected him.

Chance walked Mr. Jones to his car. Chance had never seen such a pretty car. Mr. Jones joked, "Well, this is my office, so I wanted something nice."

Chance thought to himself, well Mr. Jones certainly got something nice when he got his Coupe de Ville. Chance couldn't wait to get home to tell Ann about meeting Karl Jones. As Chance began telling Ann about Mr. Jones, he thought to himself, this man is a real gentleman. Mr. Jones was the first man Chance had ever thought about as being a gentleman.

Ann was quite impressed with the things Chance told her about Mr. Jones. She said, "Don't you think it funny that a successful lawyer would give up his law practice to become a salesman for parking meters?"

Chance replied, "Yes, it's funny, but Mr. Jones told me he loved selling meters and had starting hating practicing law. I guess if it's possible you have to do what makes you happy. Maybe you can meet Mr. Jones sometime when he comes to town. He told me he would be back in Webster next month."

About that time Chase came in and jumped up in his dad's arms. Chance thought, Ann and I are so lucky to have such a beautiful, healthy boy. Chance remembered what Mr. Jones said about him and his wife still trying to have a baby.

13

Cy true to his word, Karl Jones was back in Webster the next month. Chance was making his early-morning inspection of the parking meters and as he went by the Hilton hotel Chance saw Mr. Jones' Cadillac parked in front of the hotel.

Around ten o'clock that morning Mr. Jones arrived at Chance's office. One thing Chance was to learn about Karl Jones was sometime he took the long way around to say what he wanted to say. After talking around the subject for a long time, Mr. Jones finally said, "Do you think you and your wife could get away for a few days to visit Superior's factory in Chicago and do some advance training on the meters?"

"I'm sure we could work it out, but I would have to have the chief 's approval to make such a trip."

"Let's go talk to him about it right now."

The two of them went downstairs to talk with the chief about Chance going for advance training at Superior's factory in Chicago. Chief Spruce thought having Chance go to the factory was a great idea. Mr. Jones told the chief he would send a formal letter of invitation for Chance and his wife to visit the factory in Chicago and with all of their expenses being paid by Superior.

The letter came to the chief three days later and a copy was also sent to Chance. Ann and Chance would be in Chicago for four nights. The chief sent back a letter the same day accepting the invitation for Chance.

Ten days later Chance received a large brown envelope at the police station with their tickets, hotel reservations and instructions on how to get to the hotel from Midway Airport and to Superior's plant in Chicago. They were to leave Webster the next Monday on a Continental flight to Kansas City change planes to TWA from Kansas City to Chicago. Chance went home for lunch early to show Ann all the information on their trip, so she could make arrangements with her mother to take care of Chase while they were gone.

On Monday morning, Chance and Ann's flight from Webster to Kansas City was leaving at six-thirty. Ann was up at 4 a.m., making sure she was ready to go. Did she have the right clothes? Had she packed the right shoes to go with her various outfits? Had she written down all of the instructions for her mother about looking after Chase? Would he be too lonesome without her for five days?

Chance was out of bed by 5 a.m., showered, dressed and made sure he had pictures of his shop to show the people at Superior. He threw his shaving kit into his suitcase, closed and locked it and was ready to go by five-thirty.

Ann was still not dressed. She had been so busy making sure she had everything for her trip and instructions for her mother on taking care of Chase that she hadn't gotten dressed.

Chance said, "Ann, quit worrying and get dressed. We have to go to the airport. Your dad's already out in the car."

With that announcement, Ann began dressing in her travel clothes, already laid out on the chair next to the bed. Ann could get ready in a hurry if she had to. She put her make-up kit in her suitcase and closed it. She asked Chance to put Chase in bed with her mom.

Chance picked Chase up out of his bed and took him into Ann's folks' bedroom. Chance was pleased at how much Chase had grown from the little five-pound, six-ounce baby he had been at birth. At twenty months, Chase was so tall his legs were below Chance's waist when he carried him around. Chance put Chase into Ann's mother's bed, kissed Chase on the cheek and told him good-bye.

Ann came into the bedroom and kissed Chase. She told her mom, "I left all of the instructions for Chase on his bed. I also left the telephone number for the hotel in Chicago in case I need to come home."

Mrs. Harris said, "Ann, would you just go and have a good time? Chase will be fine here with me. I raised you, didn't I and you came through it all right. You didn't turn out so bad, did you?"

"OK, bye mom," she kissed Chase good-bye again.

Jack Harris drove Chance and Ann to the Webster airport. It only took about ten minutes to get there since there were hardly any cars on the street that early in the morning. Chance took their suitcases out of the trunk of the car while Ann was telling her father good-bye. She gave her dad a kiss and told him to help mom take care of Chase.

This would be the first time either of them had ever flown on an airplane, or at least on a commercial airline. Chance had been in a little two-seater, L-19 Bird-Dog at guard camp the summer before. The artillery used these planes for their forward observers to direct artillery fire, but Chance didn't think his fifteen-minute ride counted for much.

After checking their luggage and getting their seat assignments they were ready to go, except their airplane wasn't there yet. Chance paced the floor hoping their plane would arrive soon. He was concerned that if they didn't get to Kansas City on time, they would miss their plane to Chicago. Their plane finally landed and Chance and Ann stood by the fence watching as it taxied to the terminal. They watched as three people got off the plane and then the agent who had checked them in told them, "We're ready to get you on board the plane."

Chance and Ann walked out on the tarmac to board their plane, a DC-3. It was so shiny in the rising sun Chance was having problems seeing due to the reflection of the sun on its silver skin. They got on the plane and the stewardess showed them their seats. She asked if they would like some gum before taking off and explained that it helps the ears during take-off and landing. They both took the sticks of gum she offered.

Ann looked out the window and saw her suitcase being loaded into the baggage compartment of the plane. She said, "Well, at least I will have some clothes when we get to Chicago."

"Yeah, if they get your suitcase off of this plane in Kansas City and put it on the plane to Chicago."

The door closed and the pilot started up the left engine, then the right one and they soon taxied down to the end of the runway. When they reached the end of the runway, the pilot stopped the plane and began revving up the engines. The plane shuddered, the pilot released the brakes and the DC-3 began speeding down the runway. The tail came up first and then Chance could feel the front of the plane beginning to shudder and then lift off of the runway.

Ann grabbed Chance's arm as the plane lifted off the ground and they grabbed each other when the plane began to shake as the pilot put up the landing gear. The plane continued gaining altitude and before long they were flying straight and level.

The stewardess asked them if they would like to have coffee or a soft drink. Both Chance and Ann asked for a coke. When they had their cokes, Chance looked around at the other passengers on the plane and noted that all of the other passengers were men. Ann was the only female passenger on the plane. Chance figured normally only businessmen flew on planes.

Ann asked the stewardess where this plane came from before its arrival in Webster. The stewardess explained they came from Denver and after they arrived in Kansas City, they would turn around and return to Denver. Ann thought the stewardess must live an exciting life, going to so many different cities in a day. From her very first flight, Ann loved flying.

Chance was much less adventurous than Ann and he kept listening to all the various noises the plane made.

The captain's voice came over the intercom, advising the passengers they would be landing in Kansas City in about fifteen minutes. Chance watched through the window as the plane began its descent into Kansas City Municipal Airport. Each time they passed through one of the fluffy white clouds, the plane would rock and Chance wondered if this was normal. As the pilot turned the plane, he again used the intercom to advise the passengers they were now on their final approach for landing. Just then, Chance heard a noise coming from below them. As the stewardess walked by, checking to see that everyone had their seat belts fastened.

Chance asked her what the noise was. The stewardess smiled and told him it was nothing to worry about, it was just the landing gear going down.

The noises on the plane didn't appear to be bothering Ann at all. She said to Chance, "Boy, flying to Kansas City sure is a lot faster than driving up here."

The plane was landing from the south of the airport and as they got closer to the airport, Chance saw they were flying lower than some of the buildings they flew by. Chance sure hoped their pilot knew where he was going. Just about that time, the plane crossed the river and touched down on the runway. A few minutes later, the captain had the plane parked at the gate. The stewardess opened the door and the passengers began filing out of the plane. Chance and Ann followed the rest of the passengers inside the terminal.

Chance looked around to see where to go for their TWA flight to Chicago. When he saw the counters for TWA, he and Ann walked over to one of the agents and presented their tickets to him. The agent checked them in for the flight and said they would be boarding in about an hour. He said they hadn't posted a gate for their flight yet, but they should listen for the announcement of their flight number and gate over the public address system.

Chance and Ann started to sit down and wait for their flight, when Ann decided to telephone her Aunt Elizabeth and tell her about flying from Webster on their way to Chicago. Ann found a telephone and gave her aunt a call. Aunt Elizabeth was surprised to hear from Ann and even more surprised to hear they were on their way to Chicago. After talking with her aunt for a few minutes, Ann came back to where Chance was sitting and sat down next to him to wait for their flight's announcement. She told him her aunt was exciting for them about them going to Chicago.

Over the loudspeaker, they heard a fabulous voice saying, "Trans World Airlines, flight number fifty-six to Chicago is now ready for boarding at gate number one."

Chance thought this guy must have the best announcer's voice of all time. Chance was just fascinated by the man's voice. Chance and Ann soon found gate one and got into the line of people traveling on their flight.

As they left the terminal building, Chance looked up at their plane and was shocked by its size. It was a Super G Constellation; it had four engines and a tri-cycle landing gear, which meant it, had wheels under the wings and one under the nose of the plane. Chance looked back at the tail and found it had three tails. Chance wondered if it could really fly as big as it was. They had to climb a stairway mounted on a truck to get inside the plane and when Chance and Ann got into the plane, they saw how big the plane really was. The stewardess checked their seat assignments and directed them to their seats. Chance decided he liked this plane a lot better than the little DC-3 they arrived on from Webster.

Chance liked everything about this airplane from its white- painted exterior with "Trans World Airlines" painted in red on the body of the plane, to its red "TWA" on the tails. Inside, all of the seats were covered in a blue material and had white cloth seat covers on the back of the seats, with red "TWA" printed on each one. There were six stewardesses on this plane and Chance and Ann thought they must have all come from the same mold. They were all very young none could have been older than in her mid - twenties. They were almost exactly the same height and weight. Chance said to Ann, "TWA must have got a good deal on their uniforms because it looks like they are all one size, so TWA only hires girls who can fit in them."

Chance and Ann were ready to take off this time. They had their seat belts fastened and they understood when the plane taxied onto the runway that the captain stop at the end of the runway and rev up the engines, release the brakes and take off. This plane seemed to almost jump into the air. In a few minutes one of the stewardesses asked what they wanted to drink. Of course, they wanted Coca-Cola, after all this was the Clark's family drink.

A few minutes later, two other stewardesses came down the aisle pushing a metal cart, offering people breakfast. Chance and Ann were ready for something to eat since they hadn't had time for breakfast.

After breakfast, the stewardess picked up their trays and put them back inside the metal carts. Chance was amazed at how they had everything so organized. Everything on the plane had been carefully designed to use every inch of space.

Chance told Ann that when he was five or six years old, he went on a train trip from Oklahoma to Kansas City and then from Kansas City to western Kansas so his dad could help his aunt and uncle harvest their wheat. Chance said the best part of the trip for him was to get up from his seat and get water from a huge water bottle mounted on a metal stand, using small paper cups from a cup holder. Then he would have to go to the bathroom on the train. He guessed Ann and he were experiencing the same kind of excitement flying on this plane as he did traveling on the train as a youngster.

Before long, the captain announced they would soon be landing at Midway Airport in Chicago. Chance and Ann watched through the window as the plane descended through the white clouds and they began flying over the rooftops of apartment buildings. When the landing gear was lowered this time, Chance understood what the noise was. A few minutes more and the big Super G Constellation's wheels touched down on the runway. The plane taxied to its gate and Chance could see the ground crew bringing up the steps so the passengers could disembark. As they were coming down the steps, Chance saw people unloading luggage from the plane. The young woman at the bottom of the steps told them they could pick up their luggage inside the terminal in baggage area three.

Chance and Ann made their way through the terminal following signs directing them to the baggage area. By the time they arrived at area three, suitcases were being set on a stainless steel rack so people would be able to pick up their suitcases. Chance spotted Ann's suitcase and retrieved it.

Ann said, "I got my clothes anyway."

They waited and the luggage handlers continued setting luggage out on the baggage rack, but not Chance's. The men finished unloading the carts they brought in from the plane and Chance said, "I'm glad you got your clothes, but it looks like I may be wearing what I have on all week."

Another baggage cart came into the terminal and Chance saw his bag.

After they had their suitcases, they went outside the terminal looking for a taxi to take them to their hotel. They got into a line formed for people wanting taxis. The airport had people to help direct the taxis to come and pick up passengers and then tell the drivers where the people wanted to go. When Chance and Ann made their way to the head of the line, the director of the taxis asked them where they were going and after checking Karl Jones' instructions, Chance told the man, "The North Park Hotel."

The taxi driver loaded their suitcases in the trunk and was told by the taxi line director these kids are going to the North Park Hotel. Off they went. Chance asked the driver if he knew where the hotel was and the driver said, "Yeah, I know it."

Chance looked at his instructions from Karl Jones again and told the driver, "My friend gave me some directions on how to get there. He said we should go up Ogden Avenue."

The taxi driver responded, "That's what we're on right now."

Chance thought perhaps this was a good time to shut up and let the driver take them to the hotel. As they continued up Ogden Avenue, it began raining very hard. Chance and Ann had never seen so much traffic. Trucks, cars, and buses all trying to occupy the same space on the street, horns sounded if the cars didn't starting moving the split second after the traffic lights changed from red to green. A truck pulled out in front of their taxi and their driver began cursing the truck driver, questioning the legitimacy of the truck driver's birth, something about being the son of a female dog.

Chance told Ann, "Cover your ears!"

They started laughing and only quit when the driver pulled up in front of their hotel and announced they had arrived at the North Park Hotel.

A doorman took their suitcases from the trunk of the taxi and another man opened an umbrella for Ann when she got out of the taxi. Chance paid the taxi driver and caught up with Ann. They went to the desk to register. Chance wondered if the desk clerk here would give them as bad a time as the one in Colorado Springs who questioned them about being married since they were so young. Chance told the desk clerk their name and that they had reservations. The desk clerk found their name and asked Chance to sign the guest register.

Then he said, "Mr. and Mrs. Clark, your reservations were made by the Superior Parking Meter Corporation and they asked me to advise you that if there was anything you wanted, you should just sign your name and Superior will take care of it for you."

A bellman took their room key from the desk clerk and asked Chance and Ann to follow him. He directed them to a bank of elevators. One of the elevator doors was open and they got in.

The bellman said, "You folks are in room 725. You will have a good view of Lincoln Park if it stops raining."

They followed the bellman to room 725. It was a corner room at the front of the hotel and Chance could tell they would have a nice view of the park across the street when it wasn't raining. The bellman put their suitcases on a luggage rack at the end of the double bed and then checked to make sure everything in the room was in order. He asked Chance if there would be anything else or if they needed ice. Chance said no and gave the bellman a dollar tip.

Chance and Ann began unpacking their suitcases and hanging their clothes in the closet. They put their shaving and make-up kits in the bathroom and the rest of their things in the drawers. Chance lay down on the bed and Ann said, "What are we going to do with our suitcases?"

"Why can't they just stay on the luggage rack?"

"Because they don't look neat."

Chance got off the bed and tried to find room in the closet for them, but they wouldn't fit. He finally managed to put them under the bed and out of sight.

Ann announced with pride, "Now our room looks a lot better."

Chance told people he worked with how neat Ann was and that everything had to be organized just so! He told them he was afraid to get up and go to the bathroom at night, because by the time he got back in bed his side of the bed would be made. This always got a laugh from his co-workers. Of course, it wasn't true, but it wasn't far off either!

Ann said she needed to take a bath after traveling all day and wanted time to rest before they had supper. Ann corrected herself and said, "Since we're in the big city, I meant "dinner," of course!" Chance got off the bed. Ann had turned away from him and was working at getting undressed for her bath. Chance put his arms around her standing behind her and kissed her on the right cheek. As he did so, he pulled her backwards and they fell onto the bed. Ann's bath was delayed for awhile.

Chance woke up as Ann came out of the bathroom after taking her bath. She leaned over the bed and kissed him ever so gently and asked, "Are you getting hungry? I am."

Chance and Ann went downstairs to the restaurant for dinner. The waitress asked them if they would like a cocktail before dinner. Chance thought for a minute and said, "Bring us two martinis."

When she came back with their drinks they ordered their food. When the waitress left, Chance said, "Here's a toast to my love and to our trip."

They touched glasses and took a drink of their cocktail. They both almost spit the liquid out of their mouths.

Ann said, "This tastes like hairspray smells."

They set aside the martinis and when the waitress returned with their salads they ordered cokes. The martinis sat untouched.

Chance and Ann were up early the next morning. They went to breakfast and were soon on their way to visit the Superior plant. Chance told the taxi driver they were going to 835 North Wood Street, just a little north of Chicago Avenue. When they arrived at the plant, Chance looked over the building and thought it looked like a four- or five-story redbrick apartment building. On the glass entrance door the name of the company was painted in gold, "Superior Parking Meter Corporation," and below that, it said, "Superior Toy Company."

Chance held the door open for Ann and she went inside with Chance close behind. Once inside the building they had to climb stairs up to a landing. Chance saw a window with a young woman sitting behind the glass. On each side of the landing were doors. Chance approached the window and the young woman slid open the window and asked if she could help them.

Chance said, "We're here to see Bob Ellsworth."

The young woman asked Chance's name and he told her he was Chance Clark from Webster, Kansas. She pushed a button on the telephone and said, "Mr. Ellsworth, a Mr. Chance Clark from Webster, Kansas is here to see you."

Chance heard her say, "Yes sir, I will tell him."

The young woman turned back to Chance and said, "Mr. Ellsworth will be with you in a few minutes. Please sit down.

Chance and Ann hadn't waited long when one of the doors opened and a man about forty years old came out. He was very thin, about five-foot-ten. He had thinning hair and was wearing a pair of gold-rimmed glasses sitting on the end of his nose.

He said to Chance, "You must be Chance Clark. I'm Bob Ellsworth and this young lady must be your wife, unless you just picked her up at the hotel last night."

"This is my wife Ann."

Bob shook hands with both of them and said they would go to his office and then he would take them on a tour of the factory. The receptionist pushed a button and the door Bob just came through unlocked and Chance and Ann followed Bob Ellsworth to his office. When they arrived at Bob's office, he asked them to sit down and then asked if they would like to have a cup of coffee. Since Chance started working at the police department he had learned to drink coffee and he replied, "That would be very nice."

"Good, I need a cup before we get started on the tour."

He called his secretary into his office and asked if she would please bring them all a cup of coffee. Bob asked if they had any trouble getting to Chicago and whether their hotel room was all right.

Ann replied, "The trip was without any problems and the hotel is very nice."

"I'm really happy to hear that. Karl Jones called here three times yesterday to make sure everything had been arranged for your visit."

Just as Bob finished speaking, his phone rang. Bob picked it up and said hello. Chance heard him say, "Yes Karl, they're here now, sitting across from my desk. Yes Karl, we will take good care of them for you. OK, I'll let you talk to Chance."

Bob handed the phone to Chance and said, "Karl wants to speak with you."

Chance took the telephone and said, "Hello Karl. Yes Karl. No we didn't have any problems with our flights. Yes, the hotel is just fine. Ann is doing OK. We are just getting ready to go on a tour of the plant. OK Karl, if we need anything, I will call you. Yes, you sent me your office and home phone numbers. Yes, it's good to talk to you too. Good-bye."

Chance found someone who could rival Ann at worrying! Chance asked Bob if Karl always worried about everything.

Bob said, "Yes, but I can tell you this. You have certainly become one of Karl's favorite people. He wants everything to be perfect for your trip here."

As they finished their coffee and started to leave Bob's office another man came into the office. Bob said, "Chance and Ann Clark, this is one of our accountants, David Dawson."

David shook hands with both of them and welcomed them to Chicago and Superior. He said he would probably see them again before they returned to Kansas.

Chance couldn't wait any longer to ask Bob, "What is the Superior Toy Company?"

"You didn't know? We are Superior Yo-yos."

"You have to be kidding."

"No, sir, I'm not kidding. Before the parking meter business started, Mr. Donald was making and selling millions of yo-yos."

Chance could certainly remember playing with Superior yoyos when he was little. The local Woolworth's Store used to have Filipino men come in once or twice a year giving demonstrations of all of the tricks you could do with a Superior yo-yo. After Chance bought a new Superior Yo-yo he knew for certain someone had taken out all of the tricks out of his before he got it, because he could never make them do the tricks the yo-yo demo men did.

Bob started the tour in the engineering department. Bob explained how they began by drawing up a part on a sheet of paper and he told them Superior's engineers generally made the tools needed to actually manufacture the part. Bob continued, saying the engineering department also made up the bills of material to make each one of the time and rate combinations for the meters the cities wanted. He said they had over five thousand different time and rate combinations they had made for cities. Chance shook his head he couldn't believe they could have made that many different kinds of meters.

Bob told them a Mr. Miller had designed the original Superior meter and patented it in about 1931 or 1932. However, Mr. Miller was an inventor of different products and never did make a parking meter and he sold the rights to Mr. Donald an only acted as a consultant to Superior. Superior began making and selling parking meters in 1936. Chance looked at Ann and smiled since that was the year they were born.

Bob said the first parking meter ever installed was in Oklahoma City in 1935. These meters were made by a company in Oklahoma City, the Magic Meter Company. Superior's first installation was made in 1936 in Pocatello, Idaho and the next one was in Atlantic City, New Jersey.

Bob Ellsworth took them into a machine shop, where all kinds of small parts were being made, some with punch presses and others by machines bending and cutting notches in the stainless steel winding rings.

The next stop on their tour was the assembly of the housings. Chance watched the people putting assemblies of parts onto the housing and then moving them up to the next person in the line. From the housing assembly line, they went upstairs to where the timers were being made. Chance watched the women assembling and adjusting the timers. He thought to himself there is no way I could ever do that as fast as these women.

Chance told Ann, "After watching these ladies put clocks together, I see your dad has been working with the wrong person in our family."

Ann retorted, "Forget it! I'm not fixing clocks for you and my dad."

Chance and Bob both broke out laughing, because of the way Ann said that. It was not only a fast answer it was as firm an answer as they had ever heard.

Bob said, "Well, if we can't put Ann to work helping you, maybe we better go to lunch. You go downstairs and I'll get my car and pick you up in front of the plant."

Chance and Ann made their way down the front steps until they got to the front door and waited there for Bob to pick them up. Soon Bob pulled up in front of the plant and Chance and Ann got into his car. Bob went around the corner and headed down Chicago Avenue. In a few minutes they arrived at the Como Inn. Bob said, "I hope you both like Italian food."

Chance replied, "We sure do."

Bob pulled the car in front of the restaurant and they got out. Bob gave his car keys to a young man who handed Bob a ticket and then got in the car and drove away. This was Chance's first experience with valet parking. He was not so sure he would be ready to hand his car keys and car over to someone in front of a restaurant, because he was not sure they would bring it back.

They walked inside the restaurant, which was much larger inside then it looked from the outside. They had at least two, maybe three large dining rooms and these were flanked by small dining rooms all along the outside of the restaurant. Private dining rooms were really what these rooms were, because they had doors that could be locked from the inside if the people didn't want to be disturbed.

The waiter showed them to Mr. Ellsworth's table, which was already set-up for the three of them.

Bob said, "I hope you don't mind, but I took the liberty of ordering for us."

Chance and Ann both said in unison, "That's fine."

They began bringing food to the table, starting with wonderful bread and butter. Chance thought it was not quite as good as the bread he and Ann used to get at the Rainbow Bakery after school, but it was very good. Then they brought minestrone soup that was out of this world. After the soup, a pasta dish was served, and last, but not least, they brought spumoni ice cream made at the Como Inn. Chance and Ann thought this ice cream was spectacular. The meal was great, but the spumoni was unlike anything they had ever eaten in their life.

Back at the plant after lunch, they went upstairs to the mechanism assembly line. Chance was taken back by the fact the production lines were so different from what he pictured in his mind. There was so much more work done by hand on the meter lines and far less movement of the mechanism downs an assembly line as he visioned. Chance expected one person would put on a part and then the mechanism would move down some type of a conveyor belt to the next person, who would put on a part, and so forth until at the end of the line you had a finished product. In truth, one person took the components of the back half of the mechanism and put that half together then moved it to another person who assembled the front half of the mechanism. After that an adjuster coin-checked the mechanism and made any final adjustments to it. They put their initials on it and the mechanism was ready to go to either be packed in a box or placed in the housing for shipment to the customer cities.

Chance spent a couple of hours watching the mechanism assembly line, Bob Ellsworth said, "What if I have someone take you back to your hotel and then my wife and I would like to take you to dinner tonight. We'll pick you up at the hotel at seven - fifteen."

Chance and Ann went with a driver who took them back to the North Park Hotel. They lay down for awhile then showered and dressed for dinner. By seven o'clock, they were waiting in the lobby for Bob and his wife.

A little before seven-fifteen, Chance saw Bob's car pull up in front of the hotel. They went out to the car and got in.

Bob said, "This is my wife Mary. Mary, this is Chance and Ann Clark," and with that, Bob pulled the car away from the curb and started driving toward downtown Chicago. He told them he made reservations at the Sherman House for dinner and a show.

When they arrived at the Sherman House, Bob and Mary led them into a huge ballroom and they were shown to their table. After sitting down, Bob said, "I would recommend the New York strip steak here; it's the best thing on their menu."

Chance and Ann both replied, "That's fine with us."

During dinner they were entertained by a variety show. Chance liked a young woman singer and thought she was very good. Mary told Ann she and Bob had four children, two boys and two girls. After dinner, Chance saw the check the waiter gave Bob. Bob paid the waiter and picked up a receipt. As soon as Chance and Ann were back in their room, Chance asked Ann, "Do you know how much the bill was for our dinner?"

"No, not really."

"It was one hundred and thirty-eight dollars! That's more money then we spend on food in two months."

The next few days Chance spent learning a lot more about Superior then just how to fix meters. Just before they left, Bob said he wanted to introduce them to Larry Lamb, the Vice President of Sales for Superior. Larry had just returned from Los Angeles. Bob brought Larry into his office and introduced him to Chance and Ann. Chance was very impressed with Larry, he had a very bubbly personality. Larry asked if everything had been all right with their stay in Chicago and if there was anything more Superior could do to help Chance or if they needed anything. Chance assured him Bob Ellsworth had done a very good job of looking after them during their stay.

The next morning as they checked out of the hotel, the desk clerk said, "Mr. Clark, if you will please sign the bill, everything will be taken care of by Superior."

Chance signed his name.

The trip home was uneventful. On the flight from Kansas City to Webster, Chance told Ann, "I want to work for Superior. I'd love to be a part of that company. I was born to be in this business. Just think I was born in Oklahoma where the first parking meter in the world was installed and we were born in 1936, the year the first Superior meter was put on the street."

"OK, Chance, if that's what you want to do, you can do it."

When their plane touched down on the runway in Webster, Ann said, "I want to see my baby."

She didn't have to wait long. When they got off the plane, the gate opened and as Chance and Ann were walking from the plane, Chase came running to meet them. They both reached down for him, but Chance would get him second-his mommy already had him in her arms. No matter how much fun she had in Chicago, it was a lot better for her to be home with her baby boy.

14

Chase was growing up fast and was so much fun to be with that Chance and Ann couldn't believe it was already his third birthday on August 6, 1957.

Chance had become one of the best parking meter servicemen in Karl Jones' territory. Karl came to see Chance at least every other month and, sometimes, every month. They become very close friends by this time. The city bought another seven hundred meters from Karl and Chance finished installing them over the Labor Day weekend. Everything was going along very good in Chance and Ann's life.

November came and Jack Harris asked Chance if he would like to go hunting with him the second weekend after pheasant season opened.

Jack said, "There are too many crazy hunters out there on opening day."

Chance agreed to go with him the following weekend. They left Webster early Saturday morning, just a little after three in the morning, headed for Western Kansas.

Jack said, "I don't feel very good this morning. I have an awful headache, but it will probably go away after while.

Jack told Chance a story about hunting one time in this area with his brother-in-law, Robert Keane. They were walking back to their car when Jack saw a car pull up next to where his car was parked.

Jack said, "I told Robert that has to be a game warden. We counted the number of birds we had and realized we had too many for just the two of us. We were hunting with two friends from Webster, but they went into town to buy some shells and their birds were in the back of my car. I told Robert to give me the two birds he was carrying and I stuck those two and two of those I had up inside my empty pant leg where my leg was missing. We walked onto the car and, sure enough, it was a game warden."

Jack continued his story, "The game warden asked for our hunting licenses and then wanted to look in the trunk of the car. When he did, he counted the number of birds and we still had two more then we were allowed."

The game warden said, "I think you boys must be through hunting for the day."

Jack said, "He told him you know you're right."

Jack then said to Chance, "The game warden started to leave and would you believe it, one of the roosters I stuck up inside my pant leg wasn't completely dead. He moved and my pant leg fell down, dropping those four other birds on the ground!"

Chance started laughing thinking about how Jack must have looked when his pant leg fell down and out popped four more pheasants.

Jack continued, "It cost me four hundred dollars, but the worst part was it happened right after we first moved to Webster from Kansas City and I gave the judge a check on my Kansas City bank. I got all the way home to Webster before Julie told me we had closed that account!"

Chance said, "My god! What did you do then?"

"I got on the telephone and called the judge and explained what had happened. He told me it would be OK if I just sent him a check on the right bank."

Daylight came and Jack turned the car down a dirt road somewhere west of Gove, Kansas. As they were driving along this road, Jack spotted three pheasants crossing the road and duck down in a small ditch next to the road. Jack stopped the car and told Chance, "I think you might be able to get one of those birds. Just walk down the road and before you come to that cross-road, I'm sure they will get up and you will have a chance to get at least one of them."

Chance slowly and quietly got out of the car and took Jack's twelve gauge Winchester pump shotgun out of the trunk. He loaded it with five shells and put some more shells in his coat pocket. Slowly Chance began walking down the side of the road, with Jack following him in the car. Just before Chance got to the crossroads as Jack had told the three pheasants flew up in front of Chance. Chance took aim with his shotgun and fired, dropping one of the birds like a rock. Chance took aim at a second bird and got him, too. It was the first time Chance ever got two birds with two shots. The other bird sailed away Chance knew he couldn't get him so he didn't fire. Chance found the birds, picked them up and loaded them into a box in the trunk. He unloaded the shotgun and put it back in the trunk.

When Chance got back in the car, Jack said, "That's as good shooting as I've ever seen."

"It must be your gun, because I've never been able to do that before."

Jack said, "Let's just keep going down this road and see what we can find. I don't feel much like getting out of the car, my head is killing me."

Jack drove on down the road and Chance saw the bright white ring on the neck of a pheasant rooster.

Jack said, "I think it will be better if I drive on by him and then let you walk back and try to get him up out of those weeds."

Chance got out of the car and got Jack's gun out of the trunk. He loaded the gun and starting walking back about a quarter of a mile to where he first spotted the pheasant. Chance walked down the edge of the road where he had good visibility of the ditch.

Just before Chance got to where he had first seen the pheasant, the pheasant flew up, coming straight at Chance. Chance pulled the shotgun up and fired. The bird was hit and began falling, but then started flying again. Chance took aim again and fired and this time, the pheasant fell to the ground.

Chance walked down into the ditch and began looking for his bird Just as Chance found the pheasant and picked him up, he heard a very loud sound behind him. He turned in time to watch twenty or thirty pheasants fly away from the ditch he just walked past.

Chance came back to the car and put his third pheasant in the trunk. Chance unloaded the shotgun again and put it back in the trunk. When he got into the car, Jack asked, "You didn't like any of those other thirty pheasants that flew away behind you huh?"

Chance grinned, "I guess not, but they sure scared the heck out of me when they took off." Jack said, "I'm feeling worse, why don't we go back to Gove and have some lunch?"

He turned the car around and drove back to town and parked in front of the only cafe in town. They both ordered the plate lunch specials. Chance finished his, but Jack took only a couple of bites. He drank his coffee and took some more aspirin.

Chance asked, "Do you want me to drive?"

"I think that's a good idea, I'm going to lie down in the back seat."

Jack gave Chance the car keys, opened the back door and lay down on the back seat. Jack never let anyone drive when he was in the car, so Chance knew he was really sick.

"Dad, I think we better go home until you get to feeling better."

"Maybe that's a good idea."

Chance backed the car out of its parking space and turned onto the highway headed back toward Hays. When Chance got to Hays, he asked Jack, "How are you doing? Maybe we better stop at the hospital here and let someone check you out."

"No, let's go on home I'll be all right."

Two-and-a-half hours later Chance pulled into the driveway at the Harris's home. Chance helped Jack out of the back seat and into the house. Julie and Ann were surprised to see them back, since they had planned to stay until Sunday night before coming home.

Chance said, "Dad's not doing very well, he has an awful headache. I tried to get him to let me stop at the hospital in Hays, but he said he just wanted to come home."

Julie got a cold washcloth and placed it on Jack's head as he had lain down on the couch in the living room. She brought Jack a glass of water and four more aspirin.

The next day when Chance and Ann checked on Jack, he was on the couch watching a football game on TV. Chase started to get on the couch with his grandpa, but Ann told him, "Chase, don't get on grandpa. He's not feeling good, he's sick."

Chase went over to his grandpa and gently laid his hand on Jack's hands and then he came back to his daddy and wanted to be picked up. Chase didn't like to see his grandpa sick.

The Monday morning Chance stopped by the jewelry store to have coffee with Jack as he did every morning at this time. Jack was working on a watch when Chance came into the store. Jack put down the watch and they walked over to a small cafe two doors from the jewelry store. Jack said he was feeling a lot better, but still wasn't able to get rid of his headache. When they finished their coffee, Chance walked back to the jewelry store with Jack and said, "I'll see you later dad. Hope you get over that headache pretty soon."

"I'm sure I will. I'll see you tonight."

Jack headed back inside the glass doors of the jewelry store.

Chance got into his jeep and started driving back to his shop at the police department. Before he got two blocks away from the store, he met an ambulance coming from the fire station located next door to the police station.

As Chance pulled into his parking space behind the police station, Chief Spruce came running out the door to meet him.

The chief said, "They are taking your father-in-law to the hospital. He just collapsed at the jewelry store."

Chance got back into his jeep and started to the hospital.

The chief said, "I'll call your wife and let her know what's going on.

By the time Chance got to the hospital, Ann and her mother were coming in the door. The store called Julie and told her about Jack.

Chance said, "Where's Chase?"

Ann said, "Your mother was over and she took Chase home with her."

They waited outside the emergency room for what seemed like hours to hear how Jack was doing in fact, it was hours. They kept asking about Jack, but no one could tell them anything. Finally a doctor came out to talk with them.

The doctor said, "Jack's had some type of seizure. Does he have epilepsy?"

Julie said, "No."

The doctor said, "Well, we have him stabilized now and after we get him cleaned up, we'll take him to a room. I'll have a nurse come and get you when we are ready to move him to a room."

Chance was saying prayers in his mind as fast as he could, "Please Father, let Jack be all right."

He knew Ann was doing the same, sending prayers up to God to help her father to be OK.

They waited for another hour before a nurse came to get them. They went up to Jack's room and all three of them gathered around his bed. Jack was still unconscious. The three of them just stood watching him. He was breathing very hard and once in awhile a nurse would come in to check on him. The hours dragged by. A doctor came in about nine o'clock that evening and said, "Well, I thought he would have regained consciousness by now. I'm sure he'll be coming around pretty soon."

Julie kept talking to Jack and rubbing his hands. Instead of Jack regaining consciousness, his breathing continued to get worse. About one-thirty in the morning the nurse on duty called another doctor to come up from the emergency room to check on Jack. When the doctor came in to look at him, he asked Chance and Ann to leave the room. He told Julie it would be all right if she stayed with her husband.

Ann began pacing the floor in the hallway just outside Jack's room. A nurse who was working on the other end of the floor came up and told Ann she would have to sit down or leave the hospital, because she was bothering the patients. Chance couldn't believe what he just heard. He told the nurse his wife's father was not doing very well right now and Ann was very worried and upset. Chance and Ann sat down on a couple of chairs at the end of the hall. The doctor and two nurses were still in Jack's room along with Ann's mother.

Shortly before 3 a.m., the doctor came out of the room, walked over to Ann and said, "I'm sorry, but there was nothing else we could do for your father. He passed away a few minutes ago."

Ann began to cry and Chance held her. They went back into Jack's room. Julie was sitting by his bed holding his hand. She was softly saying, "Why did you leave me like this?"

Hearing this, Chance began crying with Ann and they held each other as close together as they could get.

Chance kept thinking this is my fault if only I had taken him to the hospital in Hays on Saturday they could have saved him. Chance would carry this thought with him for the rest of his life.

Jack Harris was forty-seven years old when he died on November 15, 1957, leaving Julie a widow at only forty-three years old. They would never get over losing Jack, he meant so much to all of them. Jack died from a cerebral hemorrhage. Chance always wondered if it might have helped if the doctors would have treated Jack for something besides a seizure. Jack's funeral was on Friday morning and the police department turned out in force to support Chance and Ann.

Chance was lost. He didn't just lose his father-in-law; he lost his teacher and his friend. By Monday Chance was in worse shape then Ann and her mother. Finally, Ann called Chance's father to come over to see if he could help Chance. Chance's dad was never one to spend a lot of time talking and almost never showed any kind of open affection to Chance, but when Ann told him Chance needed him, he came.

Chance was in the kitchen crying with his head on the kitchen table, when his dad came to the house.

Ann said, "Dad, see if you can talk to Chance and help him.

I can't, I've tried."

Chance's father came into the kitchen and spoke to Chance, "Chance, you've got to get a hold of yourself. You have a family to take care of and I'm sure you are going to have to help Ann's mother too."

Chance continued crying. His dad put his hand on Chance's shoulder and said, "Son, Jack wouldn't want you to carry on like this."

Chance got up from the table and continued to cry. He said to his dad, "Jack taught me so much, I don't know how I can make it without him."

Mr. Clark put his arms around Chance and pulled him close. He said to Chance, "It will be all right. You have Ann and Chase to look after."

Hearing that, Chance stopped crying but he continued to let his dad hold him, because he could never remember his dad doing something like this before, except maybe when he was a baby. After Chance's dad came over to help him, Chance felt much closer to his father. His father really surprised him with his tenderness and caring when Chance needed him most.

No matter how one tries to stop time, they can't. Thanksgiving came and Chance, Ann, and Julie couldn't find anything to be thankful for on that day. Julie and Ann fixed a turkey, but the three of them could only see Jack's empty chair at the end of the table. Later in the day they went out to the cemetery. Julie had been going out every day since the funeral, but this was the first time Chance and Ann had been there since the funeral.

It had been over two weeks since the funeral and you could still see the fresh grave covered with flowers. At a distance the flowers still looked pretty good, but as they walked up to Jack's grave they could see the flowers were getting to be in bad shape. Chance read the headstone that said, "Father - Jack Harris: 1909-1957."

Chance turned and went back to the car and began crying.

Ann soon returned to the car out of the cold Kansas wind. They embraced as they cried together. Julie stayed at Jack's grave until Chance regained his composure and got out of the car. He took her hand and said, "Mom, let's go before you freeze."

Julie replied, "I can't believe he would leave me like this."

Chance said, "Mom, I know he wouldn't have left you if he could have kept from doing it."

Chance wondered why God would take someone as good and kind as Jack while they were so young and Chance decided right then life was not fair. Christmas was better for them since they had to put on a happy front for Chase. Besides, Chase was so full of life he caused everyone around him to get caught up in some his happiness.

The new year of 1958 arrived and Webster hired a new city manager. The new city manager was coming from some city in Ohio, according to the newspaper and his name was Allen Winfield. Mr. Winfield had not been in Webster for more then a few weeks, when one cold January day as Chance was leaving his shop for lunch, he saw Mr. Winfield getting out of his city car.

Chance said hello to him.

Mr. Winfield said to Chance, "May I talk with you for a few minutes?"

"Yes, sir."

Mr. Winfield explained he was staying at the Hilton Hotel and wondered if Chance could join him for dinner and some conversation that evening.

"I would be happy to meet you for dinner. What time do you want me to meet you and where would you like to meet?"

"How about six-thirty, just come up to my hotel room at the Hilton, I'm in room 620."

"All right, sir. I'll see you at six-thirty."

Chance drove his jeep home as soon as he left Mr. Winfield to tell Ann the news. When he told Ann about his conversation with Mr. Winfield, she said, "I wonder what he wants to talk to you about."

"I don't have the slightest idea, but I guess I'll know tonight."

Chance was excited about this meeting, but he couldn't think of why Mr. Winfield wanted to meet with him. If it had something to do with the parking meter operations, why wasn't he meeting with Chief Spruce? After all, the chief had been in charge of the meters since they were installed in 1947. It was going to be a long afternoon. At six-twenty, Chance parked near the Hilton Hotel and began walking to the front door. When he got to the door, he met Mr. Winfield coming into the hotel.

Mr. Winfield said, "Hi, Chance. I'm just getting here I've been tied up with a planning committee meeting. Why don't you come on up with me?"

Chance followed Mr. Winfield into the elevator. When they gotinside his room, Mr. Winfield said, "I want to wash up a bit and change shirts before we go for dinner. I could sure use a drink, how about you Chance?"

"That would be nice."

Mr. Winfield went over to dresser, picked up a bottle of J&B Scotch, poured two water glasses almost full of scotch and handed Chance one of the glasses. Mr. Winfield proceeded into the bathroom with his glass.

Chance took a drink and almost choked. He tried to say something, but his voice was just a whisper.

Mr. Winfield asked, "Did you say something, Chance?"

The best Chance could do was to say, "No, sir."

In a few minutes Mr. Winfield came back into the room and asked Chance if he wanted another drink.

"I'm not used to drinking, I think I had enough."

Mr. Winfield smiled and finished his drink. They went to dinner in the hotel dining room and after ordering, Mr. Winfield began to tell Chance what he had in mind.

Mr. Winfield said he had been a city manager for over twenty-five years and during that time he found the three biggest problems came from the three "P's": purchasing, police and parking.

He said, "I took charge of purchasing this afternoon. I promoted Vern Miller to city clerk and I have personally taken over purchasing. I think Chief Spruce is one of the best police chiefs I have ever worked with, but he doesn't need to oversee parking, that's not a job for the police chief."

Mr. Winfield continued, "I have decided to move parking out of the police department and put you in charge of a new department. Do you want the job?"

Chance thought to himself, do I want the job! I sure do, but he responded to Mr. Winfield by saying, "Do you think I can do the job for you?"

"Chance, I'm going to give you some advice. When someone offers you a job they think you can do it, so if it's a better job take it."

"I want the job!"

Mr. Winfield extended his hand and said to Chance, "Congratulations! You are my new Director of Parking."

Chance took Mr. Winfield's hand and shook it with a very firm grip.

Chance asked, "Have you talked to Chief Spruce about this yet?"

Mr. Winfield said, "No, but I'll take care of that. You just develop a plan to take over all the jobs being done by other departments in the city for parking. I'm sure you are going to need some help, so start thinking about someone to hire to help you."

Chance's mind was now traveling at the speed of light. He knew somebody in the National Guard who he would like to work with. Where could he move his shop? Bingo!

Chance asked, "Do you have some place in mind where my department can operate?"

"I think I have found a place for you in the back of city hall."

They finished eating and Chance told Mr. Winfield, "Thank you for dinner and I really appreciate the new job."

Chance couldn't get home fast enough to tell Ann the news. He went flying into the house yelling for Ann. "Annie!"

"OK, what's the news?"

"I just got promoted to Director of Parking for the City of Webster."

Chance sat down and told Ann the whole conversation.

When he finished, Ann asked, "Can he do that?"

"Ann, he's the city manager he can do almost anything he wants to do about running the city."

Late the next afternoon Chance went to the city manager's office and asked to speak to Mr. Winfield. His secretary was about to tell Chance Mr. Winfield was busy, when Mr. Winfield came out of the office with the people he had been talking to. As they were leaving, Mr. Winfield saw Chance and said, "Come on in, Chance."

Chance said, "Well, I believe I have put together a plan to consolidate all of the functions for a parking department."

Chance began by showing Mr. Winfield the various functions needed by the parking department and which departments were currently doing the jobs:

Function	Department
Maintenance	Police Department
Meter Collections	City Clerk Office
Counting Coins City	Treasurer
Enforcement Police	Department
Processing Unpaid Tickets	Police Department
Post Maintenance	Street Department

Chance said, "I will need one full-time person and one part- time person to take over all these jobs, plus I'm going to need the four current enforcement officers and the two people who process the unpaid tickets and I'm going to need another vehicle."

Mr. Winfield asked, "Do you think you need another jeep wagon?"

"No, they're too expensive to repair and besides, it would be better to have something with an automatic transmission to drive checking meters."

"Come on, Chance and I'll show you where your department can be set up and we can talk as we go."

Mr. Winfield and Chance left Mr. Winfield's office and walked downstairs and into an area on the ground floor of city hall. Mr. Winfield took out his keys and opened a door into a very large room filled with chairs and tables.

Mr. Winfield said, "Chance, I don't know why this wouldn't work for you. It's going to have to be painted and we'll get some lights installed for you. What do you think? Is it big enough?"

"I think so. It looks like a pretty big area."

"That settles it. This is your new office."

"Mr. Winfield, have you talked with the chief yet about these changes?"

"No, I haven't had a chance today, but I'll take care of it."

Two days later Mr. Winfield sent word to Chance he could start moving into his new office whenever he was ready. Chance had been talking with Joe Carver about coming to work with him in the parking department. Chance told Joe he wanted him to start as soon as he could get approval from the city manager. Chance picked up a key for his new office and talked to Mr. Winfield about hiring Joe Carver. Mr. Winfield gave Chance the papers to put Joe on the payroll and told Chance if he was happy with Joe Carver, then to go ahead and hire him.

Chance called Joe and told him he could start to work the next morning. Joe Carver was almost a copy of Chance. His hair was a little lighter in color, he wore glasses and he certainly didn't have Chance's freckles, so he didn't have problems with sunburns all the time like Chance did.

When Joe arrived at the police station the next morning, Chance had him fill out the papers they needed to get Joe on the city payroll. After Joe finished filling them out, Chance signed them and told Joe he would take them over to the manager's office. Chance told Joe to begin packing up all the tools and parts in the shop for their move from the police station to city hall.

When Chance returned, Joe had already filled several boxes with parts and tools. Chance said, "I guess it makes sense to go ahead and load these in the back of the jeep so we can take them over to our new office in city hall."

Chance and Joe began carrying the boxes down the steep stairs of the police station and loading the boxes into the jeep. After they had the jeep loaded with as many boxes as it would carry, they closed up the back and drove over to city hall. They found it was a lot easier to unload the jeep and take the boxes into their city hall office on the ground floor.

About the time they loaded the jeep for the third time that morning, Chief Spruce came down the stairs and said to Chance,

"What in the hell are you doing? Where are you going with all your stuff.

"Chief, didn't Mr. Winfield talk to you about moving my shop and things?"

"He sure as hell hasn't talked to me about any such thing."

Chance didn't want any hard feelings between the chief and himself. He thought far too much of the chief to want to make him mad at him.

"Chief, I'm sorry, but Mr. Winfield told me he would talk with you about him making changes in the parking operations."

The chief started walking toward city hall and as he was walking away, he said to Chance, "I'm on my way over to talk with Mr. Winfield and get this whole thing straightened out."

Chance never knew exactly how the conversation went between the chief and the city manager. He only knew the chief never quite forgave Chance for the way things happened with the transferring of people from the police department to a new parking department. Although Chance didn't know how the conversation went between the chief and the city manager. What he did know was he got full cooperation in making the changeover.

Within a month, Chance had all of the people and the responsibility for a fully integrated parking department. He had collections, maintenance, parking enforcement, ticket processing and follow-up and budgeting. In other words, every function relating to the parking operation was in his department. Year's later Chance would hear how some guy in Washington, DC claimed to have had the first fully integrated parking department in the world in the mid-sixties. Chance's department was fully organized and operational by April 1958.

Chance thought Ann's dad could never dreamed about how his idea for Chance would turned out, by training Chance to get the job as the meter repairman turned into Chance being something far more then the meter repairman and his fatherin-law deserved the credit. Chance was so sorry he wasn't with them to see how his plan worked out.

Chance was twenty-one years old and head of his own department. Chance would never have believed what was ahead for himself in this business.

15

Chance and Ann joined a new Sunday school class at the Methodist Church for young married couples and instead of going to church every Sunday, as they used to do before they were married. They went to Sunday school every Sunday and it gave Chase a chance to be with children his own age for at least one hour each week. Part of the idea of this young couple's class was to get together socially because most of the couples didn't have much money and were struggling to make ends meet. They certainly didn't have money for entertainment.

One Sunday Chance and Ann were told they and another young couple in class, by the name of Schmidt was to be in charge of next month's social event. Ann talked with Susan Schmidt after Sunday school and Susan invited the Clarks to come over to their house the next Friday evening after supper, so they could plan the social. Chance was not big on going to people's homes, but Ann told the Schmidt's they would come over Friday and work on the plans for next month's social so they were going.

After supper on Friday, Ann almost had to drag Chance out of the door to go to the Schmidt's house. Chance and Chase finally got in the car and Ann said, "We'll probably only be there for about an hour, so you start thinking of what we can do for the party next month and we can come home sooner."

They were met at the door by Susan Schmidt and her daughter Sherry. Sherry was a year younger then Chase. She looked like a little doll, with big blue eyes and golden curls. Chance fell for her the moment he saw her hanging onto her mother's skirt. Chase and Sherry soon found some of Sherry's toys to keep them busy. Susan and Ann began to talk about things at the church and Chance took a seat at the kitchen table. Susan's husband had worked late and just got home a few minutes before they arrived. He was in the bathroom getting cleaned up.

A few minutes later Susan's husband came into the room. Although they had all seen each other at Sunday school, they had never been introduced. Susan said, "Chance, this is my husband E. R., but everybody calls him Doc. Doc, this is Chance and Ann Clark and their little boy, Chase."

Doc reached over to shake hands with Chance and told everyone to please sit down.

Chance asked, "How did you get your nickname, Doc?"

"In high school I was pretty good at fixing cars and the kids starting calling me the Auto Doc and then just doc."

Chance thought that was pretty funny and he liked Doc and Susan right away. They were friendly and down to earth. Doc was about five-foot-ten with black hair and a round face. Susan was not as tall as Ann and had very dark black hair and dark eyes behind very thick glasses. Chance thought she was a beautiful young woman.

As they all began to get acquainted, Chance learned Doc recently got out of the army and was now working for a company remanufacturing Ford engines. Doc was three years older then Chance and both of them were born in September. Susan was a year older then Chance and Ann and was born on the same day his parents were married.

Susan made a pot of coffee and they sat around the table planning the social event for their Sunday school class the next month. The longer they talked, the more they liked each other. The four of them were having so much fun talking, they didn't even notice Chase and Sherry had crawled up on the couch in the living room and went to sleep.

Chance looked at his watch and couldn't believe it was after midnight and said, "Ann, we better get Chase and go him home and get him to bed. I didn't realize it was this late."

Doc said, "Well, there's no need to hurry off now. We're going to have breakfast here in a little while."

The four of them started laughing and it took Chance and Ann another half-hour to actually start out to the car. Doc and Susan followed them to their car and Doc said, "I don't know why you are rushing away so soon, I told you Susan would be fixing breakfast pretty soon."

Susan said, "Doc! You're going to wake up the whole neighborhood."

With Susan having the last word, Chance put Chase into the back seat and they finally headed home. Chance and Ann had just met their lifetime best friends.

Time passed quickly it was August 1959 and soon it would be time for Chase to start school. Ann asked Chance to go with her to enroll Chase, Chance came home early and went with Ann to sign Chase up for kindergarten. After Ann finished filling out the papers in the office to get Chase enrolled, Chance and Ann took Chase to see his room. Chance thought it would be a good idea to help Chase get familiar with things and places in the school. After they found Chase's room, Chance took him outside and they played on the swings, the merry-go-round and the jungle gym.

On the first day of school, Chance came home from work so he could go with Ann to take Chase to his first day of school. Chance took movies of Chase going to the car and opening the driver's side door. In the movie, it looked like Chase was going to drive himself to school. Chase didn't just walk up to school he pranced like he was in a parade. Chance and Ann let him walk in front of them and he found his room without any problem and went inside with Chance and Ann close behind him.

A little girl and her mother came into the room just behind them and as the girl's mother was telling her daughter good-bye, the little girl started crying. The teacher came over and tried to talk to the little girl as her mother was leaving the room, but the little girl just kept crying and yelling for her mother. Chase came over and put his arm around the little girl's shoulders and said, "It's OK your mommy will be back to get you after while."

Chase led her away from the door and over to some toys and she quit crying.

Chance and Ann looked at each other with so much pride in their eyes as to how Chase helped the little girl to stop crying for her mother.

The next day, Ann's mother took Chase to school by herself. Chance took movies of Mrs. Harris and Chase walking to her car and driving away from the house.

On the third day of school Chance's mother had her turn taking Chase to school. Again, Chance took movies of them leaving for school.

Chance thought Ann and he were so lucky to have a son like Chase. He was perfect in his looks, he was always just a little taller then average for his age and he had a great personality. He worked hard at whatever he did, including playing. Chance would never forget when Chase was about three years old he had been playing in the backyard all morning and by lunchtime was very tired. Ann put him in his high chair and he began eating his lunch. A few minutes later Chance and Ann looked over at him and Chase had a spoon in his hand, but his head was down on his plate. He played so hard all morning he had just fallen asleep. He looked so cute they almost couldn't pick him up and wash his face so they could put him in his bed. Chance and Ann looked at each other and then at Chase. They were so pleased with Chase and with themselves for having a child like him.

Chance and Ann's love was as deep as ever, each year they grew closer. They knew they had the best kind of love because they were not only husband and wife they were lovers and best friends. Doc and Susan were their best and closest friends, but no one could be friends like Chance and Ann.

Chance learned when things seem they are going along too good, you either don't know what's happening or you have overlooked something.

Just before Thanksgiving 1959 Ann began to have all kinds of bruises on her legs and arms. She didn't think a lot about it, but she began to feel tired all of the time. She was having a hard time keeping up with Chase and being able to do her housework. After talking with Chance about it, he suggested she go to the doctor and get a check up.

Chance said, "Maybe you just need some vitamins."

Ann waited a few more days, but she kept feeling worse so she finally made an appointment with Dr. Jones. When she told the doctor what was wrong, she didn't have enough energy to keep up with her five-year-old, and he looked at the bruises on her arms and legs.

Dr. Jones told Ann, "I want you to go to a new doctor in town who is a specialist in internal medicine. I'll have my nurse make an appointment for you with Dr. Henry Mendel."

The following day Ann went to see Dr. Mendel. He was young, only in his late thirties or early forties. Ann like him at once because she didn't have to wait long to get in to see him and, unlike most of the other doctors in town who talked down to you, he actually talked to her as if she was a real person.

Dr. Mendel looked over her medical records Dr. Jones sent with her and said, "I see you have a son who was born in 1954, you had your tonsils out in 1956 and had an ovarian cyst removed last year. It looks to me like we doctors are not being very kind to you, as young as you are."

The doctor said, "Let's take a look at you and see what's going on.

He called in a nurse and told her to get Ann ready for a complete physical. Dr. Mendel left the examining room and the nurse gave Ann a gown to put on. The nurse told Ann to take off all her clothes and put them in this basket.

Ann did as she was told and by the time she had on her gown, she was so tired, she lay down on the examining table. A few minutes later, Dr. Mendel and his nurse came back into the room. Ann had never had an examination like this one. The doctor started with her hair and worked his way down to each one of her toes and everywhere in between. He asked questions about her parents, their health, and all the time during the examination he kept writing down information about Ann.

The doctor asked Ann about her white hair and told his nurse to come take a look at it.

He said, "Her hair is white there because there is no pigment in this part of her skin."

Dr. Mendel told her most of the people who have this white hair, or who lack skin pigment, is prone to losing their hearing at a very early age. He said no one knew why or what the connection was between the two things, it just happened.

Dr. Mendel told the nurse he wanted a urine sample and a complete work-up on Ann's blood. The nurse took out two very large needles to take the blood sample and filled the vials with Ann's blood. She apologized and said she promised not to take so much blood again. Then the nurse asked if Ann could give a urine sample right then. Ann said she thought so and the nurse took her down a hall to a bathroom. When Ann gave the nurse the sample, the nurse told her she could get dressed and wait in the examining room for the doctor.

Ann got dressed and by the time she was finished, she was exhausted and lay back down on the examining table. When the doctor came back into the room, Ann was actually asleep. The doctor told her he wanted to start her on some medication. He said her platelet count was much to low and gave her a prescription for medicine.

Dr. Mendel said, "I want to see you again in a couple of weeks. Ann, I hope you get to feeling better soon."

That was the first time Ann ever remembered having a doctor say that to her.

Two weeks went by and Ann was not feeling any better. She went back to Dr. Mendel and he had another blood test done. Her platelet count was even lower then the last test.

Dr. Mendel said, "I'm going to put you on a type of steroid to see if that helps you, but you can't stay on them for very long as they have a tendency to change your whole metabolism."

Ann had always been slim and trim. She weighed only one hundred twenty-five pounds, which was well proportioned over her five-foot-seven frame. The doctor gave her the pills and asked her to be back in a week.

Ann went back the next week and they took a blood test again.

The doctor told her, "The platelets are just a little below normal."

He told Ann to take one of the pills every other day and that she should have enough to last for another two weeks. He asked her to come back at the end of January.

Christmas came and the New Year started. It was 1960, a new decade. Chance and Ann had a lot to be happy about. She was feeling better and she had even begun to gain weight. Chance thought she looked healthier with the addition of five pounds.

By the end of January, she was feeling bad again, the bruises were back and she was tired all the time. When she went back to Dr. Mendel, he gave her a new type of steroid and told her to stay on it for six weeks. During the spring and summer Ann didn't get worse, but she didn't get better. In August, Dr. Mendel ordered Ann to go to the hospital for a bone marrow test.

Chance took Ann to the hospital and went with her to talk with the doctor who would be doing the test. The doctor told them she would be taken into one of the surgical rooms for the test and told Ann it wasn't going to be a fun deal. He said they would not put her to sleep for the test. They would put medicine on her breastplate to prevent any type of infection and then they would take a large needle and go directly into the breastplate to extract bone marrow from it.

Chance didn't know how Ann would be able to stand this kind of test, but she told him, "You just wait outside for me. I'll be all right."

The doctor said he could wait right outside the door.

About fifteen minutes later, the doctor came out and told Chance the test was over and Ann could go home in about an hour. Ann was soon brought out in a wheelchair and the nurse said she could go home. Chance looked at how pale Ann was and wondering why is God putting her through this?

The first part of September Chance got a call from David Dawson, the new Director of Service for Superior parking meters. David told Chance that Bob Ellsworth left the company to buy a plastic company and he was promoted to Bob's job. David told Chance, Superior has an opening for a service engineer and Chance was their number one choice. Chance remembered meeting David when he visited Superior in 1956. At that time, David was in the accounting department.

Chance was just been offered the job he had been dreaming of since he and Ann went to visit Superior. Chance liked the idea of traveling and going to new places. He was getting bored running the Webster parking department and besides it would give Joe Carver a promotion, because Chance had been training him for this day.

Chance went home at lunchtime and told Ann he just got the call from Superior he had been waiting for a long time.

Ann knew there was only one thing to say to Chance, "Take the job."

She knew how much Chance wanted to be a part of Superior. She never liked changes in her life and she didn't want Chance on the road, but she wouldn't tell him that.

Later that afternoon Chance called David Dawson back and said he wanted the job. David asked him if he could start in two weeks and Chance said he could.

Then Chance went in to see Mr. Winfield to tell him the news. Mr. Winfield was as happy as Chance because he felt this opportunity came about partially because of his own efforts in setting Chance up running his own department. Chance told Mr. Winfield Joe Carver is ready to take over running the department. Chance went back to his parking department and had a long conversation with Joe, telling him he would be taking over the department in two weeks and that he was going to work for Superior.

Two weeks later Chance at age 23 was hired by Superior and became the youngest service engineer Superior ever had. He spent a week in Chicago working on the mechanism line and then he traveled to St. Louis to meet another of the Superior Service Engineers, Ted Monroe. He rode with Ted for a week, calling on customers. Then Chance went home to Webster. He was happy to see Ann and Chase and they were sure ready to see him.

Chance resigned from the National Guard because he just didn't have time to serve anymore while traveling all the time.

Chance started traveling Monday through Friday and came home every weekend. Ann continued to see Dr. Mendel, and she was better as long as she was on the steroids. The minute she was off, her platelet count dropped.

Chance and Ann were excited about the presidential election. This would be the first time they would be able to vote for the president.

Chance told Ann, "I guess in Kansas, by voting for Jack Kennedy we will be making a protest vote."

Jack Kennedy won the election, but Nixon carried Kansas. Ann was now going to the doctor every week for blood tests.

She was getting worse and after the first part of 1961, the doctor was having her come in every day for a platelet count.

The steroids were not helping her anymore. Dr. Mendel began contacting specialists at the University of Kansas Medical Center, Johns Hopkins and Mayo Clinic. All of the doctors he spoke with felt Ann had leukemia.

Dr. Mendel just wouldn't agree to that diagnosis. He knew if that was what it was it was a death sentence for the twenty- four- year old Ann. Dr. Mendel still felt there was some part of the puzzle that didn't fit the leukemia diagnosis, but he wasn't sure what it was.

In early April 1961, Dr. Mendel made the decision to have Ann's spleen removed. The doctor held a conference with Chance and Ann and told them what he wanted to do and informed them that none of his advisors felt this would help Ann. But, he said, she can't go on much longer the way she is.

Ann checked into the hospital the next day. They gave her a simple test, by pricking her finger with a pin. After twenty minutes her blood still would not coagulate. Normally, blood would coagulate in less then three minutes. The surgeon met with Chance and Ann and told them he would be doing the surgery, but felt they were putting her through something that wasn't going to do her any good.

He said, "I'm sorry, but I have looked over your records and I'm certain you have leukemia. This surgery may cut down on whatever time you have left."

Ann said, "I believe in Dr. Mendel and if he's wrong it doesn't seem like it going to makes much difference anyway does it."

They had flown in several units of Ann's type of whole blood from Wichita to have it on hand for the surgery. The nurse came into her room and said they were ready for Ann in surgery. Ann sat up and

Chance held her for several minutes. He told her he loved her and he knew she would be all right.

Ann said, "I know, I'll see you after while."

They took Ann down the hallway to surgery. Ann's mother and Chance's mother and dad all waited with him outside the surgical ward. The operation took almost three hours and when it was over, Dr. Mendel and the surgeon came out together. Chance became concerned when he saw both doctors coming out to talk with him. Dr. Mendel said, "Chance, Ann's all right. The minute her spleen was removed, her platelet count started improving. We did another bone marrow puncture while she was asleep and everything looks good."

Ann's surgeon said, "Dr. Mendel is right. As soon as her spleen was removed, she began to improve. We didn't even have to give her any of the blood we had flown in for her."

Later, Dr. Mendel wrote a "White Paper" on Ann that would become the standard treatment for what is now called "Idiophatic Thrombocyte Penia Purpura or ITP."

Later that evening Dr. Mendel explained to Chance and Ann that one of the spleen's jobs is to act as a reservoir of blood if you are in an accident. Another one of the spleen's job is to kill off damaged blood platelets. In Ann's case however, the spleen was overactive and was killing all of her platelets.

Ann recovered quickly from the surgery. She was released from the hospital in less then a week and her strength began to return, even the color in her cheeks was back to normal. In a month she was feeling as good as she had before she became ill.

Chance continued to travel and when he returned on the weekends, their lovemaking was intense. Chance was told by some of his fellow travelers this was called the "honeymoon syndrome."

They said being apart meant coming home was like going on a honeymoon. Chance didn't know if that was true, he only knew he missed being with Ann. Although he loved traveling and going to new places, it wasn't the same without her.

Superior found having Chance on the payroll helped them a lot with their customer cities, since he had experience running a parking department for a city himself and with his background in clocks, Superior became more and more dependent on him to do their trouble-shooting. Chance's territory was Kansas, Oklahoma, Missouri, the panhandle of Texas, and a little part of western Arkansas. Before long, Superior had Chance working in New York, Illinois, Pennsylvania, Ohio, South Dakota, and anywhere else they had a problem. Chance was driving from Webster to all of these different states and sometimes couldn't even get home on weekends.

After working as a service engineer for Superior for a couple of years, Chance was asked by his friend Karl Jones to come and work with him in sales. Chance met with Karl in Kansas City on the way home from one of his extended trips. Chance had been working in Illinois for two weeks and was ready to get home to Ann and Chase.

Karl told Chance he wanted to cut down on his personal travel and was working with Superior to expand his distributorship to include eight states in the middle of the USA he said, "I want to build a real sales organization and you are one of the people who can help me. At the same time you're helping me build this company, you will have a chance to earn a lot more money then you're making now."

Karl went on, "I want you to take over Kansas for me."

Chance told Karl, "I'm on my way home tonight and I'll call you tomorrow after I talk with Ann, but that would certainly cut down my travel and I want to be home a lot more then I am now.

When Chance got home to Webster, he and Ann spent part of the night looking at maps and studying the potential for selling parking meters to the cities Chance would have. After some time, they began studying each other and found what they saw in each other was more enjoyable and rewarding then studying maps. They would think about Karl's offer some more tomorrow. Tonight they had a much better offer for each other.

The next day Chance called Karl and told him he would come to work with him and help build his organization. When Chance made the transfer from Superior to sales for the Karl Jones Company, he continued his pattern of achievement by becoming the youngest salesman who ever sold Superior Parking Meters.

16

*I*n Chance's new job working with Karl Jones, he would not only have the opportunity to learn about selling parking meters, he would have a chance to learn about some of the finer things in life.

Karl knew everyone in city government in Kansas. City Officials told Chance, Karl Jones was the "Mayor of Kansas." Chance didn't know about that, but he did know Karl was well liked and highly respected. One day while they were having lunch in a restaurant in downtown Topeka. A gentleman came over to their table and said, "Karl, Karl Jones. I haven't seen you for a long time, how have you been?"

Karl told the man he was doing just fine and that he wanted to introduce his associate. Karl turned to Chance, who had gotten up from his chair.

Karl said, "This is Chance Clark. Chance, I'd like you to meet Mr. Alf Landon."

Karl and Mr. Landon continued their conversation for several more minutes, talking about their mutual friends.

Afterward, Mr. Landon said to Chance, "You have one of the best person you could ever fine to work with if you are working with Karl."

After Mr. Landon left, Karl said, "If you didn't know, Alf Landon was the Republican candidate for president who ran against Franklin Roosevelt in 1936."

Chance knew Mr. Landon's name, but never expected to be introduced to him or have a chance to meet him. Karl ended the subject by saying in his typical fashion, "I'm not sure how he even knows me."

Over the next several years, Chance was always surprised by how many important people just "happened" to know Karl Jones.

Working with Karl gave Chance the knowledge of how to work with city officials and Karl was able to transfer the good will he earned over the years to Chance. Very few people have this kind of ability. In his own right, Chance could provide the expertise to help cities with their parking programs, because unlike most salesmen who sold parking meters he had actually ran a parking system himself.

Chance began to provide cities with studies and written recommendations to improve their parking systems. Providing this type of service allowed him to earn his own place in the sun. Chance could never replace Karl Jones, but Karl couldn't provide the know-how Chance brought to the job. The two of them were a winning team.

Karl continued to work with Superior to increase the size of his distributorship and after Superior fired several distributors, the Karl Jones Company was getting a new contract which would include the states of Kansas, Missouri, Oklahoma, Texas, New Mexico, Colorado, Wyoming, and Iowa.

When Chance left Superior, he got his friend and former employee in the Webster Parking Department, Joe Carver to take his job as a Superior Service Engineer. After Texas was added to Karl's distributorship, Karl decided to hire Joe to become his salesman for Texas. Karl contacted Joe and set up a meeting with him to discuss the possibility of joining the Karl Jones Company to sell in Texas for him. Joe had not been married very long at that time and his wife Jill recently gave birth to twin girls. After he and Karl met, Joe had to spend some time talking with Jill to decide if they wanted to move to Texas and away from their families in Webster.

It took Joe and Jill almost a week to make the decision to pull up stakes and move away from their friends and families. Karl agreed to pay their moving expenses and loan them money to buy a house in Texas until they could sell their house in Webster. If they didn't make enough from their house in Webster for the down payment, Karl agreed they could pay him back out of Joe's commissions in the future.

Karl already had a salesman working in Missouri for him, Albert Douglas. Albert had been with Karl for two or three years and had been doing a good job for him. But Albert loved Colorado, so Karl agreed to let Albert work Colorado and Wyoming as well.

Last, but not least, Karl had hired a former competitor with the Magic Meter Company, Dillon Redding. Karl assigned him to work Oklahoma and New Mexico. Dillon was an ex-Marine and was, as far as Chance was concerned, a wild man! He drank all the time, got into fights and just didn't fit in any way with Karl Jones or the Karl Jones Company. He was as far from Karl's personality and morality as one could get. It wasn't that Chance didn't like him, it was just so unbelievable Karl would have someone this different as part of his organization. Dillon just didn't fit in with the rest of the organization.

The only state not covered was Iowa. This state was "owned"

by a competitor. If Kansas, was owned by Superior, Iowa was owned by the Magic Meter Distributor. Superior had only four installations of their parking meters in Iowa and all of them were along the Mississippi River. The Magic Meter's Distributor was from Minnesota a man named Tommy Thompson. Tommy had Iowa, Minnesota, and the Dakotas for his sales territory for the Magic Meter Company.

Everyone at Superior knew Iowa was the most difficult state in the America for Superior, because everyone in the state of Iowa knew a story about a Superior Distributor and the city of Baxter City. The story went that many, many years ago; Baxter City had a government headed by three commissioners. These three people decided they would improve their life style by getting a commission on every product the city purchased.

They had a great plan; when people went to the purchasing agent to sell any kind of product with a fairly high price tag, the purchasing agent instructed the salesmen to contact a local company that the city did exclusive business with. When the salesman went to see this local company, they were told they needed to pay them a five-percent commission for acting as the local representative.

At the time, Superior had a distributor from Omaha who was told if he wanted to sell parking meters in Baxter City, he needed to hire this local company. The distributor agreed to hire them and he got his parking meter order. He paid the local company their five-percent commission and then promptly turned them in to the Internal Revenue Service. By the time the IRS was finished in Baxter City, the three commissioners were all arrested for income tax evasion. Their pictures, in handcuffs were in every newspaper in Iowa. Since that time, city officials were afraid to do business with Superior, because they thought someone might think they were being paid off.

Karl decided the only chance Superior had to break into Iowa and get any sales was to have Chance move to Iowa and work the state. Karl knew all the stories about Baxter City, but he also knew that when all of this was going on Chance was in the second grade. Karl felt Chance's youth and innocence would serve him well. Karl's plan was to have Chance move to Iowa, but he would let him keep Kansas since he was already established there.

Karl met with Chance and Ann and began telling them about this great opportunity in Iowa. Chance would have believed anything Karl told him and besides he loved changes and challenges. Ann hated any and all changes and she didn't know why people just didn't leave them alone. One thing about Ann, however, was that no matter what Chance wanted to do with his life, she was going to support him no matter how much she disliked doing it. If Ann wanted a quiet simple life, she was married to the wrong man. The other side of the coin was that her husband was working for someone who could change his mind in the middle of a sentence. Chance and Ann agreed to move to Iowa, but then they began a series of moves between Des Moines and Webster. They moved every thirteen months from 1963 to 1967. In 1967, they broke the pattern and moved to Kansas City. They stayed there for thirteen months before moving back to Des Moines. Poor Chase, just about the time he knew something about his school, he was suddenly the new kid who just moved to town.

Chance made a deal with Karl to bring his friend, Doc Schmidt, into the company to help him sell parking meters in Iowa. Doc and

Susan moved their family to Des Moines and for nearly six months Chance and Doc worked Iowa together while Chance still looked after sales in Kansas.

Karl finally had enough of the antics of Dillon Redding and fired him. Apparently, one night Dillon was drunk and called the President of Superior at his home at two o'clock in the morning to tell him what a jerk he was. That was simply the last straw for Karl. Karl was always a gentleman and even if the President of Superior had been a jerk, Karl would never condone that type of behavior. Besides, the President of Superior was a very good man.

Karl flew to Des Moines to talk things over with Chance and Doc. Karl said he thought it would be better if Doc and Susan to move to Oklahoma and took over Dillon's old territory. When Karl wanted someone to do something it was very hard to say no to him. Doc and Susan agreed to move to Oklahoma.

Chance continued working Iowa and Kansas, but was not too happy with the way things were going. A lot of small towns in Iowa and Kansas began removing their parking meters and Chance's potential customer base was being eroded. At the same time, Chance and Karl were not getting along too well. They were like father and son and sometimes that's the way they acted toward each other. In other words, they had their conflicts.

Chance had made a lot of sales in Iowa and was a success. Chance knew it and that made some of the conflicts worse.

One Saturday morning late in December 1968, Chance got a telephone call from one of his biggest customers in Iowa, the University of Iowa. It was the Director of Traffic and Parking and he asked if Chance would consider becoming the Assistant Director of Traffic and Parking for the University. Chance agreed to come to Iowa City and talk about the job offer.

After Chance met with Terry Brown, the Director of Traffic and Parking for the University of Iowa, he agreed to accept the position. On January 2, 1969, Chance began his tour of duty with the University.

Chance and Ann agreed to let Chase finish up his sophomore year before moving him to yet another new school. Chance liked the idea of being home with Chase during his last couple of years of high school instead of traveling all the time as he had done for nearly all the years Chase had been going to school.

Chance rented a room from an old lady in Iowa City to use for the months before Chase was out of school. It was a very depressing time for Chance. Ann had taken a job in a jewelry store in the Merle Hay Mall and between her work and Chase's schooling they couldn't come to Iowa City very often. Chance would go home on weekends unless the basketball team at the University was playing at home, then he would have to look after the parking for the game. The result of all this was Ann and Chance were not seeing enough of each other. Ann was trying to sell their house in Des Moines and Chance was trying to buy one in the Iowa City area.

Spring came. Ann sold the house in Des Moines, Chase finished school, and Chance finally found a new house in a little town fourteen miles east of Iowa City. As part of the down payment, Chance agreed to paint the walls and stain and finish the woodwork. This gave Chance plenty to do when he was not working at the University.

Their new house was off a main street, with two other new homes built by the same contractor. The contractor promised to put in a concrete street for the three new homes in this area. Somehow, he never got time to finish the street, so when the spring rains came water and mud were everywhere. One day the water came down the driveway and into Chance and Ann's new home. They had mud and water everywhere on the lower level of their house. The carpet looked as if they had been making mud pies on it.

The next day Chance went to see a local attorney to see what he would suggest about how they could get the contractor to finish their street. Chance showed the attorney all of the papers relating to the purchase of their home, which clearly stated the contractor would build a street in front of their house.

Chance said, "I'm sure the contractor has good intentions about putting in our street, but somehow he just never gets time to do it."

The attorney, who was at least seventy-five years old leaned back in his chair and said something to Chance he would never forget: "Son, the road to hell is paved with good intentions."

Chance could only laugh. The lawyer wrote a letter to the contractor and sent it registered mail. The next day the contractor started building their street.

17

Running the day-to-day operations of the University of Iowa's parking system was very demanding. One of the biggest problems Chance faced was with the thirty women working in his department. They were always fighting with each other about something. His department operated twenty-four hours a day, seven days a week. The only day his department wasn't in operation was Christmas Day.

Not a month went by that Karl Jones didn't ask Chance to come back with his company. No matter how mad Chance got with Karl, the truth was he loved him like a father. Actually, Karl was old enough to be Chance's grandfather. Karl came to see Chance every few months, so Chance kept in close contact with how things were going with his friends. Chance always told Karl he liked working at the University, but someday he might consider coming back to work with him.

In April 1971, Ann went to Texas to help Joe Carver's wife, Jill to help take care of their children while Jill was having another baby. Joe and Jill already had four children, three girls and a boy. While Ann was staying in Texas helping Jill, Ann kept feeling sick and throwing up. After Jill had another baby girl, Ann told Jill she had to go home to see her doctor because she was so sick. Ann had an awful trip home. Chance drove to the Cedar Rapids airport to pick her up and when he saw her, he couldn't believe how bad she looked. Ann had an appointment with her doctor the next day. When Ann arrived at the doctor's office, the doctor began checking her over and running various blood and urine tests. After about an hour, the doctor came back to talk with her, he said, "Ann, you're pregnant you're going to have a baby!"

Ann said, "Are you sure?"

The doctor said, "Well, I'm as sure as any doctor can ever be about these things."

Ann was shocked. Chase would be a high school senior in the fall and she was going to have a baby. She was thirty-four years old and she had already raised a child. Ann remembered what Dr. Mendel told her when they wanted to have another baby when Chase was in the fourth or fifth grade. Both Ann and Chance went through tests to see if they could have another child. The doctor would only say, maybe. Dr. Mendel did say to them, "About the time Chase is graduating from high school, you'll probably have another baby."

Ann didn't know if he was a prophet or had just said that at the time to make them feel better. What was Chance going to think? She had to tell him as soon as she could get over to the University. Dr. Taylor said to Ann, "I want you to go to a specialist if you intend to carry this baby to term. With your medical history, you'll need the best doctor looking after you and the baby. I will have my nurse make an appointment for you with Dr. Ross Schiller."

Ann left Dr. Taylor's office and drove straight to Chance's office in the parking garage at the University. Ann never went to Chance's office. He was always so busy she never wanted to bother him. This was different; she had to see him right away. She pulled her car into the parking garage and stopped her car in the parking area for the parking department's vehicles. She got out of her car and went into Chance's office. When she got there, he was actually there and talking on the phone. He looked up at Ann and she could see the concern on his face. Ann just didn't come around when he was working. He thought the worst, somehow she must be sick like she was years ago.

Chance told whomever he was talking to that he had an emergency and would call back later. Chance hung up the phone and said to Ann, "What's wrong? What did the doctor say?"

Ann came around the desk and leaned on it and said, "You're not going to believe it!"

Chance could only think something bad was wrong with Ann. Then Ann said, "I'm going to have a baby!" Ann was right, Chance couldn't believe it.

"Are you sure?"

"That's what the doctor told me."

Chance got out of his chair and put his arms around his wife.

"Annie, that's wonderful. I just can't believe it. We wanted another baby so much, but I never thought we would ever have one.

Chance thought back to when Chase was born and how he had prayed Ann would never have to go through that pain again. Maybe God had forgiven him for that prayer and would really let them have this baby.

Ann told him Dr. Taylor made an appointment for her with a specialist, Dr. Ross Schiller. Ann said the doctor wanted her to have the best if she intended to carry this baby to term.

"Chance, what do you think he meant by that? Do you think he thought we would want to abort this baby?"

"I don't know. Maybe he thinks with the health problems you had in the past, carrying this baby might be too much of a risk for you."

"I've got an appointment with Dr. Schiller tomorrow afternoon.

I guess we will know more then."

Ann's appointment was at two o'clock in the afternoon and Chance met her at the doctor's office. They went in and sat down until her name was called. A nurse took Ann back to one of the examining rooms. Some time passed and the nurse came back to the waiting room and asked Chance to come with her. She led him to the examining room where Ann was and told him to sit down and the doctor would be with them in a few minutes.

"It's OK, Chance, Dr. Schiller won't bite you. He's a nice guy." Chance sat down and waited with Ann.

Dr. Schiller came into the room, introduced himself and offered his hand to Chance, he shook hands with the doctor, who said, "It's OK, please sit down."

Chance wondered what was coming next.

Dr. Schiller said, "I have examined Ann and she is definitely going to have a baby. She is about two months along at this time. The question for you two is do you want to carry this baby to term? I understand you have a son who's a junior in high school, and I have read over Ann's medical history."

Chance asked, "Based on her medical history do you think it's a risk for Ann to have the baby?"

Dr. Schiller replied, "Having a baby always holds some risk for the mother and with Ann's history, her risks are going to be higher then normal. Why don't I let you two talk this over and I'll come back and talk with you both a little later?"

Dr. Schiller left Chance and Ann alone in the examining room.

"Ann, I want this baby, but I don't want risk losing you."

Ann paused for a minute and said, "Chance, this baby is a miracle. We have to have it."

Chance went to the examining table where Ann was sitting, put his arms around her and said, "The baby will be fine and so will you. I know it, I just know it!"

Dr. Schiller came back into the examining room and Chance and Ann were sitting on the examining table holding hands.

The doctor asked, "Have you decided what you want to do about the baby or do you need some more time?"

Ann said, "We're having our baby and you need to take really good care of us."

"Great," Dr. Schiller replied, "That's settled. I'm going to do everything possible to look after both of you. One other thing, I don't plan to treat your pregnancy quite the same as we normally do. To start with, I want to see you every other week. I feel I have to keep a much closer watch on your progress then we would routinely do."

As he got ready to leave the room, he said, "I'll see you in two weeks, and you made the decision I would have made after waiting all the years you two have waited for another baby."

They left feeling very good about everything and then wondered how Chase was going to take this news. He had been an only child for all these years.

Chance and Ann were waiting for Chase when he came home from school. They told him he was going to have a new baby sister or brother. Chase's reaction could be summed up in one word, "thrilled." Chase thought he would spend his whole life without any sisters or brothers. He couldn't wait to tell his girlfriend. After dinner, Chase said he was going to tell his girlfriend Marie he was going to be a brother. Chance and Ann were so happy about the new baby and how Chase reacted and they wanted everything to be perfect.

Chase was working with his dad part-time at the University that summer and they had lunch together every day. One day they took a walk along the Iowa River and Chase told his dad, "I'm really in love with Marie and one day I want to marry her."

Chance said, "Marie is a very nice girl, but I hope you are not thinking about getting married until after you finish college."

Chance had spent all of Chase's life pushing him and trying to instill in his mind that he had to get a college education.

"Well, I don't mean right now dad, but she's the girl I want to marry."

Chance could hear himself telling Grandma Cooper the very same words about marrying Ann.

Ann was doing wonderfully carrying the baby. Dr. Schiller was taking every precaution with both Ann and the baby. He told them if Chance wanted to be with her when the baby was born, the hospital insisted they both attend childbirth classes at the hospital.

Chance thought about this and kept remembering how much he hated seeing Ann in pain when Chase was born. He didn't want to go, but he wouldn't tell Ann that. Ann told the doctor that of course they would attend the classes, because she wanted Chance with her when their baby was born.

Chance planned to take off the whole month of December off so he would be available when the baby was born. Ann's birthday was on December 4th and Chance hoped their baby would be born on her birthday. Ann's thirty-five birthday it came and went, but no baby. Early

December 8th, Chance heard Ann taking a shower. She fixed her hair and did her nails and then calmly announced to Chance, "The baby is ready to be born."

Then, just as calmly Ann put on her clothes and checked out the suitcase she had prepared to take to the hospital to be sure she had everything she needed.

Chance flew around getting dressed. He went into Chase's room and told him he was taking mom to the hospital, it was time for the baby to be born.

Chase said, "OK, I'll see you after while."

It was amazing to Chance that Ann and Chase were both so calm. Chance got the car out of the garage, put Ann's suitcase in the car and Ann carefully came out to the car and got in.

Chance drove the fourteen miles into Iowa City as quickly as possible. When they arrived at the hospital, Chance took Ann and her suitcase inside. Ann was already pre-registered so they took her directly to the maternity ward. Chance went outside to park the car and by the time he got back into the hospital and went upstairs to the maternity ward Ann was already in her hospital gown.

It was almost seven-thirty in the morning by now and Dr. Schiller was in the hospital checking on other patients. He was told Ann Clark was now in the maternity ward. Chance was in a labor room with Ann and remembering all the things they learned in the classes about the birthing of their baby. About eight o'clock, Dr. Schiller came into the labor room and checked Ann's progress. He said he was going to call his office and tell them he would not be in until after Ann's baby was born. Chance couldn't believe it. Dr. Schiller's office was only about six blocks from the hospital and he had patients coming in that morning, but that's exactly what Dr. Schiller did, he waited until Ann's baby was born before he went to his office.

Chance and Ann had the maternity ward to themselves. No one else was there except for a couple of nurses and Dr. Schiller.

Chance stayed with Ann encouraging her and holding her hand. He wiped her lips with ice in a washcloth. Dr. Schiller would come in every fifteen minutes or so to check on Ann. Then he would go back into an office next to the labor room.

Chance could see the doctor sitting there with a deck of cards, playing solitaire. He was just passing time until Ann's baby was ready to come into this world. Dr. Schiller was not going to take any chances with Ann or her baby. He had gotten her to the point of carrying this baby full term and nothing was going to go wrong now.

About twelve-thirty, Dr. Schiller told Chance it was time to get his "greens" on, because they were ready to move Ann into the delivery room. One of the nurses took Chance into a room next door and gave him a complete outfit that looked just like what the doctors wore, including little green covers for his shoes. He put on the surgical uniform and went into the delivery room to be with Ann. Dr. Schiller told him to stand next to Ann's head and help her with her breathing. Ann was working hard, the pain was getting worse with each contraction, but having Chance with her and Dr. Schiller talking to her helped. Dr. Schiller kept telling Ann, you're doing great, the baby's just about here.

Chance kept telling her, "You're doing great, you're almost through. We almost have our miracle baby."

Dr. Schiller asked Chance, "Did you want a girl or boy?"

"I guess a girl since we have a great son already."

Just as Ann thought she had pushed about as much as she could, Dr. Schiller said, "Well, I guess you'll have to come back next year for your girl."

Chance saw their baby in Dr. Schiller's hands and then he laid their baby boy on Ann's abdomen.

Dr. Schiller cut the cord and handed the baby to a nurse who weighed him, seven pounds, eight ounces, and twenty-two inches long. The nurse cleaned up the baby and handed him back to Ann.

She said, "What do you think of your new son?"

Chance thought this was the most wonderful day in his life. As the tears ran down his cheeks, he knew he would never forget December 8, 1971. He was so thrilled and thankful everything had gone perfect.

Ann's pain was forgotten as she held their baby. When Ann looked her baby over, she found he also had the white skin on his forehead, just like hers and Chase's. She told Chance, "Our baby is going to be Shane."

Then she gave Shane to his daddy.

Chance held his new son for the first time and thought how different this time was from the time when Chase was born. Chance had been so afraid for Ann then and now everything had changed. Chance couldn't believe the way fathers were now treated. This time he had been a part of bringing this new life into the world and before he had been treated as someone who was only in the way. Chance would never forget this day it was one of the happiest of his life.

The nurses told Ann she would be moved into her room in a few minutes. Ann told Chance, "You need to see if you can get in touch with Chase and let him know I'm OK and he has a new baby brother."

Chance left the room to call Chase, but Chase was waiting outside the delivery room. Chase was as excited about Shane as Chance and Ann were. Soon the nurses took Ann to her room and Chance and Chase went in to see her. Chase gave his mother a hug and a kiss and told her he loved her. Not long after they were in Ann's room, the nurse brought Shane in and she asked Chase if he wanted to hold his new brother. She handed Shane to Chase and they instantly bonded.

Chance went to the hospital gift shop and found the cutest little red dog with a green Christmas stocking in his mouth. He brought it back up to Shane. It was Shane's first present and every Christmas from then on, Shane's doggie could be found sitting under the Clark's Christmas tree.

The changes in hospital policies between the time Chase was born and Shane was born was simply unbelievable. Ann and Chance could have Shane in Ann's room anytime they wanted him. They would have brought Shane a bed in her room, if she wanted him with her all the time. Ann decided she was really tired after dinner, so Shane went back to the nursery and Chance and Chase went home.

Two days later, Dr. Schiller told Ann she and Shane could go home whenever she was ready. Chance arrived at the hospital around ten-thirty that morning and Ann and Shane were dressed, packed and ready to go home.

Chance and Ann only thought they had undergone changes in their lives with a new baby. The following Friday night, Chase and Marie told them they would finish high school at the end of the first semester and they decided they wanted to get married right after Christmas. Ann couldn't believe their timing. She had been home for less then a week and now Chase wanted to get married the same month she had a new baby.

Chance told Ann last summer about his conversation with Chase about him wanting to marry Marie. Chase and Marie original plan to get married sometime after school was out, next spring or summer. Chase told his mother they couldn't wait any longer that was too many months to wait. Chance knew too well how that felt.

Ann asked Marie, "Have you talked with your mother and dad about getting married?"

Marie said she hadn't talked with her folks yet, but she and Chase were going to her folks to talk with them next.

The following Monday, Ann called Marie's mother and asked if she and her husband would come over to discuss their children's desire to get married. Marie's mother said they would come over at seven that evening.

Marie's parents, Mr. and Mrs. Burton, arrived with Marie promptly at seven o'clock. Marie's folks were a lot older then Chance and Ann. In fact, they were as old as Chance's parents. They had five daughters and three of them were already married, so having a daughter wanting to get married was not something new to them. The only difference was that their three older daughters finished college before getting married. Chance couldn't believe how cool and calm the Burtons were. It was as though they went through this every day.

Mrs. Burton said, "I don't know if you know this, but I'm Catholic and so is Marie. I understand Chase has been raised in the Methodist Church. Chase would have to take instructions in the Catholic Church before he and Marie could get married."

Mrs. Burton said to Chase, "If you want to marry my daughter will you agree to do this?"

Without any hesitation, Chase replied, "I love Marie and if that's what you want me to do I will."

Mrs. Burton said, "I understand you want to get married this month. I'll call the priest and make arrangements for him to give you instructions right away. I'll take care of getting the church for the wedding. We have a lot to do in a short period of time, but we'll get it done."

Mr. Burton had sat quietly through all of this and finally he said to Chase, "Everything will be all right. I've been married to this Catholic woman for a long time and I'm still a Methodist myself." Chance and Ann had to smile to themselves at Mr. Burton's statement. Mr. Burton continued, "Marie, I don't know what your plans are about continuing your education, but I will help pay for you to get your college degree, even if you are getting married."

Marie answered, "Thanks, dad. Chase and I appreciate that."

Ann had fixed coffee and cookies, so the evening ended with all of them sitting around the Clark's kitchen table. Chance and Ann liked the Burtons and they knew they would love Marie.

Chance, Ann, Chase, Shane, and Marie drove to Webster two days before Christmas to show Chance's parent and Ann's mother Shane and to introduce them to their soon-to-be new daughter- in-law. They were going to spend Christmas Day with Chance's parents and Ann's mother.

On the way back to Iowa City, they stopped in Kansas City to see Karl Jones and his wife Kathy. They wanted them to meet Marie and they wanted to show off their new baby. Kathy Jones instantly fell in love with Shane. She thought he was the most beautiful baby she had ever seen. Before leaving Kansas City, Karl talked Chance into coming back to work for him, as his sales and service manager working and living in Kansas City. Chance agreed to start on February 1, 1972.

Ann asked Chance if it would be all right if she loaned Chase the Keepsake engagement and wedding rings her father had given to them. Ann said, "Maybe it would bring Chase and Marie the luck and happiness they brought us."

Chance said, "I think that's a great idea. Chase will appreciate that."

Several years before, Chance designed a special wedding band for Ann. It was a wide, white gold band with a diamond star on each side of her initials, set in diamonds. Ann liked her ring so well she put her Keepsake set back in the little blue cloth- covered ring box her father had given her. Ann loved her ring because it was totally unique, unlike any ring anyone else had in the world. Two years later, Ann had a ring made for Chance to match hers with his initials in diamonds on it.

Later that evening, Chase and Marie came back to the house from Chase's instructions at the Catholic Church. Chase hated taking these instructions, but Chance told him since he agreed to take them and if he wanted to marry Marie he needed to finish them.

Ann asked Chase, "Would you and Marie like to borrow my wedding ring set?"

She handed the box to Chase and when he opened it, he replied, "Mom, we sure would."

Ann told them, "I hope these rings bring you a lot of luck and as much happiness as they brought to dad and me."

Marie said, "Thanks I love them and I promise to take good care of them."

Chase said, "Mom, some day we'll return them to you."

Later that night after Chase took Marie home he came into his parent's bedroom and told his mother, "Mom, thanks. Marie loved the rings and we really appreciate you letting us use them."

Chase and Marie were married on December 29, 1971. In the space of three weeks, Chance and Ann gained a new son and a new daughter. Their new daughter was a little older then they planned, but she was the sweetest thing and she fit perfectly into their family.

The two things Chance would always remember about Chase and Marie's wedding was Marie made her own wedding gown and Chance kidded her about sewing the hem up on the way down the aisle. She made a beautiful dress and she looked beautiful in it. The other thing that made an impression on Chance was the crisp, clear reciting of the wedding vows by Chase and Marie. Chance never heard anyone do them better in his life.

After the wedding, Chance and Ann made arrangements for the newlyweds to spend their wedding night and a few days at Johnny and Kay's in Des Moines. Johnny and Kay's were one of the nicest motels complexes in Iowa and their restaurant was a good as anywhere in the United States.

18

Chance, Ann and Shane left Iowa City in February 1972 to move to Kansas City and Chase and Marie moved to Webster so they could establish Kansas residency to enroll as instate students at Webster Community College in the fall. Chance found a small house in Webster and made the down payment so Chase and Marie would have a place to live that would not cost them too much every month. It would also give them a way to build up some equity so they could buy a house in the future. Chance told them when they were ready to move they could have half of the money the house sold for.

It was hard for Chance to believe, but Chase got a job working at Robinson's Printing & Stationery store in Webster. This sounded like the second verse of an old song to Chance. After Chase worked at Robinson's for about six months, he got the opportunity to join the Webster Parking Department as a serviceman on the parking meters. Chase had worked on meters with his dad from the time he was five year sold. Chance started teaching Chase about parking meters by having him take the mechanisms apart. In addition, Chase worked on the meters at the University of Iowa for the last two summers, so he was well qualified for the job.

Chance saw Chase following in every step he made, but at least Chase was seventeen years old and he and Marie had finished high school. Chance and Mr. Burton were pushing them to go on to college and they promised to help them all they could.

Chase and Marie had been in Webster for only a short while when they found out Marie was going to have a baby. The doctor said she would be due in September. They were both very happy with the news and felt they knew all about having a baby after being around Chase's baby brother.

The months passed quickly that spring and summer but before Marie got to September her baby decided August 24, 1972 was long enough to wait to come into this world. Chance had hoped his grandbaby would be born on his birthday, September 20. When Chase and Marie's baby was born Chance was working with one of their customer cities in Iowa. Chance checked into a motel in Clinton, Iowa and was surprised while he was checking in the desk clerk said, "Mr. Clark, I have a call for you. You can take it right here if you like."

The desk clerk handed the phone to Chance and as he said hello, he was really surprised when Ann answered, although he shouldn't have been surprised because he knew Karl Jones could find him no matter where he was.

Ann said, "Chance, Marie had her baby, we've go a boy."

Chance asked, "Are they OK?"

"Yes, they're both fine. They named the baby Curt. Curt Clark." Chance thought the name sounded fine, maybe like a baseball player; maybe someday he would play for the Kansas City Royals. Chance said to Ann, "Well, he didn't make it to my birthday Grandma!"

"No, he sure didn't ... Grandpa!"

They were thirty-five years old with a new baby of their own and now they were grandparents. Life was moving along too fast, way too fast.

If Chance thought life was moving along too fast that August, he sure wasn't ready for the next few months. In late November, Karl asked his salesmen to come to Kansas City for a meeting. Chance assumed Karl wanted to get everyone together to discuss their business in general and to give everyone a pep talk. They were having a great year. In fact, they were number one in sales for Superior that year. In the past they had always been second or third, but moving into the top spot was hard to believe since they didn't have a major customer like a New York, Chicago or Los Angeles in their territory.

After everyone was assembled in his office, Karl calmly announced he was disbanding the company as of December 31.

Karl said, "I've talked with Superior and they have agreed to make each of you their distributor for the territory you are now working in."

He said Superior would not agree to let them form a new company and keep the territory together, because Superior didn't want any more big distributors. Chance could figure out pretty easy why Superior didn't want any more big distributors since they had too much power by controlling their sales.

Chance was lost. He didn't have a territory he felt could make a living for him he had been going to Iowa to look after a few customers. Chance's closest friend, Doc Schmidt, now covered Oklahoma, Kansas and New Mexico, so there was no way he would try to get Kansas. Chance didn't know what he would do.

It took some time before Chance found out why Karl at eighty years old suddenly decided to quit the business he loved.

Kathy told him Karl developed hardening of the arteries and it had begun to affect his reasoning. He didn't want to embarrass himself or his company and decided to quit before he got worse.

Chance and Ann didn't know what they were going to do. Chance had been back with Karl for less then a year and left a good job at the University of Iowa he could have had until he retired. Chance thought about talking to Superior about going to work directly for them.

Before Chance did anything about finding a job, the telephone in the office rang and Chance answered it, "Karl Jones Company."

A voice said, "I would like to speak with Chance Clark."

"This is Chance Clark."

The person on the other end of the phone line said, "This is Charles Stacy with Donald Engineering in Chicago. Chance, I have been talking with several people in the parking industry because we need to hire the best parking operations person in the country for a job we have available. Everyone I talked with said they could give me a short list and the only name on the list was Chance Clark."

"Well, that's awfully nice to hear, but I doubt I'm the only parking operations person in America."

Charles Stacy asked, "Would you consider flying to Chicago at our expense and talking with us about the job?"

"I would certainly consider talking with you about a job."

"Do you think you could come to Chicago in the next few days?" "I guess I could," Chance said, "How long do you think we would need for this conversation?"

"I think you could come up in the morning and return to Kansas City in the afternoon."

"I'll check on flights and get back with you. What is your telephone number?"

Mr. Stacy gave Chance his direct number. Chance called him back and said he would come to see him on Friday, if that was a OK. It was.

Chance called Ann and said, "You're never going to believe the telephone call I just got."

"Chance, I don't believe half of the things that happen to us."

"Well, this is going to be another one you are not going to believe." then Chance told her about his conversation with Charles Stacy.

On Friday, Chance flew to Chicago and took a taxi to downtown Chicago where Donald Engineering Company's offices was located on the sixteenth and seventeenth floors of a nondescript building on Wacker Drive, it was directly across the Chicago River from the Merchandise Mart. Chance met Charles Stacy and found he liked him a lot.

Charles Stacy was a typical engineer. He was careful with his conversation. He took his time answering questions, to be sure he thought out his answers. Sometimes, he would hold his pipe in his hand and just stare at Chance before he spoke. Chance learned Charles Stacy was a very smart man and felt some of his pauses were part of a facade.

By the time they went to lunch together, Chance was sure he wanted the job. Mr. Stacy told him his main job would be as parking consultant to the City of Chicago's Parking Program. Chicago had the second largest parking operation in the world, only New York City's was bigger.

Chicago had issued fifty million dollars in revenue bonds to build parking garages in the city and part of the requirement to get the money was that the city had to have an independent parking consulting company oversee the parking operation to be sure it was run properly. In truth, Donald Engineering was the watchdog for the bondholders to be sure they got back their fifty million dollars, plus interest.

Mr. Stacy offered Chance the job at a substantial increase over his current salary with the Karl Jones Company, plus they would pay the Clarks' moving expenses to come to Chicago and also offered fringe benefits equal to or better then he had with the university. Chance agreed to start in a month.

Chance found a home in Olympia Fields, Illinois with a beautifully landscaped yard. Chance was fascinated by a tree in their backyard that the former owner of the home had grafted several types of trees to make a perfectly shaped tree. The previous owner used two different types of apples--one red and one green, a cherry, and a pear. Chance didn't know how you could do this, but the Clarks now owned the tree. Chance could hardly wait for spring to see the blossoms such a tree would produce. The house was about twenty-five years old. It had three bedrooms, two baths, and a very large living room with a fireplace. The house was in excellent condition so they wouldn't need to do anything to it before they moved it.

Chance began working with Donald Engineering on January 2, 1973. He had never worked in an office with so many people before. In the Chicago office alone, they had almost three hundred people. Donald Engineering had their own company travel agent, which worked directly in their office. In addition, they had a large computer department, with the largest mainframe IBM computers available. They also had their own printing company, art department and report editing department. Chance learned Donald Engineering had a complete organization of transportation engineers and could produce reports for their clients anywhere in the world. The more Chance found out about the company he was now working for the more impressed he became.

Donald Engineering had over twelve hundred engineers working for them in offices around the world, plus their support staff. They had offices throughout the United States, as well as offices in Europe, Asia, Australia, and Africa.

Chance found his job to be interesting and boring at the same time. Reading ten to fifteen reports on the Chicago parking operation was pretty dull after running his own parking systems in Webster and the University of Iowa. Chance liked Charles Stacy and the twenty-some people in his department. Most of the other employees in the department were younger then Chance and Ann and all were graduated engineers, except for the two secretaries and Chance.

Almost all of these young men were working on projects involving some type of mass transit. They were doing a lot of studies for minibus service and vanpools. Chance was told the federal government was paying for ninety percent of all of these studies in an effort to reduce travel by private automobiles.

Chance was intrigued by the vanpools. Apparently, the 3M Company started this program. The company purchased company vans and assigned the van to a driver and an assistant driver. Using the 3M Company's computer, they matched people living near the driver. The driver would pick up these fellow employees each day and drive them to work and take them back home at the end of their workday. The program was said to be working very well and Chance only wondered how long it would last.

He knew how much a person's car meant to them. Taking away an American's car was like taking away their freedom. Chance felt in the long term, such a program would be doomed to failure.

Donald Engineering was also involved in designing and supervising various subway construction projects, including extending the subway out to O'Hare Airport from downtown Chicago; the Second Street subway extension in New York City; the subway system in Atlanta; the Metro system in Washington, DC, and the subway in Athens, Greece.

Donald Engineering was, without a doubt one of the premier transportation engineering companies in the world.

Chance liked the idea of being with a company that did projects all over the world. One project he found very interesting was the construction of the first bridge in Istanbul, Turkey, over the Bosporus Straits. This bridge would link Europe and Asia together for the first time in history. This had to be one of the longest- delayed projects in the history of the world.

Chance discovered the first design and proposal to build a bridge over the Bosporus Straits was done by Leonardo da Vinci. Chance knew governments moved slowly but centuries of delay was really slow. The bridge now under construction was located only a few feet from the site da Vinci had chosen to build his bridge. It was good to be able to use other people's efforts when you work on a project Chance thought with amusement. He was sure Leonardo would not mind as long as the project was finally completed. Completed it was, under Chance's company's direction, after Leonardo da Vinci had been dead for more then four hundred and sixty years.

Chance and Ann settled into the routine of living the normal life of people with eight-to-five jobs. Every morning Ann took him to catch the Illinois Central at 6:38, and she picked him up every evening at 6:45. They had a good income; a decent older home, a new car, and each other. In addition, they had a wonderful bonus of a fifteen-month-old son and a grandson.

Chase and Marie were going to college in Webster and Chase had a full-time job working for the Webster Parking Meter Department.

Chance and Ann's love continued to grow. Sometimes Chance would bring her flowers he picked up at the train station. They were still like kids in love, touching each other as they passed in the hallway, holding hands at dinner and watching TV. Their lovemaking continued to improve. Still, with all of this Chance was restless.

Ann was capable of adapting to every move. She made a home for them wherever Chance took her. However, if it had been up to Ann, Chance would still be working for the City of Webster.

She hated change and Chance had to have change to grow and to survive.

One change was coming in Chance's life he didn't expect. Chance's mother called him at work and told him she was in Miami, Oklahoma and that Grandma Cooper died this morning. Chance was heartbroken. Before Ann, his grandma had always been his biggest supporter and was the one person other then Ann, who always made him, feel special.

Ann's role in Chance's life had just taken on even more responsibility. She was now the only person, who always built him up, cared for him and with whom Chance was totally relaxed. Ann was his girl, his wife, his nurse and his lover. Now she had to be the one person who overlooked his shortcomings and build him up when he was down. She had to start right now, after hearing his grandmother died.

Chance called Ann at home to break the news to her and to ask her to pick him up at the train, because he was on his way home to pack so they could go to Miami for his grandmother's funeral. Ann could sense Chance's loss as soon as she saw him walking from the train. He walked differently; he lost the swagger she first noticed in the ninth grade. Chance's swagger was almost like a John Wayne walk he had a self-confidence about him that showed in his walk. His swagger was gone.

When Chance got in the car, Shane hugged him, as he always did when his daddy came home from work. Chance kissed Ann and she could see he had been crying. Chance started crying again as soon as their lips parted. Shane put his arm around his daddy as if to say don't cry daddy, it will be OK. It reminded Chance of when Chase put his arms around the little girl on his first day of kindergarten and told her, "it will be all right; your mommy will come back and get you after while."

Chance was being comforted by a loving, caring fifteenmonth-old baby.

During the funeral, Chance kept thinking of how proud his grandmother would be to see all of her children here, as well as her grandkids and most of her great-grandkids. Chase and Marie hadn't been able to come, since they were in the middle of a test period in community college. Their son Curt was the first and only great-great grandchild for Grandma Cooper.

Chance watched his cousins walk down the aisle of the First Baptist Church to have their final look at their grandmother. Chance was six-foot-two and almost every one of his cousins was taller. Even two of his girl cousins were taller then Chance. But one thing was sure; Chance would always be the first and oldest of his Grandma Cooper's grandchildren, even if he wasn't the tallest.

It took a lot of Ann's tender loving care to get Chance back to his normal optimistic self. As the days turned into weeks and the weeks into months, Chance was back to his old self. Whoever said "time heals," knew what they were talking about.

One day Tom Reed, Donald Engineering's Vice President of International Projects called Chance into his office and asked Chance to read a proposal Donald had submitted to a prospective client. Chance quickly looked over the proposal and said it looked pretty straightforward to him. At this point, Mr. Reed asked Chance if he would agree to be the project manager for the job and Chance said he would be glad to help in anyway he could.

Mr. Reed said, "Great, you need to be in Perth, Western Australia in ten days. This job should take sixty to ninety days to complete."

Mr. Reed told Chance the company would pay for his wife and son to accompany him on the assignment.

Chance called Ann and said, "Guess what? We're going to Australia and we have to be there in ten days."

Ann said, "You're kidding!"

"No, I'm not. It's true. You know Australia is the one place in the world I always wanted to go and we're going."

Ann was almost in a panic. They were going to an assignment overseas--to Australia, halfway around the world--and they had only ten days to get there. Ann thought with Chance why should I ever be surprised at what we're going to be doing next?

Mr. Reed told Chance to get in touch with the company travel agent and see what they needed to get into the country and have her make airline reservations and get their tickets issued. Chance's next stop was to visit the company travel agent. She told Chance she would take care of the airline tickets and reservations, but Chance would need to get a U.S. passport for himself, his wife and son, as well as visas to visit Australia. Chance was told they would need four passport pictures and each of their birth certificates for them to process their passports.

That evening Chance and Ann searched until they finally found all of their birth certificates. Ann and Shane would take the train into the city the next day and get their passport pictures taken at a place next to the passport office and they would process the pictures in fifteen minutes. It was a good thing they lived in Chicago, since they could get their passports in fortyeight hours and there was also an Australian Consul office there that could issue their visas. The next morning Ann and Shane arrived at the Illinois Central Station at 11:08, right on time. Chance met them and they took a taxi to the photographer's shop. They got all of their pictures done in less then an hour and then went to the passport office. There were several people in the passport office waiting for their passports. Chance took a number to obtain service and the three of them sat down to wait. The people were being served much faster then Chance thought they would be and before another hour past their number was displayed for their turn.

Chance confidently went to the counter with Ann carrying Shane right behind him. Chance laid down the completed passport applications, their photos and their birth certificates on the counter. The clerk looked over their applications, they were fine, she looked at their passport photos they were fine. Next, she looked over their birth certificates and Chance could sense a problem. The clerk said Chance Clark's birth certificate was OK, because it was a certified copy issued by the state of Oklahoma. Shane Clark's was not acceptable, because it was issued by the Iowa City hospital and Ann's was not acceptable because it was issued by the Bureau of Census of the United States of America.

She explained, "To get a passport, you must have a certified birth certificate issued by the state in which you were born."

Chance asked the clerk, "You mean you won't accept a birth certificate issued by the U.S. Government?"

"I don't make the rules, I just follow them."

She told Chance, "Your passport will be ready to pick up anytime after two o'clock tomorrow afternoon. You will have to contact the states where your wife and son were born and have certified birth certificates sent to you."

Ann and Shane took the train back home and Chance went back to work. Before the afternoon was over, Chance had talked to the Bureau of Vital Statistics in Des Moines and Jefferson City and both agreed to Federal Express him certified copies of Ann and Shane's birth certificates. Chance couldn't believe they would agree to send them by Federal Express and he could simply mail them a check to cover the cost of the certificates and the Federal Express charges after he received the birth certificates.

The following day Chance received birth certificates from Missouri and Iowa for Ann and Shane. This seemed to be unbelievable service provided by two different state's agencies. He took all of the papers to the passport office with the newly acquired birth certificates. The same clerk who had helped him the day before also expressed disbelief Chance got two states to Federal Express birth certificates on the same day Chance called them and without payment in advance. The clerk told Chance he could pick up Ann and Shane's passports the next day.

The following day Chance arranged to pick up the passports and to meet Ann and Shane at the train station. Chance met them and from the train station they took a taxi to the Australian Consulate office. They walked into the office and there didn't appear to be anyone around. They sat down on a big brown leather couch to wait and see if someone would return to the reception area. After ten or fifteen minutes Chance got up from the couch and opened a door leading to the inner offices of the consulate.

Chance said, "Hello is anyone here?"

He got no reply, so he kept walking down a corridor and he could see there were offices behind doors on each side of the corridor. Finally, he head people talking and laughing behind one of the doors. Chance knocked on the door, opened it, and said, "Hello?"

Three women were sitting around a desk and obviously had been talking about something other then Australian Consulate business. A woman behind the desk asked curtly, "May I help you?" Chance replied, "I hope so. I need visas for myself, my wife, and my son to visit Australia."

One of the other women said, "I can help you with visas. I need your passports, the completed visa applications forms and to see your round-trip airline tickets."

Chance had no idea they would want to see the airline tickets and he said, "I don't have our airline tickets with me. I didn't know you would need to see them."

The woman said, "I'm sorry, but we can't process your visas without them. You know, you might go to Australia and like it so much you wouldn't come back!"

Chance asked, "Can you please look over what we have so far to see if we need to do anything else. I want to be sure we have everything done right so we can get our visas?"

The woman got up from her chair and said, "Follow me back to my desk."

Chance followed the woman back to her desk in the reception area where Ann and Shane were waiting. The woman sat down at her desk and said, "Let's see your papers."

Chance handed her the documents; he had the applications for their Australia visas, passports and two photos of each of them. The woman checked everything over and proclaimed, "Everything is all right here; you just need your airline tickets and then I can start processing your visas."

Chance asked, "Is it possible to start processing our visas now, since we want to go as soon as possible?"

Mr. Reed told Chance they would have to go on tourist visas because it would take too long to get any other type of visa. He cautioned Chance not to say he was going to work in Australia when applying for a visa, because they would make them wait for a different type of visa and Chance wouldn't get to Australia in time to start the project.

Just as the woman started to reply, Ann and Shane walked up to Chance. Chance reached over and took Shane from Ann. The woman said, "Is this your little boy? He so cute!"

Shane ducked his head down on his dad's shoulder.

Chance said, "Yes, he is."

The woman seemed to soften a little and she said, "OK, I'll tell you what. I'll get the processing of the visas started and you bring me the airline tickets as soon as you can."

Chance said, "That's great. I'll get them and bring them back this afternoon. How long does it take to process the visas?"

"About four or five days," the woman replied.

"Is there any way to speed things up?"

"You get me your airline tickets and I'll see what I can do."

With that, Chance felt he better not push his luck. Chance, Ann and Shane left the office and Chance promised to be back soon. They took a taxi to the Illinois Central station, where Ann and Shane got out of the taxi to take the train back to Olympia Fields. Chance then had the taxi take him to the offices of Donald Engineering.

Chance went directly to the company travel agent to check on the tickets they needed to get their Australian visas. The travel agent told Chance she had confirmed all the reservations for him and his family for the trip to Australia. She said, "There is just one thing I'm not sure about; it's your British Overseas Air Corporation flight from Honolulu to Fiji and then on to Sydney."

Chance asked, "What are you concerned about?"

"Well, they list the plane as a VC-10. I don't know what kind of a plane that is maybe it's a British model of a DC-10. Here's your schedule. You leave from Wichita, Kansas on a TWA flight to Los Angeles, then on a flight from Los Angeles to Honolulu. You are going to stay two days and one night in Honolulu and then you leave at 11:30 at night and make a refueling stop in Fiji. After a two-hour stay there, you fly on to Sydney. You will arrive in Sydney at 6:15 a.m., two days later."

Chance said, "That sounds OK, but right now I need the tickets so I can get our Australian Visas."

The travel agent said, "It's going to take me twenty or thirty minutes to write the tickets, maybe an hour if I make any kind of mistake on them."

Chance said, "OK, I'll go to my office and let you get started. I only have a week left to get to Perth."

"I'll call you when they're ready."

Chance left to go downstairs to his office.

Before Chance could get to his office, Tom Reed asked, "How's it going, Chance? Is their anything I can do to help you?"

"I don't think so, unless you can issue Australian Visas."

"Well, I can't do that, how about anything else?"

"It would help if I could get an advance on my expenses to help cover some of my travel costs."

"I thought I arranged that for you already."

"I don't think so Mr. Reed."

Then Mr. Reed said, "I'll go up to the seventeenth floor and have them cut you a check for twenty-five hundred dollars, do you think that will be enough?

"That should be enough to take care of the cost of the trip." Mr. Reed went to take care of the check right away.

Chance continued on to his office and began going through the daily reports from the Chicago Parking System. Charles Stacy, Chance's boss, had assigned Lee Walter to help Chance with the Chicago Parking System while Chance was on assignment in Perth. Chance asked Lee Walter to come into his office so he could show Lee what to look for on the Chicago reports. Chance just finished going over the reports with Lee when his telephone rang.

Chance picked up the phone, "Chance Clark."

The voice on the other end of the line told him his Australian tickets were ready and Chance replied, "Thanks, I'm on my way up to get them."

Chance told Lee he had to go pick up his airline tickets.

Chance picked up the airline tickets, hurried out of the building, hailed a taxi and took the tickets to the Australian Consulate as quickly as possible.

The woman who had been helping Chance was sitting at her desk in the reception area when Chance came in. She looked up at Chance and said, "Well, Mr. Clark, you must have your airline tickets."

Chance smiled and said, "You're right."

The clerk told him, "I'm going to do everything possible to have your visas ready tomorrow."

Chance said, "Thank you we really appreciate your help."

The clerk from the consulate called the next day and said the visas were ready. The Clarks now had six days left to get to Perth, Australia.

Chance picked up their passports, visas and airline tickets from the Chicago office of the Australian Consulate. Chance thanked the clerk profusely for her help him in getting the visas and then he headed back to the office, picked up his expense advance check for twenty-five hundred dollars, and told everyone good-bye and left the office bound for Australia.

Ann had their suitcases packed and she had packed one big box with towels, sheets, dishes and a few toys for Shane to be airshipped to Perth. Chance had called the real estate lady who had sold them their house in Olympia Fields and listed the house. He made arrangements with a local moving and storage company to pack up and move their household goods to storage, if the house sold while they were gone. Chance and Ann decided to buy a newer home when they returned from Australia.

Chance packed up the car to drive to Webster. They were leaving their car for Chase and Marie to use while they were gone. Chance made arrangements with his company to send his paychecks to Chase and Chase would pay their bills for them while they were out of the country. Chance, Ann and Shane left their home in Olympia Fields around eight o'clock that evening headed for Webster. They were all dead tired, but Chance said they would need to drive as close to St. Louis as possible in order for them to make the drive to Webster the next day. Chance knew they could drive all the way to Webster in one day, but they needed to have some time to say good-bye to Chase, Marie and Curt, as well as Chance's folks and Ann's mother. Chance's mother was not happy about them going to Australia and taking her grandson, Shane. Chance drove as far as Effingham, Illinois and both Ann and Shane were already asleep in the car. Chance was just too tired to go any further. He pulled the car into the Ramada Inn and checked in. He carried Shane to their room and since Ann had put on Shane's pajamas in the car, Chance put him right into bed. Ann managed to take care of her nightly routine of washing off her make-up, brushing her teeth, combing her hair and putting on her gown, but she almost fell back asleep before her head hit the pillow. Chance's head was spinning, trying to realize all they had gone through in the last four days. He needed sleep worse then he thought, because the next thing he knew the alarm clock in his head was telling him it was 6:30 a.m. and time to get up. This morning Chance couldn't decide whether having a built-in alarm clock was a blessing or a curse. Whichever it was Chance got up and went to the bathroom to take his shower, shaved and get dressed. He woke Ann up at six forty-five and before seven-thirty, they were rolling down Interstate 55 heading to St. Louis.

When they got to Kansas City, Chance said to Ann, "We'll have to stop and tell Karl and Kathy good-bye, Kathy will have to see Shane before we leave the country."

Chance continued, "One thing it's going to have to be a short stay there."

It was a short stay. Chance told Karl all about the kind of project he would be doing in Perth. Ann and Kathy talked and played with Shane and when they got ready to leave, Kathy could hardly let Shane go.

She told Ann, "You take good care of my little chicken while you're gone."

Ann promised she would.

<h1 style="text-align:center">19</h1>

Chance, Ann and Shane arrived in Webster from Kansas City in early evening. They went directly to Chase's house to see Marie and Curt. They knew when they arrived; Chase would be in class at the community college. Shane was happy to able to get out of the car and play after having spent another four hours in the car driving from Kansas City. Curt already had his supper and bath and was already in bed.

Marie opened his bedroom door and they went into his room. Even though Shane shook the side rails of his crib, Curt didn't even stir.

Chance and Ann were amazed at how much Curt had grown since they saw him last. Marie told them she took Curt to the doctor for a check-up and the doctor said he was doing great. She said she and Chase were both fine and were doing well in school. This didn't surprise Chance, since both of them were honor students in high school.

Shane played on the floor with some of Curt's toys while Chance brought in all the information so Chase could pay their bills while they were in Australia.

Then Chance said, "We had better go to Grandma Harris's house and later we'll be at Grandma and Grandpa Clark's house."

Chance picked Shane up and they gave Marie hugs and kisses good-bye since she would be in school when they left the next day.

After spending some time with Ann's mother, they told her good-bye and said they would see her in two or three months. Mrs. Harris had to go to work early the next morning so they wouldn't see her tomorrow either. She put a bag of cookies in Shane's hand as he was going out the door.

Then they drove to Chance's folks to spend the night. When they arrived, Mrs. Clark opened the door and came out to the car to get Shane. She carried him into the house where his grandpa was waiting for him. Chance and Ann unloaded the things from the car they would need to spend the night. By the time they got in the house, Shane was playing with building blocks on the floor with his grandma and grandpa. He had a half-of-a-sandwich in one hand and a block in the other. He looked like he was having a great time.

Chance's mother had food and cokes waiting for them after they finished their sandwiches she had a birthday cake for Chance. In all of the excitement and work of getting ready for their trip to Australia, they forgot tomorrow Chance's birthday. In addition to his cake and ice cream his folks gave him his birthday presents, two new pairs of slacks and matching shirts. Before long, Ann said, "I think it's time for Shane's bath."

Shane loved his bath. In a flash, he began taking off his clothes and headed for the bathroom, with Ann in hot pursuit. Ann started his bath water and poured in some bubble bath. She tested the water to make sure the temperature was just right, and then she picked Shane up and put him in the tub. He began moving the bubbles around the tub and splashing the water to break the bubbles.

Just then Chase came into Grandma Clark's house. Chance gave him a hug and a kiss and told him they had been to his house earlier and saw Marie and Curt.

Chase asked, "Where's mom and Shane?"

Chance told him, "Mom's giving Shane's a bath and getting him ready for bed."

Chase went into the bathroom and saw his mother leaning over the tub washing Shane with a washcloth. When Chase came in, Ann got up to give him a hug and a kiss. When Shane saw Chase he got up from the tub and after Chase kissed his mom, he leaned over the tub and Shane put his arms around Chase's neck and held on as Chase picked him up from the tub, dripping water and bubbles all over him.

After drying Shane off, Ann put his pajamas on and Shane ran into the living room. Shane's pajamas were a blue, lightweight summer material. When he got into the living room he took his left arm out of the sleeve of his pajamas and with his right arm, he held the sleeve up to his nose, pretending he was an elephant and the sleeve was his trunk. Shane's grandmother and grandfather and Chase were laughing at him so hard, they almost fell off the couch. Finally, Chance grabbed up his little elephant and told him it was time for all good little elephants to go to bed. Chance took Shane and his "Teddy" into the bedroom. Teddy played his tune three times as dad patted Shane and the little elephant was soon asleep.

Chance and Ann said their good-byes to Chase and then Chance walked him to his car. Chance told Chase he left all the information about paying their bills with Marie and that he could pick up their car the next day and use it while they were in Australia. After one more hug good-bye Chase got into his car and headed home.

Chance and Ann had never been as far away from Chase as they would be in Australia. They had never gone more then a month without seeing Chase. Chance suddenly felt sad about going to Australia without Chase, Marie and Curt going with them. No matter how excited Chance was about traveling to the one place in the world he always wanted to go he would be leaving behind one of his best friends. Chase was not only his son, but one of his closest friends.

It seemed Chance and Ann had just gotten into bed when Chance's mom opened their bedroom door and softly said, "Chance."

The sound of his mother's voice was all it took to wake Chance.

"Mom is it time to get up?"

"I'm afraid it is."

"Thanks mom."

It didn't take long for Chance, Ann and Shane to get up dress and be ready to go.

Chance's mom had breakfast ready for them by the time they got to the kitchen. Chance's mom said, "Happy Birthday son."

It was September 20, 1974. Chance was thirty-eight years old and was starting on a new world adventure.

Chance's mom drove them to Wichita for their flight to Los Angeles. They would then go to Honolulu. Chance thought it would be great traveling to Hawaii on his birthday. He thought with the time changes it will make my birthday last longer than any birthday I've ever had before.

When they arrived in Honolulu the weather was beautiful. Tour groups were having leis put around their necks. Chance and Ann felt a little left out because they weren't getting lei's. When they got to their hotel room they discovered why this was called the tropics. Their room had a musty smell and the humidity was awful. Their air conditioner couldn't even begin to keep up with the humidity. Their hotel room did however, look directly out on Waikiki Beach and they could see Diamond Head in the background. Hawaii was great. They had the rest of that day to look around and the next day to explore Hawaii.

Their flight to Australia was to leave at midnight the next evening. They took a walk on the beach and played in the ocean. By the time they got back to their room, it was time to shower and dress for dinner. After dinner they went straight to bed. Shane almost didn't get his pajamas on before he was asleep and Chance and Ann were close behind him.

The next morning they strolled downtown looking in the shops and trying to think what they might need that they had forgotten to pack. Finally they decided they couldn't carry anything else with them on the trip anyway. After lunch they went back to their hotel room and they all fell asleep watching TV.

Chance thought they should have dinner in the hotel before going back to the airport. After dinner they packed their bags and proceeded to the airport. By ten o'clock they had their seat assignments their bags were checked in and they were ready to go. About eleven o'clock Shane got sick and threw up all over his shirt and his dad's shirt. Chance took Shane into the bathroom and washed him and washed off their shirts.

When they came out of the bathroom Ann said, "We need to get Shane another shirt this one still smells bad." Chance told her, "I did the best I could to get his shirt clean." "I'm sure you did but it still smells."

They finally found a tee shirt that was way too big for Shane in the only shop in the airport that was still open that late and bought it. Ann changed Shane's shirt and put the dirty one in the plastic bag the new shirt came in and then put it into one of her carry-on bags.

When they finally got on the plane it was almost two o'clock in the morning. Their plane arrived late in Honolulu. The airline's boarding staff told them their plane started in London with its first stop in Los Angeles. The stewardess had to wake people up to move them out of the Clarks' assigned seats when they boarded the plane. The cabin crew kept asking if Shane had a paid seat and Chance kept telling them yes. The sights and smells inside the BOAC VC-10 were unbelievable as nearly all of the people on this flight were migrating to Australia and had everything they owned with them. Chance expected to see live chickens coming down the aisle at any time.

By the time they finally got seated Shane was sleeping in Chance's arms. Ann sat next to the window with Shane propped up between them for takeoff. As soon as they were airborne Shane stirred and made a soft crying sound. Chance folded up the arm rest between them and turned Shane around so Chance could cradled him in his arms with Shane's legs and feet stretched out on his seat. Early the next morning, the plane was beginning its approach to land in the Fiji Islands.

Ann was looking out the window and told Chance in an excited voice, "Chance, I can see a large pod of whales just below us.

Quick, Chance, look at them!"

Chance tried to move his right arm the one Shane had been sleeping on since they left Hawaii. It was numb and Chance couldn't move it.

He told Ann, "You have to get Shane off my arm, it's asleep and I can't move it."

Ann picked up Shane and Chance began rubbing his arm,

trying to get the blood circulating. After about five minutes, Chance could feel his arm beginning to feel alive again. Chance missed one of the most wonderful sights of the whole trip.

Ann said, "With the sun just coming up and shining on those whales it was just beautiful."

"Thanks."

When the plane landed at Fiji the left side of the plane was bright with the rising sun and the right side of the plane was in total darkness. They were told the plane would be here for an hour-and-a-half, because they were changing crews and refueling the plane. They got off the plane and their first stop was the restroom. Chance was sure that as clean as the Fiji airport looked the bathrooms would be a whole lot cleaner and better then the ones on the plane.

Chance thought back to his conversation with the company travel agent about the British Overseas Airline Corporation's VC- 10 airplane he could now tell her and he would, that a VC- 10 is nothing like a DC-10 airplane. It was more like a DC-9.

After stopping in the rest rooms they looked through the shops. They found a lot of interesting items, but they didn't buy anything. They were afraid to spend their money, because they didn't want to run out of cash and they had no place to carry anything else anyway. Soon they were back on the plane, next stop Sydney. They landed in Sydney just before six in the morning local time. The steward announced for everyone to stay in their seats, because all aircraft coming from overseas into Australia had to be sprayed with an insect killer.

The steward said, "The spray is not harmful to people, but you may want to cover your nose and mouth during the spraying of the aircraft."

Ann took out tissues and gave some to Chance. She told Shane they were going to play a game and when the people came down the aisle of the plane, "We're going to hide our faces so they can't see us."

Two men came onto the plane. One went to the back of the plane and the other stayed at the front. The man at the front of the plane took out two spray cans of insect killer and began walking toward the back of the plane, spraying insecticide as he went.

Ann told Shane, "OK, let's hide from these people."

Shane took his tissue and put it over his face. After the spray settled, Ann said "OK" and then she saw the other man coming from the back of the plane and she said, "OK, let's hide again" and again, Shane put his tissue over his face. When they finished spraying the airplane, Chance and Shane both started coughing.

About that time the steward announced they could now disembark the aircraft.

They cleared customs and immigration with little problem and took a taxi to the hotel after exchanging fifty dollars the exchange rate was two dollars and fifty cents U.S. dollars for one Australian dollar.

After taking their showers Chance decided they should go to Donald's Sydney office and report in. They took a taxi to the office and met with the country manager of Australia, Mr. Clive Cartel.

He was happy to see Chance and told them he would advise the manager of the Perth office, Mr. Trevor Lawrence that Chance and his family would arrive in Perth tomorrow. He said if he could help in any way to just let him know. They would telex Chance's flight number and arrival time in Perth so they could be picked up at the airport.

By the time they returned to their hotel room it was eleven-thirty in the morning. They turned on the television and decided to wait until a little after twelve before having lunch. Ann got some of Shane's toys out of his carry-on bag and he was playing with them on the floor by the foot of their bed. Chance and Ann lay down on the bed to watch TV. Chance woke up and looked at his watch it was three o'clock they missed lunch. Chance got up off of the bed and Ann was still sleeping and Shane was sleeping on the other bed. Chance went to the window and looked out, it was dark. Chance looked at his watch again and picked up the phone. The operator said, "May I help you?"

"Could you please tell me the time?"

She replied, "Yes, sir. It's a few minutes past three in the morning.

Chance just got a lesson about jet lag. He remembered watching people on The Jack Parr Show talking about jet lag and he used to think what a bunch of bull! Another lesson learned by experience. Chance turned off the television since it only had snow on a blank screen anyway. He went into the bathroom and by the time he came out, Ann was awake.

She asked "Chance what time is it?"

"Well you're never going to believe it, but it's a little after three in the morning."

"Three a.m.?"

"That's right."

"Did you put Shane in bed?"

"No," Chance said, "didn't you?"

"You mean our two-and-a-half year old put himself to bed?" "I guess he did."

Chance picked up the phone and asked the operator if they could get room service.

"I'm sorry, sir, but our kitchen doesn't open until six o'clock."

Shane woke up and said, "I'm hungry."

With that, Chance and Ann began looking for something to eat and they discovered their mini bar refrigerator was stocked with juices, candy, crackers, chips, nuts, cokes, wine, whisky and some cheese. They emptied all of the food, drank all of the juices and drank all of the cokes. A plague of locusts could not have done a better job of emptying that refrigerator. They took everything but the whisky and wine!

They took showers or baths, got dressed, packed their bags and waited for the restaurant to open. They were walking the floor in front of the restaurant when a man finally came and unlocked the door.

The waiter looked knowingly at them and said, "I'll bet you folks just came in from America yesterday."

Chance said, "Yes and we're starving!"

The waiter said, "That happens a lot around here." They ordered almost everything on the menu since the breakfast choices were "a full breakfast" or "a Continental breakfast."

They ordered the full breakfast, which consisted of eggs, potatoes, cereal, juice, coffee, and a rasher of bacon--whatever a rasher of bacon was. They ate almost everything that was brought to them. What Shane didn't eat, Chance finished.

After breakfast they took a walk and then went back to their room. Chance called a porter, as Chance found the bellmen were called in Australia and checked out of the hotel. They're mini bar charges were almost half of the cost of their one-night stay at the hotel.

When they arrived at the airport a porter took their bags to BOAC to check in for the flight to Perth. Chance gave the porter a tip and waited his turn in line or, as he found out later, in the queue, as a line is called in Australia. Chance approached the counter and handed the agent their three tickets.

The airline agent said, "That flights canceled, come back day after tomorrow."

Chance said, "What do you mean canceled?"

"I mean it is not flying today."

"We can't wait two more days to go to Perth I have a deadline to make. Can't you book us on another flight?"

The clerk told Chance, "We don't have another flight to Perth for two days."

"Put us on another airline. There must be someone who goes to Perth."

The clerk said, "I can't do that. If you want to talk with another airline, that's up to you."

Chance couldn't believe what the man told him or that they were still four or five hours' flying time to Perth without an airplane.

What Chance could believe was this guy was not going to help him. The clerk closed up the little window on his counter and left them standing there.

Chance went over to a Trans Australian Airline desk and began talking with a clerk. She said she would check with her supervisor to see if they could take the BOAC tickets for their flight to Perth.

She came back in a few minutes and said they could use their BOAC tickets and then she began trying to find them seats on a plane to Perth from Sydney that day. She told them they missed the only direct flight for the day since it was already gone. The clerk got them on a flight leaving a little after three o'clock and making stops in Melbourne and Adelaide on its way to Perth.

As they sat down to wait for their plane they began talking to a young man wearing a wraparound sarong. He told them he was from Tonga, an island east of Fiji. In fact, it was just across the International Date Line.

He said proudly, "Tonga is where the day begins!"

He was selected by his chief to come to Australia to study animal husbandry on a cattle station in Queensland. He had never been off his island before and it was very easy to tell he was very frightened. Chance and Ann did what they could to make him feel more comfortable, but Shane was a bigger help just because he was there. The young man had three young daughters and the youngest was about the same age as Shane. Shane made him feel more at home; but at the same time more lonely. He said he was to stay on the cattle station for six months and he had to learn a lot, because he couldn't let his king down.

Chance understood well about the pressure of not letting his king down. Chance never had a king, but he never wanted to let anyone down, his parents, Ann, his bosses, or his sons. He never let his guard down. To just relax was something he had never been able to do. He always had to be "doing" he could never just sit down.

It was time for their plane. They wished the man from Tonga good luck and said good-bye.

Chance told him, "I know you will do well because you want to."

The flights were long and after they had been flying for some time, Ann asked a stewardess when they would be serving something to eat. The stewardess said they couldn't serve meals in coach, because Trans Australian Airline was a government-owned airline and their competitor in Australia was Ansett Airline since Colonel Ansett filed a lawsuit against Trans Australian, claiming unfair competition because he quit serving meals in coach on his planes. Chance and Ann were learning that there were a lot of things that were "unbelievable" in Australia.

Ann said, "My little boy is starving. Can't you find him something to eat from first class?"

The stewardess said, "I'll try to find him some biscuits." Ann looked at Chance and they both said, "Biscuits?"

The stewardess soon came back with two small packages of cookies. The Clarks were learning a new English language, biscuits were cookies.

The plane landed in Melbourne, then in Adelaide. It seemed the trip would take forever to get to Perth. By the time they landed at the Perth Airport, it was after ten o'clock in the evening. They gathered up their carry on luggage and started down the walkway stairs that had been moved into place to unload the passengers from the plane. The night air felt wonderful after being inside the airplane for so many hours. As they began walking across the tarmac, they could smell the fragrance of the flowers growing outside the terminal building. It smelled as good as Hawaii had when they first stepped off the plane there. Before they arrived at the door to enter the terminal, a very British voice said, "You must be the Clarks from America."

Chance replied, "Yes sir, we are or at least what's left of them after our trip!"

The gentleman behind the voice was the Perth manager for Donald Engineering. He said, "I'm Trevor Lawrence, how do you do?"

"I'm Chance Clark and this is my wife Ann and our son, Shane."

Chance extended his right hand and Mr. Lawrence took it and shook it firmly. Chance begin telling Mr. Lawrence how sorry he was for their late arrival and Mr. Lawrence kept saying it was OK.

By the time they got their luggage loaded into Mr. Lawrence's car, it was a little after eleven. Mr. Lawrence told them the Western Australian Annual Show was going on and the only room he could find for them was in a very small hotel that was more like a bed and breakfast then a hotel. Chance surmised this show must be something like the Kansas State Fair. They arrived at the small hotel and Mr. Lawrence had already picked up their room key and he needed it to unlock an outside door that led them to the stairway to their room.

The room was tiny, just large enough for a three-quarter-size bed and a folding cot that had been set up for Shane. After they carried up their luggage and things the room was completely filled. It reminded Chance of the old joke about, "My room is so small, I have to go outside to change my mind."

Finally between Chance and Mr. Lawrence, they got everything transported from the car and up the stairs to their room.

Mr. Lawrence said, "If you want to order breakfast, just fill out this card and hang it outside on the doorknob. Good night, we'll see you tomorrow, half past eleven."

Chance and Ann were really hungry and they knew poor Shane must be starving, even though he was sleeping. They filled out the breakfast card, eggs and rashers of bacon, toast and cereal for Shane. The cereal choices were corn flakes or rice bubbles. They decided rice bubbles must be like Rice Krispies.

They went to bed but by 3 a.m. they were awake. How can you be so tired when you lie down to sleep after midnight and then be awake by 3 a.m.? Obviously they were not acclimated to the local time.

A few minutes later Shane was awake. He climbed over his mother and lay down between them. He had only been there a few minutes when he began squirming and pushing, first on his dad, then on his mom. It didn't take long before Chance was about to fall out of the tiny bed.

Chance exclaimed, "OK you guys, I give up. I'm getting up."

Shane just giggled and kept pushing on his mother until she got out of bed, too. Then Shane lay spread eagle, with his arms and legs extended full out and just smiled. This was too much for Chance, so he jumped back on the bed, straddled Shane and began tickling him.

"OK Shane, if you want to play, I'm just going to eat you all up," and Chance started mouthing Shane's face and neck, acting as if he were eating him. Shane just kept wiggling and giggling.

In the meantime, Ann went into the bathroom and came back dressed. She said, "Are you two just going to stay in bed all day?"

With that, Chance got out of bed and started for the bathroom, except Shane ducked in front of him and got into the bathroom first, laughing about beating his daddy.

After they were dressed, they went down the stairs and out onto the street. It was now a little after five in the morning and the sun was just coming up. The three of them walked slowly down the street. The houses were all one-story homes in this area of Perth, except for their hotel. The yards were fenced and each yard was filled with flowers and little or no grass. Chance and Ann liked the looks of these houses. They all had large front porches and tin roofs. Chance looked again; if the roofs weren't tin, they were certainly some kind of metal.

Ann said, "It must never hail here or these people would all go crazy listening to the rain and hail on these roofs."

The longer they walked around, the more they thought Perth looked a lot like California, except the plants were types they had never seen before. In over an hour of walking the streets around the hotel, they never saw one person, nor did one car go by. It was like being plunked down in a strange new beautiful world and they were the only people there.

At seven o'clock, they had a knock on their door and a nice lady in her fifties brought them their breakfast. It didn't take them long to finish everything she had delivered and rice bubbles were indeed, Rice Krispies.

Eleven-thirty came and Mr. Lawrence arrived. He said Chance would go with him to the office and his secretary, Mrs. Fenella Crane, would pick up Mrs. Clark to show her some of the flats available. "Sorry, "he continued, "you Americans call them apartments, don't you? Anyway, we think we have found several nice flats you can look at."

Chance and Mr. Lawrence left to go the office so Chance could meet the local staff and he could take some of his things to the office. It was only about a five-minute drive to the office.

Chance and Ann had walked within a block of the office earlier that morning. Chance was properly introduced to the staff and was shown his office, which although small was much nicer then Chance expected.

As Chance was putting things away in his new office, he was surprised to see Ann and Shane coming into the office with a lady Chance knew must be Fenella Crane.

Ann introduced her to Chance and said, "I think I have found us a place to live."

Chance said, "Already? I left you less then an hour ago."

I know, but the apartment is just next door."

The three of them went next door and went up to the second floor of a very modern building. The apartment, or flat as the Australians called them, was on the southwest corner of the building. This building was built by Alan Bond, Ann told him, whoever Alan Bond was. Ann had the key to the apartment she unlocked the door and let Chance inside.

The apartment had a lounge, which was the living room, two bedrooms, a kitchen, and one bath with a washer and a small glassed-in balcony. It was furnished with new- looking modern furniture. Chance thought it looked great but was puzzled about the upper kitchen cabinets not having any doors on them.

Ann said she asked Mrs. Crane about that and was told that's the way kitchen cabinets were made in Australia.

They decided to take the apartment and Ann was told they could move in right away. Ann told Chance the lady who owned the apartment was an English woman by the name of Hannah White.

When they walked back to the office, Mr. Lawrence told them the airline called and said their box from the States was available for pick up. Mr. Lawrence said if it was all right with them, he would have one of his staff, Brian Noel take them to the airport to pick up the box and help them move into the flat. Brian Noel was a young man in his twenties and had a very difficult accent for Chance to understand. Brian told them he was from Cornwall, England. Chance had heard of Cornish accents, but never heard one before. With Brian's help by late that afternoon they moved into their apartment.

Shane, of course, was a big help too. He helped by carrying in his "Teddy" and the toys he brought with them on the plane.

By the time the beds were made, dishes put up and the clothes unpacked from the suitcases, it was bedtime again. After Shane was asleep, Chance put his arms around Ann and began kissing her and telling her how much he loved her and how much he appreciated all of the things she went through for him.

Ann smiled a knowing smile and said, "Well, I don't think we're in Kansas any more."

With both of them laughing Chance picked Ann up, closed the bedroom door and gently placed her on the bed.

Chance said, "You know, we have to see if there is any difference making love "Down Under." You know there might be, the water drains counter-clockwise, so it may be different and we need to find out."

The next morning Mr. Lawrence took Chance to meet with the government officials in charge of the parking project. It was very important for them to meet Chance so they knew the project would be started on time. Chance assured them he would soon get the project underway.

When they returned to the office, Chance was introduced to two people who had been out of the office the day before working on other assignments. Drake Stevens was the deputy manager of the Perth office and Scott Trier was to be Chance's assistant on this project.

Chance met with Scott Trier, explaining what they needed to do to get started. First, they needed to hire people to work with Scott surveying every parking space in the central business district of Perth. Next, they would be required to put together all of the inventory of the parking spaces on computer punch cards so the information could be entered into a computer.

Late that afternoon, Chance met with Mr. Lawrence to discuss the details of hiring people to help with the survey work. Mr. Lawrence told Chance to work with Scott and Heidi Ott, the bookkeeper for the office and have them get started hiring people.

By the time they meeting was over everyone else had left the office for the night.

Mr. Lawrence said, "You met Drake Stevens this afternoon didn't you?

Chance replied, "Yes, nice fellow."

Mr. Lawrence told Chance, Drake and his missionary parents were captured by the Japanese in Indonesia during the Second World War. His father was taken with the men and his mother was put with the other women prisoners. Drake was five years old at the time and he was put with other captured children, he didn't see his parents again until 1947. Each of them thought the other had been killed. All three of them were returned to England before they knew the other ones were alive and before they were reunited. Mr. Lawrence said after Drake got his engineering degree in England, he moved to Australia and married an Australian girl. Mr. Lawrence continued, "I'll tell you she leads him a merry chase. Her name is Patricia and she's the All-Australian Girl!"

That evening, Chance told Ann about his day and the people he met at work. He told her the story Mr. Lawrence told him about Drake

Stevens and his wife Patricia. Then Chance asked what Ann had done with her day.

Ann told Chance she and Shane went shopping for food. She said, "Chance, you don't know how many stores we had to go before I could fix dinner this evening. We went to the butcher shop for meat, the bakery for bread, the grocery store for tins, that's what they call canned food and to the green grocers for fresh vegetables. Buying food is an adventure here.

After we got the food put up, Shane and I were so cold in the apartment we went out to the pool. It has a lot of beautiful flowers and a big wall around it and it's on the north side of the building, so the sun warms it up very nicely.

That night after they were in bed, Ann said, "I'm cold Chance turn on some heat for me."

Chance got out of bed and began looking for the thermostat to turn on the heat. He couldn't find a thermostat, so Chance thought they must have baseboard heaters and he began crawling around the perimeter of each room, but found nothing. Ann got up and tried to help, but to no avail. Chance lit the gas oven in the kitchen and turned on all four burners on the stove. Then they took raincoats to put over Shane and themselves.

Chance told Ann, "I know this apartment must have heat, we just don't know how to turn it on. I'll call Hannah White in the morning and ask her how to do it. Everybody in Chicago told me that living in Perth would be like living in San Diego, but it feels more like San Francisco to me."

Ann said, "You know it's because we're on the south side of the building and we don't ever get any sun into the apartment. The sun is in the north here. We have to start thinking backwards from when we were in the northern hemisphere."

The next morning Chance called Hannah White and asked her how to turn on the heat in the apartment.

Hannah replied, "The flat does not have any heat, you poor dears must be freezing. I'll bring around a fire this afternoon."

Chance visualized Hannah White bringing a box of some type with a fire in it, maybe like a small barbecue. At lunch time he told Ann what Hannah White told him?

Ann said, "I guess we will wait to see what she brings."

When Chance returned to the flat that evening, the first thing he did was ask Ann, "Did our landlady bring us a fire?"

"Yes, there it is."

Chance looked and the "fire" was a Hoover electric heater, the size of a shoebox.

The next afternoon Chance met Patricia Stevens and she certainly lived up to Mr. Lawrence's advance billing. She came to pick up Drake, because his car was in the repair shop. Patricia walked into Chance's office while he was talking with Scott.

She said, "Hi, I'm Patricia Stevens, Drake's wife you must be Chance Clark, the American that's come to show us Aussies how to do things."

Chance got up from his desk, extended his hand to her and said, "Hi, I'm glad to meet you. I'm Chance Clark and I confess to being an American, but I'm not sure I'm here to show anyone how to do anything. I think I'm here to help do a parking study for the government."

Patricia took his hand and said, "You sure are a tall one, aren't you?"

Chance could only smile and Patricia popped out of his office as quickly as she had come in.

Scott said, "Well Chance, you've met our All-Australian Girl!"

Chance shook his head and said, "I sure did."

Two minutes later, Patricia stuck her head back inside the door and said, "I'll pop over and meet your wife next week. Cheers!"

She was off again this time with Drake in tow. Chance heard her say to Drake, "Come on love, you know I don't have all day." Chance told Ann about his brief encounter with Patricia Stevens and Ann said, "I don't know if I'm up to her or not."

Chance said, "I'm sure you'll do your best to be nice to her you are to everyone else."

Chance added, "I think if I were married to her, I might have to hold her under water once in awhile to slow her down."

True to her word, Patricia came to see Ann the next week.

When Chance got home that night, Ann said, "I see what you mean about Patricia Stevens."

Ann whistled. "She's something, but I like her."

"Ann you like everybody. Sometimes you are just too nice."

Ann said, "Sure I'm!"

With that, Chance pulled her down on his lap, kissed her and said, "It's true, Annie, you're just too nice to some people, but I'll let you be nice to me," and he kept holding her on his lap.

The following Friday at lunchtime, Chance, Ann and Shane went to downtown Perth to pick up a rental car. After a lot of conversations with Trevor Lawrence, Mr. Lawrence agreed to let Chance rent a car every other weekend at the company's expense and this would be the first time they would be picking up a car.

After getting all the paperwork done they went to get into the car.

Ann went to the right side of the little red, two-door Ford to get in and discovered there was a steering wheel on her side of the car. At the same time, Chance went to the left side and opened the door.

Ann said, "No way, I'm not driving."

Chance said, "I guess since someone stole my steering wheel, I'll have to come around and use yours."

Chance got into the car. It was a stick shift with all of the controls just opposite to what he was used to. Chance got the engine started; he took his right hand and shifted the turn signal, let out the clutch and the car died.

Ann started laughing, Chance started laughing and Shane began laughing at both of them. Chance was pleased that, at least, the turn signal he had shifted was still blinking. Chance looked the car over some more. The gearshift was on the floor at Chance's left hand. That meant Chance would have to shift gears with his left hand, which he had never done before. He also noticed the hand brake was on and that's why the engine stalled when he let out the clutch.

Chance started the engine again. He released the brake and shifted the gear. Ann was still laughing at him. Chance carefully let out the clutch and the little red Ford lunged forward and died again. Chance had shifted the car into fourth gear. Ann's laughter got even louder and all Chance could do was laugh with her. Two more tries before Chance got the car out of the door of the Hertz garage. Now he only needed to get into the Friday noontime traffic in downtown Perth.

Chance edged the car into the traffic lane and began to move with the traffic. Ann just kept watching him and laughing. When he tried to make his first right turn, he killed the engine again; he hadn't down shifted the gears.

Ann said, "Chance, you're making me laugh so hard, I'm going to wet my pants."

Shane said, "Mommy is going to wet her pants!"

With that, Chance couldn't stop laughing long enough to even try to get the car started again. After some time passed, somehow he got the car going and got them back to their apartment building.

After the car was parked, Chance said, "Annie, you got me laughing so much I just about couldn't drive us home."

They continued to sit in the car laughing away; just when they thought they were going to stop, they looked at each other and start all over again.

Chance said, "I'm not going to look at you. I'm just going to get out of the car. If people see us sitting out in this car laughing, they'll say, see those crazy Americans!"

Ann cackled even louder. Chance opened his door and got out, wondering how he was going to be able to work that afternoon he was so weak from laughing. They would never get a car with a right-hand drive again without thinking about the first time Chance tried to drive one in Perth.

Sometimes when you do a job too well, unexpected things happen to you. It was now the middle of November and the way things were moving on this project, Chance told Ann, "We'll be back in the States before yours and Shane's birthdays."

Trevor Lawrence returned from a meeting with government officials that same afternoon and when Chance saw him come in the office door he was smiling. Trevor Lawrence rarely smiled, but he was smiling this afternoon. He asked Chance to come into his office. Chance followed him in and sat down across the desk from Mr. Lawrence.

Trevor Lawrence said, "Chance, please call me Trevor."

"OK, Trevor."

Trevor continued, "I've just come back from a meeting with the officials in charge of the parking project. Great news! They are really pleased with the job you are doing and I must say, I am, too.

"Thank you, Trevor."

Trevor kept going, "They just signed the contract to complete phases two and three of the parking study. Isn't that great news?" Chance replied, "It certainly sounds like it to me."

But Chance was not prepared for the next thing Trevor said to him.

"That means you'll have to stay for another six to nine months to finish these contracts."

When Chance told Ann, she just said, "I don't think we're going to be home before my birthday, do you?"

"No, I guess not."

"Look at it this way," Ann said," at least you're doing a good job for them and it got them two more contracts. Maybe they'll give you a raise."

Chance thought, well, Chase would like that since their paycheck went directly to him and Chance and Ann were living off of a twenty-Australian-dollar-a-day per diem, a whole one hundred forty dollars a week. After paying the apartment rent, rent for their television, the electric bill and their food, they never had any money left. Once every other month or so, they used their American Express card to buy some Australian gifts from the Sheraton Hotel for their families. They were just small things since they wouldn't have room to pack much when they went home.

They were invited to an office Christmas party and their landlady agreed to stay with Shane while they were gone. The Christmas party fell on Ann's birthday, so she at least got to go out on her birthday. Chance got her a card and a small pin with a painting of Western Australian wildflowers on it. As Chance thought back to the first birthday present he bought for Ann, he felt very sorry for her. Her father was gone, her eldest son and mother were 13,500 miles away from her and her birthday present was as small as she ever received since he had known her. At least she still has Shane and me with her he thought.

The first course of the dinner was octopus, pickled, of course.

Chance and Ann tried some of it and it wasn't that bad, but it wasn't that good either. The dinner continued. Everyone was drinking wine or beer, except Chance and Ann. They almost never drank. They danced a few dances and then made excuses they had to get home so their baby-sitting landlady could go home early.

After their landlady left and Shane was asleep, Chance told Ann, "I'm sorry I couldn't do more for your birthday."

"It's OK, as long as I have you nothing else matters."

The next Monday, Chance was told the office would be closed for the Christmas Holidays from the middle of December until the middle of January. Trevor Lawrence relented and gave Chance permission to rent a car for the whole Christmas holiday. Chance assumed either getting the two additional contracts or the spirit of Christmas must have moved Trevor. Chance thought Trevor was the tightest manager he ever met while working for Donald Engineering Company. One would think every penny spent came directly out of Trevor's pocket and maybe it did by reducing his bonus for managing the Perth operation.

Chance, Ann and Shane celebrated Shane's third birthday by themselves. Ann made a birthday cake and decorated it herself. It looked really cute. Grandma and Grandpa Clark sent Shane a birthday present that arrived two days before Shane's birthday. Chance and Ann bought him some neat little cars made by Corigi in England. Ann did all she could to give Shane a real birthday party. Shane had a great time unwrapping his presents. Three days later, Ann's mother's birthday present arrived, so he got to open another present. Shane also got a card from Chase, Marie and Curt, saying they were keeping Shane's birthday present until he returned home.

Chance wrote to his folks and Ann wrote to her mother and Chase, suggesting everyone exchange their Christmas presents after they returned to America. Chance and Ann found a very small artificial Christmas tree at Boan's department store, as well as some neat Christmas ornaments. They found some more ornaments at Coles, a five and dime store that was Australia's Woolworth's. Christmas was not much at the Clarks that year, but Santa still found Shane all the way in Western Australia. Shane was happy with his Christmas presents and Ann and Chance each received a gift. Chance also had the opportunity to make one of his all-time wishes come true, he had watermelon on Christmas Day.

The Clarks spent most of the day in the park, having a picnic and letting Shane play in the pool. The temperature was one hundred and four degrees. They telephoned Chase, Ann's mom and Chance's folks. They had to call from the office since they didn't have a telephone in their flat, but they got a chance to wish all of their family a Merry Christmas.

It came as a big surprise to Chance and Ann that both the milkman and the bread man delivered to them on Christmas Day. They also got the chance to celebrate "Boxing Day," an old English tradition adopted in Australia. Boxing Day is the day after Christmas and presents are given to all of the people who served them, such as the men who delivered milk and bread.

Between Christmas and New Years, they drove to the southwest part of the state, to the city of Bunbury, to see the Karri trees.

Only the redwood trees in California are larger then the Western Australia Karri trees. The trees were very impressive, but to Chance the drive from Perth to Bunbury was even more so, for it had taken them along the coast. The coast was beautiful with hundreds, really thousands of miles of the cleanest, most unpopulated coastline in the world. The Indian Ocean looked as if it went on forever.

Looking at it brought goose bumps to the back of Chance's neck; just thinking about that on the other side of the water was Africa.

Drake and Patricia invited them to a New Year's Eve party at their home. Patricia told them to bring Shane along; he could play with the other children and then go to bed in one of their bedrooms.

By the time Chance and Ann arrived at the Stevens home on New Year's Eve, both Drake and Patricia had been enjoying a good bit of white wine. As soon as they got in the house, Patricia started in on Chance about the Americans being so materialistic.

She said, "They got us into their bloody Vietnam War along with them and the only thing Americans care about is how to get more things."

Patricia and Chance seemed to always be debating about Australia and America every time they were together. Ann, Drake and anyone else around tried not to get in the between them. They all just sat back and listened. Chance knew Patricia had never been to the United States, so she really only knew about it and the people from books, movies and television.

The Australians who Chance had met who had been to the States all said the same thing, "I've been to America and we didn't like it."

After Chance questioned these people, he always found they had been to New York City or Los Angeles. Chance could understand why they didn't like America. If he had only been to New York City for four or five days, he probably would have had the same opinion. He wasn't so sure why people didn't like Los Angeles, other then their comment, "It's so spread out and it's nothing but freeways. It's not a real city, you know."

Chance said to Patricia, "Americans are materialistic! What about the Australians?"

Patricia said, "What about the Australians?"

"Just look around your beautiful home. You live less then four blocks from one of the most beautiful beaches in the entire world, yet you have a big swimming pool in your backyard. You have two cars, a dishwasher, several televisions, all kinds of stereo equipment, clothes of all kinds and you go to Europe every year. Ann and I have never owned a home with a swimming pool. We have one car and no dishwasher, yet we are the ones who are materialistic? I don't think Americans are any more materialistic then any Australians I've met"

Patricia was taken back she didn't have a comeback for his statement. Instead she said, "Come on; let's have a drink and something to eat."

Drake said, "I guess this one goes to the All-American Boy. Sorry, love," he said to Patricia, "but I think he got you this time." Chance thought to himself, no Drake my friend, I think she got you.

Patricia took Chance by the arm and led him through the house and back to the pool where several tables were set up with all kinds of food and drinks. The evening was brilliant it was warm with a light breeze blowing in from the Indian Ocean. Chance thought what a different way of spending New Year's Eve and what a difference the weather was in Perth than it was in Kansas, Iowa, or Illinois on New Year's Eve.

Ann took Shane in to play with the Stevens' three children. They had two boys and a girl. The boys were already in school, but their little girl was only about six months older than Shane. Shane sat down on the bedroom floor and began playing with some of the toys scattered around the room. Ann came out to the pool as Chance was working his way around the table of food Ann found a plate and joined him.

She whispered, "Take it easy on Patricia, she's become my friend and we do things together."

"Sorry, I'll watch it."

Drake had stereo speakers set up around the pool, with soft romantic music playing. After people finished eating, couples were dancing. Chance looked up in the sky and could see the Southern Cross, something else he had always wanted to see. An hour later a full moon was shining, its light made the New Year's Eve party even more romantic. Chance and Ann danced several dances together when Patricia announced everyone should put on their swimsuits and get into the pool. Patricia was wearing shorts and a blouse and as she made her announcement, she took off her blouse and dropped her shorts, revealing a bikini she was wearing under them.

Drake shouted, "I thought we were really going to see something, but you're wearing a bikini!"

People began going into the house to don their swimsuits.

Chance and Ann were the last to make their way into the house to change into the swimsuits they brought with them from their flat.

By the time they returned, everyone else was already in the pool.

Chance and Ann went to the shallow end and began wading into the water hand in hand. Chance knew he was probably the only one at this party who couldn't swim, but the water felt warm and wonderful to him.

At midnight, everyone wished everyone else "Happy New Year 1975" followed by many hugs, kisses and handshakes with so many people Chance and Ann didn't know. Shane came out to the pool and told Ann, "Happy New Year!"

Ann got out of the pool, dried herself off and got Shane something to eat and drink. Then she took Shane back to the bedroom Patricia had fixed for him for the night.

Chance was sitting on the side of the pool with his feet and legs dangling in the warm water. Patricia came up to him and sat down next to him an started talking.

She said, "I didn't get to wish you a Happy New Year," and she leaned up and kissed him.

Chance smiled and said to her, "Happy New Year Patricia.
You know, you are The All-Australian Girl."

Patricia looked him in the eyes and said something no one else had ever said to him before, "You never let go do you? You never relax. Do you ever just have fun?"

Chance replied, "No, I don't suppose I ever just let go or become completely relaxed, but I do have fun. Maybe not like you Australians, you're much more open and carefree then I could ever be."

Chance thought to himself without saying it, you Australians like drinking beer, going to the beach, gambling, sports and sex and not necessarily in that order.

Just then Ann came back and told Chance, "I think we are going to have to go home because I don't think Shane will ever go to sleep in a strange house."

Chance got up from the side of the pool, told Patricia and Drake, "Thanks for a nice time," and the Clarks left to go back to their apartment.

20

When they finally got back to work after the Christmas break, Chance got things rolling. They completed the personal interviews to see where people parking in Perth came from and where they were going in the central business district. Next they did the license plate recording of every vehicle entering and parking in the central business district over a two-day period. Using their computer program, they could track each stop every car in Perth made in the central business district over the two-day period.

They had only one problem with this survey. One of Chance's people got arrested for recording the vehicle license numbers of cars coming out of the parking lot of the Criminal Investigating Department of the Police Department. It seems these were unmarked detective cars and their chief thought we might sell this information to the criminals in Western Australia. Chance had to get the Commissioner of Transportation to talk to the Commissioner of Police to get his man released from jail and to obtain permission to do their parking study on the police parking lot.

The next problem Chance and Ann faced was trying to get their visas extended so they could stay in the country to finish the parking study. This time it took the Commissioner of Transportation appealing to the Australian Director of Transportation to "ring up" the Australian Director of Immigration to get the Clarks' visas extended for an additional six months.

Before this was accomplished, Chance and Ann were afraid to answer their door, thinking they would be deported any day. Sometimes the mail brings good things and it did when their passports, with their new visas were returned to them. Life looked better. They had been in the country two months past the time their visas expired before they received their new visas.

Another good thing that came in the mail was news of the sale of their house in Olympia Fields. Not only did they get back their investment, but they made a little money, even after paying the commission and all the other costs of selling a home.

The day came when they finished the project and were leaving Australia, but not before Chance got strep throat. He was determined to get on the plane and go home anyway. This time, they flew non-stop to Sydney on a Quanta's flight that just came from Johannesburg, South Africa. It took them a little over three hours for their 747 to make the crossing to Sydney. In Sydney, they changed to another terminal and when Chance saw the Pan Am 747 with the American Flag on its tail waiting for them, he thought it was one of the most beautiful sights he had ever seen.

Their last Australian surprise was trading their Aussie dollars for U.S. dollars. It cost a dollar-and-a-half Australian for every U.S. Dollar. When they arrived in Australia less then a year ago, it cost the Clark's two and a half US Dollars for every Australia Dollar. What a change!

Chance got on the plane and when he heard the American accents, he felt like crying. After they were airborne Chance took one last look out his window at the Sydney Harbor Bridge and the Opera House, he had a coke and then didn't move until they landed in Fiji. Chance bought a small wooden model of an outrigger canoe made in Fiji and then he settled back down in his seat and didn't move again until they landed in Hawaii. Chance thought Patricia Stevens was wrong, he could lay back and let go when he was sick and exhausted.

Chance and Ann had studied the U.S. customs regulations very carefully while they were in Australia. They brought a customs book with them and followed the regulations to the letter, they purchased original oil paintings of Western Australian homes for themselves and oil paintings of the so-called "black boy" trees found only in Western Australia. The first white men to explore the area thought these trees looked like black tribesmen carrying spears. They were told it took a wildfire to make these trees grow and Chance was told it took a hundred years for them to grow an inch. The trees in their paintings would have been thousands of years old. All original artwork could be brought into the USA Duty Free.

They had brought a kangaroo skin for Shane and a dideroo for Chase, a musical instrument of sorts made by the Aborigines. They had opal pins for Chance and Ann's moms and several other things for everyone else. They packed all of the items they purchased in one suitcase with the customs regulations book laying on the top of their gifts. They also had every receipt for their purchases and they hadn't exceeded the twelve hundred dollars they were allowed.

The customs agent in Honolulu said, "Let's have a look at your bags. You've been out of the country for a long time." He took one look at the customs regulations book on top of their purchases and said, "Well, you two must know what you can bring into the States."

With that he closed their bag and said, "You can go."

They stayed in Honolulu for two days and were in culture shock. The stores had products they could actually buy. Levi jeans weren't selling for seventy-five dollars a pair as they were in Perth.

Food tasted great. They took tours and were real tourists. They had a great time.

When they arrived in Kansas, it was Christmas--without the cold or the Christmas tree. Everyone loved their Christmas presents.

Chase gave them the best Christmas of all. While they were gone he paid off all of their debts, everything! He did it without using any of the money from the sale of their house that was all in a savings account and they had several thousand dollars left over in their checking account. It was the first time Chance and Ann had been debt free since they first went into debt to buy the little blonde radio-phonograph player when they were sixteen years old. The bank with their checking account probably didn't know how to act with the Clark's account having more then a few dollars, but neither did they!

When Chance went back to Chicago to work, the International Department gave him the use of one of the two apartments the company owned in the Marina Towers. The apartment was just across from the company's offices and they told Chance he could use the apartment for two or three months before they would need it again. Chance got the key and moved into the apartment. It was on the forty-seventh floor and faced northeast. At night, the view of the lights of North Michigan Avenue was spectacular.

Ann and Shane stayed in Kansas for awhile to rest and visit with family and friends. Besides, Chance had to buy them another house. That's the way it worked. Chance went first to find and buy a house and Ann sold them. As they had been told so many times before, "Good housekeepers sell more houses then good houses."

They made a great team. Chance knew how to buy a house using his three rules, location, location, location and Ann was a great housekeeper. She knew how to always keep the house clean and neat and have food cooking on the stove when the house was being shown by a realtor.

Chance found a new home in Homewood, only a few minutes away from the Illinois Central Railway Station and close to Interstate 57 and the Tri-State Tollway. The location was excellent for transportation and he got a good buy on the house. Ann flew to Chicago to close the deal on the house and Chance picked her up at O'Hare Airport. It was late in the evening, so they went directly to the Marina Towers and the apartment on the forty- seventh floor.

Chance left the drapes open with the wonderful view of North Michigan Avenue waiting for Ann. On the dining room table he had flowers for her and a short black nightgown on her bed. He worked hard to have everything perfect for her and to make it as romantic as possible. After all, they had been apart now for several weeks.

Chance opened the door to the apartment and Ann could see a fairyland of lights on display only for her. Chance later turned on some lights so she could see her flowers.

Chance told her, "Come on I want to show you the rest of the apartment."

They explored the kitchen. It was stocked with all kinds of wines, liquor and food. The apartment was outfitted with beautiful china, crystal and silver.

Ann said, "You've really been roughing it here, I see."

Chance showed her the bedroom with its king size bed, a couch, two chairs and plenty of lamps.

The next day they closed the loan on their new house and made arrangements to have their furniture moved from storage into their new house.

Chance's folks brought Shane to his new home in Homewood the next weekend. He was really happy to see his mom and dad after being only with them so much of the time he had a very hard time being away from them.

The new home got good reviews from everyone. The Clarks were settling down into a routine again with Chance back working full-time on the Chicago project. In addition Chance served as project manager on two small parking studies in Detroit and Fort Wayne. Each day Chance worked in the office required the same routine. Ann drove him to the railroad station, about five minutes from home unless the traffic was extra heavy, then it might take ten minutes. His train ride would take an hour and fifteen minutes and then he had a ten to fifteen minute walk on lower Wacker Drive to his office building.

At night the trip home was the reverse of the same routine with the only difference being people would fall asleep and lean over on Chance for almost the whole train trip home. Chance hated that.

He was too private to have strangers leaning on him every day. This went on for four months before Chance took his calculator and started adding up the time it took him to go to and from work.

Let's see, two hours and thirty minutes a day on the train,

thirty minutes of walking to and from the office to the train station, that's three hours plus another ten minutes from home to the station and back home at the end of the day, plus at least twenty minutes every day waiting to get on trains.

Chance calculated he was spending a minimum of three hours and thirty minutes a day to and from work, so five times a week amounted to seventeen-and-a-half hours a week of commuting time. He thought if I go to the office an average of forty weeks a year that amounts to 700 hours a year or almost thirty days a year just going back and forth to work. Chance had another twenty-five years to work before reaching a normal retirement age. At this rate more than two years of his life would be lost commuting. Chance thought no way, baby! He walked into his boss's office the next day and said, "I'm giving my notice. I'm quitting."

The first words out of his boss's mouth were, "You can't quit. Is some other consulting company offering you more money?"

"No, I just don't want to live and work in Chicago anymore."

After an hour's discussion Chance agreed to continue working every other week and the company would pay his transportation back and forth from where ever he decided to move to as well as all of his expenses while he was working for them.

Chance called Ann on the phone and calmly told her, "Honey, I quit my job. I just can't stand this three-and-a-half hour commute every day."

"Well, I'm not surprised since I knew you haven't been happy since we got back from Australia. What are you going to do?"

Chance told her what his boss said to him. "I guess for awhile I'll still be working half-time as a consultant with Donald Engineering." When Chance got home that night he told Ann he thought they should move back to Webster to be with the rest of their family and friends.

Chance called a friend he made while at the University of Iowa that owned a small manufacturing plant that made grain storage products and grain-handling equipment for grain elevators. Chance told his friend he was starting a sales company in Kansas and wanted to sell his grain equipment products there. Needless to say, his friend, Todd Grimley, was delighted. Todd told Chance he could have the whole State of Kansas, as his exclusive agent, since they had never sold one product in Kansas.

Chance told him, "Ann and I are moving back to Webster and they certainly have a lot of grain elevators in Kansas."

The next day Ann called the same real estate company they bought two houses from and who sold one for them. When she asked for their agent Dorothy Straker, she was told Dorothy died two months ago from cancer. Ann was stunned.

The gentleman Ann was talking with said, "Can I help you? I'm the broker for the Century 21 agency."

When Ann told him her name, he said, "I certainly know who you are, Mrs. Clark and I will be glad to personally help you, if I can."

That evening, Mr. Russell Potter, the Century 21 broker came to the Clark's home. Chance showed him the house and Mr. Potter said to Ann, "You're certainly a good housekeeper Mrs. Clark."

Mr. Potter suggested a price almost nine thousand dollars more then they had paid for the house six months ago. They agreed with the listing price and signed the listing contract. Before lunch the next day they sold the house for cash at the full listed price.

They bought a new house in Webster and Chance started his new company. Chance continued doing consulting work every other week in Chicago. Chance left home on Monday morning and came back on Friday night when he worked in Chicago.

After three months, he began to get one or two small sales of the grain-handling equipment. Chance needed financing for the equipment he was selling. He only needed the money for about sixty days this was about how long it would take to make the equipment and for Chance to go to Iowa to pick up the equipment and install it. Chance contacted the First Security Bank in Webster and was introduced to the vice president in charge of commercial loans, Mr. Paul Black.

Mr. Black said, "Chance I need a cup of coffee let's go to the employee's lounge and talk."

Chance said, "That sounds good."

They took the elevator up to the second floor and Mr. Black led Chance into a luxurious dining room. A neatly uniformed lady came over to take their orders, and they both said, "Just black coffee, thank you."

Chance began explaining what kind of help he needed from the bank for his new business. Paul Black listened carefully. Chance showed him a purchase order he just received from one of the larger grain companies in Kansas. After seeing the purchase order, Paul Black leaned directly over in front of Chance's face not more then three or four inches away and said, "Chance I work on the KISS system."

With that, Chance moved back in his chair as far as possible away from Paul Black. He never a banker act like this guy and Chance didn't like it.

Paul Black continued, "KISS, you know, Keep it Simple, Stupid."

Chance smiled, because he thought Paul Black was making a pass at him with his kiss statement.

"Call me, Paul, how much of the bank's money can I give you today?"

That was the start of a great working relationship that continued right up to the time Paul bought his own bank and moved away from Webster.

Chance kept working and getting bigger and bigger contracts. He finally got started with one of the biggest co-ops in Kansas and their manager helped him sell his products to other co-ops. He was rolling and things were looking really good.

One night his friend Todd Grimley called and said, "I know you are working in Chicago next week. How about if I pick you up in my plane in St. Louis on your way home next Friday? I've got a proposal for you. We will have a chance to talk while I fly you home."

Chance told him, "It sounds good to me. See you next Friday." Chance flew into St. Louis the next Friday and found his way from TWA over to the fixed base operators' waiting room. Todd told him he would meet him around seven-thirty. Promptly at ten- thirty, Todd landed. He told Chance he was sorry for being late, but he was having all kinds of problems at the plant with a new product they were making.

Todd had his twin engine Aero Commander refueled and they took off, with Chance in the right seat of the cockpit. Todd began telling Chance he wanted him to come to work full-time with his company. Todd said the orders and the money is coming in so fast he had to have help. He said Chance could buy into the company if he wanted to and he would pay Chance whatever he wanted.

Before they landed in Webster, Chance agreed to go to work with Todd and buy a small share of the company, mainly from bonuses he would get from the company. Chance would be the second largest stockholder in the company and would be the company's vice president.

By the time Chance got home to Ann in Webster, it was almost three in the morning on Saturday morning. Ann was sleeping, but when Chance opened the bedroom door, she woke up. The first thing he said to Ann was, "We will never have to worry about money again."

If there were ever some famous last words, those were the words! "We will never have to worry about money again."

During the next several years, things went from bad to worse for the Clarks. They moved from Webster back to Iowa City. Todd Grimley found a way to spend the company's money--he bought bigger and faster airplanes. At work, Todd hid behind closed doors and would only talk with a couple of young women who had worked for him for several years. Todd had these women telling Chance what to do. Chance couldn't believe it.

Chance could go home call Todd at home on the phone and talk for hours. Then he could go to work the next morning and he couldn't even get into his office to see him. The last straw for Chance was when Todd bought another new plane that cost more then their yearly company's sales. Chance resigned and the Clarks moved back to Webster.

Chance wasn't doing very well working with his friends. Before he moved back to Webster, he agreed to join another company owned by another friend, Baxter Godfrey. Before the next year was over, the First Security Bank told him they wanted him to borrow twenty-five thousand dollars to put into Baxter's company. With this additional investment the bank could help Baxter get a Small Business Administration loan approved for the company and Chance's note would be paid off by the new loan. Things were so bad at the company Chance agreed to do it for a small percentage of the company.

The note was signed and thirty days later the bank said, sorry they couldn't get approval for the SBA loan and they were calling all of the company's loans. The result was that Chance and Ann were in hock for twenty-five thousand dollars of which they had never seen a penny. The bank applied the money on the interest owed the bank on previous company loans. Both Baxter and his company filed for bankruptcy.

Chance sometimes wasn't a quick learner when it came to people. After that he and Baxter started another company with Chance and Ann owning all of the company. They agreed that after Baxter's bankruptcy was over, they would give him an interest in the new company. They started working out of Chance's house. Then they got a small office in an old hospital building which had been converted into offices and apartments, this was the same hospital Chase and Curt had been born in. As the business grew they kept adding more and more products. If they had any money left over after buying products Chance and Baxter divided it and that's what they were living on.

Chance let Baxter take over all of the purchasing of products and Chance concentrated on selling products and building the company. One day the fellow who owned the building came in to their offices and said he wanted to sell them the building. They agreed to purchase the building for three hundred thousand dollars, on a ten-year land contract with a small down payment. The business continued to grow and they needed more and more money to build their product line. They hired additional employees and Chance and Baxter got less and less income from the company. Chance failed to control or to pay attention to purchasing and Baxter kept them broke.

Chance had to borrow more and more money to keep the company going. On paper Chance's financial position looked great.

With the growing value of the company, his house, the building, etc., it "looked" as if his net worth was now more then a million dollars. Interest rates continued to climb; their interest rates were now over twenty-two percent. It kept getting harder and harder to pay back the banks. One day Baxter told Chance he had people who wanted to buy the building.

Chance said, "That sounds good to me."

Baxter said, "We should have the building appraised."

Chance agreed to hire an appraiser and the building and property were appraised at seven hundred fifty thousand dollars.

Chance felt really good because if they could get that much for the building, they could pay off the land contract and have almost half a million dollars left.

The next week, two businessmen from New York City came to see the building. After three days of tough negotiations, Chance and Baxter agreed to sell the building for one million dollars worth of investment gemstones and one hundred thousand dollars in cash and the buyer would take over the note due on the land contract. Papers were drawn up by their attorney and the deal was closed.

The following week Chance and his attorney flew to Houston to pick up the gems from a certified gem appraiser. Chance chartered a plane and the two of them flew to Houston to meet with the appraisers. Chance got to pick out the gems, each one had its own certificate of retail value. It took almost five hours of going through the stones to make the selection. They were to get all of them for the wholesale value or fifty percent of the certified appraisal.

There were not only stones, but all kinds of rings, bracelets, pins, etc. Chance chose carefully, mixing stones with rings and bracelets.

They flew back to Webster around midnight with all of the investment gems packed in Chance's briefcase. Chance felt like they were jewel thieves or smugglers or something. Chance got home that night and dumped the gemstones all over Ann's bed where she lay sleeping. It certainly looked like the loot from a jewel heist.

The next morning Chance showed the jewelry to Baxter and they deposited the gems in a safety deposit box at the bank. They received a cashier's check, by Federal Express, that same morning and the sale of the building was complete.

It didn't take them long to go through a hundred thousand dollars. Chance made a deal to borrow money from a Wichita bank for forty percent of the value of the gemstones. A little later Chance decided to send some of the gems to Christie's in New York to be auctioned off. Chance got the bank to agree to let him ship several highly appraised gemstones by Federal Express to Christie's for the auction.

Christie's sent back a message to them that said that they would put in a minimum bid of less then five thousand dollars on the entire lot of gems. The certificates said the gems were valued at almost five hundred thousand dollars. Chance didn't know what to do except to have them returned to the bank, because the bank had given him a loan for almost one hundred seventy-five thousand dollars on these stones. When the loan was due the bank agreed to renew it, but they wanted another two hundred thousand dollars worth of stones put in escrow to hold against the loan.

Baxter kept buying more and more products until Chance exploded one day and told Baxter they were through. He would buy him out of the company. Baxter agreed to take gemstones and products for his share of the company and the deal was done. But far too late. The rapid growth and overextending of their assets doomed the company there was soon no doubt he would have to close the company.

During all this, Chance's mother who had been complaining about being sick for the last three years was finally diagnosed as having cancer. The doctor told her they would start her on chemotherapy on Monday morning. Chance and Ann went to the hospital Sunday night to see her. Mrs. Clark was worried about losing her hair, but Ann told her not to worry because she would get her a wig that would look just like her own hair.

Chance's mother was having fluid drained from her lungs during the last two days and the doctor had removed the tubes just before Chance and Ann arrived at the hospital that Sunday evening. The doctor said she needed to do some walking, so Ann helped her put on her house slippers and Chance held her arm and walked her down the hospital corridor. When they got back to her room, Chance asked if she wanted to get back in bed. She said, "No, I just want to sit here in the chair and watch TV for awhile."

Chance and Ann told her, "Good night, Mom, we'll see you tomorrow.

They drove home from the hospital which took just a little more then ten minutes and when they walked in the door, the phone was ringing. It was Chance's dad and he told Chance the hospital just called and said we needed to come to the hospital right away.

Chance said, "Don't you think it could wait until tomorrow? We just came from the hospital and Ann's mom was bringing Shane home in a few minutes."

Mr. Clark said, "I don't know. They said they needed us come right now."

Chance said, "OK, we'll go back to the hospital."

Ann called her mother to tell her they had to go back to the hospital and they would pick up Shane a little bit later.

Ten minutes later and they were back at the hospital. Chance's dad was waiting for them outside his mother's room. A few minutes passed and a doctor came out and said, "I'm sorry, but she is gone. We did everything we could."

Chance and Ann were in shock. They left his mom less then thirty minutes before; she couldn't have died just like that. The doctor took them into her room. Chance's mother was on the bed, looking as if she were sleeping just like Chance had seen her a hundred times before. She had a big bruise on the right side of her forehead.

The doctor said, "She was sitting in her chair when a nurse came in to help get her back in bed. Mrs. Clark had a blood clot go through her heart and it killed her instantly. Her head was bruised when she fell out of the chair before a nurse could reach her; she was gone before her head hit the floor."

Chance found a chair and sat down next to his mom's head and just stared in disbelief. Ann came over and stood next to him and his dad stood at the foot of her bed. No one said a word for the next two hours. They just sat or stood in shock.

The next morning Chance took a red suit Chance's father had picked out for his wife's burial to the funeral home. Chance's folks had their picture taken recently and his mother worn this suit for the picture.

Chance couldn't comprehend how she was alive one minute and gone the next. Why did she have to die at only sixty-five years old? Chance knew there were no answers to these questions, at least not here on earth.

The day of the funeral and when the family was with his mother's body for the last time, Chance heard his father say the most eloquent thing he had ever heard his father say to his mother. His father said these simple words: "I'm sure going to miss you honey."

All of them had tears flowing. Those few words told Chance more about the love his father had for his mother then anything he ever heard his father say before. Chance knew about the love between a man and a woman, because he loved Ann so much.

The first eight months of 1982 were some of the worst months of Chance and Ann's life. Chance's mother died on April 4 and by June, they closed their business.

The assets they had left were few. They had a car that had been refinanced twice. They had their furniture, which was worth very little by this time after all the moves and its age since all of the furniture was at least ten years old and most of it was over twenty years old. They had clothes and their house. They couldn't sell the house, they owed almost as much on it as it was now worth, and besides, if they did where would they live?

All Chance knew for sure was he and Annie was still together and they had Shane and a lot of love and support from Chase, Marie and their grandson Curt.

Chance had learned a lot of hard lessons, some he hoped he would never let happen to him again. Chance didn't have a job and they had no money. Ann's mom had been an angel about giving them money if they asked, but unless they didn't have food in the house, they didn't ask.

Chance thought back to when he was sixteen and he came to the realization that the only thing that mattered in his life was Ann. He still had her so whatever else happened they would face it together. One thing for sure in 1982, unless something happened to one of them or to one of their kids, things couldn't get much worse, but they could sure get a lot better.

21

The Great Eighties, so far were certainly not great for the Clarks. They lost almost everything. They had seen three businesses go under that they either owned or owned part of. Chance lost his mother and two years before that he lost one of his closest and dearest friends and his mentor, Karl W. Jones. Karl died June 10, 1980; it was like losing his own father. No, so far the Eighties had not been kind to the Clarks.

One thing in Chance and Ann's life that had always been true was when one door closed another door opened. Another door was about to open when the telephone rang. Chance answered it.

It was his old friend Joe Carver, his friend and assistant when he worked in the parking department in Webster.

Joe Carver said, "I've got a big contract in Houston to increase the parking rates on all of the parking meters. What are the chances of you coming to help me?"

"The chances are really good since I don't have a job or a company to work for at the moment."

Joe said, "I'll tell you what I'll do. I'll pay you three dollars for each mechanism you convert, plus I'll pay your expenses while you are here."

"When do you want me to start?"

"Next week. I should have the parts we'll need this Friday. You can fly into Dallas and we can go to Houston in my van. By the way Chance, are you as fast working on the mechanisms as you used to be?"

"I doubt it since I haven't worked on a parking meter mechanism for years."

The following Monday, Chance flew to Dallas to meet Joe Carver. After Chance picked up his luggage from the baggage carousel, he walked out of the terminal and his old friend Joe was sitting in his van waiting for him.

Chance opened the door of the van and said, "It's good to see a friendly face for a change."

They shook hands and started off to Houston.

Joe spent the entire trip talking about his family and what was happening in the parking meter business, what kind of sales he was going to have this year in his territory. Cars and whatever else came into his mind. Chance was happy and content to just sit and listen. It didn't require any thinking and Chance was happy to be away from Webster and all of the problems he been through. The other nice thing for Chance was that his friend did all of the talking and he didn't even have to answer.

They arrived in Houston late in the afternoon. They checked into the motel and took an extra room and make it into a workshop. Joe brought folding tables, lights, floor covers for the carpet, hand cleaner, tools, parts and cases of pop for them along with two big ice chests. By the time they unloaded everything and ready to start work on the meter mechanisms it was time for dinner. Joe said he knew a great Mexican restaurant and Chance replied it sounds good to me. When they returned to their hotel room, Chance called Ann to see how she and Shane and were doing. Ann answered the phone and Chance said, "Hi,

sweetheart how are you doing?"

"I miss you, that's how I am it's been so long since you were not home every night I forgot how lonesome it is without you."

"I know I miss you too and for one thing you don't talk all the time."

Ann laughed and said, "You mean Joe does?"

"What do you think?"

The next morning Joe and Chance had breakfast at seven and by eight-thirty; they began working on the parking meter mechanisms.

Chance began slowly; it took him all morning just to get used to working with tools again. The only tools he had used for several years were a pen and a phone. As the day went on he began to pick up speed. He was adjusting the meters' winding ring for the coins much easier and faster on the last three meters then the time it took him to do the first one he worked on that morning.

He had set a goal of converting fifty mechanisms the first day. It was after nine o'clock in the evening before he finished the fifty, and he was finished as well!

His goal for the next day was to convert seventy-five meter mechanisms. He had those completed by eight o'clock that night and had time to stop for dinner. Chance's third-day goal was to get a hundred meter mechanisms converted. Again, he had reached his goal before eight that evening. Chance's confidence and speed were coming back to him. Every day after that Chance was knocking out 100 meters a day and doing it before six o'clock in the evening. Chance began thinking of how much he missed the parking meter business. He loved this business and couldn't remember why he ever left the business. Before ten days were over they finished the conversion and Joe wrote Chance a check for two thousand, nine hundred and twenty- five dollars. This was more money than Chance had earned at one time then he had seen in years.

Chance asked Joe "Is there anyone left at Superior Meters that I might know?"

Joe started naming names and most of the people Chance knew were still at the company.

Chance said, "Joe would you call Tom Watts and see if there are any sales territories open in the United States?

"Sure, I'll give him a call right now," he picked up the phone and called.

Tom Watts said, "Let me talk to Chance."

Chance took the phone from Joe and said, "Hi Tom, how are you?

"I'm doing great and Joe tells me you are looking for a job."

"Not only am I looking for one I need a job."

"Would you take the job as Superior's Customer Service Manager and move to Big Springs, Arkansas, where our manufacturing plant is?"

"I'm sure interested in the job."

"How soon could you come to Chicago? Today is Wednesday."

"How about Friday?"

"That's great. I'll see you Friday."

On Friday Tom picked Chance up from O'Hare Airport and drove him to Superior Meter's Chicago office. In thirty minutes Chance was back in the parking business. He would become the customer service manager, but first they planned to hide Chance in the engineering department, because they had not fired the guy who was their current customer service manager in Chicago.

Tom said, "I'll introduce you to your new boss, the company's chief engineer, Tim Hunt."

Chance already knew Tim Hunt; he used to be the President of the Magic Meter Company. Their plant was also in Arkansas, at Woodlake. Chance was introduced to Tim, and Tom told him, "I've just hired you a new engineer, Chance Clark."

"You did what?"

Tom laughed, "Don't worry he is on my payroll. I'm just loaning him to you."

"Well, I can always use a good man. How are you, Chance? It's been a long time since the last time I saw you.

Chance smiled and said, "It sure has been; you were with Magic Meter the last time I saw you in San Francisco at the International Parking Conference."

"Well, they lost some of their magic."

Chance laughed and Tim continued, "Our Director of Manufacturing is here with me. Let me introduce you to him. Chance Clark, this is Frank Spencer. Frank, this is Chance." They shook hands and exchanged greetings.

Tom said, "By the way, you guys are flying out of O'Hare after while, aren't you? It would help me if you could take Chance to the airport with you, because I've got a bid to get out so the plant has some work to do."

Tom said to Chance, "Let me show you around and let you say hello to some of your old friends."

Tom took him into the Chairman of the Board's office and said, "Morley, you remember Chance Clark? He's coming back to work with us."

Morley Penny took Chance's hand and gave it a vigorous shake and said, "Chance, it's good to see you. We don't get many of our good people to come back to work with us. It's great to see you again. I just want you to know, I'm very happy to have you back in the organization and if you need anything, just let me know. I'll see you later, good luck Chance!"

Next, they went to meet Chris Goodhand, the President of Superior Products, the holding company that owned Superior Meters and two other operating companies. Mr. Goodhand's secretary told them he was somewhere out in the factory. They went out into the plant and found Mr. Goodhand playing pingpong with one of the foremen. As they walked up to the table, the foreman sent a ping pong ball flying past Mr. Goodhand.

Tom said, "Chris, I would like to introduce you to our newest employee."

Mr. Goodhand looked at Chance and Tom and said, "Can't you see I'm busy? If it's necessary I'll meet him some other time."

Chance looked at Tom and Tom looked back at Chris Goodhand and said, "OK thanks," and they walked away.

Chance said, "He thinks he's pretty important, doesn't he?"

"He certainly thinks he is. What can I tell you? He's an exuniversity business professor from the University of Chicago."

"I think he missed the classes on human interpersonal relations when he was a student."

Tom grinned, "Also the one on human kindness. Chris Goodhand has written and published books on company management. One of his ideas is if you throw enough money at a problem you can either fix it or it will go away. Another of his ideas is that anybody who has worked in the same job in a company for more then three years and hasn't been promoted or assigned to a different job should be fired."

"How long has he been at Superior?"

"Almost three years."

Hearing that, Chance said, "Maybe he's right, maybe after three years you should be fired."

Tom and Chance laughed together. Then Chance asked, "Why does he think you should be fired if you have worked on a job for more than three years?"

"His theory is after three years in a job you become too comfortable and you don't bring any new ideas to the job."

"Some jobs you can hardly learn about them in three years, much less hone a real skill doing them."

Tim and Frank dropped Chance off at O'Hare Airport at the TWA check-in entrance. Chance flew back to Wichita and Ann and Shane picked him up and drove back to Webster.

Ann asked, "How does it feel to have a job?"

"Wonderful. I'm never going to go back in business for myself again. It's the company life for us from now on."

On Saturday Chance found a 1971 VW bug advertised in the paper. He had to be at work in Big Springs, Arkansas Monday and Ann needed to have a car. Chance bought the VW for seven hundred fifty dollars.

Sunday, Chance and Ann packed as much of his clothes and things in the VW bug as it would hold. Chance told Ann he should leave by lunchtime since he thought it would take about nine hours to drive to Big Springs. Once again as he had done so many times before, Chance was going ahead to find some place for them to live. This time it was different, in the past they had been moving up, now they were starting over.

Before Chance left, he and Ann held each other in an embrace for a long time. They divided up what cash they had left. Chance insisted Ann take an extra twenty dollar bill, but Ann turned it around and said, "No you keep the twenty and you take twenty more out of my half. If Shane and I need money, I'll ask my mom." Chance finally agreed.

Chance figured right, it took him almost nine hours to drive from Webster to Big Springs. The company made a hotel reservation for him at the Ramada Inn in Big Springs and the charges were to be billed directly to the company, which would big a help to Chance.

Chance was pleased that the little VW ran as well as it did and it took less then a tank of gas to make the trip.

Chance's thoughts kept going back over the events of the last few years. He kept thinking about his mother and Karl Jones.

These people meant so much to him. Like his Grandma Cooper, they were major supporters of Chance. Chance thought that a boy or in Chance's case a man, probably never gets over losing his mother. Karl Jones had been like a father to him. In fact, in many ways he was closer to Chance then his own father.

He also was feeling bad for Annie. He couldn't believe what he had put her through over the past thirty years of their marriage.

Truthfully, he didn't know how or why she continued to love him. She hated change and he thrived on it. They say opposites attract, so it must be true. Chance didn't know why she still loved him, but he knew he was sure glad she did. As soon as Chance got into his room, he called Ann to tell her he was in Big Springs safe and sound.

Before Ann hung up, she asked Chance what Big Springs looked like. Chance told her so far all he had seen was the motel and it was all right. Also, he could tell it was just a little town in the Ozark Mountains. Chance started to say good-bye when Ann said, "Chance, in all that's gone on, I forgot tomorrow is your birthday, Happy Birthday my love!"

"Thanks, baby. Maybe starting this new job on my birthday will be lucky for us."

Monday, September 20, 1982, Chance started back to work with Superior Meters, on his forty-sixth birthday. He first started with the company in September of 1960. Chance had breakfast that morning at the hotel and went directly to the Superior plant.

It took Chance only about ten minutes to drive from the Ramada Inn to the plant. Boy! It was nice being in a small town. Big Springs may have been the name of the town, but big it wasn't. Less then ten thousand people lived there. By the time Chance arrived at the Superior plant a few minutes before eight o'clock, Tim Hunt was already at work. Chance walked up the steps to the plant's front entrance, opened the glass door, and walked inside to a small waiting area with glass sliding windows on each side of the entrance way and a locked security door in front of him.

Chance looked inside the sliding glass windows and saw a lady working at a desk on his left as he came in the door. When she saw Chance, she opened the window and asked Chance if she could help him. Chance told her, his name was Chance Clark and he was here to see Tim Hunt, the chief engineer. She picked up the phone and called Tim. He promptly answered and said he would be right out. Just as the lady was telling Chance that Tim would be right out, the security door opened and there was Tim Hunt saying, "Hey, Chance, how are you? Come on in."

Tim extended his hand and Chance reached out to shake it. As Chance and Tim walked through the security door, Tim said, "I guess while we are here, I should introduce you to Tilly Rich, our personnel manager."

It turned out Tilly was the lady Chance had been talking to through the sliding glass window.

Tim said, "Tilly, I want you to meet Chance Clark. He's my new senior product engineer and starting with us today."

Tim turned to Chance and said, "Chance, I want to introduce you to the person who really runs this plant; Tilly Rich, our personnel manager."

Tilly extended her hand and Chance shook hands with her. She said, "Chance, I want to welcome you to Superior and to Big Springs. I hope you will like both."

Tilly was either in her late fifties or early sixties. She was a very sharp lady, very petite and well dressed. Chance immediately liked her.

Tim said, "Tilly, I guess you better do your magic with the papers, so Chance is on the payroll beginning today."

"OK, I'll take care of Chance and his paperwork and when we've finished, I'll bring him back to you."

Tilly asked Chance to sit down as she got out an application for employment form and some other forms for Chance to sign, regarding taxes, social security, etc.

Chance began filling out the papers and when he wrote down the date, it was Monday, September 20, 1982, Chance's forty- sixth birthday. If Tilly noticed it was Chance's birthday, she never mentioned it and Chance refrained from saying anything about it being his birthday.

After Chance finished filling out the paperwork to put him on the payroll, Tilly led him back to the engineering department.

When they arrived, Tim Hunt had two of his engineers in his office discussing a problem with the operation of some meters in Montreal, Canada.

Tilly said, "Chance, I think we should wait until they finish their conversation. I don't think you want any part of this problem."

Then Tilly said, "Here, let me introduce you to the engineering secretary. She's the only one besides Tim Hunt who knows anything back here anyway!"

Tilly said, "Brandy, this is Chance Clark, one of your new boys."

Brandy looked up from her desk and said, "Hi, Chance. I needed one more person to look after in this department," and she smiled at Chance with her mouth and her eyes. Chance felt as though he had known Brandy for a long time, even though they just met.

Chance said, "Well, I sure need a lot of looking after."

Brandy continued to smile and replied "I'm sure you do. All of you engineers are just alike--basically, helpless!"

With that, Chance had to smile. He had been accused of a lot of things, being helpless had never been one of them.

Tilly said, "OK, Chance, mother will look after you. I've got to get back to my desk to see if I can get some more help for the second and third shift tonight."

Tilly left Chance with Brandy.

Brandy told Chance she had a desk for him and took him over to the only empty desk in the whole department. Counting Chance and Tim, they had ten people working in the engineering department.

Brandy told him she was sure Tim would be finished with his meeting in a few minutes. Chance sat down at his new desk. He was facing a blank wall, so he was sure he wouldn't be looking out a window. Brandy said if there was anything he needed, he should just let her know. Chance thought this wouldn't be very hard to do since her desk was less than ten feet away from his. After about thirty minutes, the meeting ended in Tim's office and Tim came out and asked if Brandy had gotten Chance fixed up with a desk. Chance assured him that Brandy had taken good care of him.

Chance had never been in this plant before. He told Tim he had been in the old Big Springs plant in 1962. He heard that the company sold the old plant and made a lot of money on the deal since they sold it to a company that tore it down and built the Big Springs shopping mall on the site.

Tim said, "Come on let me show you around the plant."

Chance got up and followed Tim out a door located at the back of the engineering department. The door took them directly into the tool room. Tim explained they had seven full-time tool makers who could make any kind of tool to make either diecasting or punch press tools. Next, they went into the die-casting department. Tim explained they had five die-casting machines, ranging in size from fifty tons to five hundred tons. In addition, they had a zinc recovery system used as a break down furnace that melted down the excess material from the parts, so as Tim explained they were able to recycle all of the excess zinc material. Tim went on to say that they sent samples of various meter parts to an outside lab to be sure the raw materials they used in the diecast parts met the specifications for the Zamac material, which was a blend of various metals used in die casting. By blending the materials, the parking meter parts could last for twenty, thirty, or even fifty years without breaking.

Next, they watched the biggest die-cast machine operate. Each machine had an operator who watched each part as it was cast. The die-cast molds had two sides; one side was hot where the molten Zamac material flowed into the mold and the other side of the mold had cold water continuously flowing into it. Each part had a cycle time required for the two parts of the mold to come together to form the part.

Tim said, "You know, it's kind of like sex--you got one hot side and one cold side. The only difference is that you don't have to wait nine months to see the results, only about ninety seconds."

About that time the mold separated and the operator reached in with a long steel rod and knocked the part loose from the cold side of the mold. The part dropped onto a conveyor belt submerged in water which was used to cool the part off and then it was dumped into a holding rack at the end of the conveyor belt. Then the part was picked up by a break off and trim person, who placed the part into a punch press to trim off the excess material. The excess material was then dropped onto a conveyor belt under the floor, which took the material back to an upright conveyor belt that dropped it back into the break down furnace. From the break down machine, there was a long laundry-type chute that was heated all along its route, taking the molten zinc back to the die-cast machines.

The trimmed parts went into a large metal basket on a wooden pallet. The pallets with the baskets were picked up by a forklift operator and taken to the vibrator department. Every stamped or die-cast part made in the plant came to be processed in the vibrator department to smooth off burrs and get the die-cast parts cleaned and ready for painting. The vibrator department had one operator with a variety of machines, all which generally worked on the same principle. Each machine had smooth, man-made stones made in various sizes, shapes and textures, depending on the size and material of the part to be prepared. Chance thought this process was very interesting as he watched the die-cast parts being shaken, turned and moved through these stones, he though it was kind of like watching people swimming in the ocean through a lot of waves; one minute you could see them, the next minute they disappeared under the water. It was the same with the parts; one minute you saw them, the next minute they were under the stones.

The parts kept going up and down in the stones. Each machine also had water or some type of chemical to clean the part.

The next stop on the plant tour was the buff and polish department. This department processed all of the zinc housing parts. The parts were polished as brightly as if they were silver.

Again, this process was to smooth the parts and make paint adhere better. Chance realized the whole process took a lot of time and effort just to get a part ready to paint.

The next department was the machining department. This department processed the iron housings, drilling holes for mounting the hardware for the door and mechanism lock-up cap. They also machined the parts to make all of the iron parts the same size, so if the part was being sent out as a replacement part it would fit any housing made by Superior ten or fifteen years ago.

The fabrication department was the next one Tim and Chance visited. Chance was amazed that even though Superior had been making parking meters for forty-six years, so many parts were literally being hand made in this department. The coin segments were being measured, cut and ground down to the proper size by hand. Chance thought, no wonder I had problems with coin segments not working in the field, there has to be a better way of making these parts.

The "fab" department had dozens of punch presses used to stamp out various meter parts. There were about twenty operators working in the department in addition to a foreman and two set-up men. The set-up people were like sub-foremen, preparing the next machine for the operator to make whatever part was needed for production or for a parts order.

From the "fab" department, they went to the paint department where there was a continuous running chain to hang parts on to be painted. The parts were placed on paint fixtures,

called trees by the department employees due to the shape of the fixtures. Each fixture was designed to hold a certain type of part. Tim explained they used a wet on wet paint system using an electrostatic system to make the paint cover each part completely. The concept was simple. The paint fixtures, through contact with the chain, carried a negative electrical charge and the paint, as it was shot through paint guns, had a positive electrical charge. The paint wrapped around each part as the negative charge attracted the positively charged paint. Tim said since the government mandated removal of lead from paint, the paint manufacturers were having a really hard time providing paint with the same quality of finish for the parking meters Superior provided twenty years ago.

Chance and Tim went next to the timer room where Superior made the clocks for the meters. The only two parts in a timer or clock Superior didn't make, were the hairsprings which were imported from Switzerland and the jewels for the balance wheels.

Next, they looked in the lock room where the special parking meter locks and keys were made. Tim explained only two people in the company had access to the lock and key combinations assigned to the cities. Superior felt this was one of the highest security points in the company, since Superior didn't want any ex-employees going into partnership with the cities with keys stolen from the plant.

This had never happened and they wanted to be sure it never did. The last two stops on the tour were the areas Chance knew the most about, assembling the housings and mechanisms. Again Chance was surprised that everything about this process was still being done by hand. The only difference from Chance doing assembly in the field was that the factory had air-powered screw drivers to put the parts together. Each mechanism was coin tested and adjusted by a final adjustor. After the mechanism was adjusted properly, each was sent to a run-down inspector to be sure that each mechanism gave not only the correct amount of time, but so many minutes extra so the motorist was assured they got the time they paid for. Tim said the only thing left in the process is for the meters to go into the box and get shipped out the door. Just as Tim said this, a forklift cut in front of them and picked up a pallet of meters being shipped to New York City.

"Well," Tim said, "I guess we took the whole morning on our tour. It's lunchtime. I go home for lunch, so I'll see you after lunch."

Chance took his keys and headed out the front door of the plant. The rest of the day went by quickly and at five o'clock, Brandy said, "Chance, it's time to go home."

In five minutes the engineering department was empty. This was the first time Chance had ever been alone on his birthday. He was as lonesome as he had ever felt in all his life. He had dinner by himself, but all he could think about was how everyone else who worked in the engineering department was at home with their family. The more he thought about it, the sorrier he felt for himself. Chance felt so lonely. When he got to his room, he called Ann.

Shane answered the phone and when he found out it was his daddy, Shane said, "Happy Birthday daddy! Did you have a birthday cake at work?"

"No, no birthday cake."

Shane asked, "Why not?"

"Well, the people at work didn't know it was my birthday." "I'm sorry, daddy. I miss you. Here's mom."

Ann wished him happy birthday. Ann had been wishing Chance happy birthday for the past thirty years, so this made him feel better. Chance and Ann talked for almost an hour and the whole conversation came down to how much they missed each other and loved each other. Everything else they said meant nothing.

Ann said, "I almost forgot, tell me the telephone number for the motel? Chase wants to call you."

Chance gave her the number. He could sense she was as lonesome as he was, but he didn't want to say anything about it. He knew it would only make both of them feel worse. They finally hung up the phone since both of them could tell the other was about to break down in tears.

Chance tried to think about the day, but all he could think about was being alone on his birthday and for the first time in his life his mother would not be wishing him "Happy Birthday."

He would never hear his mother's voice for the rest of his life. Chance turned on the Monday night football game on TV, but he couldn't get interested. His phone rang and it was Chase calling to wish his dad happy birthday. Then Marie and Curt got on the phone to wish him happy birthday. After talking with Chase for twenty or thirty minutes, Chance felt better.

After Chance hung up from his conversation with Chase, he realized how lucky he was to have a family that loved him and he decided to stop feeling sorry for himself. Before he went to sleep, he called Ann again to tell her how much he loved her and thanked her for loving him and giving him two wonderful sons.

22

The next morning Chance was up early and ready to get things done at work. The sun was shining and it was already warm. Chance was not the kind of person to sit around feeling sorry for himself very long no matter what happened to him. He was ready for fast-paced action and changes, but on September 21, 1982, Chance couldn't have had any concept of what lay in store for him over the next five years.

Chance's first week back with Superior went quickly and he decided to stay over the weekend to try and find a house they could buy or rent. Early Saturday morning, Chance went to the local Century 21 Agency to begin looking for a house that they could assume a loan on. The real estate agent, Shirley Jones took him around to see several homes that were on the market, but nothing was what Chance was looking for. The agent said she would keep looking for something for him. Chance told Ms. Jones his wife would be coming to Big Springs in a couple of weeks and they would work with her then.

On Sunday Chance drove around the countryside exploring areas around Big Springs. He decided although the Ozarks were not the Rocky Mountains they were very beautiful. No matter what direction from Big Springs Chance drove the mountain views were great. He was sorry Ann wasn't here to share them with him.

Chance talked on the telephone with Ann everyday so they could share with each other their day. On Sunday they talked twice; it seemed to both of them it was the hardest day of the week for them to be apart.

Monday, Chance was in the plant by seven-thirty in the morning and Tim Hunt was already hard at work. When Tim saw Chance, he asked him to come into his office.

Tim asked Chance, "Do you still have a valid passport? I know you were working in Australia for about a year."

"As far as I know it's still good and we did have them renewed." "Good. We have some problems with seven thousand mechanisms in Dublin, Ireland and I think you're the person to take charge of getting them fixed."

Chance asked, "What's the matter with the meters?"

"To tell you the truth, I'm not sure we really know. Listening to our distributor over there you would think they are falling off the post. What I need for you to do is to get there as soon as possible." "I'll need to get my passport from Kansas and then I can leave whenever you want me to."

"OK. I think it would be good if you could leave by next Monday and I think it would be a good idea to stop in London to see our distributor for the UK on your way to Dublin."

Chance said, "If you think it's all right, I will go to Webster tomorrow and be back on Sunday, ready to leave on Monday."

"That will be great!"

Chance went to his desk and called Ann. Ann answered on the second ring and Chance asked her if she had Shane ready for school.

"Not yet, but he is up and in the shower. Why are you calling so early on Monday morning? Aren't you afraid the company will think you are spending too much money on the telephone calling me all of the time? I love to talk to you, but I don't want you to get in trouble the second week you're back with the company."

"Well, this is business. I need you to find my passport and make sure it's still valid, because I've got to go to England and Ireland for the company next week."

"You're kidding aren't you?"

"No, I'm not kidding. They're having a lot of trouble with some meters in Dublin and they want me to find out what's wrong with them.

"I don't know where our passports are!"

Chance told her he thought they were in the top dresser drawer in their bedroom.

Ann said, "OK, let me look for them."

A few seconds later Ann came back on the line and said she found the passports. She checked the expiration date and found their passports were good until September 1983. Chance told Ann he was coming home tomorrow to get things ready to leave next Monday for Ireland and England.

Chance spent the rest of the day reviewing the bills of materials for the Dublin meters. He also found samples of the mechanisms that had been built for the Dublin order. As he checked the samples he found several times when he ran the Irish coins through the meters, they skipped. In other words, they didn't give the right amount of time for the coins. The winding pawl did not engage into the winding ring's teeth to wind up the clock in the meter.

Chance also found these meters were nothing like any meters he had ever worked with. They had an overtime feature. After talking with the engineer who designed the bill of material and built the sample mechanisms for the Dublin order, Chance discovered this overtime feature was something unique used only in England and Ireland.

The concept of the overtime feature in England was to give an indication of what was called excess time. This was a thirtyminute period of time after legal paid parking time expired. During the excess period, if you got a parking ticket you paid about five pounds to the local council. However, if you got a ticket in the one-hour penalty time, you had to pay an additional fifteen pounds and this was paid to the British Government. That was the way it worked in England and no one at Superior knew for sure how the two overtimes worked in Ireland.

Later that day Chance got his plane tickets from Tim. His flight schedule took him from Big Springs to St. Louis, then to New York, then to London. He would be in London for two nights and go on to Dublin from there.

In London he was to meet Graham Rommey, Vice President and Director of Operations for Superior's Distributor for the United Kingdom, UK Parking Controls. Chance was just to get acquainted and make sure they were not having the same problems they were having in Ireland with the overtime meters.

Mr. Ian Stark, Superior's Vice President of International Sales, would meet Chance in Dublin and introduce Chance to the Distributor for Ireland, Sean Sommers and help him however he could. Chance met Ian when Ian first joined Superior. In fact, Chance took Ian on his very first sales call after joining the company. So Chance knew Ian very well and they had always liked each other. In fact, Ian tried to get Chance to come back to Superior when he was at the University of Iowa to run Superior's Canadian Company. They couldn't get together on a salary so Chance turned down the job.

Chance didn't get a lot of sleep that night, worrying about whether he could really solve the meter problems in Dublin. He felt his future with the company would be greatly enhanced if he could. The next morning, Chance was on the road before six o'clock on his way to Webster. Chance thought Tim had been very thoughtful by getting Chance a travel advance in cash to cover his expenses for his trip to Europe. Chance was pleased with the way the little green VW bug handled and by changing his route between Big Springs and Webster he made it into his driveway at home in eight hours.

Ann met him at the door and they fell into each other's arms. They quickly closed and locked the front door and kept kissing and holding each other until they were in their bedroom. Their clothes were off in record time and were soon on their bed with loving on their mind; only their actions were quicker then their thoughts. As they lay together holding each other, they became one and whole again, they were where they belonged- -together. After they made love, they talked about how much they missed each other. They knew they had to get dressed to pick up Shane from school and they dressed almost as quickly as they undressed, but not with the same urgency.

They left their bedroom hand in hand and took the VW bug to pick up Shane. Shane ran quickly to the car and gave his dad a big hug and kiss. God, Chance thought, it was wonderful to be home.

Chance would leave early Sunday morning to be sure he was in Big Springs to get his flight on Monday. Chance was excited about going to England and Ireland, but he was filled with mixed emotions since he hated being away from Ann. Each time they said good-bye, each was concerned something could happen to the other. Chance's mother once told him during the time Ann was so seriously ill. "I don't know what would happen to you if you ever lost Ann."

These words haunted Chance every time he was away from Ann. He didn't know how he could go on, how he could even function without his other half, his better half. Chance also knew they were getting older and every day away from Ann was a day he could never get back. Both Chance and Ann did their best to put on a brave front when they said their good-byes. Chance made it out of town before the tears were running down his cheeks.

Chance tried to think of the great adventure and the opportunity to prove his worth once more to his old company. Lord, he needed some new successes, not only for himself, but for Ann.

Chance got to Big Springs, checked back in to the Ramada Inn and called Ann to let her know he was safely there. Their conversation was short because each of them was afraid they might start crying on the phone and let the other one know how badly they really felt about being apart.

Chance said, "I love you, I'll call you tomorrow before I leave the country."

Early the next morning, Chance stopped by the plant to pick up telephone numbers for the companies in England and Ireland, as well as any other bits of information regarding the Dublin meters.

Tim asked Chance to call him as soon as he had an idea on how to make the Dublin mechanisms work right and Chance said he would certainly do that.

Chance's flight from Big Springs to St. Louis left a little after nine o'clock, so he drove over to the airport. He thought it was sure easier to get to the airport in Big Springs then when he lived in Chicago and flew out of O'Hare. From the plant in Big Springs to the airport took less then five minutes. When he arrived at the airport, there was no one waiting to check in. He walked up the counter, they checked him in for the flight, tagged his suitcase for London and in less then ten minutes from the time he left Superior's Parking Meter plant, he was checked in for his flight and ready to go to London.

Chance took his seat on the airplane and almost before the wheels were up and locked Chance was fast asleep. The next thing he knew, the pilot came on over the intercom to tell the passengers to be sure their seat belts were fastened they were landing at St. Louis's Lambert Field.

Chance took the shuttle bus from the east terminal to the main terminal. He went to the TWA counter and checked in for his flight to New York's Kennedy Airport and they also gave him his boarding pass and seat assignment for the JFK to London flight. Chance made his way through security and started his long walk to gate 48 on the "C" concourse. Chance wondered if any airport in the world had longer concourses then St. Louis's Lambert Field, surely not. His flight to JFK was one of the best kinds of flights to have--it was uneventful. He walked off his plane and found his flight to London Heathrow was only two gates from his arrival gate.

Chance's experience with overnight flights was limited to the trip to Australia almost ten years ago. He couldn't remember much about that flight, except holding Shane all night and how uncomfortable he had been. He discovered without holding a two- year old, these overnight flights were still damned uncomfortable. About six in the morning, Chance raised his window shade and looked out. He could see the English countryside as their plane began its approach into Heathrow Airport. Chance had always heard how beautiful the English countryside was and it was beautiful! Chance had the feeling he was coming home since most of his ancestors came from England.

When they arrived at the gate, he went to clear customs and immigrations, and he instantly experienced the British system of organization. People were coming into Heathrow from every corner of the world. As Chance approached the immigration hall, everyone was lined up in several lines. They had several officers on duty checking passports. As each line moved up, there was an officer directing people to an immigration officer, so the lines moved quickly and orderly. Soon after this experience, Chance learned in England you never had "lines," you had "queues" just like he remembered in Australia. Whatever they called them.

Chance, was impressed by their organization and how quickly they handled the thousands of people coming into Heathrow Airport every day.

For whatever reasons his ancestors left England, he was already falling in love with it. Chance collected his suitcase and left the customs area without any problem or delay. Then he exchanged his US dollars for British pounds. He found this a little tough, as one hundred US dollars got him just over sixty pounds.

Chance went outside for his first breath of English air. Although, it was only late September the air was nippy. No, it was cold! After coming from Arkansas the air felt really cold to him. Chance located a taxi stand, called a taxi rank in England and waited his turn in the queue. He soon got into one of the famous black London cabs he had always heard about. The cabby placed his suitcase on the left front seat of the taxi and went around and got into the right front seat. The cabby used the actual words Chance had heard in the movies, "Where to governor?"

Chance held his laughter inside and told the driver the name of his hotel. The cabby replied, "Right, governor."

Chance's hotel was located in an industrial area of London and Chance thought to himself, I sure wouldn't recommend this hotel to anyone. He knew he could stay here all right for a couple of nights, since he lived and slept in a lot worse places growing up. When Chance got to his room, he telephoned the office of UK Parking Controls and asked to speak to Graham Rommey. When Mr. Rommey came on the line, Chance told him it was Chance Clark with Superior Meters. Mr. Rommey said he would pick Chance up the next morning to take him on meter checks with him if he would like to see their parking meter operations. Chance told him he would love to see his operation. Mr.

Rommey said he would be at the hotel at four-thirty. Chance said he would be happy to see him.

The next morning Chance was waiting in the lobby of the hotel at the appointed time and it was completely empty except for him. Even the desk clerk was in a little room behind the desk. Chance could see the desk clerk sleeping in a chair. At exactly four-thirty a car pulled up in front of the hotel and a man in his forties hopped out. Chance went out the front door of the hotel and said to the man coming around the car, "You must be Graham Rommey."

The man replied, "And you must be Chance Clark."

They shook hands and Graham motioned for Chance to get into the car. Chance started to go around and get into the right front seat of the car when Graham said, "Did you want to drive?"

Chance stopped in mid-step and turned around to get into the left side of the car. Both men were laughing as they took their proper seats in the car.

Graham began driving toward Westminster and as they drove, Graham explained to Chance Westminster was the part of the city that everyone thinks of as London since it is the most recognized area of Greater London. He went on to say that the city of London is a very small part of Greater London. The city itself is where Lloyd's of London is located and is the financial district of the city. Westminster is the part of London that is always pictured in the movies, Piccadilly Circus, Bond Street, Big Ben, Westminster Abbey, the Parliament Building, Victoria Station, and 10 Downing Street.

Graham said, "Even 007, James Bond has his headquarters, "Whitehall," in Westminster. Although it was still very dark, Chance began to see places that looked very familiar to him from seeing them in the movies.

Graham knew London like Chance knew Webster. When you work and live on the street as parking meter people do you soon know everything that is going on in the city and every building and store in it. As they drove along Graham explained he had ten "blokes" who worked on the streets checking and repairing every meter before it was time for the meters to begin operating at eight o'clock in the morning.

That sounded familiar since that's how Chance ran his meter operation back in Kansas. Chance knew he was a long way from Kansas and it certainly had been a long road since his first trip checking meters on that cold Christmas Eve morning in Webster in 1955.

After driving past Lord Nelson's statue, Graham headed his car down a small dark street and before long he stopped the car in front of a small cafe. Graham told Chance that this was where he met six of his chaps each morning at six-thirty and they had a cuppa.

He continued, "I give them information on any reported meters out of service and they give me their service reports from the day before."

They went into the cafe and Graham introduced Chance to six of his "blokes," as Graham called them. Chance shook hands with each of the men and sat down in a chair at a large round table.

Graham began handing out various sheets of paper with out- of-service meter information to each man and in turn, received a daily report from each one. After the business was finished the men joshed Chance about coming over from the factory in Arkansas to check up on them. Chance gave it back to them by telling them Graham had asked him to come over to help him because he was having so much trouble keeping his chaps in line. With that, the men soon began picking on one of their own coworkers, saying, "David, we knew you were a trouble-maker and Graham couldn't handle you, but we never thought he would have to call in the damn Yanks to keep you line."

The man they were kidding just smiled and ducked his head.

Chance picked up the bill for all of the men and they promptly told Chance, "You can come back again, soon Yank."

The men left the cafe and began walking back to their inspection routes.

Graham and Chance got into the car and after about another ten to fifteen minute drive they came to a large square. Graham said, "This is where I meet my other four men."

Graham pointed out the four men standing on the corner. Graham pulled his car up and parked next to them. Graham got out of the car, so Chance did the same. Graham introduced him to the four parking meter servicemen. Graham spoke with each of the men and at the same time dispensed report sheets and picked up their reports. They didn't stay long. Graham and Chance were soon back in the car, headed to Graham's office. Graham told him as they were leaving the square, "This is Grosvenor Square and that's the American Embassy over there."

Chance just caught sight of the Embassy as they turned the corner. After they arrived at Graham's office, they sat down and talked about parking meter operations for two hours or more. Chance enjoyed having an opportunity to talk with someone who was as knowledgeable about meters and how to run a meter operation as Chance was. Chance hadn't found that many people in the parking meter business that were his equal, Chance considered Graham to be.

Graham said he wanted to introduce Chance to the Managing Director of the Company, Mr. Bryan Fitzfield. Graham telephoned Mr. Fitzfield and told him Chance Clark from Superior Meters was in London and wanted to meet him and say hello. Mr. Fitzfield said he would come over in a few minutes. The few minutes turned into twenty, thirty and finally after another call from Graham, Mr. Fitzfield showed up after an hour and a half. Bryan Fitzfield came into Graham's office. Graham introduced him to Chance. Mr. Fitzfield said, "I understand you recently came back to work for Superior."

Chance replied that was correct, and Mr. Fitzfield said, "I'm very busy and if we need something from you, we'll let you know." With that, he turned around and walked out the door. In the space of less then a month, Chance had been ignored and treated rudely by two people. First, the President of Superior and now by UK Parking Control's Managing Director. Oh well, it was the Eighties!

Graham said to Chance, "Well, you've met our glorious leader, Bryan Fitzfield."

Chance laughed and replied, "I sure have."

"It's past time for me to go home, so I'll take you back by your hotel. I hope you don't judge our company and the UK by the kind of treatment you received from Bryan."

"Don't worry the UK doesn't have a lock on rude people." They laughed and headed for Graham's car. On the way out of the office, they met a woman in the hallway.

Graham said, "Chance, this is Mr. Fitzfield's secretary, Ruby.

Chance, I want you to know I slept with her last night."

Ruby said, "Graham!"

Graham continued, "This woman is my first wife."

Chance smiled at Ruby, who was miffed at Graham and Chance asked, "Graham, how many times have you been married?"

"Once!"

The next morning Chance left London on the short flight to Dublin. On his arrival in Dublin and as soon as he cleared passport control, he was met by Sean Sommers. Chance guessed Mr. Sommers was in his late sixties. He was as slim as a rail, with thinning white hair and to Chance, Mr. Sommers looked like someone who had spent his life in show business. Mr. Sommers had a twinkle in his eye, a look of devilment in his eyes if Chance had ever seen anyone with that look.

Mr. Sommers was having a real problem with the 7,500 new meters made by Superior that they recently installed in Dublin.

Chance knew his assignment was to get the customer satisfied and with the problem fixed as quickly as possible, and with the least amount of cost to Superior. Mr. Sommers was truly the "actor" Chance thought. He began to dramatically describe the problems with the meters. He told Chance if they couldn't get this problem resolved soon, he might not only lose his business,

but the corporation might even take his home.

Chance asked, "Who is the corporation?"

Mr. Sommers replied, "The Dublin Corporation," Chance understood now that the Dublin Corporation was the City of Dublin's Government.

After they checked Chance into the Berkeley Court Hotel they went directly to Mr. Sommers' office. Chance soon discovered Mr. Sommers' company was also a wholesale company that supplied nearly all brands of clocks and watches in Ireland. In addition, they were in the time clock business and supplied and maintained time clocks for the major offices, department stores, government offices and manufacturing plants, so parking meter sales and service was only one of the three businesses Mr. Sommers owned.

Chance suspected Mr. Sommers was probably very well off and he doubted the problems with the meters would cost him either his business or his home. Chance found out some time later that Sean had lived in New York and Chicago for several years and his knowledge of America was excellent. Sean also loved horses and owned several.

Mr. Sommers introduced Chance to Shamus Murphy, his Director of Parking Meter Services. Shamus Murphy was a little taller then Mr. Sommers and Chance guessed a little younger. Mr. Murphy began to explain their problems with the new meters to Chance. The Dublin Corporation had increased the parking rates, so all of the new meters were manufactured with the new parking rates. In addition, since they increased the rates, they added the fifty pence coin.

As Chance began studying the meters, he could see the problem. Due to the overtime feature on the meter, it had a lot of extra parts to make it work. Chance tried adjusting the meters and if he got the five and ten pence coins to work right, the fifty pence coin would either skip or give too much time. After spending several hours trying to adjust the meters to get them to work right, Chance concluded the coin segments were not made correctly; they were too short and the teeth on the winding rings were not spaced right. Chance kept finding more and more things that were not right on the front half of the meter mechanism--the coin-handling portion of the meter.

Many of the front mechanism frames were poorly made which was contributing to the problem. The floor of the mechanism frames, where the coin segment attached to the frames were in some cases too thin and others too thick. Even the hole where the handle shaft went through the frame was not properly lined up. Chance concluded, but didn't say it, that these were some of the poorest made parking meters he had ever seen. Chance was shocked Superior would have ever let these meters leave the factory.

Mr. Sommers came back to the meter repair shop and asked Chance how he was doing. Chance explained he was still working to evaluate the total problem and should reach his conclusions by tomorrow.

Mr. Sommers said, "I've been told you're one of the most knowledgeable people on Superior Parking Meters in the world."

"I don't know about that, but I will tell you this; I will do everything possible to get the problems fixed on these meters for you and the Dublin Corporation."

"Chance if you say you can get the meters fixed that are good enough for me."

Chance heard the words being said, but doubted that at the moment what Mr. Sommers said was what he truly believed.

Chance could sense the doubt in Mr. Sommers' voice.

Mr. Sommers said, "I'm going to take you back to the Berkeley Court Hotel and I will be back at six-thirty to pick you and Mr. and Mrs. Stark up for a dinner party at my house with the officials from the Dublin Corporation. I want them to know that Sommers Company and Superior are working on the meter problem.

When Chance returned to his room, the message light on his telephone was blinking. He called the operator and Chance was told to call Ian Stark in room 512. Chance called Ian and they made arrangements to meet in the lobby bar at six o'clock to give Chance some time to fill Ian in on what he had found with the meters. Six o'clock came quickly and Chance rushed down to meet Ian. It had been a long time since they had seen each other and a lot had happened since that time.

Chance had taken Ian on his first sales call in the parking meter business out in Western Iowa. Ian was ten to fifteen years older then Chance. Chance always liked Ian a lot and although Chance thought it was a mutual feeling, sometimes it was hard to separate Ian's real feelings from his sales persona. Ian had been the President of Superior until about four months ago, when he had stepped down to become Vice President of International Sales.

Nine months before Chance came back to Superior, the company had been sold to Cayler Company, a big furniture manufacturer and Ian exercised all of the stock options he held in Superior and got rich. Chance remembered the few shares of Superior stock he held for almost fifteen years and he finally sold them for a loss. That's what you call it when you buy a stock at fourteen dollars and fifty cents and sell it for nine dollars and seventy-five cents. The really amazing part of the company sale was within six months, his friend Morley Penny became Chairman of the Board of Cayler. Along with one other outside Director, they had taken control of Cayler. All the other directors were voted out and Penny and the other Director began liquidating Cayler by selling all of the thirty- two furniture factories they owned in the United States.

Waiting in the lobby bar was Chance's friend, Ian and his wife, Betty. Chance and Ian rushed to meet each other and shook hands. Ian said, "Boy am I happy to have you here to help with the Dublin problem. Chance, tell me what you think we can do solve this problem. Sean has been all over me like a wet horse blanket, so you've got to get this problem fixed right now."

Ian introduced Chance to his wife and they sat back down at the Stark's table.

Chance quickly explained about the two problems with the Dublin meters; first, the design and second, the poor quality of manufacturing of the meters.

Ian said, "Let's keep this to ourselves. Just say you are still analyzing the problem and we'll make the meters right."

23

When they arrived at Sean Sommers' home, the moon was just coming up and it reminded Chance of the moonrise Chance and Ann experienced on Kanopolis Lake in Kansas long ago. It was a beautiful old brick house built in the 1700s. The backyard had a commanding view as the yard sloped down to the Irish Sea. When they went inside, the house was filled with people, all friends of Sean and his wife, Patricia.

These folks were officials with the Dublin Corporation, who were in charge of the parking meter program. The Dublin Corporation Delegation was headed by Paddy O'Hara. After the introductions, Chance was soon in a conversation with Paddy O'Hara about the problems with the Dublin meters.

Chance assured him that Superior would take care of the problem and fix the meters. Chance began to question Paddy about how Dublin used the overtime feature on the Dublin meters.

Paddy asked one of the junior officials, Shannon O'Connor, how the overtime was used. Shannon said it wasn't used at all. These were the words Chance wanted to hear.

After a "wee bit" more conversation, and being in a house full of Irish politicians that takes a lot longer than a "New York minute"- it was decided since they had had the overtime feature on their meters since they first got meters from an English manufacturer made with the overtime feature. So when the Corporation ordered meters from

Superior they just copied what they had used in the past and although their old meters had the overtime feature it was never used by them. Just as Chance thought! They also concluded that those English meters never worked right for as long as they had them.

Chance got an agreement right then and there that Superior could take the overtime feature off all of the meters since the Dublin Corporation had never used this feature. Now Chance knew how to fix the rest of the problems, he had full confidence now.

Three weeks later Chance returned to Dublin. The new meter parts needed to fix the Dublin meters were scheduled to arrive by airfreight the following day. Chance wanted to spend the rest of the day recovering from his overnight flight from the States and get everything set up to begin changing out the meter parts the next morning. After Chance cleared customs and immigration at the Dublin airport, Sean Sommers met him and drove him to the Berkeley Court Hotel, Chance's Dublin home. Chance liked this hotel as well as any hotel he had ever stayed in. The rooms were very well done and the service was exceptional. Sean told Chance he would come back in two hours to take him to the meter shop to get set up for the next day and he added that he would have Shamus Murphy waiting for his arrival to organize whatever Chance needed.

When Chance arrived at the meter shop, Shamus Murphy was waiting for him as promised. The two of them quickly organized everything for the next day's activities. Shamus was dressed in a blue blazer, a sweater vest, gray slacks and a white shirt with blue tie. Chance thought this was very formal attire for a parking meter service man. Chance discovered Shamus got into repairing parking meters the same way he had. Shamus was a watchmaker by trade and training and with their common background the two men developed a very friendly relationship.

Shamus said, "I'm sorry I was a bit standoffish when we met three weeks ago, but I was going through a personal problem that was only resolved last week."

Shamus began telling Chance an unbelievable story about his only child, his daughter Patricia. Chance thought every third woman in

Ireland must be named Patricia. Shamus' daughter Patricia had been a flight attendant for Aer Lingus, the Irish national airline. She had been based in London and then in New York. In New York, she met a young man from Jordan and after going together for some time, they were married in Ireland. Not long after they were married, she discovered she was going to have a baby. Her husband told Patricia he wanted her to quit her job and they would move to Jordan to have their baby. Patricia agreed.

Patricia's new in-laws were very wealthy and they wanted her husband to come home to help run the family business. Patricia's baby was a son and very soon after his birth, her husband and his family began treating her as if she was a third-class citizen. She tried to leave him, but he beat her and told her if she ever tried to leave him again, he would have her killed.

Shamus and his wife made a trip to Jordan to see Patricia and their new grandson when the baby was about nine months old.

When her husband was away from home, Patricia told them what was happening to her. They couldn't believe it; they didn't want to believe it. That evening when Patricia's husband came home, Shamus tried to talk with him about what his daughter told them.

The young man told Shamus what went on between a husband and wife in Jordan was between them and was none of Shamus' business. Two days later Shamus and his wife had reservations to fly home to Ireland. Patricia's husband told them to have a safe flight home and left to go to his office.

Shamus had a plan to get his daughter and grandson out of Jordan. Patricia and the baby were going to the airport to see them off and Shamus called earlier and got reservations and tickets for them both to go home to Ireland. Patricia told her folks she was always watched by the servants and her husband's security people.

So when they left her home, Patricia took nothing of hers or of the baby's to the airport. Her driver took them to the airport and she gave him instructions to wait for her while she saw her parents off.

Upon arriving inside the terminal, they checked in Shamus' luggage and then he asked for the ticket for his daughter and grandson. The agent said there was a problem with the reservations and he was checking on it. He told them to wait just a few minutes and he would see if he could get the problem resolved. A few minutes later two men in dark suits came to the counter and told Shamus and his wife to please come with them. Shamus explained he was waiting for his daughter and grandson's tickets. Hearing this, the two men opened their suit coats and put their hands on guns that were in holsters under their jackets.

One of the men said, "I don't think you understand what I just told you, please come with us."

Shamus said, "What about my daughter?"

The man replied her husband will look after her.

Just at that point, Patricia's husband came up to her, took the baby from her, and said, "Come, love, we must go home now. It's been so nice to have your parents visit. They must come again soon.

The two men escorted Shamus and his wife onto their plane. They were told as they sat down in their seats, "Your daughter's husband said to tell you not to ever come back to Jordan. It would not be good for your health or good for your daughter."

After they left Jordan they didn't hear anything from their daughter for over two years. They tried telephoning, but she was never available to take the call and she never answered any of their letters. After two years, Patricia bribed one of her servants to finally mail a letter to her parents. In the letter she told them what happened to her when she got home from the airport. Her husband beat her so badly; he broke her left arm when she tried to put it over her face to protect herself. He had a doctor come to the house to attend to her and it was several weeks before she was allowed to see her son.

In the letter, Patricia pleaded with her parents to find some way to help her get out of Jordan. She said the only thing that saved her from being killed was that she lied and told her husband she didn't know her father was going to try to take her out of Jordan. Shamus said he went to the Irish Government to see what they could do to help him find a way to get his daughter and grandson out of Jordan. After meeting with them several times. He was told to go to the British Embassy in Dublin and talk with a Mr. Jones. Explaining to whomever was working at the reception desk, that the Irish Home Office referred him to Mr. Jones. Shamus went directly to the British Embassy and asked to see Mr. Jones.

Shamus was told Mr. Jones would return to the Embassy in two days and they set up an appointment for him to see Mr. Jones. When Shamus met with Mr. Jones, Mr. Jones said he had already been briefed on the problem and, officially the Embassy could do nothing. However, Mr. Jones told Shamus he would have someone contact him that could help.

Three days later a man came to Shamus' home and said his name was Charlie and he was there to help him get his daughter and grandson out of Jordan. Charlie told them it would cost about twenty-five thousand pounds to get them out. Shamus said he did not have that much money, but he would get it. The man said he would need the money in cash and he would begin putting the plan together for his team to extract Patricia and her baby from Jordan.

Shamus continued the story. "I talked to Mr. Sommers and told him for the first time what I was going through and asked if he could help get the twenty-five thousand pounds. Mr. Sommers reacted just the way I thought he would. He shook his head and said to me, 'Shamus, that's an awful lot of money. Do you have any of it? How in the world are you ever going to pay all of that money back? You are not a young man any more. Good heavens, you've been working for me for over thirty years so I know you can't have much money saved on what I pay you'."

Shamus told Mr. Sommers he had about five thousand pounds in savings and given time, he could sell the family home that had been in his family for three generations before Shamus inherited it. Shamus said his home was worth at least fifty thousand pounds or more. Shamus told Chance he had a pretty nice house and Maureen O'Hara's home in Dublin was just a little ways from his.

Chance pictured Shamus' home in his mind and thought, if it is anything like Sean Sommers' home, it is probably worth two to three times that much. Chance was sure Shamus had never considered selling his home before, but his daughter's life was at stake and Chance knew almost any father would do anything to save their child.

Shamus told Chance the next day Mr. Sommers called him into his office and told him he had the twenty-five thousand pounds in his office safe when he needed it. Chance thought to himself this was just the man Sean Sommers was. He talked cheap and stingy, but was really a pushover when it came to crunch time. Mr. Sommers had what amounted to over fifty thousand U.S. dollars in a safe to give to Shamus one day after he asked for his help and with no questions about repayment.

Shamus went on with his story. He said three days later, the man who had been sent by the British Embassy telephoned him at home and asked if he was able to raise the money and Shamus said the money was ready. The man, who called himself Charlie, said it would take about a month before he had Patricia and his grandson home in Ireland. Two days after that conversation, Charlie called from Heathrow Airport in London and told Shamus to meet him at the Dublin Airport with the money. Shamus met Charlie and gave him a briefcase with the twenty-five thousand pounds in it. Charlie told Shamus he was on the next plane back to London and then on to Jordan.

He told Shamus don't try to contact your daughter because it might tip them off that they were trying to get Patricia out of Jordan and he might not ever see her again. Charlie took the briefcase and turned around and went directly through security and immigrations.

Shamus said he never saw or heard from Charlie again.

However, a little more then a month later, his wife got a collect telephone call from Tel Aviv, Israel from Patricia. She said she and her son were getting on a plane to London and would be Dublin later that evening. She gave her mother the flight number and the time they would arrive in Dublin.

After Patricia arrived safely in Dublin and they had put the baby to bed, she told them how Charlie got them out of Jordan. Charlie bought two tickets for them in London on a flight from Amman to London for four weeks from the time he bought the tickets. Patricia told her parents three days ago, she and her son had gone with her driver and a servant to the open-air market as she did every Friday. After shopping, they returned to the car and her driver was gone and some other Jordanian was in his place behind the wheel.

Suddenly, another man she did not know pushed her servant to the ground, showed her a pistol and told her to stay on the ground. The man got into the car with Patricia and the car began moving at once. They drove the car in the direction of the airport and the man told her don't worry that her father sent them here to help her escape.

Patricia said she told the man, "You will never get me out of here going to the airport. My husband has everyone there watching for us to try to get away."

The man said, "We know that and we're counting on that." Just before they arrived at the airport, they stopped beside a very old farm truck parked off the side of the road. The truck was positioned to shield them from view from the road. The man told her to take her son and get out of the car and into the back of the truck. The truck bed had a frame with a canvas cover over the top of it and an opening on the right side of the truck bed. Patricia and her son quickly climbed into the truck. Inside was a man who told Patricia his name was Charlie and that her father sent him to take her home. The old truck began moving; it turned around and began going back over the same road she just came down. She told us that although she knew Charlie was British, she worried that maybe her husband put this plot together to make people think she had been kidnapped so he could have her killed. Charlie kept telling her it would be all right and that things were going just like he planned.

Charlie said, "Your husband is sure going to be disappointed when he shows up at the airport, waiting for you and your son to get on the plane that I made reservations for you on. Well at least he can find his car at the airport."

After driving around for several hours, the truck finally stopped and Charlie said this was where they got out. He opened the side door on the truck bed and said from here, they would walk. They began walking and Charlie and another man who had been in the cab of the truck took turns carrying her son. They walked the rest of the night. They dodged border guards from Jordan and Israel. By early the next morning, they entered a small village and Charlie led them to a house. Once inside, he told Patricia that they would rest here and wait for someone to pick them up tomorrow.

The next morning, two people came in a car and brought clothes for her and her son, they even had cosmetics for her. Patricia bathed and dressed her son and then showered and dressed herself. She told her folks that the shower felt wonderful! When she went back into the living room, Charlie was sitting on the floor playing with her son. Then they took her picture and one of her son with a Polaroid camera. A few minutes later, one of the men handed her two British passports, one with her birth date and one for her son. The only thing different from her own passport was this one used her maiden name and it was British instead of Irish. This new passport said she was British and not Irish. Then the man gave her plane tickets from Tel Aviv to London and on to Dublin. The two men got into the front seat of their car and Charlie and her and the baby in the back seat. Then they drove toward Tel Aviv.

Less then two hours later they arrived at Ben Gurion Airport. Patricia said Charlie took them straight through passport control and security. Once through, he told her she could call her parents and advise them she was on her way home. Patricia said she was pretty much in shock when she heard her mother's voice. Then Charlie took them to their seats on the British Airways plane. He said something to the plane's captain and the chief steward. Then he came to say good-bye to Patricia and her son. He handed Patricia the tickets for the flight from Amman to London and told her she could either get a refund or keep them as a souvenir. He leaned over and kissed her on the cheek and said, "Miss Patricia, you and your son have a great life!"

Then he left.

Chance sat motionless when Shamus finished his story. He was exhausted just listening to it. He couldn't imagine the highs and low's Shamus and his wife had gone through over the past few weeks. Shamus said Patricia and her son arrived in London the previous Thursday night. One thing for sure, fixing Dublin's parking meters seemed a lot less important to Chance then it had been when he arrived yesterday.

Nevertheless, shortly after the meter parts were delivered and Chance began checking in the parts to be sure everything he had manufactured over the last two-and-a-half weeks actually arrived in Dublin. To Chance's surprise, everything was here and Chance started working. After the new parts were installed and Chance made the coin adjustment, the meters worked flawlessly.

Sean Sommers came into the shop and was delighted to see how well the meters worked. He said he was going back to his office to telephone the Dublin Corporation officials and tell them how well the meters worked with Chance's changes. Over the next two weeks, Chance, Shamus, and other employees of Sean Sommers' company installed new parts in over three thousand meters.

Sean came into the office one Friday morning after they had been working for two weeks and said to Shamus, "Don't you think we can take care of the rest of the meters by ourselves?"

Shamus replied, "We have everything in the main business center of Dublin changed over and everything is working very well."

Sean said, "Well, the people at Superior want Chance back at the plant and if we keep him here much longer, I'm afraid we might have to put him on our payroll. I think, by our standards, Chance's probably gets paid a lot more then we can afford."

Chance thought to himself he doubted he was overpaid even by Irish standards. Anyway, Chance was ready to go home to Annie and Shane. He hadn't seen them for over a month. The next day Chance flew from Dublin to London, on to New York, then to Chicago and finally to Wichita. Ann and Shane were waiting at the Wichita Airport for him. God, he was happy to see them. Chance thought Shane must have grown a foot since he saw him a month ago. Ann looked wonderful to him. He couldn't wait to hold her and make love with her. It had been far too long for him and she had been much too far away.

It was after midnight before they arrived home in Webster and Chance carried Shane into the house. He helped him into his pajamas and turned down the bed for him. Chance gave him a big hug and kiss while Shane was getting into bed. Shane said in a sleepy voice, "Daddy, I love you. Don't stay away so long anymore, OK, daddy?"

By the time Chance finished in the bathroom, Ann was already in bed. When he got into bed, she moved over as close to Chance, as she could and whispered, "Daddy, I love you. Don't stay away so long next time."

She overheard Shane while she was in the bathroom getting ready for bed and repeated what she had heard. Chance's energy quickly returned and he was ready to make love even if it had been over twenty-four hours since he got out of bed in Dublin. Ann felt so good, how could he have been away from her for such a long time?

Sunday, Ann's mother came to their house early in the afternoon and took Shane to the park to give Chance and Ann time to be alone. If their lovemaking had been good the night before, this afternoon it was much better. They could take their time to enjoy each other and satisfy each other's passion. Afterwards, they held each other for a long, long time and renewed their "oneness." Although they were two very different people, when they were together, they became one. Not only did they still have deep passionate love for each other, they liked each other and were best friends. Sure, they had other friends, but no one had ever--or could ever--assume that title for either one of them.

Monday morning they dropped Shane off at school and Ann took Chance back to the Wichita Airport. He had to be back in Big Springs as soon as he could. He was able to fly to St. Louis and then get a commuter flight into Big Springs. He landed at the Big Springs Airport at four-thirty in the afternoon. He telephoned the plant and one of his fellow engineers came to the airport and took him back to the plant. Chance went in to talk with his boss who told him he was sorry to cut Chance's stay at home so short, but they had a group of people coming to the plant tomorrow from Germany and our glorious President scheduled an all-day meeting with all of the Department Directors.

Tim said, "I just don't have anyone else in the department that I feel comfortable with looking after these people all day."

Then Tim said, "Chance, you did a great job in Dublin. I got a real nice letter from Sean Sommers thanking me for sending you to solve their problems. I hate to tell you this, but we have quality problems with the last two shipments of meters to Germany and that's what these people are coming to Big Springs to talk about.

Chance do whatever you need to do, but take care of the problems, because Gunnar Schmidt is Superior's largest international distributor.

The next morning the President of Superior, Chris Goodhand and two of his Vice Presidents from Chicago arrived by Lear jet.

They also brought Gunnar Schmidt and an official from the city of Hamburg, Mr. Knox with them on the plane. When they arrived at the Superior plant, Chance was introduced to Gunnar Schmidt and Mr. Knox. Tim told them Chance would look after them for the day and he would get the information on the problems they were having with the meters from him.

Gunnar Schmidt spoke very little English, but Mr. Knox spoke English very well. As the day dragged on, Chance felt Mr. Knox's English was too good. They started off by telling Chance that the name of his company might be Superior, but their products certainly were not. In fact, the workmanship was so poor; they were considering sending back the last two shipments of meters and getting their money back. Chance was taken back by this whole conversation and felt like the people in the President's meeting should be the ones listening to the problems and making decisions on what to do to fix the meters in Germany. After all, Chance had only been back with Superior for little more then two months.

Chance thought maybe taking a plant tour with the two Germans might cool them off a little and get them ready to go through the problems with their meters without such high emotions. Chance had been wrong before and he would be wrong many more times in the future, but he was certainly wrong with this idea. When they returned from the plant tour, Gunnar Schmidt announced, through his interpreter, that if Superior's plant was in Germany, it would be closed down. He told Chance this was the filthiest plant he had ever seen in his life. He said he toured the plant ten years before and there was not one new piece of equipment in the plant since then. Gunnar knew a lot about manufacturing since he was a design and manufacturing engineer.

Chance tried a different tack. He said he really needed to understand the problems with the meters so he could address the problems with the appropriate people and departments. Gunnar came all of the way from Germany to make his complaints and he did not intend to miss one thing; he planned to get his money's worth. He opened his black leather briefcase and took out a folder filled with neatly typed notes. Gunnar started, item by item and hardly stop for breath until Tim came into the office about one o'clock and asked them to join the President and the Company Directors in the conference room for lunch.

Chris Goodhand loved to eat fried chicken when he made his monthly visits to the Big Springs plant, and before he went back to Chicago he always looked up one of the foremen for a few games of Ping-Pong. No one realized Germans almost never ate food with their hands, so the two visitors ate little and said nothing. Chance later found out Pizza Hut almost went out of business in Germany when they first started because they didn't offer their customers silverware.

After lunch, the Germans picked up exactly where they had left off. Chance was not only getting an earful, he was getting a legal pad filled up. Finally about three-thirty, Gunnar said, "I have to go to the toilet, please."

Chance showed the men the way to the restroom. When Mr. Knox returned, he said he had a funny story to tell Chance about something that happened in World War II in his hometown of Hamburg. Chance was ready for a funny story because he sure hadn't had any fun since the Germans walked into the plant. Mr. Knox said the Nazis made a bunch of wooden barges and built copies of the railway stations and many of their most important buildings in Hamburg out of plywood. Then they put them on the lake in the center of Hamburg to fool the British fliers and keep them from destroying the real buildings with British bombs. Mr. Knox said the British dropped "wooden bombs" on the wooden buildings and then bombed the real buildings to pieces. Mr. Knox and Gunnar thought this was really funny. Any other day, Chance might have thought so too, but these two men had destroyed Chance's sense of humor for the day. Just as quickly as Mr. Knox lapsed into his story, he and Gunnar were back at Chance with all of their quality problems. They were still going at it at five-thirty when Tim came in and said the staff meeting was finally over and it was time to fly back to Chicago. The two Germans put away their papers, said good-bye to Chance, and went out the door to return to Chicago on the Lear jet. Chance sat in disbelief that this day had finally ended.

Tim came back into his office and told Chance how sorry he was to dump the Germans on him all day by himself.

Tim said, "You know, sometimes Chris Goodhand doesn't act like he cares about customers. He acts like the only thing he cares about is pumping product out the door and showing shipping dollars. I just don't understand a boss who tells the manufacturing people, "Ship it, we'll fix it later." When I was with the Magic Meter Company, Superior would never have let products out the door that was not perfect. If they had, I would have beat their ass.

Chance I've had enough of this place for the day let's go home."

Chance sat in Tim's office for a few more minutes, then picked up his papers, stuck them in his briefcase and headed for the Ramada Inn, Chance's Big Spring's home. He called Annie and as soon as she heard him say hello, she said, "What's wrong, Chance?"

As he began to tell her about his day with the Germans, she said, "Chance, you've done your best, now forget the day." Then Ann said something to Chance he had told people so many times over the years that Karl Jones used to say to him, "Chance, after you've done your best that's as much as you can do and angels can do no more."

In spite of Chance's day, he laughed and told Ann, "Thanks love, I needed that."

Before he hung up the phone, he told Ann, "Tomorrow I'm going to find us a place to live so you can get down here with me. Good night, love but let me say hello to Shane before we hang up."

Ann called Shane to the phone and Chance talked with Shane about what was he was doing in school and how much they missed each other. Chance, thought about how much Shane had grown up, he was already in the fifth grade. They said good night and that they loved each other.

After Chance had dinner alone in the Ramada's restaurant,

he thought about what Ann said and how much he missed his mother and how he missed Karl Jones. Chance thought Karl would have loved the story about the British dropping wooden bombs on the wooden buildings. Thinking about Karl, reminded Chance about a joke Karl loved to tell. It was funny how sometimes one thing reminds you of something you heard years before.

As Chance lay in bed, he remembered hearing Karl tell his joke maybe ten or fifteen times. Karl's story was about the rabbi and the priest driving back from a meeting one night. As they became better acquainted, the priest asked the rabbi if some time in his life if he hadn't eaten ham, just one time in his life. The rabbi waited a long time before finally answering, "Well, a long time ago I ate a ham sandwich, just once." Then the rabbi said, "Father, I would like to ask you a question. At some time in your life, didn't you have sex with a woman? Just once?"

The priest waited for awhile and finally said, "Well, yes, I did once. Just before I became a priest."

The rabbi said, "It sure beats ham, don't it?"

Yes, Karl would have loved the wooden bomb story.

The next day Chance went into the office and called Shirley Jones, the real estate lady he had been working with trying to find a way to buy a house. She wasn't in the office that early, but her secretary promised she would have her call Chance as soon as she came in.

Chance went into Tim's office to tell him he needed to take time away from the office to find a place for his family to live in Big Springs.

Tim told him, "Take whatever time off you need. I think you have already put in enough time to cover you for the rest of the year."

Chance promised to have his report on the problems with the German meters finished and given to Brandy to type no later then tomorrow. Just as Chance finished saying this, Brandy was at Tim's office door, telling Chance he was wanted on the telephone.

Chance went to his desk and answered the phone. It was Shirley Jones from Century 21. Chance asked if she could find some place to rent in Big Springs. Shirley said she had an idea that she would check out for him, but she told Chance rental houses in Big Springs were a pretty sad lot.

Chance went to work on making sense out of the notes he took the day before about the problems experienced with the German meters, as told to him by Gunnar Schmidt and Mr. Knox. He finished the report by lunchtime and gave it to Brandy to type.

When Chance came back from lunch at the Ramada, Brandy told him to call Shirley Jones at Century 21. Chance returned her call and she said she thought she had a great deal on a rental house. Shirley said she would come to the plant and take him to see the house. She drove to one a subdivision not far from the plant.

The house was a lot more house then they needed. It had five bedrooms and three baths. The house had a covered deck that went completely around the house. Chance thought whoever built this house really liked windows, because it had floor to ceiling windows in the combination living/dining room, the master bedroom, the downstairs family room and the downstairs bedroom.

Shirley explained the house belonged to one of the car dealers in town. He just built a new house on his ranch, but he didn't want to sell this house until he was older so he could get the tax break on selling his principal residence.

Shirley told Chance he would have to meet with the car dealer to assure him they would take good care of his house. Shirley said she would set up an appointment that afternoon for Chance to meet with this man at his car dealership. She said, "He wants five hundred fifty dollars a month if he decides to rent the house to you." Later that day Chance met with his potential new landlord and pleaded his case, telling him that his wife was an excellent housekeeper and that he could come to the house anytime and inspect it. Shirley telephoned Chance a short while later to say he had a house. She needed to collect the first and last month's rent before they could move in. Chance told Shirley he would bring the money to her the following Monday.

Chance made arrangements for a moving van and set a date for them to pick up their furniture and their other household goods to be delivered the Friday after Thanksgiving. That weekend Chance drove home to Webster and started helping Ann pack up their things once more.

Chance talked with his dad and asked if he could borrow a thousand dollars. His dad told Chance he was welcome to whatever money was in his checking account since his bills were paid for the month and his social security and company retirement checks would be coming in on first of the month. Chance's dad had about eighteen hundred dollars in his checking account.

Chance asked, "Dad, you have eighteen hundred dollars in your checking account, would it be OK if I took twelve hundred dollars to help us get moved?"

Chance's dad said, "You can take it all if you need it."

"No, I just need the twelve hundred dollars."

His dad said, "This is not a loan. It's for you and I'm only sorry I don't have more to give you."

Chance had not asked his dad for money since Ann and he got married. He knew his dad would have given him anything he ever had. It was funny how hard it was for Chance's dad to say he loved him, but he could show it in so many other ways.

Chance got a telephone call on Sunday afternoon from Tim Hunt, asking him if he could come back to Big Springs tonight, because they had to fly to Montreal the next morning. Chance asked what was going on in Montreal and was told they had ten thousand new meters that weren't working. Chance hung up the phone and turned to Ann and said, "Honey, you're not going to like this."

"I already know I'm not going to like it, if you start a conversation saying that."

"My boss, Tim Hunt, just called and said he wants me back in Big Springs tonight."

"Tonight?" Ann said, "It's already after five o'clock. Doesn't he know it takes you eight hours to drive from Webster to Big Springs?"

"I don't think he cares."

Ann said, "For goodness sake, Chance, you have only been back at Superior for three months. What in the world have they been doing for the past ten years while you were gone?"

"I don't know, but they seemed to have stayed in business without me."

When are you coming back?"

Chance answered, "I don't know. All Tim said was that we were flying to Montreal in the morning."

Ann said, "I guess their meters don't work either."

"You're right. Tim says they have ten thousand that don't work."

"Ten thousand parking meters that doesn't work, what's wrong with Superior anyway?"

Chance said, "I don't know, but I know Tim said Chris Goodhand, the Company's President, only cares about how many dollars get shipped out every month and makes statements like "Ship it. We'll fix it later."

"How can you run a manufacturing company like that?"

"I don't know, Ann," Chance replied, "but I don't think you can make much money with that kind of an attitude. That kind of statement made by the president of a company sends the wrong message to all of the employees. They think if that's what our boss thinks, why should we care about doing quality work?"

Chance stopped talking for a minute and then totally changed the subject. "Ann, you're going to have to move by yourself. The moving van is coming Tuesday and I know I can't get back here by then."

Ann told Chance, "I guess I can do it again, it won't be the first time."

Chance said, "Honey, I know it won't be and I'm really sorry. "Sure, sure. Just go on back to Big Springs and fly off to Canada and I'll do all of the work."

Chance said, "Poor baby!"

"Don't 'Poor Baby' me Chance!"

Chance began laughing and Ann soon joined him. "Chance, if I didn't love you so much I could really get mad at you."

"I know Annie that's why I love you so much."

In less then an hour, Chance loaded everything he could in the VW bug and started for Big Springs.

Ann said, "Call me when you get to Big Springs and be careful.

I guess I'll see you in Big Springs later this week."

Chance said, "I'll make reservations for you Wednesday night at the Ramada Inn. Annie, you be careful driving over those Arkansas hills." Chance was pushing the green VW bug as hard as he could. He was down shifting going up every hill to keep up as much speed as possible and he was making good time. It was now one- thirty Monday morning and Chance was only nine miles out of Big Springs. He was just topping a hill and taking a curve. He was shifting the VW back into high gear when-- Bang ... Pop--the engine died. Chance began losing speed. He down shifted into second gear and let the clutch out. The engine didn't even think about starting. Chance could hear noises that sounded as though the whole engine was coming apart. Chance pulled the car off the road and while it was coasting, he drove the VW into a lane leading up to an Ozark farmhouse.

Before the car rolled to a stop, Chance saw a car pulling in behind him. Chance looked into the rearview mirror and saw an Arkansas State Trooper getting out of his patrol car. The trooper asked Chance if he was having car trouble. Chance told him about what happened to the engine. The trooper asked Chance where he was going. Chance explained he was an employee at Superior Parking Meters in Big Springs.

The trooper told Chance he might as well get into his car and he would take him into Big Springs. Chance asked the trooper if he thought his car would be all right until morning, parked in this lane. Chance said he would try to make arrangements in the morning to have his car towed to a repair shop, but didn't know if he would have time since he was flying out in the morning with his boss to Montreal. The state trooper told Chance not to worry.

The people who lived in the house were friends of his and he would have the dispatcher call them in the morning and explain everything.

Chance took his suitcase with the clothes he needed for the trip to Montreal out of the VW and by the time the state trooper dropped Chance off at the Ramada Inn and Chance woke up the desk clerk, it was almost three am before Chance was able to call Ann.

Ann said, "Chance, where have you been? I woke up about an hour ago and have just been laying here worrying that something happened to you."

"I'm OK, but I think the engine on the VW is gone."

Then he told her about what happened and how an Arkansas State Trooper helped him.

Ann said, "You better get some rest and don't worry about the car. Goodnight, I love you."

Chance and Tim Hunt arrived at the local Superior Distributor's office in Montreal early that afternoon. Chance had met Pierre Shardue, Superior's Canadian Distributor in Chicago years ago at a sales meeting. Pierre greeted them warmly and said he was glad to have them in Montreal. He told them he really had a problem with the city; they wanted to send back all ten thousand new meters. Pierre said Tom Watts, Superior's Vice President of Sales, and Chris Goodhand, Superior's President, were scheduled to arrive in an hour and then Montreal City Officials would be in the office in less then two hours. Pierre introduced his manager of service, Pierre Le Pugh. Pierre Le Pugh was a young man, about twenty-five years old and had been managing the service department for the past four years.

Tim asked Pierre Le Pugh to explain what kind of problems they were having with the meters. Pierre said the problems were primarily with the meters not giving time for the coins. Chance began putting coins in the mechanisms and they appeared to be working all right as long as Chance turned the handle slowly.

If Chance increased the speed turning the handle, some times he did not get any time for his coin. Pierre explained that's part of the problem people on the street found out they could turn the handles very fast and not get time for their coins. Then they would call the police and report the problem. Then they would park all day without getting a parking ticket. Word got out on the street and soon the police were getting hundreds of calls a day and revenue from the meters and parking tickets drop like a rock in a shallow stream.

A few minutes later Chance's friend Tom Watts came in to greet them. He listened very carefully trying to understand the problems with the meters. Tim asked Tom if Chris Goodhand came with him from Chicago. Tom assured Tim he did and that he was in Pierre Shardue's office talking. Chance was happy to hear Chris Goodhand could actually talk to someone. He had never spoken to Chance the two times he had seen him.

About that time Pierre Shardue, Chris Goodhand and two men Chance didn't know came in and sat down at the table where Chance, Tom, Tim, and Pierre Le Pugh were sitting studying the mechanisms. Pierre Shardue introduced the two Montreal City Officials to them. Chance didn't really understand their names, but at the moment it didn't matter. After they were introduced and shook hands with each other, Chris Goodhand told the Montreal City Officials that Tim Hunt and Chance Clark had been assigned to fix the problems with their meters.

Mr. Goodhand told them Superior had another engineer who worked on their problem for the past two months and then he said he ordered Tim Hunt to fire this man, because Superior didn't keep employees who didn't perform. Next, Mr. Goodhand told them Tim Hunt had been assigned as the Montreal Project Director and Chance Clark as the Project Manager, and he personally guaranteed these two men would fix the Montreal problem.

He said, "I know they will get this problem taken care of because these men like their job and they like to eat."

Chris Goodhand then turned and started walking to the door, shouting back as he walked, "Come on Tom, we've got a plane back to Chicago and these men have work to do."

Tom got up and tried to tell everyone goodbye, but Mr.\

Goodhand shouted again, "Are you coming with me or are you going to take on this problem yourself?" Tom quickly caught up with Mr. Goodhand and they left.

Chance thought, my record is still intact. I've seen Chris Goodhand three times and he still has never spoken to me. The two Montreal Officials soon got up and left. Pierre Shardue walked out with the City Officials and then went back into his office.

Tim, Pierre Le Pugh, and Chance just kind of sat there in shock with what had just happened.

Tim finally said, "Chance, I've got to depend on you to find a way to fix these problems, you know a lot more about Superior Meters then I do. Since I've been working in engineering foe Superior I've been trying to fix some of the manufacturing problems."

Chance thought to himself, I've just had another huge problem dumped in my lap. Thanks everyone for this wonderful opportunity and your vote of confidence. Can I find a way to fix these problems, I don't know?

Pierre Le Pugh said, "Chance, if you're going to fix the problems with Montreal's Meters, you're going to have to learn how to turn the handles the way these Montreal people do."

Pierre demonstrated how they turned the handles.

Chance said, "Pierre, that's not just turning the handle fast, that's flipping them. If we don't have enough problems, now we have to contend with the Montreal Flip."

Chance asked Tim to help him gather up at least one of each one of the different time and rate combination of mechanisms to take back to the hotel, so he could study them. Tim pulled some papers out of his briefcase to see how many different time and rates were included in the Montreal meters. Chance thought, my God, how many different ones can they have? He soon found out, they had a lot! They had fifteen-minute meters, thirty-minute meters, two different rates of one-hour meters, three-hour meters, two different rates of six-hour meters and two different rates of twelve- hour meters. In all, there were nine different bills of material for the ten thousand Montreal meters. Chance was beginning to wish he were back in Dublin.

Pierre got two of the foam shipping cartons specially made for Superior mechanisms. Each special pack held six mechanisms, so they packed four mechs in one carton and five in the other one. They said good-bye to both of the Pierres and went to their hotel for the night.

The next day, Tim telephoned Pierre Shardue and said he and Chance were taking an early flight back to Big Springs.

Tim said, "We need a lot more time to study the meters and we can do it better back in the plant."

By the time they arrived back in Big Springs, it was after seven o'clock in the evening. Chance was really tired. He had a lot to do just to get ready for Ann and Shane to arrive the next day. Chance hoped Ann would like the house he rented. She surely would since it was better then the house in which they had been living in for the past five years.

Chance was sure she would love it. Chance called Ann at her mother's house and she told him the van was completely loaded. They even had to leave behind a lot of his metal shelving, because they didn't have enough room in the van to haul it.

Chance asked "Did they have a van just for our stuff?"

Ann assured him they did. She said the driver even put the tailgate down on the back of the truck and packed it full of wrought iron patio furniture.

Chance asked Ann if she had the map that he had marked the highways for her. Ann said, "It is in the front seat of the Caddy."

She told Chance she had the Caddy loaded and, in fact, didn't know where Shane and his cat "Q" would sit. Chance had forgotten about Q-cat. He didn't know how Ann could handle both Q-cat and Shane. Shane told them he was not moving, period! They could go, but he was staying in Webster.

When Chance asked Ann how in the world she was going to be able to take care of Q-cat since he hated to ride in cars, she said she got some pills from the vet to calm him for the trip.

Chance told Ann, "I love you and drive carefully, get some rest and I'll see you tomorrow."

24

Chance realized he had a problem. He had all of these errands to run and no car. The next morning he called the plant and asked to speak to Tim. When Tim answered the phone, Chance told him his problem. Tim told Chance he would call Brandy at home since she lived close to the motel and would have her pick Chance up and bring him to work. Then Chance could use his car. Thirty minutes later, Brandy knocked on his door. She drove him to the plant and after he dropped his briefcase off at his desk, he stopped in Tim's office to get his car keys.

Chance signed up for electric, gas, telephone, water and cable TV for the rental house. He dropped by the Century 21 office and gave Shirley the first and last months' rent on the house and she gave him three sets of keys for the house. Chance could see the advantage of living in a small town. In less than an hour he accomplished all of his errands. He drove over to their new house, just to check it over. It looked better to him today then it did when he first saw it. Then he realized why, because his new landlord had hired someone to come in and clean the house from top to bottom. Chance took Tim's car back to the plant and spent the rest of the day looking over the Montreal mechs. Chance kept looking at his watch, wondering where Ann was. At five-thirty, Brandy said she was going home and asked if he wanted a ride to the motel. Chance picked up his briefcase and followed her to the car. Brandy drove up to the Ramada Inn and through the parking lot. She pulled up next to his room and just as Chance was thanking Brandy for the ride, Ann parked her white Caddy in the parking space next to Brandy's car. Chance told Brandy to have a "Happy Thanksgiving" and got out of the car.

He walked over to open Ann's door. As he opened it, Ann said, "I think I must be getting to Big Springs just in time. It looks like you have a pretty good-looking driver."

Chance said, "That was Brandy, the secretary from the engineering department."

"Sure, that's your story!"

Chance leaned in the car and kissed her. Ann said, "Help me get out of the car. It's not been a wonderful trip. We gave Q-cat one of the pills the vet gave us, but it didn't have any effect on him at all. After driving for an hour, that cat was just as wild as he always was riding in the car. So we gave him another pill and ten minutes later he laid down in the back seat and hasn't moved since. I don't know if we killed him or not."

Chance looked at Q-cat in the back of the car and could see him breathing. Chance told Ann, "He's all right."

Ann got out of the car and Chance went over to Shane's side of the car and opened his door. Shane got out of the car gave his dad a kiss and said, "I'm not staying here. I'm going back home to Webster."

Chance opened the door to the motel room and Shane went into the bathroom.

Ann said, "I almost had to pick him up and put him in the car. What a trip!"

Chance took Ann in his arms and held her as close as he could and said, "I'm sorry I wasn't there to help you."

"I know, but it seems funny to me you're always needed by somebody else when I need your help."

Chance told her again, "I'm sorry, baby."

"The driver of the moving van said he would be at the house by eight o'clock Friday morning." Chance asked, "Do you want to see your new home?"

"No, it's getting dark and you know how I hate this time of day." Chance knew. They both hated this time of day, just an hour or so after sundown. Chance thought he hated it because when he was traveling by himself at this time, he knew he should be going home to Ann instead of being alone, or maybe it was because the day was dying and it reminded him of death. Either way, neither he nor Ann liked it. The only thing worse then this time of the day was this time on a Sunday that was the worst.

Just then Shane burst out of the bathroom and said, "Let's go eat, I'm hungry."

Chance said OK, but Ann said, "Just a minute. I need to go to the bathroom and get cleaned up a little."

Chance said, "OK we'll let you."

The next day, Thursday Thanksgiving Day 1982, they went to see the house.

Ann said, "Chance you always do a great job finding somewhere for us to live."

Chance told her, "I hope you like it."

Shane had been all through the house before Chance and Ann made it through the living, dining rooms and the kitchen. Even Shane liked the house and asked if he could play with a basketball he found in the storage room.

Chance said, "Why not? I think if the folks who own this house wanted it, they would have moved it with them. So you found a basketball to go with our basketball court!"

Shane asked, "What basketball court?"

Chance walked over to one of the sliding glass doors in the kitchen and pointed to a basketball court on the far edge of the property.

Shane said, "You mean our back yard goes all the way over there and the basketball court is mine?"

Chance answered, "It sure is."

Shane went downstairs and got the basketball out of the storage room, opened one of the family room sliding doors and headed to the basketball court.

Ann was still looking over the kitchen. It had a Jenn-Aire range and oven and more cabinets then her last two homes combined.

Chance said, "Come on, I want to show you the rest of the house."

Ann followed him down a central hallway. Off to the left was a small bedroom.

Chance said, "I thought I could use this for my office."

Next to this bedroom was another bedroom, just a little larger then the one Chance claimed for his office. Further down the hall on the left was a very large bathroom with a combination tub and shower and two double sinks. Next on the left was a large bedroom. Chance said, "Shane's room," and at the end of the hall were two double doors leading into the master suite. Their new bedroom was at least twice, maybe three times, larger then the one they left in Webster. The master bedroom had something neither Chance nor Ann had ever seen, a freestanding closet. The closet had two sets of sliding doors on each side; one side of the closet would be Ann's and the other side would be Chance's.

Chance told Ann, "I will have to have the closet on the other side where we have double sinks."

The sinks were built into a vanity cabinet that went completely across the length of the bedroom. Chance continued, "That way, when I get up to go to work in the morning, it won't wake you and I can find my clothes."

Ann went into the master bath. It was small, but it had a very large ceramic tile shower stall.

Next, they went out onto the deck from the bedroom. Two walls of the bedroom, the south and west walls, were floor to ceiling glass and sliding glass doors. The way the house was situated on a hillside, you could only see trees from their bedroom. It was like being in the mountains of Colorado, peaceful and restful. They walked all around the house on the deck and stopped to holler at Shane. He kept shooting the basketball, but managed a wave.

After they went back inside the house, they went downstairs where there was another bedroom as large as the master bedroom and another full bath. The family room had a fireplace, a fridge and a large built-in bar. All of the south walls of the family room and bedroom were either sliding glass doors or glass walls.

Ann said, "We better watch out running around in the nude with all of the glass this house has. Otherwise, we might have to move out of the neighborhood."

Chance said, "Right, if it is me. But if it is you, they would be camped out waiting to see you."

"Sure they would," Ann laughed.

They both laughed and started for the car, hand in hand.

Shane came running up and said, "Are you just going to leave me here?"

"Of course not," his dad replied.

After having Thanksgiving dinner in the Ramada Inn restaurant, the Clarks spent the rest of the day watching TV and resting. They wanted to be ready to meet the van with their furniture at eight o'clock the next morning.

The next morning Chance was up at five o'clock. He showered, washed his hair, shaved, and dressed as he did every morning. By the time he was finished in the bathroom, Ann was sliding out of bed. Chance went over to her, took her hands and pulled her up and gave her a good-morning kiss.

He said, "Honey, I'm sorry you had to do everything by yourself again."

Ann just gave him a slight smile and said, "Oh, it's OK, I know you didn't have any choice."

Shane looked up from his bed and said, "Hey, could you people be quiet? Q and I are trying to sleep."

Just as he said that, Q-cat stretched his body and legs as far as they could stretch, then he turned over, curled up and went back to sleep.

By seven-thirty the Clarks were waiting at the house for the moving van. They were still waiting when the clock showed eight- thirty. In the meantime they unloaded Annie's car and put things in closets. As the last trip into the house was made, the moving van drove up in front of the house. Chance and Ann had played this scene too many times already in their lives. They stood together as the driver opened up the side door and they could see what was left of their life's possessions inside the truck. In some ways, it was very sad, but they soon brushed that thought away and Chance said, "Well, we have another new beginning.

After that, they didn't have any more time to feel sorry for themselves because the moving van driver and his two local helpers began asking, "Which room does this go to?"

By the time the last item was unloaded from the truck, it was six o'clock in the evening. The movers stopped only once during the day to consume hamburgers, French fries, and cokes that Chance and Shane got from McDonalds for all of them.

The Clarks worked all weekend straightening up the house and putting things away. By the time Monday morning arrived, Chance told Ann as he was getting out of bed, "Baby, I've got to go to work to rest up. I'm so tired from moving, every muscle in my body aches."

Ann replied, "I'm not sure I can even get out of bed."

Chance said, "As tired as I am, I don't know how I'm going to find a way to fix the Montreal problem."

Ann said, "It doesn't sound like you have a whole lot of choices from what Mr. Goodhand said. You've got to find a way. We just got moved in and we can't be without a job."

Chance said, "I've found out they have been trying to fix this problem for months and nobody has been able to do it."

When Chance got to the plant, he sat down at his desk and began taking apart the meter mechanisms he brought back from Montreal. He studied each one of the mechanisms and he studied the bills of material. Chance began talking with Ben Loose, the design engineer who did all of the bills of material for the meters sold by Superior. Chance found out something very interesting; the bills of material used on the Montreal meters were not done by Ben. He was on vacation when the order came in and the production people just pulled some old bills of material from the files and built the meters for Montreal.

Chance asked Ben more questions and found the production people picked some of the worst bills of material available. In fact, three of the nine bills had been obsolete years ago, because of problems customers experienced with their meters. No one else had ever questioned Ben about the problems with the Montreal meters, why they didn't Chance never knew.

Ben suggested to Chance, using the latest bill of materials would probably fix the problems with the meters. Chance went to the plant to see how many of the special parts used in these bills of material were available so Chance could make up samples of the three meters. Chance's luck was holding the plant had all of the special parts needed to make up two of the mechanisms in inventory. The clerk in the stock room said she could have the other parts needed to make the third mechanism in a couple of days.

Chance took his box of treasures back to the engineering department. He sat down at his desk and began putting together one of the mechanisms. Chance adjusted the mechanism with the Canadian coins and it worked fine. Next, Chance tried the Montreal Flip and the coin fell out of the coin carrier and didn't give any time. Chance tried it again with the same result; the coin fell out of the coin carrier and didn't give any time for the quarter.

Chance operated the meter by turning the handle in a normal manner and the meter worked fine every time.

OK, so now what could Chance do? Chance thought about what he did to fix the old meters in Webster that just did not give time for coins. He remembered he added a second and, sometimes, a third spring to the extended coin pawls. The differences in springs used on the old meters were that they had flat leaf springs and the new springs were round wire springs. Chance didn't know if he could actually fit two of the round springs onto the extended coin pawl to double the strength on the winding pawl.

Chance took the mechanism apart again and removed the pin clip that held the pin holding the coin pawls in the coin carrier, than he removed the coin pawls. He put a second spring on the extended coin pawl. There was not enough room for the second spring between the jaws of the coin carrier where the coin pawls fit into the coin carrier. The clearance he needed to make the double spring system work was not very much. So Chance took out a small point file from his tool kit and filed down the jaw of the coin carrier. He tried to fit the coin pawls back into the coin carrier, but they still didn't fit, so he filed the jaw some more. He tried putting the pawls in again and this time they fit.

Chance put the coin pawl pin and clip back together and then reassembled the mechanism. He checked the adjustment of the coins again; they were perfect. Chance said a little prayer and tried the Montreal Flip. The coin didn't fall out of the carrier and he didn't lose the coin. The coin pawl stayed engaged into the winding ring and gave Chance the right amount of time for his quarter. Chance tried the Canadian nickel and the dime with the same results, the right amount of time for each of the coins.

As he continued testing the coins in the mechanism, Chance realized he was having a hard time turning the handle. This was due to the second spring on the ratchet pawl that engaged into the ratchet plate. This pawl kept the handle in place if you let go of it during the turning cycle. Without this system, if you let go of the handle, the coin carrier would return to its home position and throw the coins out of the coin slot and the coins would be rolling down the sidewalk.

Chance took the mechanism apart again. He took out the coin pawls and he took off the second coin pawl spring he had installed. He studied it a moment, then took a pair of side cutters and clipped off the side of the round spring that operated the ratchet pawl. He put the mechanism back together and tested it.

Now, he had no problem turning the handle and he still didn't lose the coin with the Montreal Flip. Chance did the same thing to the second mechanism that he had all of the parts he needed for the second bill of material. Same results, the mechanism worked fine.

About that time, Tim Hunt came to Chance's desk and said he got a call from Chris Goodhand wanting to know what we were doing to fix the meters in Montreal. Tim said Mr. Goodhand wanted to know how much it was going to cost Superior and how long it would take.

Tim told Chance, "This guy is something else! I told him we didn't know what we were going to do yet, but before I finished my sentence, he said you've got until Friday to get me a budget and a time schedule to get this problem fixed." Tim asked, "What have you found out so far Chance?"

Chance said, "I've only looked at two different mechanisms at this point, but maybe I have a way to fix the Montreal Flip."

Chance handed Tim one of the mechanisms with some coins. Tim tried it and it worked fine. Tim tried to do the Montreal Flip, no problem.

Tim said, "What in the hell did you do to this mech to stop the problem?"

Chance explained the double spring system. Tim told him to keep looking at all of the nine different mechanisms and build one of each one to see if he could make them all work with the double spring system.

Chance said, "I need some help getting the factory to make me some parts and help with determining our cost for the parts."

Tim said, "I'll get Frank Spencer, the Vice President of Manufacturing, to help us."

Things begin moving fast after that. Chance got all of the special parts he needed. He built the nine mechanisms over the next four days and worked out a plan to go to Montreal with one other person from the plant. He would hire people in Montreal to help re-manufacture the 10,000 meters on-site in Montreal.

Between Tim and Chance and someone from accounting, they worked out a cost and a timetable. The best guess was it would take four months in Montreal and almost two hundred thousand dollars to rebuild the ten thousand meters.

When they talked to Mr. Goodhand on the phone, after faxing him the plan and the cost, he asked only two questions, "Can you cut the cost and can you do the work quicker?"

Chance replied, "No."

Mr. Goodhand said, "OK. Get everything ready to start after the first of the year. I don't want this screwing up my warranty and operating cost in 1982."

He hung up the phone. Tim Hunt shook his head and said, "That son-of-a-bitch only cares about his bonus that's why he doesn't want the warranty cost to hit this year."

Chance said, "Well, I better get to work organizing parts to get shipped to Montreal so I can start the first week in January."

Tim said, "You've got it. It's all up to you."

January 3, 1983, Chance and Steve Heimholtz, an old Chicago employee of Superior, begin setting up an assembly line to convert the meters in Montreal. They soon had six local people hired to help them with the work. By the end of January, they were rolling out the mechanisms by the hundreds each week. Chance was going back and forth to Big Springs every other weekend and coordinating the parts. With Brandy looking after the shipments and pushing the plant, they never ran out of parts for the Montreal project. By the end of February they were over three-quarters finished with the project and Chance was bringing in the project a head of schedule and under budget. One good thing that occurred in February was that someone agreed to take over the payments on the house in Webster, but they didn't get any equity out of their house.

It was now the second week of March. Chance was leaving the plant on Monday morning enroute to Montreal, Frank Spencer Vice President of Manufacturing stopped Chance as he was walking out the door and said Mr. Goodhand asked me to have you stay at the plant, because he has someone coming from Chicago to meet with him. Chance went back inside the plant and called Steve Heimholtz and told him he was delayed in returning to Montreal because Mr. Goodhand was having him meet with someone from Chicago. Chance talked with Tim Hunt to find out what was going on, but Tim said he had no idea.

Late that afternoon, Dr. Alfred Handel introduced himself to Chance. Dr. Handel explained he was a consultant for Mr. Goodhand and he was here to give Chance a series of tests if he was agreeable. Chance told Dr. Handel, sure, no problem. Dr. Handel told Chance he would like to start first thing in the morning and Chance agreed.

Chance opened the door and walked in the house. Both Ann and Shane came out of the kitchen and said, "What are you doing here?"

Chance said, "Well, I'm not exactly sure, I only know I have to take a bunch of tests at the plant in the morning."

Chance recapped what had happened that day.

Ann asked, "Chance, what do you think this means?"

Chance replied, "Right now, I have no idea. One thing for sure, Chris Goodhand is a strange cat."

For the next three days, Chance took test after test.

Dr. Handel was a very interesting guy. He was an industrial psychologist and said he did work for a lot of major companies. On Thursday afternoon Dr. Handel sat down with Chance and told him his tests confirmed what everyone in the company thought were Chance's talents. He said Chance was very well organized, he was capable of working with all types of people, he didn't get angry easily and he was a natural leader. Dr. Handel also told Chance he had strong convictions and could not be easily influenced by other people.

Dr. Handel said, "Chance, you did very well on all my tests and I will give my report to Mr. Goodhand tonight. It was a pleasure meeting you and I want to wish you good luck in the future."

Friday morning Chance went into the plant and back to the engineering department. He called Steve Heimholtz to see how things were going in Montreal and Steve told him everything was fine. A few minutes later Frank Spencer came to Chance's desk and asked Chance if he would come into his office.

Chance said, "Certainly, since I'm trying to decide what to do next."

Chance followed Frank Spencer into his office and Frank motioned to Chance to sit down. Chance sat down in a chair across the desk from Frank.

Frank said, "I guess you have been wondering what was going on around here having you take tests for three days."

"Well, it's been a long time since I took tests for three days in a row.

Frank told Chance, "Mr. Goodhand wanted to make sure you were the right man for the job. Dr. Handel confirmed you were. Chance, I want you to take the job as my Superintendent of Manufacturing."

"I don't have any experience working in or running a manufacturing plant."

Frank said, "Chance, you know the product we're making and you can supervise the people. That's all you need to know.

"What about Albert Douglas. He's your Superintendent now. What happens to him?"

Frank replied, "He doesn't know it yet, but this is his last day at Superior. Chance, I want you know he's gone whether or not you take the job."

Chance thought for a minute and said, "I came back with Superior to do whatever I could to help and I sure need a job."

Frank said, "Congratulations, Mr. Superintendent. By the way, your pay will be increased by nine thousand dollars a year and your office will be right next to mine."

Chance walked, no he floated back to his desk in engineering. No one was around so he called Annie. When she answered the phone, Chance calmly said, "I know why I have been taking tests all week."

"Why?"

Chance whispered, "I've just gotten a big promotion. I'm the new Superintendent of Manufacturing. That's what all those stupid tests were about."

"Chance, that's wonderful. That means you won't have to travel anymore."

"Annie, you have no idea how wonderful this news is. I got a raise to go with the job. Guess how much my raise is?"

Ann said, "I don't know, twenty-five dollars a week?"

Chance said, "More."

"Fifty dollars a week?"

"How about one hundred seventy-three dollars a week," Chance crowed.

"You're kidding!"

"No, I'm not."

"Chance, that's wonderful!"

In just five months after coming back to Superior, Chance got a promotion and the biggest increase in salary he ever got in his life.

Chance thought, why did I ever leave Superior in the first place?

Chance thought about that for a minute and decided that if he had not left the company, he probably would have never got his new job.

Chance was on a roller coaster ride now. Four months later, Mr. Goodhand and several people from Chicago came to the plant for a meeting. Chance was never invited to these meetings, but late that day Frank Spencer asked Chance to come in to the conference room.

Mr. Goodhand said, "I have an announcement to make.

Effective in two weeks, Frank Spencer is leaving the company to accept a position with a company manufacturing submarine parts for the United States Government. I want to thank all of you for coming here for this announcement. You may all return to your work now."

End of discussion. The meeting was over.

Chance talked with Frank Spencer after the boys from Chicago left to go to the airport to take the Lear jet home.

Frank told Chance, "Actually, this is my last day because when I told Mr. Goodhand I was giving my two weeks notice, he said "Fine! Go ahead and leave today. There is no use in prolonging your exit from the company."

Mr. Goodhand decided he needed to hire someone with real manufacturing experience to take Frank Spencer's place. Two months later Chance was advised they hired a new Vice President of Manufacturing from St. Louis. He would arrive in two weeks.

A week later, Chance got a call on the hot line, the direct line from Chicago to Big Springs, advising him that at an afternoon meeting of Superior's major distributors and the President of the holding company that owned Superior fired Mr. Goodhand effective immediately. Chance couldn't believe it. Chance was told that a new general manger from another of the companies owned by the holding company would be in Big Springs on Monday and would be taking over the company.

On Monday afternoon, Les Rivers, Superior's new General Manager arrived at the plant. He held a meeting in the conference room with all of the department heads. When Mr. Rivers was told a new Vice President of Manufacturing had been hired, he got on the phone with the new man and told him Superior's offer for employment was withdrawn. Les Rivers arrived at the plant every Monday afternoon from Chicago and left by lunchtime on Friday. This went on week after week. Chance continued to run the plant, just as he had since he became the Superintendent of Manufacturing.

Les Rivers was a man with a dual personality. He would explode at people in the plant and then take them out for lunch or dinner and be the funniest, nicest person you would ever want to meet. That was his pattern of behavior, but he never exploded at Chance. Chance had lots of conversations with Les and he liked him a lot. He couldn't understand why Les acted the way he did. Les was a hard taskmaster, but Chance always thought he was fair with him. Two weeks before Christmas, Les asked Chance to come into his office. Les said, "Chance, close the door."

Les took a paper out of his inside coat pocket and handed it to Chance. Les said, "Chance this is your official notice that I'm promoting you to the Director of Manufacturing. With the title, you are getting a five thousand-dollar a year increase in salary and a three hundred twenty-five-dollar a month car allowance. You will also be entitled to annual bonuses for your job performance. Chance, I want to tell you what a great job you are doing and I want you to know how much I appreciate your cooperation and help."

Chance replied, "Thank you very much for the opportunity, Les. I'll do everything possible to help you."

"I know you will. The notice will be posted on the bulletin boards today announcing your promotion."

Chance reached across the desk to shake hands with Les and said, "Thanks, Les."

Chance walked out of Les' office and went straight into his own office. He picked up the phone and called Ann. When Ann answered the phone, Chance said, "Guess what just happened?"

"Knowing you and Superior, who knows?"

Chance said, "I just got promoted to Director of Manufacturing with a five thousand dollar a year raise in salary and three hundred twenty-five dollars a month car allowance."

Ann said, "You're kidding aren't you?"

Chance replied, "No I'm not kidding. With the car allowance, that's like getting another nine thousand dollars a year raise. Since the first of the year, our income has been increased eighteen thousand dollars a year."

"Chance you have almost doubled your salary since you started back with Superior fifteen months ago."

"Well, not exactly, but almost. Life sure looks better then it did a year ago."

One thing Chance didn't do was to put someone in his old job. Chance did both jobs; he was his own Superintendent of Manufacturing as well as being the Director of Manufacturing.

Nineteen eighty-four was a banner year for both Superior and Chance. Superior had sales of fourteen and a half million dollars, the company earned just over four million dollars and a lot of those earnings came as a result of Chance's efforts. Chance pulled orders from the sales people even before Superior's sales department got the orders. Every month the plant made their shipping dollar goal.

Sometimes this meant working until two, three, or four o'clock in the morning on the last day of the month, but Chance was right there on the line with his people. If they worked late, Chance ordered pizza for all of the staff. The staff liked him and he liked them. They worked hard together to help make the shipping goals.

Chance took risks and every risk worked for him. One major problem you have when you ship every order you have at the end of the month the next day you don't have any work.

Since there were thousands of different combinations of time and rate meters, all orders were custom built for each city so you couldn't start making meters until you had an order. At the end of every month a lot of the staff in the plant had to be laid off because they didn't have work. Chance thought the whole system was crazy. No matter what he did, he couldn't ever get enough orders to keep the pipeline filled.

The people in the plant didn't seem to mind though as many of them had worked for ten, fifteen, or twenty years or more for Superior. Another thing that helped keep employees was that Superior had the highest-paying jobs in town. During some months, two weeks passed before they had orders in the plant. This made it tougher and tougher for Chance and his staff.

They had to over-staff people, pay overtime and fly in parts from suppliers. All of this was done so Les looked good by hitting his profit goals each month.

Chance thought, if we could just smooth out production, profits would be even better. The fact was what they were doing actually made profits better. They were doing just-in-time deliveries of parts and supplies, so they didn't build inventory. They couldn't make mistakes on the orders, because they didn't have time to fix them. They made every production goal every month and they didn't have a lot of scrap.

Les and Tim Hunt began working with a company in New Jersey to design a new electronic parking meter. Almost all of their efforts were being put on this project. Les told Chance he planned to bring the product to market early next year. Tim told Chance they would never make that schedule. One thing Les learned from working for Mr. Goodhand, if you throw enough money and people at a project, you can get almost any project done. The product may not work, but you can fix it later. Neither Tim nor Chance knew why it was so important to get the electronic meter out early in nineteen eighty-five, but Les certainly had his reasons.

25

Les didn't come to the plant in Big Springs until the third week of January 1985. As soon as he came into the plant, he went straight to Chance's office and closed the door.

Les started his conversation by saying he wanted to review last year's results. Chance thought to himself, this should be a pleasant conversation.

Les said, "Your efficiencies and scrap were way off of what this plant has done in the past."

Chance said, "I don't think I understand what you are saying, Les."

"Well, your scrap is too high and your efficiencies are too low. In the past, efficiencies in this plant ran between ninetyseven to ninety-eight percent and scrap was only about one-half of one percent."

"Les let me tell you why they had such high efficiencies in the past it was because if they found parts that ran good, they just kept running them. And the scrap was all of the parts these people ran to get their one hundred twenty percent numbers on efficiencies, so it would average out for the whole plant. Who do you think is paying for that efficiency? We are."

Les said, "I'm telling you have to get efficiencies up to ninety-five to ninety-six percent."

Chance just looked at Les without replying.

Les continued, "The eighty-nine percent efficiency is not acceptable for nineteen eighty-five.

"I give up, Les. You have driven me all year to get out orders when we didn't have them. I've rode herd on everybody in this plant to make your shipping schedules. Les, I want another job, I sure can't satisfy you with this one."

"You have the job I have for you. If you don't want it, you can go home right now."

Chance took a long look at Les. He put his clipboard down on his desk, got up and started for his office door. Les got between him and the door and said, "Chance, let's sit down and talk about this." Chance turned around and went back behind his desk and sat down.

Les said, "What do you want to do?"

"I want back in sales."

"OK, I have an idea of what I want you to do. I want you to take over international sales. It will take a few months, but that's where I need you now."

What a change in a few seconds, first Les was telling Chance to go home and now he was telling Chance he needed him.

Les said, "I plan to introduce the new electronic meter in London in April and that's when I want you to start in international sales. Chance, I want you to put together a plan to do a market study of Europe, because I don't think our distributors are telling us the truth about how much of the business we are getting."

Chance said, "OK, Les. I'll keep running the plant and work on a marketing survey plan for Europe."

The next few months went fast. One of the men who came down from Chicago and who worked in one of the other divisions of the company was taking over Chance's job as Acting Director of Manufacturing. Chance was to become Director of International Sales after he finished the European marketing survey. Chance developed a plan to survey cities in ten countries, the United Kingdom, France, Belgium, the Netherlands, Germany, Switzerland, Italy, Monaco, Spain, and Portugal.

Chance was planning on surveying a total of thirty cities. Chance worked out all of the travel arrangements with the local travel agent. They prepaid all of his hotel reservations. All of Chance's plans were completed for the flights, trains, rental cars, etc. The only things he would need cash for were meals and incidentals. His survey plans began the Saturday after the sales meeting ended. He was would be traveling by train from London to Edinburgh, Scotland.

Chance was to fly into London on Tuesday the second week of April. With all of the traveling Chance had done, he had never been away from Ann for more then a couple of weeks at any time. No, that was not quite true; he forgot he had been in Ireland for almost a month when he repaired the meters there. Saying good- bye was never easy for them, but saying good-bye for over two months was impossible. Chance was leaving on a commuter flight from Big Springs. Chance and Ann held hands in the car all the way from home to the airport. Shane was in school and saying good-bye to him had not been easy either, but Chance told him he would see him in Frankfurt--soon.

Chance checked in his bags and the plane was ready to go. Chance and Ann kissed and held each other as tightly as possible.

Finally, the agent said, "Mr. Clark, we are ready to go."

Chance gave Ann one more kiss, turned away and started walking to the plane. He couldn't look back at her because tears were flowing down his cheeks and he knew Ann was crying too.

When he got to the top of the stairs and was about to climb into the plane, he turned and gave Ann a smile and a wave. Leaving Ann was harder then Chance ever thought it could be.

Chance flew from Big Springs to St. Louis, then on to New York. From New York, Chance's TWA flight took him directly to London's Heathrow Airport. Chance hated these overnight flights, but that's how almost every international flight to Europe was scheduled.

The introduction of the new electronic meter was to take place at the Holiday Inn, Marble Arch, in London to all of the International Superior Distributors. The decision to show it to the international market before introducing it in the United States was to try to bolster future international sales. Also, if there were problems with the new product, the competition that lived down the road in the States would not know as much about it. Also, Superior's biggest customers were all in the United States and they would not hear as much about any trouble with a new product in the international market.

The international sales meeting lasted for three days. Much of the time was spent listening to complaints about the company's changing policies. Some time was spent listening to complaints about the quality of the products and the slow delivery of the meters. All of the distributors agreed that since Chance had taken over running the plant, the quality was much better and the shipments were coming out of the plant faster then at any time in Superior's history.

The last day of the meeting was devoted to the introduction of the new electronic meter. Although all of the distributors were impressed with the development, they were cautious. There were almost as many questions left unanswered as there were answers given. They didn't know the exact selling price of the new electronic meter. They didn't know when they would be able to take orders, or after they got an order, when product could be manufactured and delivered. Before the meeting was over, Chance began feeling sorry for Les Rivers and Tim Hunt. This was to be their big show and they were falling on their faces in front of the President of the parent company and the Chairman of the Board, not to mention their entire International Distributor force.

Mercifully, the meeting finally ended when Mr. Sommers, the distributor from Ireland, got up and said, "Well, I can tell you all that this development of a new electronic parking meter is going to change our business forever. I think we should give a round of applause to Tim Hunt and his people for the work they have done developing this new product."

Everyone began applauding. Sean Sommers continued, "We also owe a round of applause to Les Rivers for putting up with us for the last three days."

Again, everyone clapped and the meeting was over.

The next morning Chance took a train from London to Edinburgh, Scotland. He picked up his rental car from Hertz and drove to the Sheraton Hotel that was at the edge of the central business district. After checking into the hotel, Chance began getting his materials ready to start his surveying the next morning.

The one thing wrong with Chance's survey plans was he didn't allow himself any room for error or delays. He had to survey every day or he would not be able to keep up with his schedule.

By seven o'clock the next morning Chance finished breakfast on this rainy Sunday morning and was ready to begin surveying the streets of Edinburgh. He was wearing his "survey uniform:" a baseball cap from the Los Angeles Olympics, new walking shoes, jeans, a lightweight jacket, and a short-sleeved shirt. He had a camera strapped around his neck, a clipboard with his survey forms and his hand counter. Chance walked for over ten hours that day in the rain.

When he took off his new shoes that night, the bottom of his feet, were solid blisters. Chance took a needle from the sewing kit he found in his hotel room and opened each of the blisters and drained them. God! How he hurt. He got into the bathtub with the hottest water his body could stand and soaked for over two hours. Then he applied Camphor Phenique to each blister, took four aspirin and went to bed. He hurt so badly he couldn't even think about eating. Chance was really hurting when he couldn't think about food.

The next morning Chance almost couldn't get into the bathroom. In fact, when he got out of bed, he couldn't stand up straight. He half-crawled and half- walked into the bathroom. It took Chance twice as long to get ready for work that day then any other time in his life. When he finally got dressed, he left his room and shuffled into the breakfast room. After breakfast he went back to his room, took four more aspirin and picked up his survey gear.

As he walked through the hotel lobby, he could see himself in the mirror and realized he was walking just like Tim Conway when he played the "old man" on TV. Chance kept going that day on pure guts and determination. He was not going to let anything stop him from completing his mission and staying on schedule.

The following morning he was doing better--he could walk at almost twice the shuffling speed of the day before. Chance finished the street survey of Edinburgh late that afternoon, right on schedule.

Chance drove to Glasgow, Scotland the following day and started surveying before he even found his hotel. After Glasgow, Chance surveyed Liverpool and Birmingham, England. After finishing with Birmingham, Chance drove back to London's Heathrow Airport, turned in his car and waited for his flight to Lille, France.

Chance was happy to be going to Lille since he had been staying in little English hotels that left a lot to be desired and in Lille he was booked into a Holiday Inn at the airport. When Chance arrived in Lille, he didn't have any problems with customs or immigration. He picked up his new Hertz rental car. It was a French car and Chance did not care much for it. He thought it was harder to drive then driving on the wrong side of the road in England. Chance found his Holiday Inn right at the airport and as he was leaving the airport, he found a lot of his old friends in the airport parking lot--Superior Parking Meters! He hadn't seen any of these since he left London in April. Chance checked into the hotel and took his luggage to his room.

Chance went to have dinner in the hotel but found the restaurant didn't open until 19:00 hours, so Chance came back at 19:00 hours. He ordered a steak and salad. The waiter said, "A bottle of wine comes with your steak tonight and no charge."

Chance thanked him. The steak tasted very good, the bread and butter was even better. The garden salad was OK and the wine was nice. Chance drank less then a glass and after paying his bill, started back to his room. The waiter carrying his wine bottle came running down the hall.

He said to Chance, "You forgot your wine."

Chance tried to tell him he didn't want it, but the waiter thrust it into Chance's arms and left.

The next night Chance left the wine bottle sitting in his room when he went to dinner. The waiter asked Chance if he wanted him to go to the room to get it.

Chance said, "No, tonight I'm drinking Perrier." The waiter gave Chance the "poor American look", but said nothing.

After Chance finished surveying Lille, he drove to Brussels. Brussels was a huge city and Chance couldn't find his Ramada Hotel. He drove and drove; he asked directions, but people didn't know the hotel. He turned a corner and POW, the right front tire was flat. Chance got out of the car and opened the trunk. He couldn't find a spare tire, a jack, a tire tool, or anything. A taxi went by and Chance hailed the taxi. Chance took all of his things from the despised French car, got in the taxi, and asked the driver to take him to the Ramada Hotel.

Within fifteen minutes, the taxi pulled up in front of the hotel.

A bellman took Chance's bags and Chance asked the taxi driver to come into the hotel so he could pay him. Chance had only American, English, and French money. The driver accompanied him inside and Chance exchanged French Francs for Belgian Francs. Chance paid the driver and included a nice tip for saving him.

Chance got the number of the Hertz office and telephoned them to tell them about his problem with the French car. The Hertz man explained that the spare tire was under the trunk of the car on that model and the tools to change the tire were in a special compartment in the trunk.

Chance said, "I don't care, I want another car, because I don't want this car!" The Hertz man said, "OK, we will bring you another car."

Chance said, "That's great, because I'm going to have the car for another two months and I didn't like the car I have."

About two hours later, someone from the front desk phoned and said, "Mr. Clark, a man from Hertz is here with your car." Chance went to the desk to meet the Hertz representative.

The Hertz man said, "Let me go over the car with you, sir."

They went out of the hotel and the representative began explaining the car. It was a red German Opel. Although it was smaller, Chance liked it better already. Chance thanked the representative and signed the papers for the new car.

Surveying Brussels took Chance three days. On his last day in Brussels, Chance was walking on a street near the main railroad station a little after five o'clock in the evening. Chance was counting the parking meters next to the curb when he noticed young women sitting in storefront windows. Chance kept walking and counting meters. When he got near the end of the block, he stopped, turned around and really looked at the storefront windows. Chance was perplexed. Here was an entire block of young women on display in the windows. Some were dressed in street clothes and others had on sexy nightgowns. About that time, a man with a briefcase went inside one of the buildings. The young woman who had been sitting in the window closed the curtains behind her as she took the man by his arm and disappeared behind the curtain. Chance just witnessed an example of the oldest profession in the world. The boy from Kansas had just walked past a block of prostitutes. Chance remembered the great line from the Wizard of Oz, "I don't think we are in Kansas anymore, Toto."

The next stop on Chance's surveying trip was Antwerp, then Rotterdam, and next Amsterdam. The weeks were going by and Chance was staying right on schedule.

Chance talked with Ann once a week. He could tell she was getting very lonely. Since Chance was walking ten to twelve hours a day, seven days a week and when he wasn't walking he was either sleeping, washing clothes, or driving, he didn't realize how lonely he was until he talked to Ann on the phone. Then it really hit him. After he hung up the phone, he would sit staring off into nothing and think, why am I doing this, why aren't I home with Annie? The weekly phone calls kept him up-to-date on how Shane, Chase, Marie, and Curt were doing, as well as how his dad was. Ann always talked to Chance's dad every week to check on him to be certain Chance knew his dad was doing all right. By now it was mid-May, Ann told Chance she and Shane were going to Webster for the Memorial Day weekend. School would be out the first week of June and then she and Shane would be flying to Frankfurt to meet him.

One of their new friends in Big Springs lived next door to them, was coming with Ann and Shane to Frankfurt. Her name was Lou Weeks. Her husband died a short time after the Clarks moved to Big Springs. Lou's husband was a retired Air Force Colonel.

Although Chance never met him, he knew a lot about him. He had been one of the first United States pilots to join the British Air Force during World War II. He was a fighter pilot and fought in the Battle of Britain.

When the United States entered the war, he transferred over to the Army Air Corp. When the war in Europe ended, he was sent back to the States for reassignment to the Pacific, but before he reached the Pacific, two atomic bombs were dropped on Japan and the war ended. After that, he was one of the people sent to occupy Japan. Lou was able to join her husband in Japan soon after the occupying forces were in control of the country. Lou told them a lot of stories about how bad a time the people of Japan had after the war ended. She had a great memory for the details of people and places she saw when she first arrived in Japan, and she told Chance how much things changed for the better in the two years they lived in Japan.

Lou offered to pay for Shane's trip to Europe, since the Clarks invited her to go with them. She had never been to Europe and said she "wanted to see it before I die."

Chance had a lot of work to do before Ann, Shane and Lou arrived in Frankfurt. He surveyed Hamburg, Cologne, Bonn, Munich, Frankfurt and Stuttgart. He drove to Zurich, Switzerland and walked for fifteen hours to survey it. The next day he had to drive back to Frankfurt because Ann, Shane and Lou would be arriving. He was ready to see Ann. He needed her; they had never been away from each other for this long.

On the big day, Chance got up at three-thirty in the morning, showered, shaved and dressed. He was on the road by four o'clock.

He couldn't be late to meet Ann. Chance was soon in Germany and on the Autobahn. His speed increased about every twenty-five miles. Chance kept pushing the little red Opel faster and faster. The closer he got to Frankfurt, the faster Chance was driving. He was up to 200K per hour and passing nearly everything on the Autobahn. Chance kept checking the time on his watch and the kilometers to Frankfurt on the road signs.

Driving in the left lane on the Autobahn, the fast lane, you have to watch your rearview mirror for cars coming up behind you. No matter how fast you were driving, someone would pass you! Chance looked in his mirror and could see lights flashing behind him. Chance moved over one lane to the right, a Jaguar convertible passed Chance like he was parked. Chance thought, my God, I'm driving 200K an hour, how fast could that Jag be going?

By nine o'clock that morning, Chance was parking the red Opel in the parking garage at the Frankfurt Airport. He had over an hour to spare before Ann's plane was scheduled to arrive. When he got inside the airport, he checked to see the time of arrival for Ann's flight the board showed Ann's TWA flight from St. Louis showed nine-thirty, over 45 minutes early. Chance was delighted and very anxious to see Ann and of course, Shane. The minutes were dragging by. The closer it got to the time for Ann's plane to land, the longer each minute took.

Finally, it was time for Ann's plane to arrive. Chance waited outside of passport control. Suddenly he saw Shane and Shane saw him. They started toward each other, Chance walking as quickly as he could and Shane running. Chance reached down, put his arms around Shane and picked him up. Just behind Shane, he saw Ann and Lou Weeks. Chance put Shane down after giving him a kiss and started toward Ann. Ann was carrying a couple of bags and pushing a luggage cart. She set the bags down and came around the cart, reaching out for Chance. Chance had her in his arms and was kissing her like there was no tomorrow. When they stopped kissing, Chance spoke to Lou Weeks. "Was the flight all right, Lou?"

Lou said, "It was a great flight; they just kept bringing me boozes all night."

Chance smiled and gave Lou a hug, too.

Ann said, "Chance, let me look at you."

"What's the matter?"

Ann said, "Nothing is the matter, but you must have lost fifty pounds."

"I don't know about fifty pounds, but with all of the walking doing the surveys, I have certainly lost weight. Besides, Annie, these Europeans don't cook like you do!"

Chance and Shane loaded the luggage into the red Opel, and they were soon on their way back to Zurich. The drive from Frankfurt to Zurich took a lot longer with Ann, Shane and Lou in the car. Chance would not push the car the way he did coming to Frankfurt to get them. It was late afternoon before they arrived back in Zurich and by that time, all the travelers were dead tired.

Chance had everything arranged at their hotel. Shane would be staying in Lou's room and she insisted she would pay for Shane's room and hers for the entire trip. Reservations for the hotels had been made in Big Springs for their entire trip, so they didn't have to worry about that.

By the time Chance got the luggage unloaded with the help of a bellman, the three cross-Atlantic travelers were ready for baths or showers and clean clothes. After Chance deposited his charges in their hotel rooms, he went out on the streets of Zurich to try to finish up his street survey. He promised Ann he would be back in two to three hours to take them for an early dinner.

Chance made it back to the hotel in about three and halfhours. Everyone looked a lot more refreshed then the last time he saw them and they were hungry. It had been a long time since they had breakfast on TWA. Chance saw a restaurant earlier that looked interesting to him. He had tried the hotel's restaurant and found it to be very expensive and not very good. Off the four of them went to the Movenpick Restaurant.

Chance found he could hardly talk above a whisper. It had been so many months since he carried on a conversation it was as if he couldn't speak. Riding from Frankfurt to Zurich he didn't have to say much because Ann, Shane and Lou were napping most of the trip. Now that he had someone to talk to, he couldn't talk! The meal at the Movenpick was OK. Shane and Chance had a hamburger and fries. Ann and Lou had some type of fish sandwich with salads. Chance looked at the back of the menu after they finished their meals and saw a picture of a banana split. It looked good to him and he pointed at the picture and showed it to Ann. They all ordered desserts. Chance and Ann ordered the banana splits, Shane had a sundae and Lou ordered a bowl of strawberries. When the banana splits were set down in front of Chance and Ann they both thought of the banana splits they got on their first date back in Webster so many years ago. Ann told Shane and Lou about how they ordered banana splits on their first date at the Cash Drug Store in Webster and when Chance went to pay for them, he was told a man sitting at the counter had paid for them. Ann also said the lady working there told them, "I guess the man just wants you to go through life wondering who paid for your banana splits."

She certainly was right; they were still wondering who had been so kind to them, Ann laughed at her own story. Chance loved Ann's voice and to hear her laugh.

When Chance and Ann were back in their hotel room, Chance said in his whisper, "I bet you never thought when we had our first banana splits; we would be having them one day in Zurich, Switzerland."

Ann laughed and said, hardly!

Chance put his arms around her and held her as tightly as he could just as he had when they parted at the Big Springs Airport months ago. He began kissing her and unfastening her blouse at the same time.

Chance said, "Annie, it's been so long since we've been together, this is almost like a first time." "Chance, you can't know how much I missed you."

He answered, "I can only know how much I missed you. If you missed me as much, you have really been lonely!"

"Ann, I need you so much," Chance whispered.

They were soon undressed and in bed.

The next morning Chance got up at his usual time of six- thirty, showered, dressed, and told Ann, "I've got a few more streets to finish surveying."

He promised to return in time for them to have breakfast together. True to his word, Chance finished his work and was back at the hotel before nine o'clock.

Ann was just finishing dressing and putting on her makeup when Chance came into their room.

She said, "Chance, I don't know how you can get up so early. It's still two o'clock in the morning at home."

"Ann, you forget how long I've been working on this time already."

Chance surprised himself because his voice was almost back to normal.

Ann said, "Your voice is back."

"It must have been spending one night with you," Chance grinned.

"Sure, I'm good for you."

"You can say that again, baby," Chance said as he gave her a good morning kiss. After breakfast with Ann, Shane and Lou, Chance turned the car into Hertz. Shane said he wanted to go with his dad. When Chance and Shane turned in the car to Hertz, Chance asked for a receipt for his charges.

The Hertz clerk said, "No, you will receive it on your credit card directly from the renting agent in Brussels."

Although Chance rented two cars from Hertz in Europe for over three months, he never received a bill.

The rest of their trip in Europe was to be by train using Eurorail tickets purchased in Big Springs before Chance left for Europe.

Chance was told by people in his company who were experienced with European trains that they ran on time, especially the Swiss trains which were like Swiss watches. They soon found that to be true. Their train was scheduled to leave at 14:04 hours. At exactly 14:04 hours, the train pulled out of the station bound for Milan, Italy. Traveling on Eurorail passes, they were in first class and they found train travel in Europe was very pleasurable and convenient. The trains were clean, well run and arrived in the heart of the cities, just where Chance needed to be. Chance was, after all, still surveying cities, even if his wife, son and a friend were on a European holiday.

The train trip from Zurich to Milan was spectacular. The Swiss Alps were unbelievably beautiful. On the train Lou engaged a Swiss woman in conversation. The lady made trips back and forth from Zurich to Milan several times a year since she was a buyer for a Swiss shoe company. She told Lou that during the trip they would be going through the longest train tunnel in Europe. It would take over thirty minutes to travel through the tunnel. Further, she explained they would pass by a church in a small Swiss village and go by it on all four of its sides.

Chance was fascinated by the concept that they could pass by one building on all four sides of it. It was true, however. It took almost an hour of climbing and going down the mountain to pass by this Swiss village, but by the time they actually traveled past the village, they had indeed, passed by all four sides of the same church.

When they arrived in Milan, they had exactly two minutes to get themselves and their luggage off the train. Chance and Shane, moved their luggage to the vestibule of the train car so that when the train stopped, Chance would get down on the platform and Shane could hand down the pieces of luggage. This was to become their standard operating procedure in getting on and off trains. The only variation was when they got on the trains. Then Chance would get in the train car and Shane would hand him the luggage. Ann and Lou would find them seats on the train; Chance and Shane would handle the luggage. Chance had his large pilot- type briefcase and one large suitcase. Ann and Shane each had one large suitcase and Lou, bless her heart, brought five small to medium-sized cases so she could take care of her own luggage, which, of course she couldn't do. She never thought about getting on and off trains in two to four minutes. Upon arrival in Milan, Chance exchanged money for Italian lira and found a taxi to take them to their hotel. After traveling about four blocks, they arrived at the hotel and the driver helped them unload their luggage. When Chance tried to pay him, Chance could not understand how much he owed. Chance learned in Europe, if you held out money in your hand if you didn't understand the amount of money owed, people would honestly take the amount you owed them. That is, until he arrived in Milan!

The driver quickly took advantage of Chance, grabbed bills out of Chance's hand, jumped in his taxi, and sped away. Chance realized that this jerk had just taken the equivalent of over one hundred U.S. dollars for a four-block taxi ride. Chance felt like a jerk for just opening his hand and letting the taxi driver steal a hundred dollars from him.

The problems in Milan were just beginning. When they got to the desk to claim rooms that they paid for over four months ago, they were told by the desk clerk, "Sorry, we are overbooked.

However, we have booked you in another hotel just a few blocks away."

Chance tried to argue with the desk clerk, but suddenly the desk clerk's English disappeared.

Finally in desperation, Chance said, "How are we going to get ourselves and our luggage over to this other hotel?"

The desk clerk's English came back as suddenly as it had disappeared. "We will pay for a taxi to take you to your hotel and the bellman will load your luggage for you."

Arriving at the new hotel, they found they had been downgraded by at least two stars in the quality of the hotel. Their stay in Milan was most unpleasant. The only thing they liked was the cathedral area of the city. They learned one thing on this trip and that was if they didn't have a good hotel, it affected the way they felt about the city. A good hotel equaled a nice city, bad hotel a bad city.

Chance later returned to Milan many times and stayed in five star hotels in other parts of the city. He felt on his first trip to Milan they never really saw anything of the city. He found Milan was, in fact, a wonderful city.

They continued traveling in Italy, touring Florence, Bologna, Venice and Rome. During their stay in Rome, Ann, Shane and Lou took bus tours to see the city and Chance took an afternoon to visit the Vatican with them. They got to see a lot of the city this way and they had a wonderful hotel situated just at the top of the Spanish Steps.

Their next stop was Nice, France and on the way, their train took them through Pisa and they saw the Leaning Tower of Pisa from the windows of the train. Shane liked that a lot. Chance and Shane developed their own saying about Nice, France: "Nice was nice!"

They managed to go to Monte Carlo for an afternoon, but Princess Grace was not receiving guests. They did go to the famous casino, but even James Bond was out.

From Nice, they traveled to Marseille. What a hole, compared to Nice. If Nice was nice, Marseille was the "pits."

Chance got a telephone call from Les Rivers telling him they wanted him to go to Lisbon as soon as he could get there. This proved what Chance was always saying, or as he put it, "Clark's Law:"

The only sure thing in life is change! Chance and Shane went to the main railroad station in Marseille to see how they could get to Lisbon. Chance discovered a new law in France, everyone goes on strike!

Chance asked the clerk if he had any idea how long this strike would last. The clerk's response was, "Who knows? Maybe a day, maybe two, who knows?"

They tried again the next day, but got the same answer, "Who knows?"

The following day Chance tried to get a flight from Marseille to Lisbon. "Sorry, there are no flights from Marseille to Lisbon."

They were trapped; they couldn't get out of Marseille, they couldn't even rent a car.

Finally, Chance got airline reservations for them from Marseille to Paris. They would have to stay overnight in Paris and then fly on to Lisbon the next day. Chance found it was expensive flying from one city to another in Europe. Two days later they arrived in Paris, but when they went to get a taxi in Paris, they were told, "Sorry, you must have a special taxi because Paris taxis are only licensed for three people. You could take two taxis."

Fortunately, a man who worked for the hotel tourist association got them a "special taxi" and arranged to have them picked up the next morning in a "special taxi" to get them back to the airport.

Chance and Ann decided they must have found the only kind person in all of France, because he worked so hard to get them rooms and taxis.

26

The next morning the taxi was waiting for them as promised. The ride to the airport was an adventure. The taxi was a station wagon with leather seats. Chance was in the front seat with the driver and Ann, Shane and Lou were in the back seat. The driver took it upon himself that he must hurry to the airport, because all Europeans were always late going to their flights.

The driver ran red lights, he turned down residential streets to bypass traffic and from the time the taxi left the hotel, Lou was sitting between Ann and Shane but, in truth, she was sliding from side to side on the seat and down on the floor. The more Chance tried to explain to the driver they had plenty of time the faster he went. Ann and Lou were laughing so hard even if the taxi had been parked Lou would not have been able to stay in her seat.

They made it to the airport in one piece except for all the bruises Lou suffered. What a ride! No roller coaster could have given Lou a ride like the one she got in the back seat of that "special French taxi."

When they arrived in Lisbon, they checked into the Lisbon Sheraton. What a difference from the hotels they checked out of in Paris and Marseille. It was wonderful.

Chance met with Superior's newest distributor. This was a large family-owned company that made water and electric meters. They decided to add parking meters to their product line since they were already working with city officials with their other meters.

They explained they needed Chance's help with a "municipal fair," the first such event ever held in Portugal. They wanted to show the parking meters in their booth along with their other products.

The distributor told Chance they would fly to Porta and then drive to a little town up in the mountains called Braga. Chance had never heard of this town, but soon found that back in history it had been a very important town. The Cardinal of Braga controlled the church in Brazil. During that period of time, the cardinal was second in power in the Catholic Church only to the Pope. Controlling Brazil with its vast wealth made the Braga Cathedral a work of art. It still maintained a museum with many treasures brought from Brazil.

Ann, Shane and Lou stayed at the Sheraton in Lisbon and Chance didn't even tell the new distributors they were traveling with him.

The municipal fair turned out to be just what its name implied, a fair. Instead of having city officials visiting the fair, it was open to the general public. Perhaps this outdoor event was good for the public, but for the exhibitors it was a bust.

Chance and the distributors returned to Lisbon after two nights in Braga. Chance was ready to be back sleeping with Ann. As the distributors were taking Chance back to his hotel, Chance told them his wife, youngest son, and a neighbor were traveling with him in Europe. The distributors insisted on taking all of them to dinner on their last night in Lisbon. When the distributors learned they were going by train from Lisbon to Madrid, they said, "This is will be a horrible trip on a very bad train."

The next morning they found out what the distributors were talking about. The Lisbon Special was four cars long, an engine and three cars; one first class car and two second class cars. The first class car was old, very old, and Chance could only imagine what the second class cars looked like. When they reached the Spanish border, Chance found out why the trip took so many hours.

First, they changed the engine, along with the crew including the engineer from Portuguese to Spanish.

Next, the Spanish immigration people checked passports and then the border and customs officials came into the train cars with machine guns and police dogs. They began going through the first class car.

Lou said, "Just look at those beautiful dogs."

Chance wished she would just stay in her seat and keep her mouth shut, but she didn't she got up and followed the dogs down the aisle after they past by her. Chance knew she loved animals and birds, but these dogs just weren't the right ones to pursue. She tried to pet one of the dogs. It was easy to see the dog and the border policeman were not happy with her.

Ann said, "Lou, would you please sit down?"

The dog turned and growled at her. Lou sat back down in a seat. The border guard ordered Lou in Spanish to open her bags.

Lou didn't understand, but when he gestured to her about opening her bags, she complied. The guard made her open each one of her five bags. He poked around and found nothing that interested him in the bags. Then he walked away and made everyone else on that end of the train car open their bags. Lou started in again about how beautiful the dogs were.

Ann said, "For goodness sake Lou, would you just sit down and shut up?"

The guard and dogs came back to the area where Chance, Ann, Shane and Lou were sitting. One of the guards pointed at Chance's luggage and then at him. Chance shook his head up and down, signifying the bags were his. Chance got up to get the bags down, but the guard shook his head "no." Their bags were the only ones in the car not searched.

The dogs stopped at the seat in front of Lou and began acting as if they found something. The guards got the train conductor and after a lengthy conversation in Spanish, they took out a large knife and shredded the material on the seat and the seat back.

They found nothing, but this time Lou kept her mouth shut. After some time passed and with the dogs and guards going back and forth in the train car again and again, they finally got off the train and let the train leave. This ordeal took more than three hours. They talked with some of the other passengers on the train who explained the border guards were looking for both drugs and weapons. The route from Lisbon into the rest of Europe was a major drug route and the Basques were doing everything possible to get weapons into Spain.

After surveying Madrid, they took a bus to Toledo, Spain.

Toledo was a famous steel center and for making swords. Shane got two swords to start a collection of swords.

Their next stop was Barcelona, where Chance would discover his caution with their passports would pay off. Before leaving Big Springs, Chance made photocopies of everyone's passport. Copies were placed inside each of the Clark's bags and in one of Lou's bags. Friday night after dinner, they were walking down one of Barcelona's most famous streets, the Ramblas.

Lou saw a lady with a small dog and the dog was doing several tricks. Chance was a little behind Lou, as he and Ann were looking at some leather goods in a small sidewalk shop. Lou's purse was hanging down on her arm. Just as Chance looked to see where Lou and Shane were, Chance saw a young woman open Lou's purse and take out her billfold and passport. Chance yelled at the woman and took off running after her, but the woman was soon lost in the crowd of people. When Chance returned from his unsuccessfully chase of the woman, Lou was still going through her purse to see what had been taken. All of her money, traveler's cheques, credit cards and passport were gone.

They walked back to the hotel, and Chance told Ann and Shane to stay at the hotel while he took Lou to the police station to file a report on the robbery. When they arrived at the police station, they were told to wait until an officer who spoke English could take their report; at least, that's what Chance got out of the sign language and gestures. He sat down, but nosy Lou started looking around.

The next thing Chance knew, she wandered into the jail. Chance saw prisoners reaching through the bars trying to grab her and other prisoners yelling at her in Spanish. One of the police officers took Lou by the arm, led her back to where Chance was sitting and gently pushed her into a chair. Thirty minutes later a police officer with some English-speaking ability came into the station and helped Lou get the report filled out. She was given a copy of the report. When they got back to the hotel, Lou said, "Daddy," mocking Shane," can I have some money? I need a drink."

Chance took some money out of his pocket and gave it to Lou.

He said, "Have one for me, too, because I think I'm going to bed. I've had enough excitement for the day."

Monday morning before breakfast, Chance and Lou walked to the American Consulate's office. They were directed to the passport department. When they opened the door, they were surprised to find the passport office filled with people. They were told it would take three days to get a new passport for Lou. Chance handed the lady behind the counter his photocopy of Lou's passport and the copy of the police report.

Chance said, "We have a flight tomorrow to Geneva and I have to get there."

The lady said, "Since you have a photocopy of Mrs. Weeks' passport and if you can get us new passport pictures, we will get a passport for her this afternoon. The lady told them to go downstairs and walk a couple of blocks east from the Consulate's office they would find a place to get passport photos made. Lou and Chance were soon back with the photos. They had to wait a few minutes until they could talk to the clerk who helped them earlier.

Lou began talking with a woman and her nineteen-year-old daughter, the lady told Lou when they arrived at Barcelona's main railroad station last night several young men took their purses, their suitcases and everything they had except the clothes they were wearing. She said they had a real problem, because they couldn't even prove they were Americans. Another young couple she spoke with told her they were attacked Friday night on the same street Lou had her things stolen on and both of them had been beaten up. Chance decided Lou was lucky after all.

Chance and Lou returned later that afternoon and picked up Lou's new passport. The clerk who was helping them said twentyseven Americans had their passports stolen over the weekend in Barcelona. Chance asked why they would steal passports and the lady replied, "We understand on the black market, an American passport can sell for up to ten thousand dollars. Now Chance understood.

The next morning, they flew to Geneva on Swiss Air. Stepping onto that plane was like taking a big breath of fresh air after being in a bar filled with blue smoke. Surveying Geneva went well. Shane went with Chance and helped with the survey and since they were staying at a Ramada Inn their accommodations were fine.

Chance thought everything in Switzerland was very pricey. After being in Geneva for three days, they would be traveling on a French TGV train non-stop to Paris leaving early in the morning. Even with the Eurorail passes they had to make seat reservations and pay a small charge to ride on the TGV train. Chance and Shane finished the Geneva street survey about eleven in the morning and Chance thought it would be fun to just get on a train and ride up into the Swiss Alps. Chance and Shane went back to the Ramada Inn and told Ann and Lou they were going train riding for the afternoon.

Chance looked over his train schedule and saw they could take a circle route to Speases, a town almost in the middle of the Swiss Alps. They took a train to Lausanne, transferred to one going to Milan, but they got off at a town just before they got to the Italian border. Then they took the train to Speases.

They were going to get off at Speases and have dinner, but found the last train of the day heading back was leaving five minutes after they arrived in Speases. They got on the train headed south from Speases and when it arrived at Gstaad, it stopped.

Chance asked, "How long will we be here?"

The reply from the conductor was "Tomorrow morning."

Chance discovered there were no trains leaving Gstaad until seven the next morning going anywhere from Gstaad.

Somehow they had to get back to Geneva that night. They walked to the Gstaad Hotel and asked if they could get a taxi to take them to Montreux tonight. The clerk telephoned a man who operated the taxi stand. He drove over to the hotel and talked to Chance and said, "Do you have five hundred Swiss Francs?" Chance said he did. The taxi driver said, "It can't be American money, it's got to be Swiss Francs."

Chance took out his money and showed it to the driver. The driver said, "OK, I'll be back later," and he left.

Chance studied his train schedule very carefully to be sure that even if they got to Montreux, that they could get a train to Lucerne, then to Geneva. It would be close; they would only have two minutes between trains in Lucerne to get on the train for Geneva. It would also depend on them getting from Gstaad to Montreux and then being able to get on the train to Lucerne! The taxi driver finally returned. He asked again, "Do you have the five hundred Swiss Francs?"

Chance assured him he did. They loaded into the taxi and the driver began driving south. The driver knew the train schedule better then Chance and knew they would have very little time even if pushed the taxi fast enough for his passengers to make the trip. Passing through the Swiss Alps at night under a full moon looked like a storybook setting. It was breathtaking! Chance was just as happy not being able to see the car's speedometer, because he would have been worrying more about getting there alive then enjoying the view. When the taxi pulled up at the station, Chance handed the driver five hundred fifty Swiss Francs.

The train was just coming into sight. Chance and Shane ran up the stairs to the train platform with Ann and Lou right behind them. Chance stood in the door so it couldn't close and waited for Ann and Lou. They made it! The train was moving two minutes after it stopped at the station. Chance marveled at Lou because he was pooped from climbing what amounted to two stories of stairway and he wasn't seventy years old.

The routine in Lucerne was just the same, only they had to go down the stairs and then back up another set to yet another platform, but they made it.

By the time they arrived at the Ramada Inn, it was after two o'clock in the morning. They were starving since they hadn't had lunch or dinner. After some conversation with the desk clerk, the man promised to see what he could find for them in the kitchen. Cheese sandwiches, potato chips, pickles and cokes never tasted as good to any of them before as now.

The next morning they were on the TGV train for Paris by seven o'clock. They arrived in Paris on July 4th. It was funny, but Chance and Ann had been invited to a high school class reunion back in Webster scheduled for this day. Although they didn't graduate with the class, they had been invited to all of their class reunions. Chance thought it was extremely kind of their classmates to invite them.

Due to the size of the city of Paris, Chance could only survey one fourth of the city. Then, by using the information he got from his actual survey, he would factor those numbers to give him a good projection of the total number of parking spaces on the streets of Paris.

Shane loved Paris. They took a day off and went to the Louvre to see all of the famous paintings, which fit right in with Shane's interest and talent. Shane was already showing great talent as an artist.

They left Paris by train, enroute to London. Les Rivers wanted Chance to go to London and meet his old friend Graham Rommey with UK Parking Controls because the British Government was working on standards for electronic parking meters. Graham and Les were concerned that unless Superior was represented at an upcoming meeting of the British Standards Commission, the English and Swedish parking meter companies would influence the standards and Superior would be left out in the cold.

If your product didn't meet British Standards, you could never sell them in the United Kingdom. Chance had dealt with British Standards before. Superior had to paint the parking meter housings special colors used only in the United Kingdom. Chance knew the British were so organized they had a British Standard for everything and parking meters came under the heading of "street furniture." Chance often joked that he bet the British even had a standard for making love.

Their train took them to Calais, France and there they got off and transferred themselves and their luggage to a very large ferry-boat. The ferry sailed almost as soon as they and the other passengers were on board. The crossing of the English Channel was very smooth. Chance couldn't help but think about the crossing made during World War II and how many men died when they landed on the beaches at Normandy.

Chance's Uncle Tommy made that crossing, but he was one of the lucky ones. He went on to be one of the first Americans to enter Paris and to cross the Rhine and he came home safely. This trip was a lot more comfortable then that one must have been and Chance was glad when they arrived at Dover and knew no one would be shooting at them. As the ferry approached Dover, they had an excellent view of the White Cliffs of Dover and Chance was happy they didn't have to climb them to land.

The ferry-boat docked and people scrambled off and headed for the waiting train to take them to London's Victoria Station. By the time they got their luggage stowed in the compartment of the train, Chance wasn't sure if climbing the cliffs would not have been easier ... but probably not. They had a first-class compartment all to themselves with a door that opened directly out onto the platform. Shane thought this was the coolest train they had been on, it was even better then the TGV.

Chance had planned to go on to Ireland to finish his survey, but now he didn't know what he could do until he met with Graham Rommey. The next morning he, rung up Graham, as the British say. Graham told him on the phone that it would be at least another week or two before the meeting. However, Graham needed Chance to help make several personal calls on people on the commission with him before the official meeting. Graham had received an advanced copy of the proposed standards for electronic meters and Superior's meter would not qualify as the standards were now written.

After five days in London waiting to see when Chance would be attending the British Standards meeting Shane asked his mom if they could go home. Chance had already canceled all of their reservations in Ireland and everyone was tired and getting bored. Chance called TWA and booked Ann, Shane and Lou on a flight the next day to St. Louis.

Ann had driven her car to St. Louis because it cost so much to fly from Big Springs to St. Louis. Her car had been parked at the St. Louis Airport the whole time they had been in Europe. Chance rode with them to Gatwick Airport the next day to see them off.

Shane and Lou were more then ready to go home, but Ann didn't want to go and leave Chance by himself and Chance really didn't want to be left, but he had no choice.

Chance and Ann put up a good front when they said their good-byes. After the appropriate number of kisses and hugs from Shane and Lou, Chance held Ann close and he told her how happy he was that she came over to be with him and that he would really miss her. They kissed again and Ann turned to go through passport control and Lou shouted back, "Thanks Chance for a wonderful trip and for putting up with me."

Chance smiled through a few tears and said, "You're welcome and I'll see you in Big Springs very soon."

Ann, Shane and Lou disappeared through the doors of immigration and out of sight. Chance was left alone again.

Chance and Graham made call after call on members of the commission, lobbying each of them for changes to the proposed British Standards. By the time the Standards Commission actually met almost three weeks later, Chance and Graham had picked up enough support to make the changes allowing Superior's electronic meters to be imported and sold in the United Kingdom. The minute the meeting was over; Chance went straight to the Marble Gate Holiday Inn and called Ann. When she answered the phone, Chance just said, "I'm coming home."

The next night he arrived in Big Springs. It was now late August and Chance had left the States in early April.

Chance had to fly to Chicago four days later and make a report to Les Rivers on his survey trip. After he filed his report and set up a slide show for Les to show the Board of Directors the type of parking equipment he saw in Europe, Chance flew back home to Big Springs. On his trip home, Chance reflected that in traveling to ten countries and surveying thirty cities, not one person ever asked him what he was doing. In the United States Chance would have been questioned within the first hour by a parking enforcement officer, the public, or by a storekeeper. Chance thought that was the strangest part of his trip.

Two weeks later a reporter called from an import-export magazine and asked him all about his market research experience in Europe. The next issue of the magazine Chance's picture was on the cover with a caption under it that read, "I'm one of the only persons that walked across Europe one street at a time."

345

27

The next year, nineteen eighty-six, Chance would spend three weeks in Europe working with his distributors and then three weeks back in the office in Big Springs. Chance would just begin adjusting to the six, seven, or eight-hour time changes between Big Springs and the various countries in Europe he was working in before he flew home. At home, the same thing would happen; he would just about get adjusted to the time in Big Springs and then would leave for Europe. Chance felt Heathrow Airport was almost home, since he spent so much time there.

Chance kept up the pace until the middle of December then Chance came home for Christmas and New Year's and didn't leave Big Springs until the end of January.

Chance's area of international sales responsibility kept growing. At first he only had Europe and then he was assigned Australia and New Zealand. He went to Australia two or three times a year, while still keeping up his trips to Europe. Hong Kong was added, then Taiwan and then came South Africa.

By December 1986, Chance covered the whole world for international sales for Superior. He had now worked in over fifty countries on six continents. He knew other people had been to more countries then he, but he had the opportunity to work in more countries then most people. When Ann and he were married he never dreamed of traveling out of the United States; that's what rich people did, not folks like Chance.

Jack Harris could never have dreamed what his idea of helping Chance get a job fixing parking meters for Webster would lead to and even to Chance, it was unbelievable.

Chase, Marie and Curt came to Big Springs on vacation in August 1987. They were living in a large suburb just outside of Chicago where Chase was President of the Chamber of Commerce and Marie was a Vice President of a medium-sized bank. Chance was very proud of both of them. Chase worked his way through university and Marie had gone through community college and banking school. Curt was growing up fast.

Although he was younger then Shane by several months, they were in the same class in school. Three days after Chase and Marie returned to Illinois from their two weeks of vacation in Arkansas, Chase called his mother and told her, "Mom, Marie and I are quitting our jobs and moving to Arkansas. We are buying a trout fishing resort."

Chance came home for lunch and Ann was visibly excited. Chance said, "What's the matter with you?"

Ann answered, "I've just finished talking with Chase."

"So?" Chance asked.

"They're both quitting their jobs and coming here to buy a trout fishing resort!"

"When is this taking place?"

Ann responded, "Before Curt starts school."

Two weeks later Chase and Curt arrived in Big Springs. Marie would stay working at the bank until such time as they could find a resort. The plan was for Curt to enroll in high school in Big Springs to start school, and then transfer to the high school district in which the resort would be located in. He and Shane were sophomores in high school that year and Chase and Curt would stay with Chance and Ann until they could locate a resort.

Ann and Chase made a trip to Sweet Home, Arkansas the next day to talk with a real estate agent about buying a trout fishing resort. The first thing they discovered was that there were a lot of different types of trout fishing resorts on the White River in Arkansas. They had ones with docks, boats, and cabins; some were outfitters, which meant they had guides that took you fishing, but with no cabins; one even had cabins without a dock. After looking at several places of the various types, Chase and Ann decided a resort with cabins and a dock would be the best type to own and operate. That evening they told Chance, Shane and Curt what they found. Chase called Marie and explained everything to her and she agreed with Chase and Ann on the type of resort they should buy.

The next day they went back to Sweet Home and had the real estate agent show them two resorts currently available. Chase made a bid on one of the resorts. It was the smallest, least expensive resort available on the river. It only had four rooms and a dock with four boats. The property was in excellent condition and fairly new and with plenty of room to expand. It was currently owned by a group of doctors who bought it just for them to go fishing at.

The biggest drawback to the resort was it was a long way by road from any of the highways in the area. The doctors wouldn't budge from their asking price. After further discussion, Chase and Marie decided to try to find another place. They also thought if they passed on this place, the doctors might change their minds and lower the price.

Chase and Ann went back the following day and had the real estate agent show them other places on the market. Late that afternoon, the agent said, "I'm going to show you a place that could be a good resort. It's one of the oldest resorts on the White River. The problem is the guy who owns it doesn't run it all the time and he has let it run down and has run off all the business."

They drove into the resort, which was only a short drive from the highway and close to a small town.

The name of the resort was "The Trout's Inn."

Both Ann and Chase were impressed with what they could see. The resort had a dock with room for ten boats; it had six units, a couple of storage sheds and an office/lodge type of building.

The real estate agent said, "I guess old Bob Friendly still wants to sell the place. As you can see, there is nobody around but I'll tell you what I'll do. Back at my office I have Bob's telephone number and if you think you might be interested, I'll make arrangements for you to see it."

Chase and Ann agreed this was the kind of place they thought they were looking for. The agent said, "I'll call you tonight in Big Springs."

Chase and Ann told Chance, Shane and Curt about, The Trout's Inn Resort and Chase once again telephoned Marie to fill her in.

Chance said, "I know that resort. In fact, I tried to go fishing there one time while my dad was visiting us last fall, but it wasn't open.

Chase said, "That's what the real estate agent told us. It's never open!"

It was almost ten o'clock before the real estate agent called and said he finally got in touch with Bob Friendly and set up an appointment for them to see the resort between ten-thirty and eleven o'clock the next day. The agent suggested they just meet there to save them from driving all the way to Sweet Home.

Chase and Ann arrived at The Trout's Inn just before ten- thirty and no one was there yet. They got out of the car and began looking around, as they had the day before. They walked down to the dock and looked it over. All in all, at least what they could see looked pretty good. Before they got back from the dock, the real estate agent arrived and a few minutes after eleven, Bob Friendly arrived. After inspecting the buildings and looking everything over, Chase decided this was the place he and Marie wanted. While Chase and Ann took another walk through the place, Mr. Friendly and the real estate agent held a heated discussion.

Chase and Ann were told by the agent to meet him at his office and he would go over the details on purchasing the resort.

They drove on to Sweet Home and went to the office. The agent said, "Mr. 'so-called' Friendly decided this morning he wanted to increase the price to two hundred thousand dollars for the resort. I told him I had already quoted the price of one hundred ninety thousand dollars that the property had been listed for."

The agent told Chase and Ann Mr. Friendly said, "Yeah, that's what it used to be listed for, but your listing ran out two months ago. Now I want two hundred thousand dollars."

Chase said, "Let's write up a contract and offer him one hundred fifty thousand dollars and see what happens."

Chase made out a check for five thousand dollars earnest money and told the agent that it was subject to their being able to get a loan for one hundred twenty-five thousand dollars.

The agent made out the offer, Chase signed it and the agent said, "I'll get in touch with you as soon as I have an answer from Mr. Friendly."

Around seven-thirty that evening, the agent called and said Mr. Friendly made a counter-offer of one hundred eighty-nine thousand dollars. Chase told the agent they would think about it.

The agent continued, "I'd try him at one hundred seventy- five thousand dollars. I think you'll get the deal."

Chase said again that they would think about it.

Chase, Chance, Ann, Shane and Curt talked about it until late that evening. Chase called Marie three times that night to get her input. They finally decided to offer one hundred seventy thousand dollars. The offer was made the next day, but Mr. Friendly turned down the offer. He didn't move from his price.

Chase told the agent, "I'm going to try one more time I'll go up to one hundred seventy-eight thousand dollars."

Mr. Friendly agreed to that price.

Chase went to a bank the real estate agent had suggested. Three days later the bank turned down the loan. They told Chase that his credit was "superior" but he didn't have any experience running a resort and they would need a fifty-percent down payment before they could make the loan. Chase went to a second bank and was told they didn't make loans on resorts. A third bank told Chase they might consider it if his dad would cosign the note, but they would need at least forty percent down. Chase asked about a Small Business Administration loan, but was told that resorts are considered entertainment property and SBA can't make loans on those.

Chance finally suggested, "Why don't we go talk to Mr. Friendly and see what he would do. Perhaps he will carry the loan himself."

"No, I need the money to payoff the lady I bought the resort from," Mr. Friendly said.

Chance asked, "How about leasing the resort with an option to buy?"

Mr. Friendly replied, "How much a month would you pay me?"

Chase answered, "How about twelve hundred dollars a month."

Mr. Friendly asked, "Twelve months a year?"

Chase said, "Yes, twelve months a year, with an option to buy in three years for one hundred seventy thousand dollars and you give us five hundred dollars a month credit on the down payment." Bob Friendly thought about it for a few minutes and said, "OK, draw up the papers and I'll have my lawyer look them over."

Chance and Chase shook Bob's hand and got in the car and left before he changed his mind. Monday, Chance got his lawyer to draw up the lease agreement they had discussed. Tuesday afternoon the papers were ready. Chase called Mr. Friendly and made an appointment to take them over that evening. Then Chase's fun with Bob Friendly really began.

First, his lawyer was gone to Little Rock, then there were some minor changes that needed to be made, one of which was to protect the lady that was holding Bob Friendly's note on the resort. Apparently the lady's lawyer was the same one used by Bob Friendly, so he was going to be sure Bob would paying her the five hundred dollars a month he was pay her. After they got all that worked out and Chase's lawyer OK'd the changes, Bob Friendly got cold feet and wanted to back out of the deal. Chase, bless his heart, spent days trying to resolve Bob Friendly's worries. Finally, after ten days, Chase just told him to either sign the papers on the deal he agreed to, or Chase would have his lawyer sue him for breach of contract."

Bob Friendly looked at Chase and said, "Would you really do that?"

Chase looked him right in the eye and said, "You're damned right I will. We had a deal and you're trying to back out of it."

Bob picked up the pen and signed the contract. His wife, who had wanted to sign the contract for a week, signed right under him.

Then she handed the papers to Chase and said, "I guess you've got yourself a resort."

Chase replied, "Yes, I guess I do and I expect to take it over on October 8, just as it says in the contract."

Chase almost flew his car to Big Springs. He was so excited he had finally gotten his deal signed, he couldn't believe it.

Chance congratulated him, shook his hand, and then gave him a big hug. "You did it, son. Great job, I didn't think Bob was ever going to sign the agreement. Chase, do you know how much your Grandfather Harris would have loved coming to "The Trout's Inn?" He probably would have just moved in."

Ann said, "I'm sure he would have, it's too bad he's missed so much."

At the same time all this was going on with Chase and Marie, Chance was planning to leave for Europe during the first week of August 1987. Chance received a telephone call late Friday afternoon, July 31, from Les Rivers who told Chance, "I want you to cancel your trip to Europe. I'll be down Monday to explain everything to you."

Chance pressed Les a little, "Les, how long do you want me to postpone my trip?"

The reply from Les was, "I don't know right now."

Monday after lunch, Les came into Chance's office and said, "Gather all of the directors for a meeting in the conference room.

Chance did as he was asked, found all of the directors and had them come to the conference room. Les closed the door and began by telling everyone the board had decided to sell Superior since it no longer fit into their long-term corporate goal.

He said the process has actually begun already. The board hired a company to sell Superior and the company had made books about Superior and had sent the books out to fifty companies that made acquisitions. The interested companies were to submit offers and then the selling company would consider the top ten offers and to actually have the top ten bidders visit the company. After the last company had their turn visiting Superior, they would have ten days to submit their best and final offer.

Chance began to figure out some of the things that had been happening since Les Rivers was made President and Chance was promoted to Vice President. They introduced the new electronic meter and hired a New York publicist. Superior had pictures and newspaper stores about it in every newspaper in the country, including the Wall Street Journal and the New York Times. Chance had even been sent to New York to be on CNN, on both domestic and international news.

Les was interviewed on Good Morning America with Joan Lunden. All of this was done to drive up the value of Superior. Value, as everyone knows, is like beauty, it's in the eye of the beholder.

The selling company got thirty-three bids for Superior and they narrowed the bidders down to ten. Some of the bidders were complaining that they still wanted to look at the company to make a final bid, so the number was increased from ten to fourteen.

Two days later, the kids from Goldsmith's Investments, arrived in Big Springs to meet with Superior's key staff members. The term "kids" referred to the fact that the Goldsmith's Investment team was headed by a young woman, Cindy Avery, twenty-nine years old and her two assistants, Bobby Jones and Will Smith. Both of these young men were in their mid-twenties. All had MBA degrees from expensive eastern universities and Chance learned Cindy Avery was one of the top earners in Goldsmith's acquisition and merger department. She was earning between $500,000 and $750,000 a year. She definitely knew her business and her potential customers who were bidding for Superior. She was good. She almost knew what every potential buyer would ask the staff. Cindy told all of the company department heads how to answer questions, emphasizing they should answer all the questions honestly. However, if a staff member didn't know an answer, they should just say they didn't know, but they would get an answer before the potential investor left the plant that afternoon. Each day the Goldsmith kids would arrive at the Big Springs airport from Chicago and every night, they flew back in their Lear jet. It was obvious they were too good to stay at Big Spring's Holiday or Ramada Inns.

The following week the potential buyers for the company began flying in to the Big Springs Airport each morning. Chance was appointed the lead for these visits. He would meet the planes each day and have his car and another one available to pick up the people coming in. The Goldsmith team always arrive at least an hour before the visitors.

Cindy Avery would go with Chance each morning to greet her visitors. Les Rivers and the rest of the company executives would wait in the conference room to meet the guests, along with Bobby Jones and

Will Smith from Goldsmith. Bobby and Will was actually just a couple of $100,000-a-year helpers for Cindy Avery.

They just watched and waited on Cindy. The routine was always the same for the visits. Les Rivers would greet the guests at the front door of the plant.

They would be shown into the conference room, where coffee, soft drinks and donuts would be waiting along with the executive staff. Les would introduce each member of his executive staff, always leaving Chance for last. Les said exactly the same thing for each presentation, including his little jokes about each of the staff members. By the time they were done with the last of these prospective buyers, Chance could have given everyone's little talk about themselves and their departments.

Chance was the only one who ever changed his presentation. Chance's presentation would depend on how interested he thought the potential buyers were in actually acquiring the company. He got a lot of clues on the five minute ride from the airport to the plant about their interest level. If Chance felt these people were really interested, he would provide them with more insight to the business. It was not that he left things out of any of his presentations he just included additional facts to the ones he considered as serious potential buyers.

Sometimes, the potential buyers made comments to each other in the car about how hard it was to get to Big Springs. Others would say things like, "I want to hurry back to the office this afternoon, because the company we are looking at tomorrow looks like it fits into our business a lot better then being in the parking meter business," or "Whose idea was this for us to be looking at this crazy company, anyway?"

After the introductions were made, Chance and Cindy took the visitors on a tour of the plant, with Bobby and Will tagging along behind the group. Chance bet they would follow Cindy into the ladies room, if she didn't watch them. After the tour, they all went back to the conference room, where a lunch would be set up. After lunch, there were more meetings with Superior's executive group and question and answer time.

Eventually, during the sessions the questions were turned over to Chance to answer, because he was the one member of the group that had grown up with Superior and had been involved in the parking business for over thirty years. The last event of the day was a private meeting with Les Rivers. These almost always got down to, "Will you stay with the company if it's sold?" "How about your staff? Are you happy with them or would you plan on replacing some of them? If we wanted them to stay on with the company after we bought the company, would they stay?"

After that meeting, Chance and Cindy took them back to the airport and by three-thirty or four o'clock in the afternoon, they were flying back home. End of this group, but the next day a new group would appear.

This routine continued until Superior had been visited by thirteen of the fourteen prospective buyers. Number fourteen canceled as Chance and Cindy waited at the airport for them.

They sent a message "sorry" we had a closing on another company today and can't come.

"Screw them," Cindy said, "I wouldn't take their bid now if they sent one in."

Cindy gathered up her helpers and jetted back to Chicago. Chance thought he had a good idea of the value of Superior. The current corporation bought it for just over $10,000,000 and since then sold off their other division for $7,000,000. Chance knew this price was inflated since the company buying this division was in the process of losing a patent suit in court to Superior over copying their products.

Chance and the company involved in the suit knew there was no doubt Superior would prevail in the case, because some of the people who had been working in the division just took the plans on how to build Superior's products and went to work for the competitor. All of the products being copied by their competitor's, were covered by patents owned by Superior. Yes, the price was inflated, but it settled the lawsuit. Chance's guess was that the company would go for about $12,000,000 to $14,000,000. He had heard that the corporation wanted sixteen to eighteen million.

Impossible, Chance thought.

Chance had his favorites of the groups that looked at Superior. One was an English banking group and the other was a company from

Memphis with its headquarters in New York City. Chance liked both of these groups and he only hoped that a leveraged buy out company from New Jersey didn't buy the company.

During the plant tour, they had said in front of Chance and Cindy, "When we buy this company, we'll get rid of all of the executive staff, what a bunch of deadhead losers. We know how to pump money out of this company."

Cindy sent letters by Federal Express to the thirteen companies who had visited the plant that they had ten days to submit their best and final bid for Superior.

Chance went to England to get back to real work. Graham and he were meeting again with the British Standards Committee.

After they had an agreement with them on how the standards would be written, the committee revised certain parts that would cause Superior problems selling their electronic meters in the United Kingdom.

After battling with the committee all day, Chance received a fax from Les Rivers that the company had been sold to by the Memphis Corporation for $30,000,000 in cash. Chance couldn't believe the number! Twice what the company was worth, by at least $14,000,000 more then the company was worth. Two days later he received a copy of an article from the Wall Street Journal, announcing the sale of Superior to the Memphis Corporation for $30,000,000.

Cindy had done her job and as hard as Chance worked helping Cindy sell the company he thought she should have sent him a percentage of her commission. She didn't.

By the time Chance returned to the States, Phillip Rider, President of the Memphis Corporation, and Josh Marshall, Treasurer of the Company had already been to Chicago and met with Les Rivers. Chance was told they would be visiting Big Springs very soon after he came back and that there would be no changes in the company. Les Rivers would continue as President and we were to carry on with business as usual.

Two weeks after Chance returned to Big Springs, he got a letter from Morley Penny, Chance's long-time friend and Chairman of Superior's former corporate owner thanking him for his help and enclosing a check for just over twelve thousand dollars. It was a nice closure for the years of association with Mr. Penny.

Chance could sense a big change in Les Rivers the next time they met in Big Springs after the Memphis Corporation bought Superior. He was even more demanding then he had been before when he ran the company for their old corporation. At one point in a meeting with his executive committee, he flatly stated, "This is my company and I'll run it the way I want to."

Chance was shocked at his attitude.

Chance continued to do his job as well as he could and orders for electronic meters from the international market exceeded all of their expectations. Production was having a problem producing the new meters. Engineering kept working on glitches in the new product. International distributors were complaining about how slow deliveries of the electronic meters were.

In November, the department heads and Les Rivers went to Memphis to present their 1988-business plan to Phillip Rider and Josh Marshall. The forecast was for about $18,000,000 in sales with profits of almost $5,000,000. The forecast was a stretch in Chance's mind since about $16,000,000 was the best the company ever sold in its history. Mr. Rider and Josh Marshall listened carefully and asked some very pertinent questions, some about the business plan and some about the performance of the electronic meter. Les told a good story as every answer seemed plausible.

When the meeting ended, Mr. Rider simply said, "I'm looking forward to seeing how you track with your forecast. I'm not sure if you are not counting too much on your new electronic meters to give you the profit margins you've forecast. Good luck and have a great year."

As they left the offices of the Memphis Corporation, Les said, "Did you hear what Phillip Rider said? He acts like he knows more about our business then we do and he just bought the company two months ago."

Sales for the first quarter of nineteen eighty-eight were nonexistent. There wasn't any profit. Superior just rolled up three straight months of losses, big losses. Les had to ask Josh Marshall for money to be transferred to cover their operating expenses.

In April there were a few bright spots. Chance got major orders for electronic meters in Australia and South Africa. In addition, Chance had been advised that he and Superior were being awarded the President of the United States' "E" Award for excellence in exporting. Les Rivers invited Phillip Rider to the award presentation.

Chance offered to let either Les or Mr. Rider accept the award on behalf of the company. They both declined, saying Chance earned the award and he should receive it. Chance gladly accepted the award. To qualify for this award you had to have increased your exporting of product by twenty percent a year for three years in a row. You had to enter new markets and introduce new products to the export market. In addition, the area's International Trade Representative from the Department of Commerce must recommend the award.

Chance felt this was a great victory for him and for Superior. Les and Phillip Rider were all smiles at the ceremony, congratulating Chance for his achievement. Chance could sense these two men didn't like each other at all.

As the year went by, it got tougher and tougher. Sales in the domestic market were awful. People were waiting to see how the new electronic meters were going to work before they bought. The patents on Superior's mechanical meters that had protected their products from their competitors expired in nineteen eightyseven. A competitor copied Superior's mechanical meter and were undercutting Superior prices for both meters and parts.

Suddenly the Magic Meter Company was alive and well and taking orders from Superior by using Superior's own product to get the orders. Superior's electronic meter wasn't working right. One time you would put a coin in it and it worked perfectly, the next time it wouldn't work. The company was making change after change on the product. They were replacing the product two or three times. Every time the engineering department thought they had a fix for the electronic meter, something else went wrong with it. Warranty expenses were going over the top.

It was getting harder and harder to talk to Les Rivers. He had to keep asking Memphis Corporation for more and more money. The monthly reports he was sending to Memphis were getting shorter and shorter.

Chance was in Les Rivers' office one day, talking to him about the electronic meter problems and Chance said, "Les, I think we have the wrong technology in our electronic meter to read the coins."

Les went into orbit. He screamed, "Don't ever say that to anybody!"

By now it was time to put together the 1989 business plan to present to Memphis. After Chance put together his international budget and sales forecast and the domestic team had their forecast and budget together, they submitted them to the Company Treasurer. The Treasurer assembled the 1989 sales and business plan which showed sales of $13,800,000 and profits of about $600,000.

Les Rivers took one look the plan and dumped the whole thing in the wastebasket. He assembled his department heads in the conference room and read them the riot act. He said, "If you think I'm going to take this plan to Memphis, you people are out of your minds. I'm going to tell you what the sales forecast is for nineteen eighty-nine, it's $19,800,000. Profits are going to be right at $3,000,000. If you think I'm going to show Phillip Rider a profit of less then ten percent of what he paid for this company, you're nuts. Re-do your forecasts to hit these numbers."

They did as they were told. When they presented the 1989 business plan, Phillip Rider looked at them in total surprise. At the end of the meeting, Phillip said, "Gentlemen, the foundation of this corporation are based on trust between our companies and the parent corporation. We have to know the truth about how our companies our doing, good or bad and we don't like surprises.

On Tuesday, December 6, 1988, Chance received a telephone call from Phillip Rider. Mr. Rider said, "I want you to come to our office on Thursday. Make any excuse you have to be out of the office; just don't tell anyone you are coming to see me."

Chance arrived by ten o'clock in the morning on December 7. Mr. Rider said, "We have decided to make a change of Presidents at Superior and I want you to take the job."

Chance didn't expect this at all. He was not surprised about the decision made to fire Les Rivers, but to offer him the job was something Chance never expected. Chance slowly answered, "Mr. Rider, the job of President of Superior has always been a revolving door that said "enter here, exit here." I will agree to take the job on one condition, if you are not happy with me or I can't do the job, then let me go back to my job as Vice President of International Sales."

Mr. Rider said, "Chance, if I think you need help running the company, you can go back to the job you have now. Frankly, I can't afford for the company to lose you."

Mr. Rider continued, "Chance, the way this corporation functions is that we let each president run the company just like he owned it. In its thirty-year history, no president who was removed from his job was allowed to stay with the company. So, if things don't work out for you, you will be unique by staying with the company and going back to your previous job. Let's fly to Chicago and I'll meet with Les River and then with the Chicago staff, announcing your appointment as President."

Airline and hotel reservations had already been made for them.

Phillip Rider telephoned Les and told him to meet him at a hotel in the morning at eight o'clock. Ten minutes after Phillip met with Les, he said, "Let's go to the office so I can make the announcement of your appointment."Upon arriving at the office Mr. Rider called all of the employees into the conference room and told them Les Rivers' employment with the company had been terminated and that Chance Clark was President of the Company, effective immediately.

Next, Mr. Rider had Chance call Big Springs on the hot line and asks the Department Directors to assemble in the conference room. When they were all there, they were to call Chance back on the hot line. In less then five minutes they were all assembled and Chance asked to be put on the speaker phone. Then he said Mr. Rider had an announcement to make. Phillip Rider made exactly the same announcement he made earlier. Chance was told later that when the announcement was made in the plant; a loud cheer went up from the employees. Less then an hour later, Chance and Mr. Rider were enroute to Memphis.

Chance's appointment was made official on December 8. Chance now had two exceptional events take place on the eighth of December--the birth of his son Shane and being made President of his Company.

Chance picked up his car at the Memphis Airport and nearly flew home to Big Springs. When he drove in his driveway, he saw a huge sign hung completely across the double garage door that said "Welcome Home, Mr. President!" Chance couldn't contain his excitement. He had been born for this job. He was born in Oklahoma where the first parking meter was installed and he was born in nineteen thirty-six, the year Superior Meter Company started and installed its first meters.

The Clarks had a double celebration, Shane's birthday and Chance's new job. All of Chance's family was here with him, Ann, Chase, Shane, Marie and Curt. It was wonderful! Clark's Law was certainly working this day, "The only sure thing in life is change."

Ann finally said, "In all the excitement, no one even asked if you got a raise in salary."

Chance said, "I guess I did. I forgot about that, how about an increase of twenty-five thousand dollars a year!"

"Yeah!" Shane said.

Chance held a staff meeting with the Department Directors on Monday morning to go over several things. He announced he was closing the Chicago office and moving everything to Big Springs.

On Tuesday he flew to Chicago and made the announcement that he was closing the office. He met with each person and to discuss whether they would consider moving to Big Springs. Only one person agreed to move.

He told everyone else that a package would be put together with a severance payment plan consistent with the amount of service they had with the company. He also offered them assistance in obtaining other positions, such as employment agency fees, resume services, etc. It would take until the end of January to make all of the arrangements to actually close the office and ship everything to Big Springs.

Chance flew back to Big Springs and met with Tim Hunt, his old boss from the engineering department. He asked him a very pointed question about the electronic meter can you make the electronic meter work? Tim felt sure they could solve the problems with the electronic meter. Chance was not as sure.

Chance talked to Tim in depth about what worked well on the meter and what did not work.

Tim said, "The electronic programming, time keeping and all of the electronic functions work flawlessly."

Chance said, "I agree with that. What doesn't work well?"

"The coin handling. Ninety-nine percent of the time it works fine, then it won't work at all."

Chance told Tim, "I'll tell you what I want you to do. I've studied our mechanical meter and the electronic meter and I want you to marry them together. Superior's mechanical coin handling has set the standard in this industry for the past forty years.

Chance showed Tim his idea of putting in switches for the coins to strike instead of having winding rings.

Tim said, "You know, I think that will work."

Chance said, "I know it will! You can keep your people working on the old electronic meter to try and find a solution to its problems, but I want you to make me a combination electronic mechanical parking meter mechanism."

Four months later Tim had a beautiful hand-made prototype meter that was an electronic mechanical meter and it worked perfectly every time. Chance took it to a meeting of the Presidents of the various Memphis Corporation companies. Phillip Rider was impressed.

He said, "That's the step your company should have made developing an electronic meter in the first place. They tried to skip a step in developing from a mechanical product company to an electronic product company."

It would still take them another four months before all of the tooling was finished to make the electronic mechanical meter. In the meantime, while they were waiting for the tooling to be completed, the engineering department continued to try to find a way to fix all of the electronic meters that were in operation. Improvements had been made on the product, but there wasn't any break-through development that fixed the problem. Engineering kept telling him they thought they had it fixed. Chance would report it to Phillip Rider, but then it didn't fix the problem.

Chance told Tim to get with his electronic consultant and find a different type of technology for reading the coins.

Trying to fix the electronic meters was still killing them in nineteen eighty-nine and Chance had his people cut prices on mechanical meters and parts to meet competition from Magic Meter. He put more people into the field selling product. Their sales volume began to increase, but they certainly weren't making money and in addition, they had to pay severance pay to Les Rivers, for a whole year, plus vacation, etc. This might not have hurt Chance as much if they weren't paying Les $40,000 a year more then Chance was making while he was working his heart out and Les was doing nothing. In spite of all this, they ended the year with a small profit and forecasted a much improved year in nineteen ninety.

Chance received a telephone call in January of 1990 from his Mexican distributor, Carlos Espinosa, who stated that with Superior's help, he could get a contract to operate 35,000 meters in Mexico City for ten years. After several telephone calls and faxes, between Chance and Carlos to clearly understand all of the details of the proposal, Chance had his Chief Financial Officer prepare a detailed profit and loss statement for such a proposed operation.

It was unbelievable---Superior would own 95% of the operating company and Carlos would have 5%. Superior's gross profit for ten years would amount to almost $50,000,000 and that didn't include the profit made by selling the 35,000 meters to Superior's Mexican Company. Chance was excited; he put together a report outlining all of the details of the proposal including his Chief Financial Officer's analysis of the deal. He Federal Expressed, the report to Phillip Rider, his boss at Memphis Corporation.

Before ten o'clock the next morning, Chance called Phillip to see if he received his report. Phillip said he received it and had already read it. Phillip stated perhaps they should fly to Mexico City and meet with Carlos Espinosa and some of the city officials in charge of the project. Chance thought that was a great idea.

Two days later, Chance and Phillip were in Mexico City. They met with Carlos, who was flying high, because even with only a 5% ownership in the Mexico City project, he would get rich over the ten year period of the contract.

Next, they met with city officials who were also flying high, because for whatever profit Superior was making, the City was making more then ten times the amount without investing one peso or taking any risk.

That evening they met with the Mayor's Chief of Staff who told them the Mayor was in favor of the project. First, because the City needed parking control on the streets and second, the City could certainly use the money the meter's system would give them. The Mayor's Chief of Staff told them the Mayor was concerned that there was not more Mexican ownership of the project, but he was sure they could work around this problem. They were asked to submit a formal proposal directly from Superior, explaining how they would establish a Mexican Corporation to operate the meters and pay taxes in Mexico.

When they left the meeting, they went back to their hotel.

Carlos left Chance and Phillip to go home since it was now almost midnight. Phillip said that he would like to talk with Chance some more about this proposed project if Chance was not too tired. Chance was high on adrenaline, so he was ready to talk all night about a project that would make more money in a year then Superior had made in its history.

Phillip started the conversation by saying, "Chance, I know you think this project could be the savior that Superior needs. However, it would require help from the Memphis Corporation to fund you up to ten million dollars for the project. Is that right, Chance?"

Chance replied, "Yes, sir. That's exactly right and our projections shows we could repay all of the money within two years and still make more profit per year then Superior ever made during those two years."

Phillip retorted, "Chance, Memphis companies are manufacturing companies. We make products, put them in boxes, ship them out and send out a statement and in 30 days we get paid and make our profit. That's the way Memphis companies work and we're not interested in investing another ten million dollars in Superior. Chance, stick with the manufacturing business and let somebody else take the risk of these projects. They are not for Memphis and they're not for Superior."

Chance knew one thing, when Phillip spoke he meant what he said and no matter what Chance thought or said, this potential wonderful opportunity was history.

Chance put on his best face and said to Phillip, "I want to thank you for making the trip with me and I'm sorry you can't see the opportunity, but I understand what has worked for Memphis in the past has built a great company."

The flight back to Dallas the next morning was very quiet.

Neither, Phillip or Chance had much to say. When they parted company in Dallas, for each of their flights home, Phillip told Chance, "I am sorry this did not work out for Superior, but just stick to your manufacturing and it will all work out."

Chance was not so sure, since Chance felt that privatization was the way of the future.

Soon after that meeting, the company had its new electronic mechanical meter in their bag of products to sell and it began selling. They could now make them and they worked flawlessly when the cities installed them. Orders were coming in. Chance still was trying to wear two hats in the company, President and International Sales.

While the company was attending the most important parking equipment show of the year in Toronto, Canada in early May that year Chance got a call from his office.

His Executive Secretary called to say, "I'm sending you a fax of a lawsuit Magic Meter Company has filed in Little Rock against us."

Chance told her to send a copy to their attorney in Little Rock, Sam Scott, and she said she had already done that. Chance was told by someone at the convention that C. K. Deering, Jr., President of Magic Meters said, "This is the last time Superior Meters will be coming to the parking conference. We're taking care of them."

Chance read the complaint. This lawsuit was not one lawsuit, it was a giant economy size lawsuit it was really eight lawsuits in one.

It alleged that Superior had:

Count One	Unlawfully stolen employees from Magic Meter Company;
Count Two	Obtained and used confidential customer records, stolen by former employees of Magic Meter Company, to obtain orders;
Count Three	Violated numerous anti-trust laws;
Count Four	Violated patents owned by Magic Meter Company;
Count Five	Conspired with city officials to keep Magic Meter Company from obtaining contracts;
Count Six	Interfered with contractual agreements between the company and its exclusive distributors;
Count Seven	Illegally set prices below cost to put Magic Meter Company out of business;
Count Eight	Filed frivolous lawsuits against Magic Meter Company and cities to keep the company from receiving orders of which it was entitled.

It was irony that the two largest parking meter companies in the world would end up headquartered in Arkansas since neither company began there. The Magic Meter Company started in Oklahoma City and after it was sold to a large conglomerate, the company was moved to Ohio, back to Tulsa, Oklahoma and when one of the parent companies plants was merged with another similar company, they had an empty plant in Arkansas, so they move the parking meter division there.

Superior Parking Meter Company started in Chicago, but after a problem with two different unions shortly after World War II trying to organize the employees. The president of the company told the employees he would work with only one union and since the majority of the employees wanted to belong to the AFL-CIO he agreed that he would work with them.

However, the folks working in the die cast department said they would join the Teamsters Union. The president told the die casting people to either join with the rest of the employees in the AFL-CIO or he would move die casting out of the plant. They wouldn't budge, so the president closed the die casting department and moved it to Big Springs, Arkansas. The president knew that Arkansas wouldn't allow judicial strikes between unions. The company continued moving departments to Big Springs until now the entire company was in Arkansas. So, this lawsuit would be between two Arkansas companies with major implications in the world of parking meters.

Chance called Phillip Rider and advised him he had received notice of the lawsuit. Phillip had already been sent a copy by a company employed by Memphis to protect and advise them of any lawsuits filed against Memphis or one of their sixty-plus companies. Chance then called Superior's patent attorney, Peter Reed in Chicago and set up a meeting for the next week and asked for all of their attorneys to meet there.

After returning to Big Springs, Chance asked his staff to begin thinking of ways to cut costs and improve the company's bottom line. He wanted to have ideas on why their costs had grown so much in the past six or seven years. Business stayed very poor for all of the second quarter. Problems with the electronic meters didn't get any better and they begin replacing them with the electronic mechanical meters, at a service charge of twenty dollars per meter to cover some of their handling costs.

Superior was a victim of its own successful marketing of the electronic meters. They now had over forty-three thousands of them out on the streets around the world and Chance knew they would all have to be replaced. This would take them some time to accomplish and over two million dollars from Memphis to cover the cost.

Chance then made a fatal mistake. He asked Phillip Rider and Josh Marshall to come to Big Springs to listen to what his staff came up with about what had changed that caused them so much trouble making any real improvement to their bottom line. Phillip and Josh flew in. Chance picked them up at the airport and they met all day at the Holiday Inn with the Department Heads. The Department Heads had done a great job determining how and why their costs had increased so much over the past few years.

Phillip and Josh understood the problem, probably better then they did. One option was to move the plant. The cost of the last two union contracts was really hurting them. Chance ended the day by saying it would be another three weeks before they could tell Phillip and Josh what they planned to do to solve their bottom line problem.

Phillip said, "Chance you can't run away from your problems, how come it's going to take you three weeks to present your plan to start working yourself out of this hole?"

Chance explained he was committed to attend the Australian Parking Conference for more than a year and he couldn't let the distributor down. He promised to be there and Superior always looked after their customers.

When Phillip and Josh got in Chance's car to return to the airport, he knew Phillip planned to replace him as President.

The first morning Chance was back in the office from Australia, he got a telephone call from Phillip. Phillip told him he was in Big Springs at the Ramada Inn and he wanted Chance to come to meet him.

Chance knew the drill. He had seen it with Les Rivers. Chance drove to the Ramada Inn and went directly to Phillip's room. Chance was shaking as he knocked on the door of Phillip's room. Phillip opened the door and Chance went inside.

Phillip said, "Chance, I hated to see this day come, but I want your resignation as President of Superior."

He continued, "You know I like you a lot, but I feel I need someone with more experience running the company. You can stay with the company as Vice President, or I will pay you for a year and help you find some other job. It's up to you, Chance."

Chance said, "Phillip, you know what I told you when I agreed to take the job in the first place. I'm not going to let C. K. Deering beat me in court. This lawsuit is really personal with me; I'm staying with the company."

Phillip said, "Sign this letter of resignation for me."

Chance took the pen and signed his name. This was the only time in Chance's life he ever failed at a job and he had to do it when he was fifty-two years old and at a job he felt he was born to do.

"Chance, I want you to know I really appreciate your staying with the company. Your current salary will remain the same for the next six months to help you make adjustments."

Chance asked, "Phillip who do you plan to put into the job?
I hope it's someone who can help us."

"I'm going to introduce you to him in a few minutes."

Chance should have known Phillip would have someone already there to take his place. Phillip left the room for about two minutes and he came back with a man Chance didn't know.

Phillip said, "This is Dak Thompson. Dak, this is Chance Clark."

The two men shook hands and Dak spoke first, "Chance, Phillip told me you agreed to stay with the company and I want you to know I appreciate that, I'm sure we can work together."

Chance said he would meet Phillip and Dak at the plant and he would get all of the Department Directors assembled in the conference room. By lunchtime Phillip was on his way back to Memphis. Sometimes, the real measure of a man is to be able to survive the low points in his life. Chance was surely being measured right now. Chance was determined to do everything possible to help Dak succeed where he failed. Going home at lunchtime to tell Ann he had been fired was not just hard for someone like Chance, but to tell his wife he had failed was a catastrophe!

When he told Ann, she just said, "I'm happy you still have a job."

Then she took him in her arms and took away a lot of the hurt he felt in his heart.

Ann said, "You got me, what else do you really need?"

Chance laughed and said, "I guess you're right, nothing else really matters anyway."

Life would go on.

28

Chance's life changed a lot over the next two years, not because he wasn't President of Superior any longer, but because of the Magic Meter Company's lawsuit. Chance had been designated to be the leader of the Superior's team to defend the company against the company's worst enemy. This was not a competition between competitors, it was an all-out war!

A war to be fought out in the federal courts in Arkansas and in Washington, DC, in this war there would be only one winner and Chance had every intention that it would be Superior. The other people in the company didn't understand how serious this fight was to the survival of their company. Chance knew. This fight started on his watch. He was the one C. K. Deering, Jr. and his brother-in-law, Sonny Wheeler was personally going after in this lawsuit.

Sonny Wheeler was a Senior Partner in the Flowers Law Firm. He was the ex-mayor of Little Rock and an ex-member of the Arkansas Supreme Court. The Flowers Law Firm was the oldest law firm west of the Mississippi River. One of his partners was the governor's wife. She had even signed the original complaint against Superior.

The lawsuit was about money! C. K. Deering, Jr. knew Memphis Corporation had money and he wanted it. As soon as he read in the Wall Street Journal Memphis paid $30,000,000 for Superior, he picked up his telephone and called Phillip Rider. He flew his twin engine airplane to Memphis and picked up Phillip to show him the Magic

Meter Company. He told Phillip he had to pay him $30,000,000 for his company too and then Phillip would have complete control of the world's parking meter business.

C. K. said, "It doesn't make any difference how much you pay me for my company, because you can charge anything you want for meters then."

C. K. made two big mistakes that day dealing with Phillip Rider. First, he told him to take a good look around his plant and he would see nothing, but good-looking women working in his company, because he fired all of the "old dogs" that used to work in the plant. Phillip was a proponent of women and women's rights. He had two daughters of his own and didn't like the inference C. K. was making about women that they were like cattle to be judged by their looks.

No, Phillip didn't like this comment at all. Phillip hated the statement and the way C. K. said it. The next thing out of C.K.'s mouth, Phillip would hate just as much and maybe more.

C. K. continued, "Well, I'll tell you what, Phillip. If you don't buy me out now, I'm going to give you so much trouble, that you will buy me out one day in the future. I've got a cheaper labor force, because I don't have a union and I've copied your mechanical meter and I'll put Superior out of business."

Phillip checked out Magic Meter Company and its owners before buying Superior. The report said, that a rich Little Rock businessman bought the company for his son to run. Phillip could see C. K. was an arrogant young man and was probably used to having his own way.

The plant tour was made with C. K. really laying it on thick about their new machinery, their production capabilities and how much faster and better they could do things then Superior. C. K. flew Phillip back to Memphis.

Just before landing, Phillip said, "Thank you for an enlightening day. I'll talk to our attorneys about anti-trust problems if Memphis were to buy your company. In the meantime, I guess we will meet you in the marketplace."

As he got out of the plane, Phillip thought the nerve of this arrogant young man, trying to blackmail me into buying his company and the ink not even dry on my contract buying Superior.

According to Phillip's research, Superior already controlled between seventy and eighty percent of the world's market for parking meters. Phillip knew there was no way the United States Government would ever approve of Superior buy Magic Meters.

No one at Superior knew anything about this trip or Phillip's conversation with C. K. until the lawsuit.

Chance assembled his team of attorneys, most of whom represented Superior already. The lead attorney was Sam Scott from Little Rock and Marilyn May, who worked with Superior on labor contracts. Marilyn was a partner of Sam Scott. Peter Reed had been Superior's patent attorney for twenty years and was considered to be one of the best patent attorneys in the country.

Peter brought from their Washington, D. C. office Mr. Sherman Oaks former head of the anti-trust department in the United States Attorney General's office. Sherman literally wrote the anti- trust laws for the government. He was Superior's secret weapon.

Lawsuits have several stages. The first is the discovery stage.

During this period of time, the plaintiff, Magic Meter Company and the defendant Superior attempted to uncover the truth about what really happened in a case. The lawyers for each side interviewed potential witnesses and took depositions. Chance found taking a deposition was just like testifying in court. Each side has an attorney present and a clerk makes a complete transcript of everything said at the deposition. Lawyers used these transcripts to build their case. Hour after hour, day after day, week after week, the depositions went on.

At the same time, lawyers do a document search. In this case, that meant Superior's attorneys went through the files of the Magic Meter Company and made copies of anything they thought might be helpful to their case. It was no surprise to Chance to find that their files had been sanitized long before this lawsuit had been filed. They were lily white. No copy of any letter threatening to file a lawsuit against a city for not buying their meters or anything like that was found. Superior had been put on notice that after the lawsuit had been filed, nothing could be taken out of their files. They did exactly as they were told. They did not remove one piece of paper from their files.

Superior's attorneys even hired a woman to help pick the jury.

Chance didn't know there were such people, as experts on the selection of prospective jurors. This woman knew more about each prospective juror then most people know about their own kids. She had at least one paragraph on each member of the panel of jurors. She rated them as being OK, questionable, you don't want them, maybe, or get this one.

The attorneys said, "We are completely in her hands when it comes to picking the jury. She's the expert."

It took one whole day to pick the jury. The jury would have nine members and two alternates. After challenges of some of the prospective jurors by the attorneys for both the plaintiff and the defendant, they ended up with seven women and two men, and a man and woman as alternates.

The next morning, the judge, Judge George Claypool, talked to the jury and the attorneys about the case. He ended his statements with the remark, "The lawyers in this case tell me this case will take six to eight weeks. I've not heard a case in my court in more than thirty years that lasted over four weeks, so we'll see."

Next came the opening remarks by the plaintiff's attorney, Sonny Wheeler. Sonny promised to prove to the jury that the people at Superior were a bunch of thieves that had stolen everything from the Magic Meter Company. Superior stole their secrets, their employees, their customers and last but not least, their electronic meter.

Sam Scott had given Chance instructions on how to dress, how to look and how not to react to anything said by the lawyers or a plaintiff's witness. In fact, just before coming into court that morning, Sam reached over and took a red silk handkerchief out of the breast pocket of Chance's suit.

Sam said, "Chance, you look too flashy with the red silk handkerchief. Remember, as far as this jury is concerned you are Superior Parking

Meter Company and I want you to only wear blue suits to court. Juries, don't like brown or black suits."

By the time Chance finished listening to Sonny Wheeler's opening remarks, he thought those guys from Superior were just awful. Throughout the remarks, Chance showed no reaction, he just kept looking at the jury. The judge called a recess for lunch before Sam Scott made his opening remarks. When court reconvened, Sam had his chance to make an opening statement.

Chance knew Sam was their lawyer, but he was convinced Sam had just blown Sonny away.

Later that evening, Chance got a telephone call from Dak Thompson, asking how he thought the trial was going. Chance gave him his impressions and then Dak said, "I got a telephone call from Phillip Rider asking if we shouldn't settle this case by paying Magic Meter $10,000,000."

Chance couldn't believe his ears. He calmly asked Dak, "What did you tell him?"

Dak said "I wanted to talk to you before I gave Phillip an answer."

Chance asked, "Dak, do you know how C. K. Deering, Sr. made a lot of his money?"

Dak replied, "No."

"By having his son-in-law, Sonny, sue people. If we paid them $10,000,000 now, these people will be back at the trough in six months wanting more. We didn't do anything wrong, Dak and we're going to win this case on appeal. You know none of our attorneys think we can win in an Arkansas court against Flower's Law Firm. For God's sake, don't let Phillip pay these people off.

We are going to win this case!"

Phillip was traveling, but he gave Dak a telephone number where he could reach him. Dak called and relayed Chance's words. Phillip said, "OK, Dak, I just hope Chance and our lawyers are right and we can win this case on appeal."

The court case dragged on. There were thousands of exhibits and almost one hundred witnesses. Along the way Superior, begin winning some issues on written arguments. The judge dismissed Count One, unlawfully stealing of employees; and Count Six, interfering with contractual agreements with exclusive distributors. The trial was in its fourth week and the plaintiff's attorneys called Chance to the stand three times as a witness. The trial was taking on a life of it's own. At the end of the fourth week, the plaintiffs rested their case.

The defense's case was scheduled to begin the following Monday. Chance talked to Ann every day since the trial began and she promised to drive to Little Rock Friday afternoon. He was anxious to see her. The strain of the trial was beginning to show on him. He didn't know how the lawyers did it. They were in court all day long and worked every night, sometimes, almost all night, getting ready for the next day. Chance was not just guessing this was the case because every night he was there with them. They worked with witnesses who were scheduled to go on the stand the next day. They reviewed the daily court transcripts for that day.

They researched laws and they wrote briefs. Chance, was in awe of the efforts required to try a case as big as this one. Not only did the lawyers and Chance work, they had a whole staff of legal aides and legal secretaries working. No doubt, this was one of the biggest, most complex cases Sam Scott and his office had ever worked on. The cost was also skyrocketing. Superior had already paid over one and a quarter million dollars and they hadn't even begun to present their case.

Chance drove out to meet Ann on Interstate 40 at a Texaco station since she didn't know her way around Little Rock. When she pulled up next to his car, Chance was standing next to his car waited for her to get out of the car. When she did, he reached out to take her hand. Funny, that same power still flowed between them as it had when they were fourteen.

They drove both of their cars into Little Rock and went directly to the downtown Holiday Inn were Chance had been staying for the past seven weeks. Although the trial just completed its fourth week, Chance had been in Little Rock working with the attorneys for three weeks before the trial began. He took Ann's suitcase up to his room. As he sat it down, he immediately began kissing her and then he said, "Well, madam, would you like to make love or go to dinner first?"

Ann grinned and said, "I've had lunch. How about making love?" Chance loved her choice.

The weekend was filled with Chance relating every detail of the trial to Ann, while they were eating and during lovemaking.

He just couldn't get away from the trial. Sunday afternoon came too quickly, much too soon, because Ann was driving back to Big Springs. Chance tried to get her to stay and attend the trial for a day, but Ann said, "Chance, I would be too nervous and besides, if one of those people said anything bad about you, I might hit them."

Chance couldn't imagine Ann hitting anyone, unless she was protecting one of her kids. She was too much of a lady. Chance guided her back to the Texaco station where they met on Friday afternoon and there she stopped long enough to say good-by. It seemed as thought half of their lives were spent saying good-by to each other.

Chance said, "Thanks for coming down for the weekend, call me when you get home. I love you."

"I love you, too," Ann replied.

Monday morning Chance was back on the stand, this time as a witness for the defense. Chance was to begin laying out step-by- step answers for all of the charges on the highly technical issues of the patent case. As the days went by the defense attorneys were laying out their case just as they planned. Sonny Wheeler wasn't well prepared for the case. He had let one of his young associates do most of the preparation and he had to have her give him notes when he was cross-examining a witness. The longer the trial went on, the more inept he appeared.

Sam Scott said, "I'm sure glad the governor's wife is out campaigning with her husband while he running for President, I've heard she is really good in the court room."

One of Superior's expert witnesses was a patent attorney from Houston who came up with a brilliant way to explain the difference between Magic Meter's electronic meter and Superior's electronic meter. Peter Reed presented the patent case for Superior and he and his expert witness were unbeatable. Peter asked the witness to explain, in layman's terms; the biggest difference, between Superior's electronic circuit and

Magic Meter's electronic circuit. The witness said, "It's like this. Magic's electronic circuit is smart and Superior's electronic circuit is dumb."

Peter said, "Could you go into more detail about what you mean when you say one is smart and the other one is dumb?"

The witness asked, "Is it possible for me to go to the chalk board and draw a little diagram to illustrate this to the jury?"

Peter said, "Your honor?"

Judge Claypool said, "Go ahead, I would like to see this myself."

The witness approached the chalkboard, picked up a long piece of chalk and began by saying, "This is a field where a family of prairie dogs lives."

On the chalkboard he drew a picture of a prairie dog peering out of a hole. He continued, "This prairie dog is a very good father. He wants to protect his family so he keeps watch for any fox that might come along. But even good fathers have to sleep sometimes."

He drew a picture of a bed with a prairie dog sleeping on it.

"Being a good father, he has to get up out of bed every few seconds to see if there is a fox outside. The father prairie dog is a good father, checking all the time to see if there are any foxes in the area, but he is not very smart."

"In fact, he's dumb. That's the same way Superior's electronic circuit works in their meters. Every few seconds, actually every millisecond, they have to check to see if someone has put a coin in the meter and if someone did they turn on a circuit so the meter works."

The witness continued, "In Magic Meter's electronic circuit, father prairie dog is smart. He doesn't have to get out of bed every few minutes to check for foxes. He set up a wire with a bell tied to the headboard of his bed."

The expert witness drew a picture of a prairie dog in bed with a tiny bell on the headboard, just above his head connected to a wire outside the prairie dog's hole. People in the jury laughed, even the judge smiled.

The witness continued, "This is how Magic Meter's electronic circuit works, when someone comes along and puts a coin in the slot. The coin slot has a little electronic switch that says, "Wake up circuit, a coin is coming to you." It's smart and Superior's circuit is dumb and the smart circuit is what Magic Meter Company's patent is written around."

No matter how hard the plaintiff's patent attorney tried to get around the prairie dog story, all the jury could see in their mind was the picture on that chalkboard. Magic Meter's patent attorney tried to find a way to show Superior's electronic consultant in some type of bad light, but it backfired on him because he didn't know his facts. He looked, like Chance's old boss Karl Jones used to say, "Like a nickel's worth of wormy cheese."

The attorney asked James Walters, Superior's electronic consultant, "I understand you were President of Delaware Research Corporation."

James answered, "Yes, sir."

Then the attorney said, "I understand you abruptly left this position. Please explain why you did that."

Before James could answer, Sam Scott objected that it was not relevant to this case. The judge said, "Overruled. You can answer the question."

James Walters looked directly at the jury and calmly said, "Because I was asked to help the company developing the first mammogram machine and I felt saving women's lives from breast cancer was more important then making money as president of a corporation. I left to help develop the technology for the first x-ray machine to perform mammograms."

The Magic Meter patent attorney said, "No more questions." The way the seven women on the jury looked at him, he should have been on the first plane back to St. Louis and that would have been too slow to suit them.

After six weeks in court, the judge was getting very impatient.

He was pushing the attorneys to finish their case. He kept the jury sometimes after six o'clock and seven o'clock at night. It was time for Sherman Oaks to shine. He wrote the proposed instructions to the jury for the judge to read.

He wrote a brief regarding lobbying cities to purchase equipment or having the city do something for special groups that included an anti-trust ruling by the Supreme Court which had just been handed down while their trial was going on regarding influencing government officials to favor their product or position. The Supreme Court ruled companies had the right to lobby to get the Government's to favor their product or position. The plaintiffs wrote their version of instructions to the jury and gave it to the judge, but only after the judge repeatedly requested them to give it to him before the attorneys presented their closing arguments to the jury.

The judge ruled in favor of the defendants on three counts: Count Two; using a confidential customer list, he ruled a list of cities was a matter of public record. Count Seven; illegally setting prices; and Count Eight, frivolous lawsuits.

Yes, sir, Sherman had done his job in spades. The only two things left for the jury now were Count Three; anti-trust, and Count Four; patent violations. The two big ones, these counts carried triple damages and these were the ones the Magic Meter Company and their lawyers were going to get rich on!

Chance called Dak Thompson and asked if he wanted to come to Little Rock to be there for the end of the trial. Dak said he would be in Little Rock the next day. Dak was in time to hear the closing statements. Chance thought Sonny Wheeler did, at best, a fair job in summation. Mr. Wheeler's mother passed away during the trial, so he didn't look or sound too impressive. On the other hand, Sam Scott and Peter Reed were as smooth as silk.

Peter didn't miss getting the prairie dogs in his closing remarks and Sam, who had said he was apprehensive about trying a case against the Flowers Law Firm wasn't apprehensive any more. He was in complete command in front of the jury.

The judge opted for the defense's instructions to the jury. The judge was very concise in his instructions. The judge went into great detail; to be sure the jury understood their instructions. In fact, a copy of the instructions was given to them to use as they considered the case.

By two-thirty in the afternoon, the case was in the hands of the jury. A little after five o'clock, Sam got a call from the clerk of the court saying the jury had gone home for the night and would continue deliberation at ten o'clock the next morning.

Chance went back to his Holiday Inn room to wait. He called Ann to let her know the jury had the case now.

She said, "Chance, you have done everything you could to help the company win this case. You've done your best."

Chance was back at Sam Scott's law office before nine-thirty the next morning. A few minutes later Dak came into the office and joined Chance in the conference room. Before long, all of the attorneys and their staff were gathered in the conference room. They were trying to guess how long it would take the jury to reach a verdict. They had sandwiches brought in for lunch. At one thirty-five, the clerk of the court called Sam and said the jury had reached a verdict. Sam shook his head. "That's fast," he said, "I don't know what it means."

Peter said, "It means it didn't take long to reach a verdict. That's all it means."

Everyone headed for the elevators and the short walk to the federal courthouse. They went upstairs to the courtroom. Chance had spent so much time in there, he felt right at home. The lawyers from the Flowers Law Firm and C. K. Deering, Jr. came into the courtroom and a few minutes later, the jury filed in. Chance stood and watched the jury as they filed in, as he had done every time the jury came into the courtroom. They didn't look at him as they always did before.

Sam leaned over and said to Chance, "That's bad; they didn't look at you when they came in."

Sam told Chance, "No matter what the verdict is, stay cool."

The judge came in and took his place. He said, "Has the jury elected a foreperson?"

"Yes we have your honor."

The judge said, "Give the verdict to the bailiff."

The bailiff took the verdict to the judge, who looked it over and gave it to the clerk. The judge said, "Clerk, please read the verdict."

"In the charge of Count Three, we, the jury, find in favor of the defendant. In the charge of Count Four, we, the jury, find in favor of the defendant.

Chance thought we won, we won it all! He just wanted to yell it out loud! They shook hands with Magic Meter's attorneys and with

C. K. Deering, Jr. They left the courthouse and walked back to Sam's office on air.

It was a great victory for all of Superior's attorneys, but it was a greater victory for Chance Clark. Chance felt somewhat vindicated for the blame he felt Phillip put on him, while he was President of Superior. He thought Peter thought the lawsuit was his fault and he was the reason the suit was filed in the first place. Chance always felt like the lawsuit was one of the major reasons he lost his job as President.

During the lawsuit, he had an opportunity to read a note Phillip Rider had written to file, after the screwed-up meeting in Big Springs that led up to his removal as President. The note said, "Chance Clark and his staff are floundering; they have completely lost direction. The trick will be to put in a replacement for him without losing him from the company. We can't afford to lose him, he is too valuable to the company, but we have to get someone who can give the company direction."

Chance had known as soon as the meeting was over that Phillip completely misread his intentions and planned to replace him. Reading the note confirmed Chance's thoughts.

Two weeks later at the annual business meeting with Memphis, Phillip went out of his way to praise Chance for winning the lawsuit. Chance was pleased in fact he was happy since he had been vindicated.

It was a grand Christmas that year at the Clarks. Shane was attending the local community college. Curt was going to Central Arkansas University in Conway and Chase and Marie had enjoyed a very good year at the resort. The Trout's Inn looked a lot better since they had taken it over. Chance loved to go there every Sunday afternoon if he was in Big Springs. They would have lunch with Chase and Marie and then Chance and Chase would go fishing. It was the one thing Chance liked to do besides work and it was the only time he was completely at rest with himself.

Chance's best friends were his two sons. He would rather spend time with them then anyone else in the world except Ann. Ann was always first and always would be.

Chase knew a lot about business. After all, he had a degree in business administration, so Chance figured he should know something about it. They discussed how things were going at the resort and how things were going with Superior. Money would solve all of the problems in both places.

In January, Magic Meter Company filed an appeal to the verdict, just as Superior's attorneys said they would. Chance didn't have any role in defending the appeal. Sherman Oaks had worked during the whole trial to win the case in appeal. Sherman would do most of the work required for the appeal.

Chance went back to traveling and working with his international distributors. He helped work the two big International Parking Trade Shows.

Shane continued to attend community college and went to Kansas City to spend several weeks each summer with his godmother, Kathy Jones. Shane had been spending time with her every summer since he was six or seven years old. Kathy Jones was the widow of Karl Jones, Chance's old boss and mentor. Kathy and Shane always had a great time together. Kathy had only one sister living and no other family. Whenever Shane was in Kansas City, he and Kathy would usually go out to dinner with one of Karl's college classmates, Mrs. Cooper. Mrs. Cooper's husband and only son had died a few years before. Mrs. Cooper was in her eighties when she first met Shane.

Chance met Mrs. Cooper twice. Both times it was just before Christmas and they would go with Kathy Jones to a dinner party she gave in a very nice restaurant. Chance, Ann, Shane and Kathy would drive over to Mrs. Cooper's apartment building and pick her up. Kathy had told them Mrs. Cooper was a retired concert violinist and her late husband was a physician. By the time Chance and Ann met her for the first time, she was in her late eighties. Kathy said she was the closest friend Mrs. Cooper had left and Mrs. Cooper didn't have any living family members.

Superior finally got notice of the hearing on the appeal it would be held the day after Election Day in November. Chance flew to Washington, DC on Election Day and watched on TV as the Governor of his state won the election as President. Chance kept thinking, I'm glad this appeal process will be over before Sonny Wheeler's ex-law partner becomes First Lady.

The next day Chance met with all of Superior's attorneys: Sam Scott, Peter Reed, Marilyn May and Sherman Oaks. The decision was made that only Sherman and Peter would speak. Sonny Wheeler was present for the Magic Meter side. Their patent attorney was not present. In less then fifteen minutes, the process was over.

As they left the appeals court, Sherman said, "It will take about a month before we hear anything."

Three days before Christmas they received a two-word ruling from the appeals court. It said, "Verdict confirmed." End of story. Superior had won a complete victory. It took two years of Chance's life and cost Superior over two million dollars. Chance later heard that Sonny Wheeler had agreed to take the case on a fifty- percent contingency fee for his brother-in-law, without consulting his partners. He had even agreed his firm would pay all of the expenses for their expert witnesses. You can believe his partners were not happy.

After that, the only thing Chance knew about Sonny Wheeler was what he read in the papers. His stay in the President's Administration didn't last long or come to a happy ending.

The Clarks enjoyed another glorious Christmas with the news that Superior had won the final victory. Between Christmas and New Year's, Chance, Ann and Shane went to Kansas City to do some shopping and, again, Kathy Jones took them all to dinner along with Mrs. Cooper.

When Mrs. Cooper greeted Shane, she said, "Shane, you know, I'm your oldest friend." Since she was ninety-six years old at the time, there was no doubt about that. Chance and Ann couldn't get over how beautiful Mrs. Cooper was. If they had to guess her age, they would have guessed her to be in her sixties or seventies, at the most.

The New Year started out like a lot of Chance's had for the past several years. He was flying off to Europe for two weeks. When he returned from his trip, Shane said he wanted to talk to him.

Chance had to make a trip to Wal-Mart to pick up several items to restock his travel case, so Shane went with him. As soon as they got in the car, Shane said he had met a girl that he really liked.

Chance said, "That's great."

Shane said it was someone he met at community college.

Chance said, "I'm glad to hear that. I'm looking forward to meeting her."

Shane said, "Well, you saw her one time. She was at our house making a film with me for my art class."

Shane continued, "She's married."

Chance said, "That's not too good."

Shane said, "She is going through a tough time right now and I'm her friend. A friend she can talk to."

Chance said, "Everybody needs someone to talk with when they have problems. Does she have any children?"

Shane replied, "Three, two boys and a little girl."

"What is she going to do?" Chance asked.

"She is getting a divorce," replied Shane.

"That's tough on the kids. Is she sure that's what she wants to do?"

"I'm sure that what she wants to do?"

"What can you do to help her at this point?" his dad asked.

"Be her friend."

By this time, they had been sitting in the Wal-Mart parking lot for some time.

Chance said, "Shane, be careful how you get involved. You're talking about a lot of lives here."

A week later Chance left on a round-the-world trip to attend several meetings over a three weeks span. He worked with his travel agent, putting together the trip. His first stop was Seoul, Korea, next Hong Kong, on to Australia, then across to South Africa, to Sao Paulo, Brazil, and finally back to Miami, St. Louis, and Big Springs.

As was his habit these days, he called home every day from wherever he was in the world. Thank goodness for ATT USA Direct. It made his telephone calls a lot less expensive, then when he first started traveling internationally. In those days, the telephone charges on his hotel bill were more every day then his room was. Ann said, "I've had several calls from this man who says Shane is breaking up his marriage. I finally told him, why don't you talk to your wife instead of calling me."

Ann continued, "I've talked with Shane and all he says is that he is supporting his friend who is in the process of getting a divorce." Chance said, "That's what I told you he said to me before I left on this trip."

When Chance returned from his three-week trip, he talked to Shane again about the woman Shane was helping to get through a divorce. The woman's husband was trying to bring Shane into the divorce procedures.

Chance said, "I think we better go see an attorney," which they did. After having a conversation with the three of them, the attorney met with Shane alone. Less then a week later, Shane's friend was granted a divorce and nothing else was heard from her ex-husband by the Clarks.

Several months later Shane wrote his dad a letter, telling him he had fallen in love with his friend, Jan. Chance was not happy about it, nor was Ann. This was not what they wanted for Shane.

They wanted him to fall in love with someone his own age, not someone older with three kids. After Chance received the letter, he had another talk with Shane about Jan.

Chance said he wanted them to wait until after Shane finished his university degree before they even thought about getting married.

Chance said to Shane, "You need to give Jan enough time to see what she really wants to do with her life."

Shane agreed to do that.

29

In the summer of 1992, Shane moved on from community college to the University of Arkansas at Fayetteville to complete his degree. He rented an apartment along with two of his friends from Big Springs. His friends had been living in university dorms since they started at the university in their freshman year.

Shane continued to see Jan after her divorce. She won custody of her three children and Ann and Chance finally met her and her children during the Clark's family Christmas dinner in 1991. Jan's two sons, Jake and Jerry, were teenagers and her daughter, Joanna, was seven. Ann and Chance had never met three nicer, loving or better behaved children in their lives.

Ann and Chance fell in love with Jan's kids in two hours and decided as nice and loving as her children were Jan had to be "OK." She had done a great job as a mother and anyone who did that must be capable of being a good wife for their son if they got married.

Chance thought it must be very hard for Jan, since she was raising three kids, working and going to community college. Shane came home to Big Springs sometimes over the weekends to see her.

Chance returned home the last weekend of January 1993 from a trip to South Africa. In South Africa, he had been working with his distributors, calling on cities and showing them the new electronic parking meter. This was Superior's third generation of electronic meters.

They had had a busy two plus weeks, going from Johannesburg, to Port Elizabeth, Durbin, Cape Town and some towns Chance had forgotten the names of.

Shane called Monday afternoon and said that his godmother, Kathy Jones telephoned and said that her friend, Mrs. Cooper, died this morning.

Chance asked, "If Shane knew when they should go to Kansas City for her funeral."

Shane said, "Mrs. Cooper donated her body to the University of Kansas Medical Center and there wouldn't be any funeral."

Three weeks passed by since they heard Mrs. Cooper passed away, when Shane called and told his folks he got a call from some lawyer in Kansas City asking him to come to meet with him. The lawyer told Shane he was the prime beneficiary of Mrs. Cooper's estate.

Chance and Ann said, "You must be kidding. Why would Mrs. Cooper leave you something in her will?"

Shane didn't know he only knew what the lawyer told him on the phone. Shane made an appointment to meet with the attorney in Kansas City on Friday to make sure his folks would be able to go with him.

Chance asked Shane, "Have you talked to Kathy Jones about this?"

Shane said, "I have, but she didn't know anything about Shane being in Mrs. Cooper's will."

Thursday, Chance, Ann and Shane drove to Kansas City.

Chance and Ann would stay at the Marriott Hotel, while Shane stayed overnight with Kathy Jones. They talked that evening over dinner with Kathy and she said she was Mrs. Cooper's closest living friend and she had never said a word to her about naming Shane in her will.

Kathy told them one of Mrs. Cooper's ex-neighbor's daughters, Martha Saxon, was also named in the will and would be coming to Kathy's house tomorrow.

Chance said since it was a long way from Kathy's house to the lawyer's office downtown she could ride with them.

Martha Saxon was already at Kathy's house when Chance and Ann arrived to pick up Shane. Martha was introduced to them and they all left to go to Mrs. Cooper's lawyer's office. During the trip downtown,

Martha told them she was almost Dr. and Mrs. Cooper's adopted daughter. She went with them sometimes on summer vacations to Mrs. Cooper's father's summer home in upper Michigan, near the Wisconsin border and close to Lake Superior.

Martha lived in Nashville now and worked for the District Attorney's Office there. She had been married twice and divorced twice. She claimed Mrs. Cooper wanted her to marry her son, Tom, but she said Tom and she were close friends, but she wouldn't marry him.

Arriving at the attorney's office, Chance, Ann and Shane were taken into a conference room by the attorney, Leonard Scotland, Jr. He was the attorney who talked to Shane on the phone. Another of the firm's attorney had taken Martha to another conference room to talk to her.

Shane, Chance and Ann sat in silence as Mr. Scotland told Shane, Martha had been left $50,000 in cash, Mrs. Cooper's car, furs and pieces of expensive jewelry and several pieces of furniture with an estimated value of more than $150,000.

Mr. Scotland said the balance of Mrs. Cooper's estate was left to Shane. He estimated after taxes it would amount to about $1.2 million. The Clark's looked at each other in total disbelief. Shane was going to inherit over a million dollars and he was just 21 years old and from a woman they hardly knew.

Chance had read stories in the newspaper about something like this happening, but couldn't believe it could happen to one of his sons. The ride back to Kathy Jones' house was made in silence.

With each of them lost in their own thoughts. If the Clark's could have had the power to read Martha Saxon's mind, Chance would have put her out of the car.

What happened over the next few weeks just proved how money could bring out the worst in people. After Mrs. Cooper's will was read, Martha Saxon talked with three different law firms in Kansas City trying to find one that would file a protest to the will. Martha thought she deserved everything of Mrs. Cooper's. After all, she was almost an adopted daughter.

She didn't have any success finding an attorney who would take her case, but what she did manage to do was to talk to enough people that she got an attorney interested in the case that specialized in locating and finding lost heirs. The story Martha told the attorneys was straight out of the movies. A real movie script with plenty of sub-plots. According to her, the Clark's, along with Kathy Jones, convinced Mrs. Cooper, Shane was her reincarnated husband. After all, she was a very old lady suffering from dementia and Kathy Jones could get her to do anything she wanted her to do.

In fact, according to Martha even Karl Jones helped to convince Mrs. Cooper to change her will to leave everything to Shane. The major problem with this story was Karl had died almost two years before Mrs. Cooper's son died. Until his death, Mrs. Cooper's son was her sole heir.

The attorneys for the estate got wind of Martha's activities and advised Shane she was trying to file a "protest" to the will. Shane called his dad and told him what the estate attorney, Mr. Scotland, had heard. Hearing this, Chance called his friend and trusted attorney, Sam Scott, in Little Rock and told him all about what was going on. Scott was to say the least, fascinated with the whole thing. Scott advised Chance he was going to need an attorney that was an expert in inheritance cases in Missouri, and quick.

Sam promised to research and "find" the best attorney to handle any potential protest case in Kansas City for Shane. Chance knew from experience in the Magic Meter case that having the best attorneys really helps you win the case.

The next day, Sam Scott called Chance and told him he was faxing a copy of his research on Kansas City attorneys that he found to be the best estate attorneys in KC.

Chance looked over the list and called Scott back. Chance said, "I don't know which one of these I should pick but from looking at all of their credentials, I think I like Tom Wilder. What do you think, Scott?"

Sam replied, "Mr. Wilder would be my pick too, since he's with a medium size firm. Sometimes it's not good to have an attorney that's with a big firm and a one man firm presents its own problems. He's the Chairperson of the Missouri Estate Law Committee which advises the state government on estate laws."

"Sam, will you give him a call and set up an appointment for Shane and myself?"

"Sure, Chance. I'll call you back with the information on an appointment."

Sam got them an appointment to see Tom Wilder two days later. Chance and Shane made the trip to Kansas City to meet with Mr. Wilder. Chance and Shane brought a copy of the will and relayed the story of what they were told by the estate attorney.

Tom Wilder said he would call Leonard Scotland, Jr. and talk with him about the will. Tom left the conference room and after about 30 minutes, he returned.

Tom said, "Well, I talked with Leonard Scotland, Jr., the attorney for the estate. He told me his version of what was going on. It seems Mrs. Cooper's will was written by Leonard's father and Mr. Scotland was not happy about anyone trying to attack a will his late father wrote."

"It appears Ms. Saxon has not endeared herself to Mr. Scotland for sure and that's good for us."

Chance asked, "Mr. Wilder, what is the next step we need to take?" Mr. Wilder replied, "I'm going to need to interview Mrs. Kathy Jones as soon as possible. She's the only one who probably knows what's going on with Ms. Saxon."

Shane said, "I don't want to involve her any more then we have to."

Mr. Wilder replied, "Shane, I understand your feelings, but we are going to need Mrs. Jones' help."

Chance said, "Shane, I am sure Kathy is going to want to help anyway she can."

"I know dad, but it's not fair she has to be involved in this."

"Shane, I don't think she is going to have much choice," Tom said. "After all, she is one of the people being attacked in this whole thing. Apparently, Ms. Saxon is putting most of the blame on herfor promoting this idea that Shane is the reincarnation of Mrs. Cooper's late husband."

Chance said, "Let me speak with Mrs. Jones and ask her to come in to talk with you."

Two days later, Mrs. Jones met with Tom Wilder and told him as much as she knew about Mrs. Cooper and about how private she was.

Mrs. Jones said, "Mrs. Cooper never discussed her will with her or that she was leaving anything to Shane Clark."

Mrs. Jones assured Mr. Wilder that it was Mrs. Cooper who influenced her, not the other way around. Mrs. Jones did confirm Mrs. Cooper believed in reincarnation. She also told Mr. Wilder, Mrs. Cooper felt a strong bond with Shane the very first time they met when Shane was about eleven years old.

Mrs. Jones said she had known Mrs. Cooper for almost all of her life, Mrs. Jones' life, not Mrs. Cooper's. She said that meant she had known her for more than sixty years and had never heard of her speak of having any brothers or sisters. Mrs. Jones also said, she had known Martha Saxon since she was a baby.

Two weeks later, two attorneys who purchased Mrs. Cooper's apartment when her apartment complex was turned into condominiums filed a suit to have her things removed from the apartment. Mrs. Cooper had a "99 year lease" on the apartment when they bought the apartment and when the owners converted the apartment building to condominiums. Mrs. Cooper refused to buy her apartment.

She had to go to court to hold on to her apartment after these two lawyers bought her apartment and they agreed to compromise with her and let her stay as long as she lived.

She was eighty years old at that time, so the lawyers figured she wouldn't last long anyway. They only had to wait seventeen years before they got to take possession of their apartment.

While Chance was working in Europe, the judge ruled that he would allow Martha and Shane to remove the items they inherited from the apartment. The only thing was they had only two days to get everything out of the apartment.

Shane, Ann and Chase drove to Kansas City in Ann's car to remove the furniture and personal property from Mrs. Cooper's apartment. They rented a truck and made arrangements to have someone in the apartment from the estate attorney's office during all of the time they were loading. This was necessary to assure that they didn't take anything that belonged to Martha Saxon.

After working for almost two days, they finally got everything packed and loaded in the moving van. They brought everything back to Big Springs and rented a large storage building to unload everything in.

When Chance returned from Europe, Ann took him over to the storage building to see what they had moved in. Chance opened the overhead door and found the building was completely full.

Another month passed and Tom Wilder called Shane to tell him Mrs. Cooper's surviving relatives had filed a "protest" to the will through a local Kansas City attorney. This attorney made his living by finding lost heirs had found them. When Chance got a copy of the filing, he found that there were 28 heirs, scattered from Maine to Oregon. They were grand nieces and grand nephew.

Mrs. Cooper probably had never met any one of them.

According to the filing, the protest said Chance and Ann Clark, along with Mrs. Kathy Jones had used undo influence on Mrs.

Cooper who was no longer in possession of her facilities and got her to name Shane Clark as her heir.

It also said the three of them convinced Mrs. Cooper that Shane was the reincarnation of her late husband, Dr. Cooper.

Chance didn't have to think long to understand where this pack of lies came from. Obviously, Ms. Martha Saxon had made a deal with the relatives and their lawyer to get a bigger cut of the estate or to just do everything possible to deny Shane his inheritance.

Kathy Jones was shocked Mrs. Cooper had so many living relatives and that she was being accused of such things. Kathy Jones was as nice a person as you could find on this earth and the last person that would have been involved in such a scheme as this. Shane was named Mrs. Cooper's beneficiary when he was thirteen years old it was that just no one knew it.

Tom Wilder went to work and found when Mrs. Cooper's mother died in Kansas City, sometime in the 1920's, Mrs. Cooper's older brother was the administrator of her mother's estate. It seems Mrs. Cooper was to have a trust fund from her mother's estate. However, her brother and two sisters decided, since she was married to a doctor and didn't need the money, they would divide her money between them. After some legal action, Mrs. Cooper dropped her case against her siblings and wrote not only the money off, but her family as well.

No wonder Kathy Jones had never heard of or met any of Mrs. Cooper's family. This all happened not long after Kathy Jones was born.

Tom Wilder was just filled with information. It seems the State of Missouri had some kind of law on the books about "consensual adoption" or some legal term like that. Which translates that, as a child, if you are allowed to move in with someone for a long period of time, even though no legal adoption papers are filed, the child could be considered adopted.

Martha had a room in the Coopers' apartment that she stayed in sometimes. She went on summer vacations with them to their home in Upper Michigan.

However, Tom said he didn't think any court would rule she had been adopted under this law since she normally lived with her natural mother.

Tom asked Shane, "If he had been served by a process server?" Shane said, "No, I haven't been."

Tom told him, "They only have a few days left under their court order which runs for sixty days. You can't hide out, Shane, but you sure can go about your normal routine. I wouldn't just sit around waiting for the knock on the door."

Tom Wilder kept Shane, Chance and Sam Scott up to date on all activities that were happening. Chance read that a process serving company in Russellville had been appointed to serve a subpoena on Shane. Chance though that was very strange that a lawyer in Kansas City would appoint someone in Rusellville to serve Shane a subpoena in Fayetteville, when it was over a hundred miles away.

Chance called Sam Scott and asked him to check on this process serving company. Later that afternoon, Sam called back to tell Chance this company was in default on their state corporate charter and they no longer could legally do business in the State of Arkansas, they couldn't legally serve papers to anyone. In addition, in Johnson County,

Arkansas you had to be registered with the District Court to serve papers and this firm wasn't registered there either. Legally, they couldn't serve papers in Fayetteville anyway even if they had been legally still in business in Arkansas.

Chance asked Sam Scott to forward all of this information to Tom Wilder. Chance was sure he would be interested in it.

The next weekend, Shane stayed Friday night with his former roommates in his old apartment because several months ago, Shane moved into a small apartment by himself. He was staying over that night with his friends to let one of his high school friends, Betty Hauser use his apartment for the weekend. She was in Fayetteville to be a bridesmaid for another one of their friends from Big Springs wedding Saturday afternoon..

Saturday morning someone knocked on Shane's door. Betty opened the door and this woman threw some papers on the floor and turned around and left. Betty of course had no idea who this person was, the woman didn't' ask for Shane or anyone. Betty said when she opened the door this woman just threw some papers on the floor and left.

Monday morning Shane called Tom Wilder to ask him if he had been legally served by having a woman throw papers on the floor of his apartment when he wasn't home.

Tom said, "No way!"

Another month went by and Tom Wilder telephoned Shane and told him that there was to be a hearing in Kansas City on the protest that had been filed in his case next week.

Chance and Shane met with Tom Wilder just prior to the start of the hearing.

Tom told Shane "He would be called to testify, but for him to just stay cool, answer the question truthfully and listen carefully to what is asked of you. Shane you're a smart person, you'll do fine."

Shane had his dad, Tom Wilder and Leonard Scotland, Jr. there to help him against a lawyer who made his living by stealing from the dead. Chance took one look at him and Chance knew this guy could never stand up to Shane's attorneys. He wasn't even in the same class, in fact the guy even looked a little like a vulture.

He began his case by calling the woman process server to the stand. The lawyer asked her to relate how she served the papers to Shane. She said she drove up from a small town in Oklahoma about fifty miles west of Fort Smith, Arkansas.

She said she tried to serve Shane two different times before the day she left the papers in his apartment, but he was hiding from her. According to her testimony on the Saturday morning she had been watching his apartment since early morning and when a young woman with a baby went into his apartment, she knocked on the door and left the subpoena with the woman who opened the door.

After she finished her testimony, Tom Wilder asked her if she didn't just throw the papers on the floor when the woman opened the door.

She said, "No, I didn't throw them, I just laid them on the floor." Tom said, "How long have you been a process server for your company in Russellville, Arkansas?"

"Three years."

Tom then asked, "Do you know your company's state corporate charter is in default and your company can no longer do business in the State of Arkansas?"

"No."

Tom continued, "Are you registered with Johnson County Circuit Court in Arkansas as a process server?"

"No."

Tom said, "I have just one more question for you. Do you know that it is illegal to act as a process server in Johnson County, Arkansas if you are not registered and approved by the Circuit Court?"

"No."

"Your Honor, I don't have any more questions for this witness."

The judge told the witness she was excused. Next the judge asked Tom Wilder if he wanted to call Shane Clark to the stand.

"Yes, I do, your Honor."

Shane got up from his chair and went to the front of the hearing room. The judge told the clerk to swear Shane in.

The clerk told Shane to raise his right hand. "Do you swear the testimony you are about to give in this case is the truth, the whole truth, and nothing but the truth, so help you God?"

Shane replied, "I do."

The clerk said, "You may be seated."

Chance closed his eyes and prayed to God to give Shane the courage to help him get through this ordeal.

Tom asked Shane, "Did the process server personally hand you any court documents."

"No, sir."

"Mr. Clark, did you try to hide from the process server?"

"No, sir."

Tom said, "What are you doing at the present time in Fayetteville, Arkansas."

"I'm a junior at the University of Arkansas," Tom said, "Your Honor, I don't have any more questions for Mr. Clark."

The judge promptly asked the vulture if he had any questions for Mr. Clark.

"Yes, your Honor," as the vulture started to the front of the hearing room to question Shane.

Chance silently pleaded for God to be with Shane for what was coming next.

The vulture said, Mr. Clark the truth is you were hiding from the process server, weren't you?"

Shane coldly replied, "No, sir, I was not."

The vulture stopped with that one question since the way he said it was more of a statement then it was a question.

"Your Honor, I don't have anymore questions for Mr. Clark."

The judge then said, "Mr. Clark, you may step down."

Next, the judge said, "You have five minutes to make your case." His remark was directed to the vulture. "After his five minutes, Mr. Wilder, you will have five minutes to respond with your comments.

The vulture didn't waste any of his time. He started in by saying Shane hid out so the process server couldn't find him and justice would best be served by moving this hearing on to a full trial, so that all of the facts in this case could be heard.

When it was Tom's turn, he made it really simple for the judge. In the first place, Shane was never served. In the second place, the vulture hired a company that had their corporate charter lifted by the State of Arkansas for violations of corporate laws. Last, but not least, the woman sent to serve Shane was operating in violation of Johnson County, Arkansas Circuit Court rules, because she was not registered as a process server in the county. End of story!

The judge said, "We will take a fifteen minute recess and then I will render my verdict on this case."

Tom, Chance and Shane left the courtroom and took a walk downstairs.

Chance asked Tom, "Well, what do you thing?"

Tom said, "I'm not sure what the judges ruling may be, but I think the laws are on our side if the case moves on."

Chance said, "God, I hope it doesn't. It's already taken almost a year now to clear this thing up and a lot of money."

They walked back into the courtroom and Tom went over to talk with Leonard Scotland, Jr. to get Mr. Scotland's views on what would happen next in this case.

Just before Leonard started to give his thoughts, the court clerk said, "All rise."

The judge came in and sat down. The judge said, "I am ready to give my ruling in this matter." The judge started off very slowly. "Perhaps Mr. Clark did make himself hard to find and maybe the process server's company was in all kinds of defaults with the State of Arkansas and even the process server herself was not registered to act as a process server in the Arkansas' county. But the plain truth is that the life of the court documents to notify Mr. Clark expired thirty days before anyone ever tried to serve him and the attorney never asked the court to grant a new subpoenas. This case is dismissed."

Tom turned to Shane and Chance and said, "It's all over."

Mr. Scotland told Shane, "We will get started on the papers Monday so the judge can sign off and you can get the rest of your inheritance in the next two or three weeks."

Tom said, "I will keep my eyes and ears open, just in case Martha Saxon tries to claim "consensual adoption."

Chance and Shane thanked Tom and Mr. Scotland for their help. As soon as Chance got in the car, he called Ann to tell her they won and Shane called Chase and Jan.

Sixty days later, Shane had the rest of his inheritance turned over to him. When the first wire transfer of some of his money was made, the Clark's along with Jan met in Eureka Springs, Arkansas at a local steakhouse to celebrate a hard fought victory that ended exactly as Mrs. Cooper willed.

30

Over the next couple of years, Chance continued to live in the fast lane traveling the world like a jet setter. The difference was Chance was jet-setting working, not playing, as the phrase implied.

Chance's home was wherever he unpacked his suitcase, regardless if it was Paris, London, Milan, Seoul, Sydney or Hong Kong, Johannesburg or Big Springs and all of the places in between.

The more Chance traveled the world, the larger the company's international business grew. Chance felt, given time, Superior's international business would account for more then half of Superior's total sales volume. He had already seen it grow from less then twenty percent to almost forty percent.

Chance knew he could grow the international business a lot more if he could convince Superior's parent company to let him do privatization. Chance had been to so many countries and cities that needed to control their parking, but lacked two major ingredients. One, they didn't have the expertise to set up and run a parking system and second, they didn't have the money to purchase the equipment needed to set up the parking control system.

Chance had seen this in city after city, in country after country.

Chance enlisted help from some of his staff at Superior to put together a privatization program. Chance would present the plan to the Memphis Corporation to try one more time to get their approval to at least to let Superior install one small test operation in some international city.

Chance's privatization committee worked hard putting together a plan. It was always difficult at Superior to get any time for planning. They were always too busy fighting off the day to day problems. As the saying went around the office, they were too busy wrestling alligators to remember that their assignment was to drain the swamp.

With Chance traveling the world and everyone else's work requirements at Superior, it took his privatization committee three months to complete the plan. However, when the job was finished, they had done a great job. They had assembled a very slick professional presentation.

Chance next needed to get Dak Thompson to agree to let them make the presentation to Phillip Rider. Chance held a meeting of his privatization committee to rehearse their presentation. Chance wanted to be sure they were ready before making a presentation to Dak. The last thing they needed to happen was to do all of this extra work and not get Dak's support. The rehearsal went off without a hitch. In fact, Chance though it went too good. That was a sure sign that it would never work as well for the real presentations.

Chance and his committee plotted to come up with the perfect time and day to give their presentation to Dak. Monday's and Friday's were out everyone was too busy. Most mornings started off bad for Dak, because everyone was always waiting to catch him as soon as he came into the office. They wanted to lay their problems on Dak before everyone else got a chance to. Since Chance had been in Dak's shoes, he knew how people put their problems in the hands of the President.

The committee determined a Thursday afternoon meeting would suit their needs best. They picked a two o'clock starting time for their presentation. The only thing left was to determine which Thursday they would make the presentation and this was left up to Chance.

Chance began working backward from his own travel plans in order to set a date for the meeting. Chance was scheduled to go to Hong Kong for meetings with his distributor and several city officials next week.

After Hong Kong, Chance was traveling to Taipei, Seoul and Guam before returning to Big Springs, three weeks later.

His trip was set and appointments had been made with cit officials halfway around the world, so there was no way of delaying the trip. Chance thought about trying to do the meeting this coming Thursday. This couldn't work, because Chance found half of his privatization team was leaving on Wednesday morning for a presentation in New York City and would not be returning until late Friday night.

Chance had no choice; the presentation to Dak would have to wait until after Chance returned from the Far East. Perhaps this would work in Chance's favor anyway, since he would be returning to Big Springs in the middle of September and the annual review with Memphis Corporation was to be the week before Thanksgiving.

Chance thought if Dak just likes and appreciates the committee's plan, this timing would work perfect for them to present it to the Memphis Board of Directors for approval.

Chance's meetings in Hong Kong went much better then anyone could have hoped for. After almost five years, the Hong Kong government approved a test of Superior's new electronic parking meters with a special electronic debit system instead of using coins to pay the parking meters.

This system could start a whole new trend on how people paid their parking fees. The system worked with a flat plastic key that had a microprocessor imbedded into the plastic. It also had some type of wires that acted as an "antennae" inside the plastic.

The concept of the parking meter system was for the city or for a parking operations company to sell the key devices to the motorist. Then the motorist would have money value loaded onto the microprocessor in the key. When the motorist parked their car, they could just hold the plastic key into an indentation on the front of the electronic mechanism. Each time the motorist placed the key next to the indentation, the electronic meter contacted the key through a magnetic type of antennae that would take away a set amount of money, like fifty cents or a dollar. The meter would continue doing this each time the key was held up next to the meter until the maximum time limit on the parking meter was reached. Also the "LCD" display on the meter mechanism told the motorist how much money was left on the key each time the meter subtracted money from the key. This way the motorist knew how much money was left on their key and if they needed to have more money loaded onto the key.

Using this payment system, the City of Hong Kong could have the use of the "float" of millions of dollars every month before any time was actually sold on the meters. In addition, there were no coins to collect or count and the security of the electronic purse was unbelievable. No one could cheat this electronic system because the encryption codes were phenomenal.

No more jammed parking meters, since there would not be any openings in the mechanisms for people to put things in. Chance had cleaned out everything from catsup to liquid metal and everything else you could think of out of parking meters. Things like buttons, tokens, foreign coins, paper clips, paper and plastic parts, flat metal fuses and meter knock-outs from electric power boxes, Coke can tabs and rings and a lot of other things. So many, he had forgotten half of them.

Hong Kong would be the first city in the world with this new parking meter system and if things went the way they should, Chance would get an order in a year to replace Hong Kong's 20,000 mechanical meters.

Chance left Hong Kong with the specifications for the test meters and a lot of high hopes. High hopes faded fast upon his arrival in Taiwan.

Taiwan had always been a problem for Superior. In an effort of achieve product purchases at competitive prices, Taiwan established purchasing laws which defeated their own purpose when it came to buying parking meters.

Potentially, Taiwan offered a huge untapped market for the sale of meters. Taiwan had lots of cars and lots of parking problems.

The real problem in them buying parking meters was Taiwan requirement for three qualified competitive bids. There were three parking meter manufacturers, but If one of them didn't bid, then Taiwan couldn't buy anything. In addition, they had very poor bid specifications and demanded the lowest price, plus free installation and free maintenance for three years.

Buying parking meters through local distributors in Taiwan became a nightmare. One company's parking meter distributor would never bid, so they would never have three bids. Therefore,

there had been no purchases of parking meters for several years. The company that didn't bid wanted to find out how low their competitors bid. Each distributor had someone who worked in the government who supplied them with the competitor's bid prices.

Bidding became an art form in Taiwan. The distributors tried everything to gain an advantage, from having three of their own companies bid on the same product, to working out an agreement between the three competitors to rotate who would submit the winning bid.

This didn't work either, because the distributor that came up with this idea decided when it was his turn to win the bid, the size of the order was not going to be as big as the other two distributors.

What did he do, he went to the city and the local newspaper and exposed the whole deal before anyone got an order. Big scandal, Chance fired his distributor over the deal and now had a new one.

When Chance arrived in Taiwan from Hong Kong, Chance's new distributor talked just the same way as his old one. The same old story, "I've got to have lower prices!"

Chance concluded the Taiwan market was not worth it. Chance told his distributor he would give him the best price he could, but Superior had no interest in losing money on each parking meter they manufactured for Taiwan.

The last time someone actually got an order, the price for the meter delivered and installed in Taipei was less then what it cost Superior to make a parking meter. One thing Chance felt was the competitor didn't know what it cost him to make his parking meter.

What Taiwan started out to accomplish in establishing its bidding process had, in fact, done the opposite. It created a totally corrupt system of purchasing. Good-bye Taiwan! And good luck! Arrival in Seoul was like a breath of fresh air. Chance's distributor in Korea was not only a good businessman, but had become Chance's good friend. Chairman Kim knew the parking meter business and he knew the city officials. Chance and Chairman Kim visited with city officials in Seoul, Pusan and Inchon. On this trip, prospects looked good in Korea for major orders next year. As Chance was checking out of his hotel, he was given a fax that had been received from his Executive Assistant, Linda Johnson, with a "News Flash" from Memphis Corporation. The Chairman of the Board retired and the President of Memphis Corporation took over as Chairman/CEO. Chance's ex-boss and friend was named President/COO effective this date. Great news for his former boss, because he deserved the job and he was a great President of Memphis' major division, not only that, but his new annual pay would be in the millions.

Great news, or was it? The new President for Superior's division was a man coming from a company that Dak used to be the President of. If Chance remembered correctly, these two men had lots of problems with each other in the past. This might not be good news for Chance's privatization program.

Upon arrival in Guam, Chance found Guam was another place ideal for Chance's privatization program. They had a lot of parking problems and no money to buy parking control equipment. The meeting with Chance's distributor and city officials went well; the city just didn't have the money to start a paid parking system.

As soon as Chance arrived home in Big Springs, he met with Dak, who told him, "Chance, with our new Divisional President, it's not the time to bring up your privatization program you've been working on at our annual review in November."

Dak said, "We've got a lot of work to do, just to present our core business to the new man."

Chance replied, "Dak, I certainly understand and I will do whatever I can to help get things ready for the review meeting."

"I know you will, Chance. Just get me some more international orders. You know your international sales are carrying the company this year."

"Dak, I'll try to get orders in from Germany, England, Australia and South Africa."

"Get them soon!"

"Ok, Dak. I'll do my best."

Before the year was over, Chance got his orders from Germany for $450,000; England for $180,000; Australia for $265,000 and South Africa for $220,000. International sales accounted for forty- eight percent of the total sales for the year for Superior and for most of their profits.

However, Chance's parking privatization program was shot down again and this time, Chance couldn't even get it out of the hangar! Chance just couldn't understand why no one else could see the potential out there for this business. Here was a "diamond" of a business that no one else could see but him. Someday he would find a "visionary" who understood what he was talking about.

Some day!

Chance was preparing his monthly report used as part of the President's report that Dak had to submit to the Memphis Company on what happened the previous month at Superior when his phone rang.

The receptionist said that a gentleman by the name of George Duncan wanted to see him. Although Chance didn't know Mr.

Duncan, Chance agreed to meet with him.

Mr. Duncan was shown into Chance's office a few minutes later. Mr. Duncan, Chance thought, was a distinguished looking gentleman that was either in his late 60's or early 70's.

Chance asked Mr. Duncan to please sit down and asked what could he do for him.

Mr. Duncan was, in fact, Dr. Duncan a retired University of Oklahoma professor of advertising and marketing. Dr. Duncan began explaining he was organizing a mission to the Soviet Union to hold a three- week seminar on advertising and trade at the University of Kiev.

Dr. Duncan told Chance this would be the first such seminar ever held in the Soviet Union on advertising and free trade.

Dr. Duncan explained he had assembled a team of colleagues. In fact, they were the leading expertise in the United States in this field. His team consisted of the head of departments in advertising and marketing from the Universities of Miami, Michigan, California at Santa Barbara and Florida.

These doctors were all contributing their time and paying their own travel expense to do this seminar.

Chance though, OK, this is interesting, but what do you want from me and Superior?

Chance didn't have long to wait to find out.

Dr. Duncan said, "I would like for Superior to send samples of your latest parking meters to the Soviet Union for our seminar."

"OK, we will be pleased to supply our new electronic meters for your seminar. All I need is for you to give me a shipping address and when you need the parking meters to arrive in Kiev."

"Great, we really appreciate your help."

Chance asked, "Can you tell me why you want parking meters for your seminar?"

Dr. Duncan explained that last week he had a meeting of the seminar team and they decided they wanted the students to work like they were a company putting together an advertising and business plan. Next, we thought we should have a product that none of the students would have any knowledge of before hand. "After I retired from the University, my wife and I moved to Big Springs and I knew about you and your company. I suggested parking meters to the team and they loved it."

"There's only one other thing. We want you to come to give equipment demonstrations and talk about patents and trademarks." Two months later Chance was at Charles de Gaulle airport trying to find his Air France flight to Kiev. Chance was at terminal one, Air France's main terminal for international flights. After some time trying to find his flight number, he went to an Air France check in counter.

The young woman working behind the counter said, "You are in the wrong terminal. All of the Aeroflot flights depart from terminal two."

Chance explained, "No, I want the Air France flight to Kiev." The young woman said, "Sir, the Air France flight to Kiev is a code share flight with Aeroflot and that flight leaves from terminal two."

"How do I get to terminal two, since I just came from the city by taxi to terminal one?"

"Go out the door behind you and find a bus stop for terminal two. A bus will come to you shortly."

Chance thanked the agent and went back out the same door he had just entered. Before too long a bus arrived and after waiting for several passengers to exit the bus, Chance boarded the bus.

After the bus made two more stops at terminal one and at the train station, the bus was on its way to terminal two. After traveling for a few minutes and winding around several turns, the bus arrived at terminal two. Chance got off at the first stop.

He soon found the check-in counter for Aeroflot was in the middle of the terminal. When he arrived at the check-in counter there were only two people in line ahead of him.

Chance took his position behind the other two passengers. The agent took very little time to process the passengers in front of him.

Chance handed his ticket and passport to the agent and placed his suitcase on the scale to be weight as he had done a hundred times before.

Somehow this was different, going into a country that was an enemy of America and with no opportunity to communicate with Ann everyday as they now were accustomed of doing. Chance was warned making telephone calls out of the Soviet Union could take days to get a call through and to send a fax was no better. Yes, going to the Soviet Union was something different for Chance.

The agent checked in Chance's suitcase, stapled a claim check for his bag to his ticket folder and issued him a boarding pass and a seat assignment. She checked over his passport and his Russian visa. Everything was in order. OK so far, there was nothing different about this flight than checking in for hundreds of other flights.

Too bad it didn't stay that way. Chance had a business class seat on this plane. As soon as he walked inside the plane, he could smell an odor like an outhouse. Something like going to the outdoor toilet at his grandparents' farm in the 1940's, only his grandparents' outhouse never smelled this bad. Chance knew this TUV-something airplane was not going to be his favorite flight. After taking off from Charles de Gaulle Airport, the plane experienced a lot of turbulence. Chance, was wishing this was a Boeing airplane instead of a Russian built plane. The plane shook and Chance heard noises he had never heard before on any plane, but it stayed together. The flight attendant offered him something to drink. From the choices, Chance chose orange juice. It was awful.

Later, the flight attendant brought him lunch. It matched the "OJ" it was awful! Chance thought well, one good thing about this trip. I should lose some weight.

On their landing approach to Kiev, Chance could see it was already dark outside and he could see the lights from the city below. Kiev looked like a very big city from the air.

Before landing, the flight attendant gave him a form to fill out regarding the types and amount of money he had with him. The flight attendant told him he had to keep track of all of the Russian money that he exchanged his money for. When he left, he would be required to turn in the form and exchange all of the Russian money he had left because you could not take any Russian money out of the country.

Chance filled out the form as he was told to do. He had about seven hundred fifty US dollars and five hundred French francs. When he presented his passport and currency form to the immigrant agent, he looked Chance over very close. He stamped his passport with the entry date next to his Soviet visa and Chance picked up his suitcase from a cart and walked out of the customs hall.

As soon as he walked through the doorway Chance was met by a young man carrying a single red rose for him. He smiled as he presented the rose to Chance. Behind him there was a lady Chance guessed was in her early forty's. She introduced herself in perfect English, as Tasha Valcenia. Tasha was not only the interpreter, but had a Doctorate in languages.

The young man who presented Chance with the red rose took Chance's suitcase and was making his way through a large crowd of people in the terminal.

Chance was then introduced by Tasha to the Business Manager from Kiev Institute of Technology, Peter Tambov. Tasha explained Dr. Duncan could not come to meet him because he was ill.

However, she assured him Dr. Duncan would be OK and would see him for breakfast at seven in the morning. After a short walk, they arrived at a small Russian car and their driver, Boris. The young man who had his suitcase was struggling to put Chance's three suitor suitcases in the trunk of the car.

Finally, Boris put the trunk lid down and tied it down with a small piece of rope from the trunk of the car. Boris opened the right front door of the car and motioned for Chance to get in. Tasha and Peter Tambov got into the back seat of the car and they were off. As they entered onto the highway, Tasha told Chance he was riding on the only four- lane highway in the Ukraine. She explained when the government found out President Nixon was coming to visit Kiev. The Soviet Government built this road before his arrival, because they didn't want him to think that they were not as up-to-date in Russia as America was.

Only Tasha could speak English. The others only smiled and pointed at things for Tasha to explain to Chance.

When they arrived at the hotel, Chance was taken to the desk to check-in, which really only meant he handed the desk clerk his passport. Since he was a guest of the University or the Government of the Soviet Union, Chance never knew which one would be billed for his stay in Kiev.

Chance asked about getting some money exchanged, but Tasha told him tomorrow they would take him to a foreign exchange in one of the international hotels for him to exchange money for Russian money.

All three of them took Chance up to his room. The hotel had ten floors and Chance's room was on the eighth floor. They took the lift up to his floor. When they got off of the lift, he saw a lady sitting at a wooden desk just across from the lifts.

Tasha handed this lady a card with Chance's name and his room number on it. The lady handed Chance a key for his room, number 812. Tasha explained when you left your floor, you had to leave your key at this desk and they would give back his card.

When you returned you gave them your card and you got your room key.

Further, Tasha explained this lady lived on this floor along with her family. In fact, there were four apartments on each floor of the hotel located next to the lifts and where the stairway came up to the floor.

Four families lived on each floor and they took care of all the rooms on that floor.

Chance quickly realized doing things this way cost the hotel forty rooms. Well, it was one way of giving people employment and a place to live. It wasn't wrong; it was a way of life in the Soviet Union.

Their driver, Boris took Chance's key and opened the door of room 812. The room was a fairly large room; Chance guessed it was about 10 foot by 12 foot. In the corner of the room was a TV set, the room had one chair and a couch with wood arms on each end of the couch, something like a daybed. This couch was to be his bed and was only about five and a half feet long, Chance was going to have a hard time fitting his six foot two body on it. One good thing, he did have a private bath with a stool, sink and a shower.

Tasha explained that Dr. Duncan would meet Chance in the morning and take him to breakfast. Tasha asked if there was anything he needed and Chance said, "No thank you, everything is fine."

So his welcoming committee left after much handshaking. Chance looked around his room and thought about how the people he worked with at Superior thought what a luxury life he had on the road. He looked at his daybed and thought about Annie alone in their king size bed and he asked himself out loud, "What am I doing here?" Chance went into the bathroom the towels were the size of wash cloths and looked like dishtowels. Toilet tissue felt like sandpaper and the soap was as gritty as that sandpaper. Thank goodness, his travel agent in Big Springs had given Chance a list of things to bring to Russia.

Chance brought several wash cloths, large soft towels, soaps and toilet paper. Just normal, everyday necessities at home.

He put his red rose in a glass and filled the glass with water. He took out his fold-up scissors from his suitcase and cut off most of the stem from the rose, since the glass was not tall enough for the rose. He placed the glass with his rose on the windowsill.

He unpacked his suitcase, he had brought plenty of hangers to be able to hang up his suits, shirts and slacks. He put his ties on one hanger and hung up his clothes. He took out his pillow which he always carried with him because he was sure going to need it on this trip.

After taking a shower, he made sure he hung up his towel to dry before morning. He took the mattress off the daybed and put it on the floor. He took the one large pillow that was on the couch and placed it at the end of the mattress. Now he had a bed long enough for him to lay down on.

He turned downed the covers, turned on the TV and got into bed. It was no problem turning the channels, because there was no remote control and all of the stations broadcast in Russian anyway.

Chance's alarm went off at 6:00 am. He reached over on the floor between the daybed and his mattress for his watch and shut of his alarm. He lay there for a few minutes and crawled out of his bed, grabbing onto the daybed to help him get to a standing position. He showered, dressed and went down to the second floor of the hotel where he was to meet Dr. Duncan at 7:00 for breakfast.

Chance took his key with him, since he wasn't leaving the hotel. After arriving at the second floor he found a long hall leading to the breakfast room. Outside of the breakfast room, Chance found a group of wooden chairs and sat down to wait since it was still just 6:45.

Promptly at 7:00 am Chance saw Dr. Duncan coming down the hallway with two other people. When Dr. Duncan saw Chance, he smiled and gave Chance a little wave with his left hand. Chance got up from his chair and proceeded down the hall to meet him.

Dr. Duncan shook Chance's hand vigorously and began apologizing for not meeting him last night at the airport. Chance assured him it was no problem and that he had been well taken care of by his welcoming committee.

Dr. Duncan introduced Chance to Dr. Don Wilson from the University of Michigan and Dr. Barbara Jackson from the University of California at Santa Barbara. They both were heads of their departments at their respective universities. Chance felt out of place with people of letters.

However, both Don and Barbara soon took care of his feelings of inadequacy, as in unison they said, "Chance, we are sure happy to have you here, because the students have so many questions about the parking meters that none of us can answer."

Dr. Duncan said, "Enough of that for now. Let's go see what adventure they have for us for breakfast this morning."

They went into the breakfast room and found a table for the four of them. Chance was surprised that the hotel didn't have a breakfast buffet set up like every hotel in Europe did.

A few minutes later, a waiter came and sat down a small dish of sliced raw turnips next to each of them.

Dr. Barbara said, "Chia."

She explained to Chance, "Chia" was her limit of Russian, which meant "tea."

Dr. Don and Dr. Duncan joined in and asked for "Chia," so Chance shook his head yes to the waiter for Chia.

The waiter soon brought tea, which was extremely hot and tasted very good to Chance. Next, the waiter brought bread and butter, then each one of them a boiled egg. Chance ate his egg, spread butter onto the bread and ate it.

Chance's companions started laughing as Barbara said, "Well, how did you like breakfast?"

"Is this it?"

Dr. Duncan quietly said, "You've just had the deluxe edition we normally don't get an egg."

Chance replied, "Well, there no decisions to make!"

Don said, "After two weeks here I would like the opportunity to make a decision on what I wanted to eat."

Dr. Duncan stated, "It's hard to believe how little they have here. Well, if you need to go back to your room we have until eight o'clock before our host will be picking us up."

With that, they got up and started out of the restaurant. It turned out that each of them, were assigned to different floors. Dr. Duncan said to them as he got off the elevator on the fifth floor, "I'll meet you in the lobby a few minutes before eight."

Chance went to his room for a few minutes, he put his mattress back on the daybed. He made sure he had his clothes hung up in the closet and his dirty clothes in a bag on the closet floor. They all arrived in the lobby about the same time. Chance made sure he turned in his room key at the eighth floor desk and the woman gave him his card back so he could get his room key back later.

Tasha said, "Good morning."

In unison, they all replied, "Good morning, Tasha."

They got into the two waiting vehicles in front of the hotel.

Tasha said to Chance, "We will stop by one of the tourist hotels so that you may exchange your money."

When they arrived at the tourist hotel, Tasha and Chance went inside the hotel and went directly to a money exchange window. Chance thought the three money exchange windows looked like old-time USA bank teller's windows, with brass grill windows between the customer and the teller.

Chance gave Tasha the five hundred French Franc note and two hundred US dollars. Tasha handed his money to the teller and asked her to exchange the money. The teller counted the US dollars, since Chance gave Tasha two hundred dollars in twenty dollar bills, then she looked at the five hundred French Franc note. The teller began speaking in Russian to Tasha and Chance wished he knew what the teller was saying. Next, the teller returned the US dollars and exchanged the French Francs for Russian currency and handed the money to Tasha.

Chance said, "What's the matter? Is there something wrong with my American money?

"No, it's not the American money, it's the Russian rubles. The teller said to me, "What does he want to exchange all of this money for, there is nothing to buy here!"

Chance did not understand, but he thought the teller just did not want to have that much American money. Chance insisted Tasha ask the teller to exchange at least one hundred US dollars. Tasha shrugged her shoulders and gave back five twenty dollar bills to Chance and five twenty's to the teller. At the same time, Tasha began speaking in Russian to the teller.

Chance could see fire in the eyes of the currency exchange teller. She counted our Rubles for eighty US dollars and gave Tasha back one twenty and a handful of Russian rubles.

The teller said something to Tasha and Tasha turned to Chance and said, "Do you have your currency declaration form you filled out at immigrations last night when you arrived?"

Chance took the currency declaration form from his pocket and gave it to Tasha, who in turn gave it to the teller.

The teller recorded the amount of money that was exchanged and the kind of money exchanged on Chance's form. The teller returned the form back to Tasha, who in turn gave it back to Chance. Chance folded the form and put it back in his pocket.

Tasha said, "Be sure to keep the currency declaration form and exchange whatever Russian money you have left over at the airport before you leave because you can't take Russian money out of the Soviet Union. They will check when you leave to be sure you don't have any Russian money."

"No problem I will do exactly as you tell me."

Chance had so much Russian money he could not fold it up and put it in his right front pocket of his pants as he always did with his money. He had to just lay it flat in his pocket, it felt like a ream of paper in his pocket. Surely, he was Russian ruble rich.

Tasha and Chance returned to the cars and got back in and Tasha told the others what had taken them so long at the currency exchange.

They all laughed and agreed that indeed there was nothing to buy here with Chance's money. Chance was still holding his Russian money in his pocket when they arrived at a memorial to the hundreds of thousands of Kiev citizens that died at the hands of Nazi Germany during World War II.

Both cars stopped and everyone got out of the cars. One of the drivers gave Tasha a wreath of flowers. Tasha took the flowers and handed the flowers to Dr. Duncan. She asked him to place the wreath at the base of the monument to all of the people killed by the Nazi's.

Dr. Duncan along with the rest of the group advanced to the monument. When he arrived at the monument, he spoke. "It is my honor to place this wreath next to the monument dedicated to the thousands of people of Kiev who lost their lives in World War II. I place this wreath in the spirit of friendship between the people of Kiev and the people of America."

When he finished speaking, he placed the wreath at the base of the monument.

Tasha translated Dr. Duncan's words for everyone who didn't understand English. When the wreath had been placed everyone clapped their hands. All of the Soviets shook hands with the Americans and gave them very big hugs. Chance had a warm feeling about how friendly and warm these people were. How could these people, who had so much in common with Americans have been a faceless enemy for almost all of Chance's life?

Chance looked away from his new found friends to reflect on his thoughts and discovered from this viewpoint, they had a wonderful vista of the City of Kiev below them.

When they returned to the cars, Tasha told Dr. Duncan that now him and President Nixon had laid flowers at the monument.

The tour group's next stop was just outside of Kiev that looked to Chance almost like it had once been a landfill. Tasha said we are going to the black market.

Chance said, "Will we get into any trouble going to a black market?"

Chance could just see him and Dr. Duncan on a train headed to Siberia and no one ever knowing what happened to them. Tasha said, "Well, black markets are illegal, but the government tolerates them."

Chance looked back at Dr. Duncan and he just winked at Chance and they got out of the cars. As they walked up a sidewalk, Chance saw a turnstile that was a coin operated entrance to the black market.

Their driver took out several small coins from a beat up leather coin purse and placed one coin into the turnstile for each of them to enter the black market area. Chance could see the entire area had a very high fence around it. The black market appeared to be a fairly large area with tents set up in rows like going to a fair or something in America.

The driver explained something to Tasha and she translated what he told her about the entrance fee paid at the turnstiles. The government charged five rubles for everyone that entered the black market. Chance felt better about his chances of being sent off to Siberia with the government collecting a fee to go into the black market. He was sure they wouldn't want to give back the five rubles! The black market had everything you could think of in the stalls, Pierre Cardin shirts, Dior lingerie, Bill Blass blazers, computers, printers and televisions. In other words you name it, it was being sold somewhere in one of the stands. How was it being sold? Everything was priced in US dollars. The lady at the currency exchange was right; you couldn't buy anything with Chance's rubles.

The driver explained to Tasha almost all of the items being sold in the black market were coming through the borders between Poland and the Soviet Union. Prices! Were they ever high, sweaters Chance could buy at Dillard's Department Store for twenty or twenty-five dollars were being sold for a hundred and twenty dollars.

These people would have gone wild if they could have shopped at a local Wal-Mart store. At Wal-Mart's prices, they could have four shopping baskets filled, instead of two items of clothing they were carrying around in one hand at the black market.

Next stop on their Sunday tour was an "arts and crafts fair" in the heart of the old town of Kiev. When they arrived near where the fair was being held, uniformed police officers had barricades blocking the streets.

It was just starting to rain when the driver stopped the car next to the two police officers manning the barricades. Tasha rolled down her window and began speaking to the officers. She told them who she was and that they had two cars of American VIP's that didn't have raincoats with them and we promised them they would have thirty minutes to look around the fair.

At first the officer hesitated letting them through the barricades, but the longer the officers hesitated, the more important the Americans became. After all, they had just come from laying a wreath at the Kiev monument for the World War II dead.

OK, the barricades were moved and away they went. Another car came up right behind as their two-car convoy pulled away. This car was quickly turned away as Chance saw as he turned back to see what would happen after they went through the barricade.

The driver proceeded down the hill to the next cross street that was the site of the Kiev Art's and Craft Fair.

They got out of the car by now the rain was now just a light sprinkle, Tasha said, "You may have thirty minutes to look around.

If you need help, please let me know."

Chance began walking around with Dr. Duncan, Dr. Barbara and Dr. Don. If one of them picked up an article being offered for sale, when they put the article down, the people who started following them would also pick it up for inspection, just to see why the item caught the eye of the Americans.

The fact that they were American VIP's quickly went through the crowd attending the fair. The longer they stayed, the bigger the crowd was following them. Chance was standing next to Dr. Barbara and he leaned over toward her and asked if she always had such a large crowd following her.

She replied, "No, I thought they were following you."

"Not unless they've got a rope with them," Chance replied.

"I'm beginning to feel like a member of some pop band."

Just then a large painting caught Chance's eye and he looked around for Tasha.

"Tasha!" he called out.

Tasha pushed her way through the crowd of people to get up next to him.

Chance said, "Please ask how much the artist wants for this painting of the church with its Kiev street scene. In fact, if you look up this street I can see the church is right up this very street and these shops are also in his painting."

Tasha said, "You have a good eye Chance, because this painting is of this street."

The artist said he wanted five hundred rubles for the framed painting.

"Tell him I will give him four hundred fifty rubles and he can keep the frame."

The artist replied through Tasha, "What would I do with the frame. I made it just for this painting. No, I will not sell it without the frame."

Chance explained he really wanted this painting, but could never get it home to America with its large frame.

Tasha tried to explain this to the artist, but he was unmoved.

Tasha told Chance the answer was still "no."

Chance said, "Tell him that I will pay four hundred seventy- five rubles for the painting without the frame."

"No," said the artist. "The frame stays with the picture."

Hearing that from Tasha, Chance tried a trick he learned in Hong Kong. He started walking away, because in Hong Kong the merchant would almost always say OK, but this wasn't Hong Kong. The crowd parted so Chance could get through them. The artist didn't change his mind; he just began packing up his paintings. A few stalls down from this one Chance found a smaller version of the same church without the street scene. He bought this one for fifty rubles with a frame that would fit in his suitcase.

Tour day was over and Chance was the only one with a prize to take home to Big Springs. He guessed the Soviet's discovered Americans could be as stubborn as the Russians.

Dinner at the hotel started with "Chia" and turnips and was downhill from there. One good thing about dining in the Soviet Union, you never had to make choices. They served you whatever they had that day.

Monday morning came quickly, with the time being eight hours ahead of Big Springs. Chance was ready to go to bed instead of getting off of his bed on the floor. He was anxious to see the University.

Chance was introduced to the class as soon as he arrived in the classroom. He was scheduled to give the second and third hour classes this morning. Chance was curious about the makeup of the class. He expected to see eighteen to twenty year old students, but everyone, but three or four looked like they were only a few years younger then him.

When the class took a break after the first hour, Chance asked Dr. Duncan about the class members. He was taken back when he found out that almost all of the members of the class were professors, business leaders and government officials.

Dr. Duncan told Chance the class was designed to have a maximum of twenty students and they had thirty-eight. The people in the class were too important to be denied access.

Chance was ready to give his first class on how patents and trademarks worked in America. What he was not prepared for was a change from Tasha doing translation to another translator. Tasha had her own classes to teach for the next three hours. Chance was accustom to working with translators all around the world and he understood how long he should speak and then stop to let the translator do their thing.

Tasha introduced him to Dr. Zorn who would be his translator this morning. Chance was told Dr. Zorn served as the translator for President Gorbachev and President Reagan.

The class bell rang everyone, was seated in their chairs and Chance assumed a very unaccustomed role as a teacher in front of a university classroom. Chance began to speak and almost as quickly as Chance began speaking, Dr. Zorn began translating simultaneously. When Chance heard Dr. Zorn speaking at the same time as he was, Chance lost his train of thought. He stopped in mid-sentence.

Chance turned and looked at Dr. Zorn.

Dr. Zorn looked at Chance and said, "Is everything OK?" Chance said, "You shocked me, because I didn't expect you to start translating until I stopped talking."

"I'm sorry I can work that way if you like."

"No, it's OK. I just never had anyone do that before."

It took fifteen minutes into Chance's presentation before he began to feel comfortable with Dr. Zorn's method of translation. At the end of his first hour of class, Chance was feeling a lot more comfortable working with Dr. Zorn.

After Chance's second hour, all of the students came up to be introduced to Chance. Poor Chance was being avalanched by questions from everyone and at the same time and being invited to visit the various departments of the university. It seemed to Chance that every department head for the entire university was a member of the class. Chance was surrounded by more doctors then if he had been out on the golf course on a Wednesday afternoon.

The day ended and the drivers took them back to the hotel. Tasha explained she would return to pick them up to go to the opera at eight o'clock.

Chance took a shower, shaved for the second time that day, put on a black suit and was just tying his shoelaces when he heard a knock on his door.

He opened the door and a man dressed in a dark blue suit was standing in his doorway. The man said something in Russian to him. Chance, of course, had no idea who the man was or what he was saying.

Chance said, "I'm sorry, but you must have the wrong room."

Chance closed the door.

The man knocked on the door again. Chance opened the door again. The man again started speaking in Russian and making motions to Chance, pointing at Chance and himself and motioning to Chance to come with him.

Chance thought maybe he is with the KGB. Chance, like everyone else in America over the age of ten knew about the KGB. Anyway, Chance decided he better go with the man, because although he couldn't understand anything the man said in Russian, he understood his own name, "Chance Clark."

Chance put on his suit coat and followed the man out of his room. Chance left his key at the desk on his floor. The unsmiling floor attendant gave him his card showing his room number.

The man had an elevator waiting for Chance. They went out of the hotel and the man pointed to a street leading away from the hotel. The man and Chance began walking down the street. After about ten minutes of walking, they arrived at a very large building.

The man pointed at the building. They went to one of many glass doors of the building. The man opened the door and pointed for Chance to go inside.

Once inside the building, Chance could see with the gold accent on the light fixtures and plush red carpet Chance thought well this sure wasn't any Russian government building. He was wrong; it was a government building, the Kiev Opera House. Just ahead of him he could see Tasha and his American friends.

It turned out that all of his associates were picked up early for a meeting at the University and brought directly back to the opera house after the meeting. It seems they had to change the schedule for the classes left in their courses, because some of the students in the class had to hold finals in their own classes soon. His friends didn't even have time to change and get ready to attend the opera.

The man who brought Chance had been sent by Tasha. But she didn't think about the man not being able to speak English.

Chance looked around to thank his guide, but he was already gone, Chance would never know who his guide was.

The thing Chance learned about the Kiev Opera House was it had been refurbished to be brought back to its original beauty.

Chance was made to understand that only the opera house in Milano was more elegant. The Russian Government spent millions of dollars to refinish the opera house.

Tickets to the opera were sold for less then ten cents. Chance could only think how much a ticket to the opera would cost in America.

Before the opera began, the manager of the opera came onstage and introduced everyone in the American party to the audience. They were asked to stand up when they were introduced, Dr. Duncan was introduced first. When Chance heard his name, he stood up. The audience began clapping loudly. The Americans sat back down and the music began.

Chance's first opera was not in Italian, but was done in Ukrainian, the first opera ever done in the Ukrainian language. Although he didn't know anything being sang he enjoyed the costumes and the music was wonderful.

When the opera was over, the cast got a standing ovation. This was the opening performance of this opera and Chance, along with the rest of the Americans and their hosts were invited to come backstage to join a cast party. The vodka flowed freely and each of the Americans, were introduced to the cast members and to the conductor and the director. The director spoke some English and was just beside himself that Americans had seen his production and praised it. Dr. Duncan was gifted in making people feel important. The time in Kiev went quickly for Chance and he was down to the last two days of the course. Plus, he found out why the lady at the currency exchange was reluctant to change more dollars, because there was nothing to buy in Kiev.

Chance put his money up as prize money for the best presentation for various categories such as: the best business plan, best media presentation, etc. until he had pledged to give away all, but about five hundred rubles. This money he gave to his driver. He did make one purchase in his hotel, a large coffeepot that was hand painted and looked very old. It was unique. Chance had seen pictures of this type of coffeepot, but he knew they only came from the Soviet Union. Chance tried to buy things that were unique to the country he was in and after much haggling over the price, he had his unique prize from Russia.

The five teams made their presentation to the judges who were the Americans and the heads of the sponsoring department. The presentations were outstanding. Each one was better then the last one. The Students grasp of advertising and the development of business plans to market parking meters throughout Russia was beautiful. The last presentation was Chance's favorite, it included a video with one of the students interviewing drivers on the street about what they thought of the idea of paying to park and limiting the time a vehicle could remain in a parking space.

The people they interviewed agreed that they city had lots of parking problems and thought that installing parking meters could help them with this problem.

The interviewer had taken one of the sample meter's which was mounted on a short post that was used to sit on a desk for demonstrations. They sit the meter on a stone wall near one of the tourist hotels. Two women parked a Mercedes in front of the meter, they got out of the car and went directly to the meter and put coins in it and walked off.

They were German tourists who were used to paying Superior meters all over Germany since there were more than 60,000 Superior Parking Meters operating in Germany. They paid the meter and went into the hotel. The interviewer couldn't believe it.

Plus, he had it all on videotape.

After a lot of discussion by the judges with the Russian department head who kept insisting that each of the five teams had to win for something. This was a political problem for him.

OK, that's the way they decided to award the prizes.

Chance made the awards to the team leader for each team. The judges found some reason to make each team a winner. Later, Dr. Duncan, the department director and Chance handed out diplomas to each of the students. Each student was so excited about getting their diplomas, they shook hands so vigorously that by the time they had handed out all of the diplomas, Chance's right hand began hurting.

That evening the Americans were guests of honor at a banquet held by the students. Vodka flowed along with dancing and singing.

The students all wanted to talk to Chance, but unfortunately almost none of them spoke English and Chance's Russian was still zero. Later that evening, he packed his suitcase, leaving his towels, soaps, shampoo and what was left of his toilet paper for the hotel staff.

The next morning Chance was up early and was waiting for Tasha and his driver to pick him up to take him to the airport. He was certainly ready to go home to Ann. When he arrived at the airport, he checked in with Austrian Air and saw his bag go on a cart to be loaded on the plane.

Soon it was time to go through security and Customs and Immigrations. Chance put his briefcase and his coffeepot on the conveyor belt to go through the security x-ray machine.

When the coffeepot went through the x-ray machine, the officer in charge pulled it off of the belt and called Tasha over to him. He began talking to Tasha explaining something to her about the coffeepot that much of what was being said Chance could figure out even if he couldn't understand Russian.

Tasha explained to Chance he couldn't take his coffeepot, because it was considered an antique, a national treasure. So the officer let Chance give his prize to Tasha to keep for him. Chance doubted that he would ever get it back, but a least the officer didn't just keep it for himself.

Chance went on through Customs, turned in his currency exchange form and next through Immigrations. No one said anything to him.

Chance found he had very few problems in countries that spoke very little English. No one wanted to admit they didn't speak English, so Chance probably could have gotten away with a lot. But he never tried to.

Chance boarded the Austrian Airline jet. What a difference it was compared to Aeroloft. It was clean, fresh and wonderful. When the plane took off, Chance felt like he had just escaped from Russia. He breathed a sigh of relief.

When they landed in Vienna, Chance ran to the phone and called Ann. When she answered the phone, Chance was so happy to hear her sweet voice, he almost started crying. Ann, hearing Chance's voice felt the same way. They talked for thirty minutes, just assuring each other they were all right and that all of the family was OK.

Chance boarded his TWA flight to New York and he was soon headed for America. One thing, Chance knew it would take a century for Russia to catch up with America in living standards for the ordinary people. Well, at least fifty years.

When his plane landed in New York, Chance wanted to kiss the ground the way the Pope did when he landed in some country. He telephoned Ann instead and said, "I'm getting closer, Baby."

They talked on the phone for another twenty minutes.

Just two more flights and Ann would be there to pick him up, New York to St. Louis, St. Louis to Springfield, Missouri. When they arrived in Springfield, Chance was the first one off the plane and went straight into Annie's arms. They kissed and held each other for a long time. They stepped back, just to look at each other before they started kissing again.

They finally stopped and said at the same time---"Maybe the luggage is available now, wrong!"

They had to wait another fifteen minutes before the bags began coming out. Chance picked up his bags and loaded them into Ann's car.

Instead of driving to Big Springs that night, they stayed at the Holiday Inn Crowne Center, University Plaza. Ann had checked in earlier that evening.

Chance could hardly wait to get his clothes off and get into the shower. God did that feel good, no matter how many hours Chance traveled or how long he had been awake, he needed to make love to Ann as soon as possible. My God, how he had missed her and needed her. She meant everything to him and he knew she felt the same way about him.

31

Not long after returning to Big Springs, Chance had a meeting with his distributor from Poland. It seems his distributor; Peter Wilicki had followed Chance's advice and made a deal for a small installation of meters in Gdansk on a privatized basis. Peter only had two problems. Now that he had a contract, he didn't have the money to buy the meters and he didn't know how to operate a parking meter system.

Chance knew Superior would never finance the meters for the installation and Chance didn't have time to go to Poland to help Peter set up the meter installation in Gdansk.

Chance and Peter met with Dak about this opportunity to get a Superior Parking Meter installation in Poland. Dak supported Chance as much as he could, considering how their parent company, the Memphis Company, felt about being involved in any type of privatization. They agreed to give Peter the meters on a trial basis for nine months without any payment being due.

After meeting with Dak, Peter and Chance went back into Chance's office. Arriving in his office, Chance remembered a telephone call he received a several weeks ago from a parking consultant, Charles Lorenzan, from Washington, DC. Charles wanted Moscow, Russia to try to get a contract to privatize the parking there. Since Chance didn't have a distributor for Russian, he told Charles to go ahead to see what he could do.

Chance met Charles Lorenzan years before, when Charles served as Director of Parking for Washington, DC. Chance had not seen or heard from Charles since he became a parking consultant until Charles called about Moscow. Chance remembered that Charles said he had a group of investors wanting to get into the parking business.

Chance told Peter what he was thinking about the question was did Peter want him to call Charles to see if his investors might want to talk about investing in Poland? Chance explained to Peter that Charles would be very good help starting the paid parking system in Gdansk.

Peter said, "I don't know what to do. Why don't you call and see if Charles and his investors would be interested in Poland."

Chance called Charles. A week later, Chance and Peter were meeting in Washington, DC with Charles and his investors. They were more then interested, they were ready to buy into the project. Chance recognized people of quality and money. Charles had found three people who had both of these qualities. The three investors were David Metzler, Solomon Getz and Rubin Swartz. David and Rubin were both big time commercial real estate developers. Solomon was a commercial building contractor and commercial off-street parking operator. Sol knew a lot about operating parking lots and garages. David and Rubin just wanted a new challenge. They had plenty of money to last them a lifetime, but liked the idea of expanding their world to become international business men.

It didn't take the parties long to put together a deal. The investor group had already formed a parking company to work on the Moscow project and they agreed to fund the Polish operation for a 75% ownership of the Polish company. Peter agreed because it seemed like a fair deal all the way around. Peter would get the contracts and the investors would finance the deal and hire Charles to start up the operation in Gdansk.

Chance got what he wanted, the sale of the parking meters.

Everybody was happy with this deal. Dak was pleased that he didn't have to report to the Memphis Company why he was putting meters in Poland for nine months and not getting paid for them.

The investors would pay for the meters when they were shipped. Chance was back in Washington, DC two weeks later with his distributor from Turkey, he had exactly the same problem, a contract to privatize parking meter operations in Istanbul with no money to buy the meters and a lack of knowhow to start the operation.

David, Rubin and Sol made a deal with Kamal Kahaztan, Chance's Turkish Distributor for a fifty- percent share of his company. Kamal did have some sales from some type of traffic safety products made in England and his privatization contract was much bigger then the Polish deal.

David called Chance a week later and asked him if he would consider coming to work for them as President of their parking company, World Star Parking Systems.

Chance had made up his mind when he rejoined Superior in 1982 that he would stay with them until they either fired him or he retired. But, here was someone who could see the future in parking like he did. The future was privatized parking systems. This was Chance's dream that he couldn't turn it down. He had a chance to be part of this company, World Star Parking Systems.

Chance flew to Washington, DC again to meet with David,

Rubin and Sol. He told them what he wanted for a salary and benefits and that he would set up the corporate office in Big Springs. They agreed.

Chance wrote out his letter of resignation from Superior to give to Dak. He told them that he thought that he had done as much for Superior as he could and thought he could do more for them working on privatization with this new company.

Dak was surprised with Chance's decision to leave Superior, with all of the years he had been associated with them. Dak knew Chance's heart was in this privatization scheme and that he had to try it.

The company had a retirement party for him at the plant. They gave him the standard parking meter bank that they gave all retiring employees. They also presented him with a beautiful gold desk set. Last, but not least to Chance, was a wall plaque in the shape of a Superior Parking Meter engraved with:

"In recognition of thirty-five years of service to Superior Parking Meter Company and the Parking Industry," from his fellow employees at Superior Industries. October 14, 1994."

Chance thanked everyone at Superior and told them how it was his father-in-law's idea so many years ago for him to go into the parking meter business in the first place. Chance said he was sorry his father-in-law never knew the opportunity he gave Chance and Ann. He explained to his audience his father-in-law died at age forty-seven, even before Chance became Director of Parking in Webster, Kansas.

Chance's, own father died just over a year ago and as Chance was making his little talk to the employees of Superior, he thought about how proud his dad was of him. It was too bad Chance discovered this only two years before his dad passed away. Chance's father told him only a few months before he died that when Chance was born was the happiest day of his life.

By the time Chance finished thanking everyone and shaking hands and got a several kisses from some of the women who worked not only in the office, but in the plant, it was time to go home.

Chance carried out the last few things from his office and loaded them into his car. Superior had been very good to him. He had been given his office chairs, his wooden file cabinets, cell phone and the right to assume the lease on his car. Yes, they had been good to Chance, but Chance hoped they knew he had been good for Superior.

When he got into his car to drive out of the parking lot for the last time as a Superior employee, he remembered how he drove onto that lot the first morning on his forty-sixth birthday in his VW Bug. Things couldn't have been much worse in 1982 for the Clark family. These last twelve years had really been good to the Clarks. He could only hope the next twelve years would be as good. He started up his black 1995 Chrysler LHS, slowly put the car in reverse, and backed out of his parking space. He felt really alone.

Chance had moved on in the past to a lot of new jobs, but leaving Superior was a lot harder for him then anyone knew. As he saw the front door of the plant in his rearview mirror with his coworkers leaving for home for the night he felt really lost. He wanted to stop the car, run back inside and yell "Just kidding. I can't leave you! You can't make it without me and I can't make it without Superior!"

Too late, the LHS was already out of the parking lot headed for home. He only knew he had his work cut out for him trying to get a new office set up and hire a staff of people.

Chance had no idea about how hard it would be coming from a corporate structure to working for people who operated by the seat of their pants. People who changed their minds even faster then his old boss, Karl Jones, if that humanly possible!

Chance arrived home at almost the same time as Ann. She couldn't come to his retirement party because she had a doctor's appointment that afternoon.

Ann helped him unload his car of all of the things he brought home from his office. He showed her his gifts and when she read his plaque, she beamed with pride for him. Chance told her he was sorry she couldn't be there for his party. He told her about his little speech and how he told everyone about how her dad got him into the parking meter business.

Ann liked hearing about that and his party. He told her he got lots of kisses from his coworkers.

She said, "Well, you probably wouldn't have gotten those if I had been there."

They both laughed.

Chance said, "You're probably right. They would have been afraid to give me the kisses if you'd been there."

They smiled at each other.

Chance told Ann this was the first time in his life that he felt afraid of leaving a job. She put down his plaque and held him close.

She knew how Chance felt; she knew how much he loved Superior. She brushed the left side of his hair back where his sunglasses had pushed it forward toward his face and said, "Sweetheart, it will be OK. You made the choice of what you really wanted to do."

"You wanted to build a company doing privatization and that's what you are going to do."

Chance replied, "Yes, I know, but it's hard."

"Sure, but that's what you wanted, right?"

The next day, Chance signed a lease for an office in the Big 7 Springs National Bank Building in downtown Big Springs.

Chance got really lucky, because he got a long time friend of his to agree to work as his Executive Secretary. She had worked for Superior in Chicago for his old friend, Ian Stark, when he was Vice President of Sales. Susan O'Hara was a terrific worker, well organized and smart. She lost her husband a few years ago and just graduated from a university that spring. She didn't know if she really wanted to work or not, but consented to help Chance with the new company.

Susan was perfect to work with Chance she didn't let him get away with anything. She made sure he returned calls even if they were calls he didn't want to return. They worked together very well. She could write letters for him, just by Chance giving her the concept of what he wanted to say.

She corrected his grammar and spelling and was a good friend of Ann's. What more could you want? She also could turn out more work then anyone who ever worked with Chance and he had had some very good Executive Secretaries in the past.

He was able to hire his old friend Doc Schmidt, because Superior wanted to get rid of their direct sales people and Chance got Superior to give him thirteen states from Missouri to Hawaii to be the Superior Distributor. In addition, he hired Linda Gilley, Superior's West Coast saleswoman. Linda was another great hire. She started out working as the Secretary for Superior's long time West Coast Distributor and when he died. Chance hired her to run Superior's west coast operation when he served as President of Superior.

Things were coming together very well. Before they moved into their new office, Chance took a trip to Korea and made a deal to buy fifty percent of the company from Superior's Distributor in Korea.

The Korean parking company's Chairman, Jimmy Kim, was a long time friend of Chance's and Kim trusted Chance completely.

Chance would find out Jimmy trusted him more then his new employers. David and Rubin decided that after Chance negotiated an agreement and Chance returned to Big Springs that they needed to fix the deal more to their favor. They flew to Seoul and after three days of renegotiating the agreement, they came away with a worse deal.

They were unhappy that Chance agreed to waive the five thousand dollars per month management fees to be paid to the US Company for the first two years. Jimmy had agreed to purchase furniture, pay for an apartment and the cost of getting it ready for a US manager to move in.

David and Rubin agreed to pay for the US manager's apartment and Jimmy agreed to pay the five thousand dollars per month management fee. David and Rubin didn't know that apartments in Seoul had to be fitted with western style toilets and the monthly rent amount to more then the five thousand a month, plus the rent had to be paid a year in advance.

David also found out Jimmy wouldn't let any changes be made in the agreement without calling Chance for his approval first.

David and Rubin were very good and smart business people, but they lacked experience in the international marketplace. They didn't understand how Korean people did business on trust and personal relationships.

Chance also learned from this. There could never be a deal unless David got to put his stamp of approval on it and have his input on the deal. Period! Chance was not as experienced at making deals as David and Rubin were, but he now knew how to work with his Board of Directors better in the future.

Next, Chance set up a meeting with Superior's Distributor for Mexico who just got a privatized contract for Mexico City, the one Chance could have had years ago. Chance suggested to David and Rubin that they should make a trip to Mexico City to see if they could put together a deal with Pedro Gonzales for part of the Mexican company. Chance knew he needed to make a deal, because he had only had enough money to put a few meters in Mexico City and he needed several thousand.

They made a deal with Pedro to buy thirty-five percent of the company and they would have an equal say in running the company.

Chance knew one of the countries that offered a great opportunity for privatized parking was Brazil. Chance contacted the people he had worked with when he was with Superior. Yes, they were interested in making a deal. They came to Washington, DC to meet with Chance's Board of Directors in early December. By the time the meeting was over, they had put together a new company to go after the parking business in Brazil.

In less then three months from the time Chance started working with David, Rubin and Sol, they now had businesses established on four continents in five countries.

The next step was to recruit country managers for each country. Professional parking administrators who had experience operating major cities in the United States.

He had Charles Lorenzan working in Poland with Peter Wilicki. They were up and running in Gdansk and another small adjoining city, Sopot. They were not making money yet, but they were at least paying their operating costs.

Chance needed to find people quickly to go to Brazil, Mexico and Korea. But first there was Christmas and New Years to celebrate with Ann, Chase, Marie, Shane and Curt.

With Shane's girlfriend, Jan and her three children Christmas had made a giant leap in the gift department. This year, Shane was bringing his godmother, Kathy Jones, to be with them for Christmas. Shane had a big surprise for Jan, a diamond engagement ring. Yes, she said, "yes" and they planned to have their wedding in September over the Labor Day weekend at the Thorncrown Chapel in Eureka Springs, Arkansas.

By this time they would have waited for four years after Jan's divorce before they wed. Chance thought if they had stayed together for that long of time, they had a good chance of making their marriage last.

Christmas time was Chance's favorite time of the year and Ann had their home looking like a Currier and Ives painting. The presents under the tree after Chase and Shane unloaded their cars filled the living room. If possible, there were even more presents then the year before.

Kathy Jones was awestruck with the number of presents, since she and Karl never had any children and both Karl's and Kathy's families were not close to them so she never saw anything like this before. Even though Kathy and Karl had plenty of money, they were not the type of people to go overboard purchasing presents like the Clarks.

Chance loved Christmas and giving presents. It hurt him so much in the early eighty's when the Clarks had so little and they could give so little. Now they were doing everything possible to make it up to their family.

What a Christmas, Ann prepared turkey and dressing, ham, Beef Wellington, Waldorf Salad, green beans, corn, a cherry salad, mashed potatoes, sweet potatoes with a marshmallow topping, pickled beets, sweet pickles, celery stuffed with cheese, green and ripe olives and then there was the desserts. Jan made a chocolate cheesecake, Marie brought chocolate pies; coconut pies and Ann baked strawberry and pecan pies.

If that wasn't enough, Annie made chocolate fudge and peanut butter fudge. Chase loved both cooking and eating. He brought peanut brittle, chocolate and caramel candy and mouthwatering caramels.

The food was wonderful.

To be able to see and appreciate everyone's presents, the Clarks established their own method of opening presents. Instead of having someone hand out all of the presents and everyone opening their presents at once, what they did was to start with the youngest person, which was Jan's daughter Joanna. She had to find a present under the tree for herself. Then she had to tell whom the present was from. Then she got to open the present.

Next came Jerry, then Jake and after that were Curt and Shane.

Jan followed Shane and next was Chase, since Marie was three months older. Chase took forever to open his first present, just to make Marie wait. It was funny to Chance that both of his sons' choices for mates were older than they were. After Marie, Ann got to open a present, then finally Chance and last was Kathy Jones. Sometimes, it didn't pay to be the oldest.

It took them over three and half- hours to get all of the presents opened that were under the tree. Finally one by one, each person dropped out of the present opening contest and only Chase and Shane were left opening presents. Chase finally won the race; he had two more presents to open then Shane this year. What a Christmas! Everyone got something they wanted and a lot of things they never expected. Each person had wonderful Christmas presents and the food was wonderful, what a feast!

Chance and Ann loved adding Shane's soon to be new family to theirs and having Kathy Jones was a great bonus for their Christmas. These were the best of times. Chance thanked God for all of the blessings he had given to the Clarks. Chance wished these times would last forever. Even though he knew his own motto, "The only sure thing in life is change."

Too bad all changes weren't for the best.

New Year's Day they were all together again, except Shane took Kathy Jones home. They spent the day eating and watching football games. Yes, Ann had fixed a large portion of black-eyed peas for good luck. Chance didn't know why black-eyed peas were supposed to be good luck, but the Clarks weren't going to take any chances, since they started having them ever since they moved to Arkansas and things had just kept getting better for them.

Building the new company was going well for Chance, but Annie's health wasn't doing the same.

Years before, Ann had been sick and going to the doctor for a long time with flu-like symptoms. Her doctor was not able to determine what was wrong with her one day her son Chase saw a story on TV about a congressman from Iowa that had Lyme's Disease. He called his mom and told her that she had to go to the doctor and have him test her for Lyme's Disease.

She told Chase, "I've just come home from the doctor. He's going to think I'm crazy telling him to run more tests on me." Chase insisted, so his mother went back to the doctor's office and had the test. Two weeks later the doctor's office called and said that she did indeed have Lyme's Disease, the first confirmed case in Arkansas. She went back to the doctor's office and got medicine to take for the Lyme's Disease.

Unfortunately, she had to have the treatment three times before it appeared to give her any relief. The long-term effect was that the Lyme's Disease left her with a heart arrhythmic problem.

Since the middle of January, Ann had not been feeling well and as the year went by, she just kept getting worse. Sometimes her heart would miss beats and Annie would think it wasn't going to restart. During these times, she would develop anxiety attacks.

In August, her doctor suggested she should go to, Mayo Clinic to let them confirm his diagnosis and treatment. Chance took off a week during the middle part of August to take Ann to Mayo Clinic. They drove to Rochester, Minnesota and checked into the Downtown Holiday Inn next to Mayo Clinic on Saturday evening.

Ann had to check in at the Clinic on Sunday afternoon. The nice thing about being in the Holiday Inn is you could use the skywalk system and never have to venture outside in the heat or the rain.

They had both during their stay in Rochester.

Monday morning Ann began her journey through Mayo Clinic. First, she met with her primary care doctor in the Cardiac Care department of the Clinic. Here her primary doctor gave her a physical and began giving her written instructions for tests in other departments of the Clinic.

Over the next week, she would be introduced to many other specialist departments of the Clinic. Some of these, Chance had never even heard of.

Before leaving the Cardiac Care Department, she was given a stress test which she passed with flying colors. All of the tests in the Cardiac Care Department went well.

The next stop was to have a blood test taken. Ann and Chance found the right department. Ann approached the reception desk for the department and gave the lady behind the desk her papers. Ann was told to take a seat and someone would be with her soon. Ann and Chance couldn't believe the size of each of the various departments and their waiting areas. Yes, they knew Mayo Clinic was one of the most famous clinics in the world, but until they saw it in operation, the whole concept and organization of it was incomprehensible.

They sat down and began expressing their impressions of the clinic between themselves. Just a few minutes passed when a nurse came out and called, "Ann Clark."

Ann got up and identified herself to the nurse and away they went through a door. Within fifteen minutes, Ann came back through the same door with a small bandage on her left arm.

Chance said, "That didn't take long."

"No," Ann replied, "They take your blood pretty fast in there." By now it was time for lunch, so they went into one of several restaurants located in or adjacent to the Clinic.

In the afternoon, Ann went through two more departments of the Clinic for tests. At the end of the day, she had been for tests in four different departments. Before they went back to their hotel room, Ann reported back to the Cardiac Care Department. Sure enough, they had a whole new set of instructions waiting for her. So it went for the entire week. Ann went through department after department of the Clinic. Friday afternoon, they had an appointment with her primary doctor in Cardiac Care to find out the results of all the tests.

Her doctor was ready for them as they came into his office for consultation. He said the Clinic found the following items regarding Ann's health:

1. The arrhythmic heart problem
2. Slight elevation in her blood pressure
3. Rheumatoid arthritis
4. Lupus
5. Sjogren Syndrome

Ann and Chance just looked at each other. No wonder Ann, was not feeling well. The doctor explained both Lupus and Sjogren's Syndrome were diseases of the central nervous system.

All of Ann's problems had been caught early and the doctors at Mayo believed with medication she should be able to live a fairly normal life.

They had prescriptions written for her, which she could get filled either in the Clinic's pharmacy or at one of the many drug stores adjacent to the clinic.

The doctor said it would also be a good idea if she lost a little weight and got more exercise. The doctor probably could give this same advice to 99.9% of every person living in America. They should all lose weight and get more exercise.

After the doctor finished giving his instructions, Ann and Chance left the doctor's office and went to the business office to check out.

Again, the organization of the Mayo Clinic prevailed within a very few minutes, they paid about 20% of the total charges on their American Express card and the clerk told them they thought their insurance company would cover the rest. If not, Mayo would send them a statement for whatever their insurance, didn't pay.

Ann took her prescriptions to one of the drug stores adjacent to the Clinic and soon after that the Clarks were back at the Holiday Inn.

They packed up their suitcases and checked out of the hotel. Ann's black Lexus was waiting for them in the Holiday Inn's parking garage. After loading the car they were on their way home.

The idea was to drive to Des Moines and spend the night. However, arriving in Des Moines, they found the State Fair opened yesterday and there weren't any rooms to be had.

They went through a McDonald's drive through in West Des Moines and picked up hamburgers, fries, cokes and chocolate shakes and headed south on Interstate 35 towards Kansas City, the perfect "diet meal" for people returning from Mayo Clinic.

By the time they reached Kansas City, it was almost three am on Saturday morning. After driving through Kansas City, they reached the southwest side of the city, Overland Park, Kansas.

They were only a few blocks from Kathy Jones' home. They tried to get a room at the Marriott hotel where they normally stayed when they came to town. No luck, the Marriott was full. However, a kindly desk clerk called a small motel just south on Metcalf Avenue and found them the last room the Sunset Inn had.

By four am the Clarks were in bed. The bad part was that by eight thirty, Chance woke up. He had a hard time sleeping much past his normal wake up time of around six-thirty every morning. He got out of bed as quickly and quietly as he could and went into the bathroom. He went to the bathroom, took his shower, washed his hair, as he did every morning, shaved, brushed his teeth and was ready to go for the day.

When Chance came out of the bathroom, Ann was setting on the edge of the bed. Chance got down on his knees and held her as close as he could. He gave her a big kiss on the mouth, even though she was protesting that she needed to brush her teeth. It was all right with Chance. Ann was his baby, she might be his wife, but she was still his baby. She had been through a lot over the last week and he didn't think she got anywhere near enough rest for her. Chance didn't need a lot of rest, but Ann did.

After Ann had taken care of herself in the bathroom and put on her makeup, she got dressed.

Chance said, "Let's go have some breakfast and stop at the Jones store at Metcalf South Shopping Center and go by Shane's house on the way home."

Ann said, "That sounds good to me. I'm always ready to go to the Jones Store and we need to see Shane's new addition to his house."

Chance said, "I sure want to see his media room and computer room he designed for his house."

Ann finished by saying, "Besides, I never get to see my baby boy much anymore. At least not enough, I miss seeing him every day." Breakfast was finished quickly and they went to the Jones Store. After spending a couple of hours shopping, they loaded up their purchases in the car and began driving to Fayetteville to the addition to Shane's house.

Ann called him on the car phone to be sure that he would be home. He would be.

During the drive to Fayetteville, Chance asked Ann, how she felt about what the doctor told her about all of the things they found wrong with her.

"I'm not as concerned knowing what's wrong with me; it's the not knowing that kills me."

Chance thought to himself, Ann's the most positive person when it comes to tackling her own health problems. Chance thought if a doctor gave him the same report as Ann got from Mayo Clinic, he would be a basket case.

She was, simply just a matter of fact, "Take my medicine and I'll be OK."

Around four o'clock Ann and Chance arrived at Shane's house. Shane had been watching out the window for them and Shane came bouncing out of his house to greet them. He always had a warm word for everyone and he kept his friends forever. In short, Shane was the kind of person who made you feel good to be around.

Quickly they were out of the car and in the house. Shane was so proud of his design for his addition to his house. In the past he made a lot of designs to add onto his folks' house, but Chance could never afford to spend the money to actually build what Shane designed.

Shane was fortunate he had the money to build the addition onto his house.

First, Shane showed his folks his media room. It was a very large room with everything electronic built into a south wall. He had a "52 inch TV," with a super sound system; VCR systems; CD systems and Laser disc systems. The room had no windows or any way for outdoor light to get into the room.

Shane loaded a laser disc into the system, he turned off the lights and when the sound of the helicopters came in from the film "Apocalypse Now" Chance was ready to hit the floor. It sounded like the helicopters were coming right through the media room.

The room was really beautiful and what Shane achieved with his design made a perfect media room.

Next, he took his folks down a hallway leading from the kitchen to the end of the new addition. Chance couldn't understand how well this long hallway looked with its blank wall on the side of the media room and glass "French" doors all along the other side when Shane had described it to him over the phone. At the end of the length of the media room wall in the hallway was an oversize door. Shane opened the door and showed his folks a four- foot wide closet type room where Shane could get behind all of his TV, video and sound system on one side, and his computers, monitors, etc. on the other side. Chance agreed it was a great concept and Ann loved it, because not only had her son designed it, the closet hid all of the multitudes of wiring for all of these devices.

After they saw Shane's operations closet, as Chance called it, Shane showed them his computer room.

This room was just as neat as the media room Shane had all of the computers built into the wall along with banks of monitors built into the wall as well. Shane had Formica work tops the length of both sides of his computer room and plenty of spaces between rows of drawers for several people to get up to the keyboards and use the computer's mouse. He did a great job designing the functionality of this room.

Chance saw a basketball lying next to the computer room door and said to Shane, "Well, show me your new basketball court.

Chance picked up the ball and followed Shane outside through one of the French doors. Ann came right behind them. When they got to the back of the new addition, Chance could see Shane's new basketball court, the concrete pad was a little less then half the length of a regular basketball court and slightly smaller then the normal width of a regular court.

Chance looked over the new backboard, goal and goal post. He threw the ball to Shane. Shane took a shot about fifteen feet from the basket and made the shot.

Chance dribbled out to about the same spot where Shane had just shot the ball from. Ann was standing between them, Shane was waiting under the basket for his dad to shoot the ball and Ann was just at the edge of the new court.

Behind her the yard had been torn up by the construction vehicles coming in and out of the yard and there was about a two- inch drop off the full length of the court where the concrete forms had been during construction of the court that hadn't been backfilled yet.

Chance shot the ball, it careened off the rim of the goal and flew directly at Ann's feet. Ann, being a basketball player when she was younger, started to back up and catch the ball. Instead, her shoe caught on the concrete edge of the basketball court and she fell backwards.

Ann put out her left hand to catch herself as she was falling backwards. She came down on her hand and she fell flat on her back onto the ground.

Almost before she hit the ground Chance and Shane were at her side. She was in terrible pain, Chance could see her left wrist was broken and she couldn't even try to get up.

Shane ran to the front of his house and drove his jeep back to where his mother was laying. Between Chance, Shane and Ann, they got Ann into the back seat of the Jeep Station Wagon and headed for the hospital a few blocks away from Shane's house. In less then twenty-four hours, Ann and Chance were back dealing with hospitals. They hadn't been in Fayetteville an hour yet.

Ann was really hurting. Shane, Chance and an emergency room nurse got her out of the car and into a wheelchair and inside the hospital.

Of course, there was no doctor on duty at the emergency room or even one in the hospital at four forty-five on a summer Saturday afternoon. The nurse began calling and was able to contact an orthopedic surgeon. In the meantime, they couldn't even give Ann something for her pain. Ann like most women had a very high tolerance for pain, but she was really hurting.

Before the doctor arrived at the hospital, he gave instructions for Ann to be x-rayed. The technicians from x-ray took her for the x-rays. They x-rayed her left wrist from different positions and x- rayed her back.

It seemed like they waited forever for the doctor to arrive and in the meantime, Shane called Jan and she and Joanna arrived at the hospital. Jan knew the emergency room at this hospital very well with her two teenage boys.

Ann was pleased to see Jan and Joanna though she was in awful pain. Finally, the doctor arrived. Ann was taken back into one of the operating rooms where the doctor examined her wrist and studied her x-rays. He had the nurse give Ann a shot for the pain. Next, he pulled her wrist back into position, and then applied a cast from her wrist up to just below her shoulder.

When this process was finished, the doctor told Ann and Chance that she also had a broken tailbone along with her twelfth vertebrae was broken. No wonder Ann was hurting so bad.

The doctor prescribed some pain pills for her. Jan said she would run up to a drug store and have the prescription filled while they were in the process of getting Ann released from the hospital. The doctor said he wanted Ann to remain at the hospital for at least thirty more minutes to be sure she didn't go into shock. Jan returned to the hospital with Ann's pain pills.

Chance asked Jan to take him over to get Ann's car while Shane stayed with Ann.

By the time Chance returned with Ann's car, Ann was ready to go home. Shane asked them to stay with him to be sure his mother would be all right.

Ann said, "No, I want to go home to my own bed."

The truth was Chance didn't have any idea how they could get Ann upstairs to his bedrooms even if she wanted to stay.

Chance told Ann, "Honey you better stop in the bathroom before we start the two hour drive home to Big Springs."

Chance had to go with Ann into the bathroom to help her with her clothes and help her get up off the stool. Between Shane and Chance, they got Ann into her car and they started for home.

Chance drove as fast as he could, but over the winding mountain roads of the Ozarks, no trip was fast.

Ann told Chance "You got to get me something to drink and some ice to suck on."

Chance stopped at service station and bought Ann a cup of ice and a bottle of water. This lasted her the rest of the way home.

When they arrived home, Chance took his car out of the garage before he could park Ann" car to give her enough room to get out of the car. They needed the right hand front door to open as wide as possible for her to get out of the car.

Chance took Ann's feet and between the two of them they turned Ann around in her seat so her feet were on the garage floor while she was still seated in the car.

Next, they got Ann out of the car and standing. The final challenge in the garage was to make the step up from the garage into the house. This step was a little higher then a normal step, but with Chance behind Ann so she wouldn't fall, somehow she got in the house.

Ann had an awful night; she could hardly get from her bed to the bathroom which was less then five feet from her side of their king size bed. She certainly couldn't do it by herself, nor could she get herself up and down to use the toilet.

Shane's wedding was less than two weeks away and Ann had made big plans for all kinds of things she wanted to do for her family and their out of town guests.

She had made hotel reservations at Eureka Springs for her mother and for her aunt and family at the Holiday Inn Express where she and Chance were staying. She planned to make baskets with wine, cheese, fruit and candy to be placed in each room of her out of town guests. Ann planned to have a big breakfast to be served in the Clark's suite Sunday morning following the Saturday wedding.

In addition to breakfast, she planned to have snacks and drinks available in their suite for their guest beginning at noon on Saturday prior to the wedding and open after the reception for everyone staying at the hotel.

Now what was she going to do, she couldn't even stand up by herself, as Ann lay in bed that awful Saturday night she was determined to be able to stand at the wedding, not only stand, but to accomplish all of her plans. Ann could be stronger then steel when it was called for. She thought about her mother of the groom's dress she had bought at The Jones Store earlier that day. Her dress was still hanging in the back seat of her car. Now, she wondered if she could even get her dress on with the cast she was wearing.

The two weeks went slowly by; Ann could now stand and walk with someone on each side of her but she still had a lot of pain. Chance had been pressed into service to help carry out Ann's plans for the wedding. In addition, Shane asked him to be the best man, avoiding picking just one of his friends for the job and at the same time honoring his father. Joanna was to be the maid of honor for her mother and sons Jake and Jerry would give their mother away.

When the Clark's arrived at the Holiday Inn Express in Eureka Springs Saturday morning every inch of Ann's car was filled. Chance helped Ann into their suite first with her riding in a wheelchair. It was still so painful for Ann just to get in and out of the car and into the wheelchair. Chance didn't know how she was going to make it from the back of Thorncrown Chapel to her seat in the front row reserved for the mother of the groom.

It took Chance over an hour to unload the car of clothing, cases of soft drinks, wine and the baskets of goodies for each of the out of town guest, which Ann and he put together yesterday. Almost by the time he got the car unloaded Ann's mother and her aunt and their families arrived at the motel. They obliviously had left very early from Webster, Kansas to get to Eureka Springs that early in the day since it would take seven hours to drive it.

After lunch, the time seemed to fly by, Chase and Marie arrived and soon after that, their son Curt and his new girl friend Shelly arrived.

Chance begin to get himself ready about three o'clock, learning as he was dressing in a tuxedo it was the first time he ever had one on in his life. After he was ready, he began helping Ann dress. She had already put on her make up and was working on her hair by the time Chance finished dressing.

Chance found it was a tough job helping Ann put on pantyhose, he had mastered fastening her bra, but he found a new challenge with the pantyhose. When he first started helping Ann with her bra after she fell he kept telling her "he only had experience unfastening her bras."

"It was a lot harder getting it fastened." He said.

Somehow by a little after four o'clock they were ready. Chance helped Ann into her wheelchair and got her into the car. She looked beautiful in her dress. Carefully, Ann got herself into the car and Chance lifted and turned her feet so they were inside the car. The leather seats of Ann's car really helped her to be turned inside the car. As she was getting turned she cried out softly in pain, but said she was all right.

Chase and Curt were acting as ushers, so at exactly five o'clock Ann stood up out of her wheelchair at the rear of Thorncrown Chapel and with her oldest son and grandson on each side of her. She began the long walk to the front row of the Chapel. It wasn't that long of a walk, since Thorncrown Chapel only held one hundred people, but that walk was probably the longest walk in Ann's life and made in shear pain. Ann was determined to make the walk and she did.

Chance and the rest of the wedding party remained outside waiting for their turn to enter the Chapel. Next the bride's mother and father were seated.

Chance turned to Jake and Jerry and said "Well are you ready to give your mother away?"

Without any hesitation Jake replied "If Shane promises not to give her back." everyone laughed with Jan laughing the hardest. Shane and Chance made their way down the aisle and took their place at the front of the Chapel.

Next come Joanna, who looked much older then her ten years of age, she was really beautiful anyway and in her bride's maid dress she was sensational.

Then, Jake, Jerry and Jan came down the aisle and the minister asked "Who gives this woman in marriage."

In unison Jake and Jerry replied "We do."

Jan's dress was "picture book perfect" with a train of laces about six or seven foot in length. She took her place next to Shane. With the four of them now facing the minister standing at the front of the Chapel, Chance could see the beauty of the sitting of Thorncrown Chapel placed in the woods. No wonder its design by Fay Jones of Fayetteville was chosen as the finest architectural building of the 1980's in America. It blended with its surroundings like it had been there forever. The beauty of the sitting was equaled only by the beauty of the ceremony and the bride and groom.

Chance could hardly stand through the ceremony. He worked so hard to help Ann do everything she wanted to do for the wedding and here was one of the most important days of his youngest son's life. Yet all he could think about was worrying about Ann. Not just her injuries, but her report on her health from Mayo Clinic.

Chance tried to put these thoughts out of his head and enjoy the happiness of the day and of the bride and groom.

The wedding was over and down the aisle the bride and groom went, followed by Chance and Joanna.

The bride's mother and father were escorted out next, and then Chase and Curt helped Ann stand up and helped her walk down the aisle to the rear of the Chapel.

Chance kissed the bride and welcomed her into the Clark family. Next, he gave Shane a hug and a kiss and told him "lot's of love and good luck son."

Then Chance got Ann's wheelchair waited for her at the back of the Chapel.

When she sat down, Chance leaned over and kissed her and said, "You made it Baby."

She said "Yeah I did it."

After what seemed hours of picture taking in the Chapel with Ann positioning herself behind Shane or someone, so her cast wouldn't show up in any of the pictures. They left to go to the reception at the country club on Holiday Island north of Eureka Springs.

The reception lasted another couple of hours with more pictures being taken and visiting with as many people as possible. Two of Chance's aunts and uncles came from Oklahoma to be at the wedding with them.

By the time they returned to the motel, Chance was exhausted.

He helped Ann get undressed and put on her nightgown and robe. She said she wanted to talk with her mother for awhile and telephoned her to come to their suite. After that Chance undressed and got into bed.

Ann talked with her mother for an hour or more before her mother was ready to go to bed. The next morning instead of serving breakfast in their suite. Chance and Ann invited their out of town guests for breakfast at a nearby restaurant. After breakfast everyone was anxious to get on the road home.

Shane and Jan left on their honeymoon flying to Orlando and staying at one of the Disney World Resorts. Jan's parents stayed with her children while Shane's and Jan were on their honeymoon.

It took Chance as long to load the car as it did for him to unload it yesterday.

When they arrived home, Ann was satisfied the wedding was prefect and that almost all of her plans were carried out.

Chance was just happy to have it over and that they were home in Big Springs.

When Chance saw the pictures of the wedding, he could see how bad he looked from the stress of the two weeks prior to the wedding and his worry about Ann's health. Ann looked great and he looked awful.

You couldn't tell she had a cast on her arm and that it was taking every bit of her strength to remain standing for the pictures.

Chance thought to himself, "What a woman."

The world would never know about a wife and mother's strength and courage since Ann wasn't famous. She was just an average American homemaker, "Average?"

Not really, she was far above being anything you could call average.

In Chance's eyes, she was an angel here on earth and how he was ever so lucky enough to have her love, he would never know.

He just knew how happy he was to have it.

32

Good things begin happening fast for World Star Parking Systems. They got privatization contracts in Warsaw, Sao Paulo, Rio de Janeiro and Seoul over the next three years.

Not every thing went perfect with World Star they lost their relationship in Turkey. David failed to send a payment on time to purchase additional shares of stock in the Turkish Company and Kamal Kahaztan threw World Star's Country Manager out of their office and ended his relations with them. One thing David learned from this experience was when you told an international partner a date you would do something, you better do it. World Star was now embroiled in lawsuits on two continents over Kamal taking over their share of the company in Turkey and the Turkish Company owed World Star over $1,500,000.

As Chance's old friend Karl Jones used to say in business if you don't have any problems, you don't have any business. World Star sure must have a lot of business, because they always had plenty of problems to deal with.

The Company was growing faster then Chance could hire parking directors for the projects. The only bad thing from Chance's perspective was after the first eighteen months of operation in Big Springs. David, Rubin and Sol met with him and asked him to move his office to Washington DC so he would be closer to them.

Their investors wanted the President of the Company located where most of the employees of the company were.

They asked Chance to rent an apartment at company expense for him to use when if was in town and to close his office in Big Springs. The worst of the move was losing Susan O'Hara; Chance knew she was one of the best assistant he ever had. Losing Susan was like cutting off his right arm.

Still Chance didn't feel he could tell his Board of Directors he wouldn't move his office to DC. He still had three years to go on his employment contract and he needed the income from his job. Telling Susan he had to close the office hurt him more then he wanted her to know. He tried to do it in as a matter of fact way, but it wasn't easy. He loved his office in Big Springs and loved having Susan working with him.

Chance made arrangements to give Susan her new computer and a picture of some very playful kittens which hung on the wall over her desk. He would have given her a lot more to keep her working with him if he could. Who knows, maybe someday they would work together again.

David had to do a lot of work to keep pace with the financing needs of the expanding company.

David made arrangements to have a private placement to raise capital, but the organizers failed miserly at raising the fifteen to twenty million dollars they promised to raise. They came up with less then half of the money and between David, Rubin and Sol using their personal contacts they raised most of the money from their investors.

Still that wasn't nearly enough money to invest in all of the projects they had going. Next, David secured a loan for almost fifty million dollars in project financing from a group of local bankers in the DC area. The biggest part of the new installations were due to be finished late in December of nineteen ninetyseven.

As the projects came on line, the money began to pour into the company. They begin repaying the bank loans six months earlier then projected.

Chance pushed his Parking Directors to move heaven and earth to get the parking equipment installed in these cities in order to give the cash flow they need at World Star.

The other result was with the installation of the equipment being made sooner then expected, the earlier cash flow reduced the amount of project financing they needed, so instead of fifty million dollars, they were able to get by with thirty-five million dollars.

Everything was coming together just as Chance always knew it would with new cities in new countries contacting World Star Parking Systems every week wanting them to make a proposal to install and operate a privatized parking system in their city.

Hiring a public relations firm in New York got Chance on the front page of the Wall Street Journal, in Business Week and on CNN World News. All of the stories were positive about this small start- up American Company helping to organize on-street parking systems for cities all around the world.

World Star Parking Systems in a little over three years and were operating parking systems on four continents, in five countries and in twenty cities. The number of parking spaces now under contract totaled almost 125,000 car spaces and with new contracts being secured almost every month.

The payoff for all of the work David, Rubin and Sol put-in, along with Chance and his staff were about to be richly rewarded.

An initial public stock offering was being planned by Brown Securities to be issued in September of nineteen ninety-eight.

Brown Securities calculated the stock would be issued at twenty times forecast earnings or between ten to fifteen dollars a share.

David was about to get a heck of a lot richer then he already was, not to mention Rubin and Sol. Chance's share of the company could be worth two to two and half million dollars. Chance wouldn't even let himself think about having an investment worth that much money.

Chance knew the best thing for him to do was to duck his head and keep working to get products installed and new contracts.

Also, to be sure the parking operations for the cities operated as World Star promised and that the cities got every penny they were owed.

He would let David take care of the rest. David certainly had done a great job of looking after Chance and World Star up to this point.

Chance just couldn't let his mind get bogged down thinking about wealth that someday might become a reality.

In addition, what more could he really want then he already had. He had a wonderful wife, two great sons. A house to live in, although being able to pay off the mortgage would be nice, and of course to be able to pay off those credit cards would be wonderful. Both Ann and he had new cars and Chance still remembered how hard it used to be to have one car. The only thing Chance could really want from such wealth was to be able to stay home with Ann.

Chance decided the first thing he needed to do was to sign over half of his World Star stock to their small family corporation owned by Chance, Ann, Chase, Marie, Shane, Jan and Curt. This was a way Chance could turn over the stock before it had any real value. This would save everyone in the future with this little bit of estate planning.

Chance reflected back on his life as he was flying home from Korea where he had been working for the past three weeks with Jimmy Kim on a contract for the city of Pusan to install 15,000 meters. After enough give and take they finally got the contract signed. The Koreans were tough negotiators, but unlike China after an agreement was worked out you didn't have to go back every month to re: negotiate the deal all over again.

His work had allowed him to travel to almost all of the famous places in the world. He had traveled completely around the world three different times. He had friends on six continents and had traveled to more then sixty countries.

Chance had been on a photo safari in Africa. He had traveled all over Europe by car, train and plane. The same in Asia and he had been to Israel and walked Christ's route to the cross. He had worked in almost every State in America and the Providence's of Canada.

Thinking back to his trips to Israel where he visited where Jesus had been crucified. He remembered how he had to get down on his knees to reach through a small hole in a clear plastic wall put there to prevent people from climbing on this sacred place. Chance touched the very stone Christ's blood had been spilled on; it was almost too much for him. His friends in Israel told him that many people developed "Jerusalem Fever" visiting Jerusalem from too much emotion and a few people actually died each year because the emotion was just too much for them.

Chance brought home a small cross made from the wood from a Jerusalem Olive Tree. He looked at many crosses, but Chance felt this simple cross-made from olive wood represented Christ's life the best.

Chance always tried to bring home something from ever country he visited so by seeing the item helped bring back the memory of the country to him.

Ann said their house looked like a museum and unless Chance knew where he was going to put whatever he was thinking about buying in the house, for him not to buy it. Chance bought things anyway and carried it home and then tried to find a place for it after he returned home.

As his flight continued winging it's way across the miles over the Pacific. Chance's mind turned to other things in his life, his love for Ann and the struggles they endured to survive the early years of their marriage. Their struggle was always a lack of money.

Chance's mother died during the same period of time when they had to close their business, so it was really a tough time in their life. Ann was so supportive of Chance during this time he would never forget how she helped him recover from both of these loses. If there was ever any truth in the old saw "When things gets tough, the tough get going" this described Ann reactions to their plight. No sitting around feeling sorry for themselves, just get going.

"Never put off until tomorrow what you could do today" was Annie motto. Chance never got the opportunity to use his old saying "Always put off until tomorrow, what you can get out of doing today" no sir, not when Ann was your wife.

They raised two fine sons. Chance always said, two only sons, since they were so many years apart.

Chase and Marie worked really hard getting their education. Chase graduated magma cum laud with a degree in business and a master degree in public administration. Marie had her degree in banking.

Shane was their true artist, he could draw, paint, write both poetry and stories. Although he hadn't received his degree yet,

dad would continue to push Shane to get his degree. One of Chance's goals in life was to have both of his sons with university degrees. Shane wanted a degree in film and to become a movie director. Chance had no doubt that some day Shane would do what he wanted to do in life and that was to direct films.

Chance was still determined to see Shane earn his degree;

Chance would never give up on his goal for his son. Chance wanted to plan an anniversary trip for Ann and his forty-fifth wedding anniversary. They planned to go on vacation for five days prior to their anniversary with their family, but Chance wanted at least one day just with Ann. Alas, it was not to be. They returned to Big Springs from Las Vegas on December seventeen and Chance had to fly on to Washington DC on the eighteenth. David planned a World Star stockholder meeting for Friday, December the nineteen.

The stockholder meeting went well with the staff getting a lot of praise and several people thanking David for all of the time he put into the company to make it a success. David certainly deserved every bit of praise he got. He had worked his heart out along with Chance and the rest of the World Star staff to make things happen for the company.

Chance returned to Big Springs on Saturday the Twenty of December and was not feeling well. He managed to pick up Ann's anniversary present. A diamond tennis bracelet set in platinum. The other present was a poem Chance wrote for her about their life together.

Chance, spent all day Sunday in bed and went to the doctor on Monday on their anniversary. He had bronchitis again. The doctor gave him a shot and some pills. This meant there would not been any day together for their anniversary liked Chance planned.

When Chance returned from the doctor he said "Annie, I'm sorry I'm sick, but I want to give you your anniversary presents."

Chance gave Ann her bracelet which was wrapped in a beautiful gold foil paper with a very silky green ribbon and bow. The bracelet was actually in a box inside this bigger box.

Ann said, "This is too pretty to open."

Chance replied, "I hope what's in the box is as pretty as the wrapping.

Ann laughed and said, "That would be nice." Ann carefully unwrapped the package saving the green ribbon and the bow and carefully cut the tape so she didn't destroy the gold foil paper.

Inside this large box was a lot of white tissue paper and nestled in the middle of the tissue paper was a blue cloth covered box, Ann carefully removed the blue box and opened it, exposing the diamond bracelet.

"Thanks, Chance it's beautiful. Help me put it on."

Chance removed the bracelet from its box and unlocked its safety lock and placed it on Ann's left wrist. He re: fastened the lock and the safety lock. It looked a lot prettier on Ann's wrist then it did in the display case at the jewelry store.

Ann inspected her new bracelet. She liked it a lot.

Chance said "These diamonds are a small symbol of my love for you. Ann there is no way to tell you how much you and your love meant to me over the forty-five years of our marriage."

Ann kissed Chance. She could see the tears forming in his eyes.

"Chance, I thought we agreed not to buy any anniversary presents!"

"Well, I lied."

With that he handed Ann another package wrapped in plain white paper with a small blue bow. This package was wrapped by Chance and lacked the beauty of the jewelry store wrapped package. Chance only hope the words of his poem could somehow match the love in his heart and the beauty of the diamond bracelet.

Ann could feel that it was obviously a picture frame through the thin white paper and thought Chance had a picture of himself taken for her or maybe it was an old picture of them enlarged and framed for her.

Ann took no care in opening this package, she torn away the white paper and looked at the content of the picture frame.

As she began reading her poem, the tears begin forming in her eyes. As Ann read Chance's words she was reading the story of their lives. Ann's poem read:

Together Forever

Annie, my love, sweet girl of sixteen.
Sparkling blue eyes and bright white smile.
Child bride, my bride, my love, my Annie

Two only sons, born and raised
One seventeen, when the other was born.
Both father and mother, while away I was working.
Yet on this earth, two finer sons you'll never see.

You've stood beside me all the time.
Good times and bad, you've never strayed.
Your love and faith always carries us on.
When lesser loves would have been all gone.
Just how and why I'll never know.
It shall remain a mystery to me.

This you shall know, I thank God and you.
For always being there for me.

You've stood the test of time.
Your blue eyes still sparkle.
Your bright white smile still shines.
Every time I see you my heart just melts away.
You're my life, my wife, my love, my Annie.

Loved ones lost along our way.
You've had sickness and suffered pain.
Lost everything, we started all over again.
Through all of this, you never complained.
Your spirit's so fine, you never quit or whined.

Along life's way we loved in oh so many places.
Laughed when nothing else was left to do.
We've lived, we've traveled, and we've dared.
Around the world, together we've shared.
We've been blessed, just to have one another.

Forty-five years have gone past.
Since our marriage vows we spoke last.
No longer my girl of sixteen.
Now called a woman, a lady, a mother.
And alas, a grandmother!

Whatever the name you're called
You're always my girl, best friend and lover.
No matter what tomorrow may bring.
Our love will always remain.

If our hundredth anniversary on earth can't be.
I'll pray for eternity!
Eternity to have my girl, my love, my Annie.
Oh lord, grant me one wish
For us to be just
Together Forever!

December 22, 1997 Chance Clark

Ann said, "Chance, I love you and I always will."

As they kissed and held each other close, Chance thought. Why should they not make it to their hundredth anniversary they had beat all of the rest of the odds against them by staying married after marrying so young. If not, there was always eternity for them to be together forever as Chance had written in his poem to Ann. Ann said as their kiss ended "Hang my poem by our bedroom door where I can see it everyday."

Following orders as all good husband do, Chance hung the framed poem just above the light switch by their bedroom door.

Christmas was just three days away and September with the stock offering would be there before they knew it. Whatever happened next wouldn't surprise Chance. Chance had coined the phrase long ago "The only sure thing in life is change!"

One thing Chance and Ann knew was whatever the future brought, if they had twenty dollars or two million they would still be one. The one thing that would remain the same was somehow, someway they would be together forever!

THE END

About The Author

CLARK SELBY began writing fiction as an outlet from his duties as a full-time caregiver for his first wife Patricia after they had been married for more than fifty years. Patricia became paralyzed from a rare disease called central nervous system vasculitis. Clark continued to care for her until she passed away. Previously, Clark had spent the past quarter of a century as an international traveler as a consultant and executive in the parking industry. His work took him to more than sixty countries on the six continents. Clark gained experience in the parking industry by serving as director of parking for the city of Hutchinson, Kansas; assistant director of parking and transportation for the University of Iowa; parking operations specialist for an international transportation consulting firm headquartered in Chicago, Illinois; president and vice president of the world's largest manufacturer of parking meters; and president of an international parking operations company.

During his tenure as vice president of the parking meter company, he was awarded the "E" Award for Excellence in exporting from the president of the United States. Clark's travels have included serving as an instructor at the first international trade and marketing seminar in the Soviet Union and as project manager for a major parking and traffic study in Perth, Western Australia. He has been listed in Marquis *Who's Who in the World 1991 to 1999* and *Who's Who in America 1996 to 1999*. Clark's first published novel *Dangerous Food* is available online at any of the major booksellers or at most retail bookstores. Clark and his wife, Karen, live in Springfield, Missouri.